"Passionate, complex,
and compelling...Highly
recommended."
—Mary Balogh

*"You will help me avert chaos, Miss Lindsey,
by standing in for the princess at my wedding . . ."*

Penny spilled tea into her saucer, but she forced herself not
to leap to her feet, not to let her teacup smash melodramatically on the carpet. The dog lurched up, staring at her, then
lay down again at a gesture from Nicholas.

She covered her shock with a bubble of laughter. "What?
You cannot be serious! It's absurd!"

"Stand with me in front of the Allied leaders and take
vows for Sophia. Diplomacy will be satisfied, my enemies
confounded."

It was too unreal to grasp. "Take vows? My life is here in
Rascall St. Mary. I've never been to London."

"Then take this chance. Afterward, you may come home
to the village and live out your days in all the obscurity you
wish."

The tea sloshed in the saucer. She couldn't seem to keep
it still. "But I don't want my life to change."

"It has already changed. I am here. I cannot be denied."

My Dark Prince

Julia Ross

JOVE BOOKS, NEW YORK

This is a work of fiction. Names, characters, places, and incidents are either the product of the author's imagination or are used fictitiously, and any resemblance to actual persons, living or dead, business establishments, events, or locales is entirely coincidental.

MY DARK PRINCE

A Jove Book / published by arrangement with the author

PRINTING HISTORY
Jove edition / August 2000

The Penguin Putnam Inc. World Wide Web site address is
http://www.penguinputnam.com

ISBN: 0-515-12883-X

A JOVE BOOK®
Jove Books are published by The Berkley Publishing Group,
a division of Penguin Putnam Inc.,
375 Hudson Street, New York, New York 10014.
JOVE and the "J" design
are trademarks belonging to Penguin Putnam Inc.

PRINTED IN THE UNITED STATES OF AMERICA

10 9 8 7 6 5 4 3 2 1

This story is gratefully dedicated to Bibiana,
who helped me name Glarien,
and to the horses that taught me to love them.

Prologue

Spring 1814

Devil's spawn!

Nicholas leaned into the breeze at the front of the ship and watched the small boat row out from the coast of England. Damp air wailed through the rigging, a high-pitched counterpoint to the creak and boom of canvas and sea-hardened timber.

Devil prince!

Lost echoes, voices from boyhood, taunted in the wind.

The ship shuddered into a trough as it caught crosscurrents running off the coast, answering the lurch of his heart. Ten years! Ten years since he had last come back to his homeland, and sixteen years since a ferocious, frail boy of eleven had first been torn from his home to be carried weeping across Europe to his destiny.

Prince of devils! The voices whined. *Ragged gypsy!*

He had bloodied his knuckles and some of the other boys' noses over that one. How absurd that their childish taunts should come back to haunt him now, when alien ways had devoured any last vestiges of his Englishness! The future offered no room for weakness or sentiment and never had. He had never expected this one final visit to the land where he had spent his boyhood. Who could have predicted that Napoleon's defeat would bring the powers of Europe to London this June and make it necessary?

Of course, when he left this last time, married and sworn irrevocably to his duty, he would be prince of devils forever.

"Which counts for more?" he asked the voices softly, knowing his knuckles shone white on the rail, knowing there would be no answer. "Blood or birthplace? Desire or destiny?"

Quest looked up and whined. Nicholas put his hand on the dog's head. She pressed into his leg, comforted.

The bowsprit thrust up again. Salt spume stung his face. Beyond the race of wave and wind-whipped froth, the small boat bobbed closer. Four men strained at the oars. One man, wrapped in a cloak, held a telescope trained on the *Royal Swan*. Behind him the coast ran low and humped, the sunrise flashing pink over church spires and dark woodland.

"Sire?" Von Gerhard stood at Nicholas's elbow, his own glass pinned on the rowboat. The scar on his cheek curled like a whiplash as he spoke. "It's Lucas, our own man!"

Nicholas already knew. The face of one of his spies, drawn with fatigue, his dark hair plastered to his head, desperately trying to intercept the *Royal Swan* while she still labored off East Anglia. A spy Nicholas had set to watch over his cousin Carl, his nemesis, his tormentor. Harbinger—obviously—of disaster.

Nicholas nodded at the small boat, closer now, and pitched his voice to show mild amusement. "Lucas appears to have been caught under a rainspout. When he arrives, allow him to sit and take wine." He smiled deliberately as he turned from the rail, for he would never display anything but confidence to his men. "Then let him bring me his calamitous news."

Major Baron Friedrich von Gerhard clicked his heels and bowed. There were times when such unquestioning and absolute obedience was annoying, but not this time.

Nicholas listened to Lucas in silence, Quest curled silently at his feet. The wine had brought some color back into the spy's face, but he still looked ill, his skin drawn about his pale blue eyes. He'd been traveling without rest for two weeks.

"There's no doubt?" Nicholas asked at last. "Carl has her?"

Lucas nodded, the clean motion of a seal bobbing in water. "But nobody knows Her Royal Highness is missing, sire. An impostor takes her place and stays retired, claiming an indisposition. One of the princess's ladies is in Carl's pay to maintain the deception. Thus the carriage travels on—but very slowly— as if Princess Sophia is still there. Nothing will be discovered until they reach London just before the wedding. At which time, sire, Carl can—"

"Yes!" Nicholas interrupted, biting back icy fury. "He can put it about that Princess Sophia refuses the marriage."

What he feared most had already happened. The ramifications would spread a swath of destruction like a cannonball through massed soldiers. His humiliation before the Tsar of Russia and the other Allied sovereigns—soon to gather in London to celebrate their victory over Napoleon—would be catastrophic: These were the men who held the future of his small country in the palms of their far mightier hands. There would be polite consternation when the wedding was canceled, veiled condolences on the fickle nature of women. Yet the balance of power would shift irrevocably into the hands of his cousin, unless it slipped away from them both to plunge Glarien—his country, his responsibility—into bloodshed and chaos.

He paced across the cabin, given up by the ship's captain to be transformed into temporary royal apartments. Stored somewhere far below lay the gifts some secretary had selected for his bride. Trunks and cases held his court uniforms, fretted with bullion like a holy chalice. The decorations, ribbons, stars, the ceremonial swords and accoutrements set with gold—symbols of his unforgiving routine of duty, chains to hold him helpless in the glitter of the London social round while the trap closed.

"Your Royal Highness will turn back?" The spy's eyes burned with intelligence. Lucas knew exactly what this meant.

Nicholas looked up. The low coast of Suffolk gleamed beyond the sweeping curve of windows. "To what purpose? To be absent when the Tsar arrives? By the time I expose what's really happened—if I could ever prove it—Carl will already have made sure his story reaches London. In fact, I imagine he will bring it himself."

"Sire," Lucas said. "To continue to London now—"

"Would leave the Grand Duke of Glarien squawking like a rooster on a dung heap, ripe for plucking? I shan't turn back and I shan't go to London." The sun caught suddenly on something metallic and bright, a weather vane, perhaps, flashing like a beacon from the land. "I shall take your boat."

Nicholas strode up the beach with Fritz von Gerhard while five other members of his personal bodyguard raced across the shingle to catch their mounts. Quest tore ahead of them, efficiently preventing the horses' escape. The *Royal Swan* had come in close enough to the coast to sling the animals over the side into the sea. Nicholas had watched their noble heads and vibrating nostrils as the seven horses swam to the shore. The sight had reverberated in his heart, in a strange shame and exhilaration: brave creatures facing their greatest terror for his sake. Now the men gathered them and began rubbing them down. Panting, Quest flopped beside the saddles and bridles waiting on the thin stretch of beach.

Lucas slept soundly—or so Nicholas trusted—on the ship, sailing on to London without him, carrying the now useless trunks and cases. Nicholas wore a plain green jacket, a red scarf tied carelessly at his neck, white breeches and his favorite hunting boots. One of the perks of rank: letting subordinates look more important.

Not quite how he'd imagined landing back in England!

He had no idea what to do, nor even if Lucas's information was trustworthy. Anger flamed in him. Rage at Carl, rage at fate, rage at his own bloody impotence! There was no obvious answer to this and almost no response Carl wouldn't have foreseen.

He stopped for a moment and took up a handful of pebbles. Memories flickered and burned. Flints like these had formed the walls of the church where he'd been christened, its squat tower visible from the windows of the house where he'd been born. The same bright, hard rock had been piled into his Norman ancestors' first home in Norfolk, an ancient manor that had lain in ruins for three centuries, ever since the new house had been built to replace it. They had found him there, an eleven-year-old boy, and told him his fate.

Sea wrack lay strewn on the beach. Seagulls whirled and shrieked. He'd been unconditionally trumped. Where the hell had Carl taken her? *Sophia.* His yearning for her lay even deeper than duty. A craving, not for love, but for understanding. Any other woman would expect warmth or passion, small attentions, something more than just courtesy. Only Sophia, with her own royal destiny, would accept he had nothing of the kind to offer. The fate of Europe depended on this marriage; and for him—His Royal Highness Nicholas Alexander, Grand Duke of Glarien, Fürst von Moritzburg, sovereign prince of Glarien, Harzburg and Winsteg—there was no other possible future.

His fist closed. Flints like these formed his other birthright, his earliest solace. It was the one place he could go now, a place he'd never thought to see again: the ruins of the old manor in the grounds of his childhood home, Rascall Hall.

"I swear," Nicholas said fiercely as his men stopped and looked back in surprise. "I swear —as God is my witness and by the hard soul of this flint—that Carl will never marry Sophia, nor take the crown of Glarien, while I have breath in my body."

He wasn't even sure he could find the way. Yet, fourteen hours later, after a headlong ride north through Suffolk and Norfolk, splashing through fords, scattering geese and chickens, Nicholas knew he was almost there. His men's dark green uniforms with the gold sashes and short cloaks seemed incongruous here, outlandish. Laborers and villagers had been helpless with surprise.

He rode up a small rise and looked down on the village of Rascall St. Mary: a cluster of houses he'd last seen through a blur of childish tears from the window of a departing carriage.

Memories burned.

The square tower of knapped flints thrust above a small grove of yews sheltering the village churchyard. It looked smaller than he remembered, like a toy. He closed his eyes. Inside, along the nave and clustered around the altar, brasses and monuments marked the graves of his ancestors, lords of Evenlode since the twelfth century.

He was Earl of Evenlode, of course, and had been since his father's death ten years earlier—something he'd known, though it hadn't held much meaning in these last years.

Past the village a lane ran beside a high brick wall. Through the largest of the gates, the ride to the front of Rascall Hall was exactly twenty-two furlongs. He had measured it once with his tutor. The tops of trees and the fluted chimneys of the house appeared to float in the distance. Beyond them green countryside, dappled with flashes of water and striped by evening shadows, rolled away to a flat horizon and the distant North Sea.

Home, a small voice said absurdly in the back of his mind. *Home.*

The scent of the orangery seemed to flood his nostrils: rich, damp, citrus, sweet with fruit and the nutty smell of tile warmed by the sun. He remembered his mother handing him an orange, ripe and heavy. Dear God, he'd been—what?—eight years old? Nineteen years ago!

With a curse he moved his horse forward, circling around the village, intercepting the road well beyond the church. His men followed without comment. Two more miles brought them to the main gates. The wrought ironwork stood open, rusted in place. The gatehouse, with its pretty bow windows, lay empty. Cracked glass winked, reflecting the low red sun.

Something shook deep inside, so deep he felt sick.

A wild urgency took him by the throat. Nicholas urged his mount to a gallop and tore up the neglected avenue of elms. Someone had been cutting firewood in the copse by the gatehouse and there were cows—*cows*—on his lawns. As the horses thundered into the formal front courtyard, geese scattered as if Rascall Hall were some common farmhouse. Yet the tall rosered facade slept quietly, content in its shabby elegance, oblivious to the commotion. If he could just tear away the curtain of time, that door would open and his mother would step out, dressed in green velvet and lace!

Somewhere inside a small boy began to weep, crying that he didn't want to go away, didn't want to leave England to live with his grandfather far, far away in a castle in the mountains. But his mother had knelt down and scolded him. His mother, Princess Anna of Glarien, who had cursed him with her unexpected inheritance.

With iron control, Nicholas choked back the memories. Though a bitter lump fouled his gullet, he kept his expression casual, even a little amused. He nodded to Fritz, who dismounted and thudded on the heavy oak door. No one answered.

"Try the handle," Nicholas said.

"It is locked, sire."

Nicholas grinned, belying his real feelings. "Thus said the servants of Ali Baba, waiting on the magic password. So we must stable the nags ourselves. After which, break a window."

In a clatter of hooves they rode around to the stables through an ornamental arch topped with the Glarian lion. Someone had been about. Deeply rutted wagon tracks marked the yard. A clear path was worn from the kitchen door to the pump. The men swung down to put away their horses in the stable block his father had built to celebrate his marriage.

The stalls were already occupied. Not with horses, but with neat piles of firewood and vegetables in crates. Nicholas dismounted to look for himself. In the last stall was something even more odd. Bright questing eyes peered out from several small cages. In others spiny brown spheres slept soundly in drifts of dead leaves. For God's sake! Who the devil was collecting hedgehogs on his land? And grazing cows on his lawns? And locking him out of his own house?

Fury pounded at him, past analyzing, past control. Forty thieves had taken over his soul and he had no magic password to find his way back in. Thanks to Carl, the future had splintered into chaos. Now he could only break windows and rip into the past, like a thief himself. One after another he opened the cages, letting the hedgehogs scurry away to freedom.

In a scarlet fog, he walked back to his horse. Quest lay panting, exhausted from the long run. He rubbed her head, consoling her, controlling himself, before he turned to his men.

"Turn your nags loose—there, through that gate. It leads to Upper Meadow. Major, get into the house by any means necessary. Lars, keep Quest with you; feed her and let her rest. Hentz, the rest of you, make the damned place habitable and find food. Slaughter a goose, if you must." He gave them a man-to-man grin, sharing reassurance, and cuffed young Alexis on the shoulder. "You'll find plenty of potatoes in the stables."

He swung onto his mount. As the others stripped the tack from their horses, Alexis ran to open the gate. Nicholas rode alone through the fields. Ahead of him jagged towers, overgrown with ivy and creeping bindweed, thrust up among a stand of English oaks. A broken roof still sheltered the great tithe barn beside them. He stopped his horse and stared through the trees. This was the one place meant to be ruined, the place that had once been filled with a little boy's dreams: the remains of the long abandoned fortified manor, home to his boyhood imagination. The music of a lost age had once echoed here. War cries and the clank of armor, where King Arthur and Lancelot clashed swords over Guinevere.

His horse jibbed nervously, picking up his emotion. Nicholas calmed it and rode forward, calling on his well-practiced derision—and stopped dead.

A woman with a basket had just stepped out of the undergrowth encircling the ruins. Bramble and dog rose reached thorned snares. She pulled her skirts tightly about her legs and pulled free a barb caught in her hem. Alternating long dark shadows and bright streamers of dying light raced across the grass, firing her hair as she walked into the open space and turned to watch the sun sink behind the towers.

Incoherent pain sank cruel fingers and twisted. An intruder! An intruder *here*—in the one place he held sacred! She had no right—*nothing* excused it—to stand in the ruins of old Rascall Manor as if she owned them!

Something rumbled like thunder, an echo of those long-ago knights.

His horse sidled, tossing its head, as his men's loose mounts streamed past and galloped down on her.

One

The earth shook. She spun about and dropped the basket. The horses bucked and kicked, snorting as they ran. The leader pinned back its ears as it spun close, kicking out. Hooves flashed within inches of her head. Another horse reared. She ducked and screamed. The smell of horse sweat and excitement crashed over her. Oh, God! She'd be trampled! Her blood turned to ice, sluggish and cold, yet her heart bounded like a March hare, racing in wild, disconnected leaps.

She put her hands over her head and huddled down. One huge bay nosed the basket, pushing at her with its shoulder, almost knocking her over. Hedgehogs spilled onto the turf. The horse snorted and threw back its head, smacking her elbow. All six jostled and nudged as another pawed the basket with a forefoot. The fabric of her sleeve tugged as the bay nipped with large yellow teeth.

"Stand up straight!" a man's voice shouted. "Don't cower!"

She couldn't look up. She couldn't. If she moved at all, the horses would annihilate her. Their hot breath steamed into her nostrils and mingled with the choking tears. Frozen in place, she was gasping, trembling, unable to act.

The man's voice spoke closer, with authority, taking no nonsense. *"Hah! Foolish fellows! Walk on!"*

The bay shook its black mane and stepped back. The others milled nervously.

"Go on now! Foolish fellows!" The voice held the hint of a tolerant laugh—a laugh! Whoever he was, this stranger, she wanted to kill him.

He snapped his fingers. As if the sun had blazed onto a scattering of ice crystals, the horses melted away. Hoofbeats thundered as they raced off.

"What the devil were you about?" the man asked. "In another moment you'd have had them striking at you."

She was fighting for breath, vaguely aware of the tails of a dark green coat and a booted leg resting against the side of a black horse. Her heart raced in great swoops and thuds, strangling her. Words wouldn't come. Her voice lay locked somewhere below her rib cage, choked with fear.

The black circled her, its spine bent around the man's leg. She shook her head, filled with incoherent fury. While she had stared death in the face, he was *amused.* Only one word croaked out. "Why?"

"They thought you had grain in the basket. When you cowered, you confused them."

The man's horse began to dance. In a steady, perfect cadence, it trotted almost in place, lifting each hoof high, seeming to hover in the air for a moment between each stride. *Thud. Thud. Thud.* The iron shoes drummed on the grass. She looked up between her fingers. The black softly mouthed the bit, bending its neck in a graceful arch, the eye limpid and brown. Relaxed. In spite of all the animal's power, its eye spoke of calm and content, a softness, exuding reassurance.

The man rocked smoothly in rhythm, melded to his saddle. He circled her again. Her gaze traveled up—past the black boot and the firm thigh in the white breeches—over the masculine hands on the reins, the long, gloved fingers caressing the leather as if talking subtle mysteries to his mount—up over his green jacket.

Oh, Lord help her! Instead of the decent, careful folds of a cravat, a careless toss of red silk was tied loosely at his neck.

Still shielding her eyes with her hands, she peeked up at his face.

Perfect. Indifferent. As beautiful as the forest gods. In the fading, fire-tinged daylight, a prince of darkness stared casually down at her, a tiny smile at the corners of his mouth. His eyes flickered with shadows and flame, like something immortal—both very young, as if removed from the real world, and very old, with the authority of the centuries.

The horse stopped and reared just a little, front legs folded together like an equestrian statue, while the rider's hard black eyes devoured her. Old and young, like a prince of Faerie. As exotic, as foreign, as any of the painful, alien whispers that had haunted her childhood and echoed of abandonment.

Her arms were still wrapped about her head, her hands folded over one another like leaves. A single shaft of red sun broke through the trees, shadowing her hidden face, but spinning her hair into copper. The highlights sparked gold and amber, like the heart of a daisy.

She dropped her hands and met his gaze.

It was impossible! *Impossible!*

In spite of the dancing lights and the shadows, he recognized the wide hazel eyes and the blunt nose, too bold to be fashionable in a woman. The cheekbones that slipped like the curve of a pear into the thick blond hair. The clean-cut jaw and the too-bountiful mouth. He had a miniature painting of those exact features in his luggage. Stubborn, sensual, like a sunning lioness irritated by the arrival of a jackal: Princess Sophia, his intended bride, who was supposed to have been kidnapped by Carl!

His vision cracked and shattered. As if a giant fist had smashed the sunset, sending shards of reality spinning into bright husks of red light and black darkness. As if the gargoyles on his grandfather's castle leaped grinning to tear apart his skull with sharp claws. God! Dear God! Not now! For next would come the invisible demon, the headache pulsing in his brain behind his right eye, until the unimaginable pain would beat him to his knees.

He brought his mount down to the square halt and dismounted, analyzing fast, while the darkness roared and mad
fears leaped and twisted.

With rigid self-control he offered his hand, his horse's reins
looped over the other arm. "You are unhurt, madam?" She nodded and stepped back, just as the sun dipped behind the trees,
plunging her into shadows. "Then come quickly. We can't risk
explanations out here—obviously, it's not safe."

"I'm a little ruffled," she said. "But I was perfectly safe until
you arrived. Please collect your horses and leave. Gypsies
aren't allowed here. It disturbs the cows."

Gypsy! Her insults and bravado were incomprehensible—
unless she had already given herself to Carl. The lights danced
and swirled, the implications spun and twisted, racing like
waves in the face of the oncoming migraine.

"I thought I faced coup d'état. Instead I find a princess in a
castle, entangled with briars. Like Prince Charming after one
hundred years in the wilderness, do I turn up on cue? Or do I
have the wrong fairy tale and have I stumbled into one full of
danger?" He nodded toward the ruined manor, rage and wild
laughter hammering and soaring, beating like a captive eagle in
his breast. "I used to come here as a boy. I didn't think Carl
knew. Though he has reached into every other crevice of my
soul and tried to pollute it, I thought this one memory at least
was inviolate. Did you all plan it together: Carl, Lucas and you?
Did you guess I'd come here? Is this the way Hercules felt
when gifted by his lover with a poisoned shirt?"

Before she could move again, he grasped her wrists.

Her eyes wide, she tried to jerk back. Her pulse throbbed in
the palms of his hands. Her hair smelled like roses and woodland. The sweet scent of treason. The danger wasn't to her; it
was to him and she knew it. He had been outwitted and his own
soul's deepest longings had betrayed him. He had raced here on
an impulse and left his bodyguard out of reach, when the whole
damned thing reeked of ambush. In a last twist of the knife,
even the old ruins were a trap.

She wrenched a wrist free. In a reflex honed by years of
training, he pinioned her hand and spun her against his chest.

The rose scent was maddening in his nostrils. Her entire body seemed to shiver. With deliberate cynicism he spun her against his horse's side, so the animal blocked them from any watchers in the ruins.

"I am sorry, Princess," he said. "Do you want to become a bone quarreled over by hounds? You have just fallen under my protection—not for love, nor even for revenge. Just to let you know I'm serious about our royal obligations."

"You are lunatic!"

He sneered, deliberately. "It's in the blood—yours and mine!"

The curve of her waist shaped firm and female in his palm, a disruptive, fearful feeling. Furious, he captured her chin in one hand. The blunt nose and rich mouth carried a bloom of panic in the deepening dusk. He wanted to kiss her, ravish her, there in the ruins where he'd once dreamed of romance. He had never had such feelings about Sophia!

He held himself on the knife edge of control, burning with anger and an odd humiliation. No doubt if he released her and moved far enough away, a bullet would slam into his back. Not something he intended to allow, even if the black need to use force twisted deep in his soul. *Devil's spawn!* The old fear surged and shifted, a demon grinning in the night. Pain beat at him. He could ravish her! Shame flooded through his bones in a dreadful, burning torrent. What he most feared and despised, he had just become. He wanted to drop to his knees and bury his head in his hands, in the quiet, in the dark. He opened his fingers.

This time when she swung back her hand, he allowed it. The blow exploded against his cheek, flaming into a hot bruise, sending drumming agony through his skull, spiking nausea. His horse jerked back. Groping for control, he looked away at the wavering leaves and the solid rock of the medieval walls. Dying sunlight glinted off flint, like a thousand rifle barrels.

"Alas that I owe it to destiny to live," he said.

He picked her up, slung her bodily onto his horse and swung into the saddle behind her. Holding her tightly against his chest, he set his mount at a gallop across the meadow toward Rascall

Hall. Her broken breathing roared as if it were his own. He felt the rattling rapidity of her heartbeat. Dog rose and woodland spiraled from her dress. As he carried her away, words spoken long ago echoed in the whispering grasses and ran sighing through the dying day.

Your ancestors were called the devil princes. Masters of underground halls. Familiars of the vampire demons of the night. Ravishers of virgins. It's your destiny, Nicholas. Your destiny!

It didn't matter, it never mattered, that he wanted to be something different. He was doomed by his blood.

Alexis leaned on the gate. Openly astonished, the boy flung it open and allowed Nicholas to ride through. Gravel crunched. Geese lifted their wings and hissed. The front door stood open with another of his men, Ludger, at attention. Nicholas rode his horse straight up the short flight of steps into the entryway and through the first antechamber, still carrying his captive pinned on the saddle in front of him. Iron-shod hooves boomed and echoed on the stone floors.

Hentz leaped to attention, hiding shock behind practiced obedience, his face blank beneath the mass of brown curls. "Sire, we have prepared the blue drawing room. The house was under dust sheets—" He flung open a door.

Leaving the man standing in the hallway, Nicholas rode through the doorway and halted his mount.

The gilt ceiling reflected a multitude of wavering candles and the dancing, innocent glow of a fire. The dust sheets had been whisked away to reveal brocade chairs embroidered with the Evenlode coat of arms. The carpet was thick and lush. Knotted wool garlands of rose and blue, intertwined with gold thread to match the sparkle of the gilding and the tassels on the drapes, spiraled away from his horse's hooves. The full glory of the formal withdrawing room of Rascall Hall, where he had once recited poetry to his mother, scintillated in a blaze of candlelight.

Somewhere deep inside something vibrated, echoing the dancing patterns of yellow light, as the migraine spread excruciating roots through the side of his skull.

Fritz von Gerhard had been lighting candles at the side of the room. Fine strands of blond hair tufted like a halo around his bald pate. Beneath the long scar that ran down one cheek, he'd turned white.

The black shook and steamed, gently mouthing the bit.

"Take the horse, Fritz," Nicholas said in Glarisch. "And put down the taper before you singe your fingers. The house is secure?"

Fritz had already snapped to attention. "Sire!" He grimaced and pinched out the taper as it burned down to his skin.

"Brandy," Nicholas ordered.

He swung the princess down and dismounted after her. Fritz took the horse and led it from the room. The echo of hoofbeats rang away down the corridor. Nicholas strode to the door and closed it. Deliberately he paused there, ignoring the rolling agony and swirling rings of colored lights, leaving her his undefended back. If she intended personal assassination she wouldn't succeed, but he'd like to know now.

"I have six men with me," he said. "They safeguard everywhere I stay. I can vouch for their efficiency. I trained them. Whatever Carl threatened, whatever madness I've offered, I promise I shall keep you safe. Were you afraid your own life might be forfeit? If I hadn't been certain it was not, I wouldn't have carried you back here. I don't know what schemes are afoot, but if you were threatened and had no choice in this, Princess, for God's sake, tell me now."

He waited, like a man awaiting execution, and listened to her shattered breathing. He had brought down a lioness and made her weep, when he had been ready to lay his life and his crown at her feet. How the devil did one mend this?

"My lord . . . Prince Nicholas . . ."

"Grand Duke Nicholas," he said. "I am also a prince, but that's a lesser title."

"How very confusing! You are also Earl of Evenlode, aren't you? I don't know what you're talking about. I don't know what I'm doing here. Unless, perhaps, you are both monarch and mad?"

"It's been known." Bloody hell! How the devil did one mend *this*?

He turned to look at her.

Her hair straggled in disheveled loops around her shoulders. Her nostrils quivered. She was wearing a plain muslin gown, practical, even severe, with the one sleeve ripped and the hem bedraggled. Why hadn't he noticed before?

A gentlewoman's dress, but not the gown a princess would wear.

She took a handkerchief out of her pocket and blew her nose.

Not the way Princess Sophia would blow her nose.

The feet of the chair behind her were shaped like little lion's paws, with neat golden claws and a carved curl of fur. She sat down on the blue-and-rose brocade as if her legs would no longer hold her.

For a long moment there was perfect silence. The brilliant room stripped away all ambiguities as reality asserted itself. Her eyes were a little greener, perhaps. Her hair was blonder, less red. Her mouth slightly more full, with an irreverent turn at the corners as if usually she found life amusing. She was not smiling now. She looked angry and frightened and embarrassed.

Yet the absurdity of the whole situation began to well up in the space left by his relief. The migraine softened as the demon retreated, then the pain simply shredded, leaving only a lonely, innocuous fragility underlying the bones of his skull. The lioness was just an English pussycat. Devil take it!

"I see." He gave her a full court bow. "My apologies, madam, if I caused you some unintended wretchedness."

"I thought you were a gypsy," she said. "Or a lunatic."

"A common mistake. Princes of Glarien have never known whether to hide or celebrate that unfortunate resemblance."

"I am not a princess." She stuffed the handkerchief away. "I don't know why you should think that I am. My name is Penelope Lindsey and I live in Rascall St. Mary with my mother. If Your Royal Highness has finished behaving like a villain in a bad novel, I would very much appreciate being allowed to go home."

The angel of death folded his wings and departed as Nicholas began to laugh.

Two

Firelight danced on white teeth and jet black hair. Shadows and flame, from the day's stubble at his jaw to the amoral amusement in his eyes. Dark eyes, unreadable, black velvet over midnight. The sensuous mouth with its deep upper curve echoed the tilt toward sarcasm in the flared nostrils. His skin seemed almost translucent, a fine, clear olive blushed to rose over the high cheekbones.

Lord Evenlode—also the lord and master, heaven help her, of a vital principality in central Europe—was home. It wasn't supposed to happen, ever. She had known all her life, even when she'd read about him in the newspaper, that he'd never come back to Rascall Hall.

And now he had.

Oh, Lord! When he discovered what she'd been doing, it would definitely set the cat among the pigeons. A great flurry of feathers and more than one dead bird—herself, most likely!

For one wild moment, she had thought they could laugh together over his mistake and her transgressions. He must have some sensible explanation and surely she could engage his sympathy if she just confessed. In the next instant, she banished the thought as he turned to her with his laughter turned to smoke. Not really surprising. After all, he was one of those dissolute gypsy princes her mother resolutely refused to discuss.

"You may not go home," he said.

"But now you know who I am—"

"I really don't care who you are. I would have brought you back here anyway."

Penny ran her hand over the chair arm. "Well, goodness! How dramatic! Why on earth did you seize me like that?"

His dark gaze swallowed the night, echoing the ice-cold shimmer of stars. "I thought there was danger."

"Good heavens! To me? I was terrified by those loose horses, I admit, but after that—"

"You were terrified by me." It was a statement, not a question.

"Well, yes. Until I realized who you were and that you might be upset that I was at the old manor, though not—well, it isn't worth dwelling on, is it? Should I offer thanks for your protective gallantry?"

"That isn't what happened. I never thought there was danger to you. I used you for my own preservation, as a shield."

It was such a bizarre confession, she felt completely lost. "How very ungentlemanly of you!"

"I am a prince. Gallant self-sacrifice would only be another name for shirking my duty. Nevertheless, you are in danger now, because I am here. I take full responsibility."

"Oh." She glanced down at her plain walking dress and heard her most immediate fear slip out in a question. "How long do you intend to stay at Rascall Hall, Your Royal Highness?"

His mood seemed to shift a little. "No doubt you wish that the uncomfortable prince and his soldiers would leave before daylight in the morning?"

A little too close to her wishes for comfort. "There's no polite answer to that."

"Exactly. How did you know who I was?"

"Your Highness's story has been the delight and gossip of the village for as long as I can remember. Though we never thought you'd come back—"

He interrupted. "We?"

"My mother and myself. She's always interested in news about your part of the world. Your upcoming marriage was in the papers. You were supposed to arrive in London with a great retinue of pomp and circumstance. No one expected you here. However, I remembered it when you rode inside, hauling me with you in that uncomfortable way."

His glance held mild surprise, but he seemed more amused than disturbed by her insolence. "I didn't believe I had time for niceties, but I trust you were suitably impressed?"

"Impressed? Well. In spite of your misleading appearance— you will admit, I trust, that your jacket and neckcloth aren't quite what one might expect a grand duke to wear—neither gypsies nor lunatics have keepers in military uniforms with gold sashes. Those keepers certainly don't jerk to attention and call them 'sire.' Neither would gypsies nor lunatics take over Rascall Hall as if they owned it."

"I do own it."

Presumably princes were not easy to upset, though she would like to upset him at least as much as he'd upset her! Penny had the distinct feeling that her bridges were burned and her goose cooked, so what did she have to lose? She pulled out her handkerchief and blew her nose again. "Though madmen can share a similar tyrannical certainty: all that irritated, arrogant haughtiness, as if you were more than a mere mortal."

"I'm only too mortal and I would prefer you not to weep. Take this."

He offered her a clean handkerchief.

And smiled.

She felt the impact right down to her toes. His smile cast a spell: a sensuous, magical spell, curving his lips in a promise of interest and warmth. In spite of her alarm, she thought she might melt into an undignified puddle—a puddle wearing muslin and sensible boots. Of course, the charm was empty, with no real interest and no real warmth. His mercurial changes of mood were apparently all on the surface, like sun glancing over a cold, dark pool.

"Take it, please," he said, still smiling.

His handkerchief settled in her hand in soft, luxurious folds of white. An intricate crest was embroidered on one corner. Such a casual display of wealth: a handkerchief worth more than her mother's best tablecloth!

The silk smelled faintly of sea and horse, leather and oranges—reminding her of that sharply defined, cleanly muscled maleness as he'd held her across his lap on the horse. The memory of his arm about her waist burned and flickered somewhere, with an absurd whisper of forbidden sins. Her mouth felt sensitive suddenly, almost painfully aware. She had thought for a moment he was going to kiss her. Force his lips over hers. But of course he had believed she was someone else. She tried to remember the details of the conversation they'd had at the ruins, but it was blurred by her terror and fury and the odd, unnamable mixture of emotions she'd felt when she'd realized his identity.

"As I would prefer not to have been abducted," she said. "Unfortunately I seem to be displaying a most inappropriate desire to give way to hysteria. That isn't my wish. A woman's tears can denote anger as much as fear—"

"You felt both, of course." He walked away across the room, touching chair backs and tables, then stopped to caress the brass spirals of an intricate model of the solar system. Power and arrogance lay in every line, from the tall boots to the careless toss of red neckcloth. His expression was remote, entirely free from concern.

Anger immediately won the battle. "What on earth did you expect me to feel?"

"Passion, perhaps?" His voice was deeply self-derisive, though he gave her that bone-melting half smile again—a smile offering warmth and succor and sorcery. "An uncomfortable surge of heat in the blood?"

A flood of dreadful, hot embarrassment drowned all her annoyance. Presumably this was what it meant to be royal. To be entirely above common feelings, even common courtesy. To speak and act with the most outrageous arrogance and be immune to the consequences. *Of course,* a small voice said. *What else can you expect?*

"It's part of your royal prerogative to abduct innocent females?"

"So you don't think being seized by a grand duke an honor?" His fingers rested for a moment on the sensuous metal curves—Venus and Mars spiraling on wire tracks about a brass sun, orbits and planets spinning with a rub of his thumb. "Most ladies of the court would give their eyeteeth for my glance."

"And go toothless for life, no doubt, for your personal attention?"

His derision deepened into open mockery. "I did almost kiss you. I wanted to. But royal favors shouldn't have to mean gumming one's food for the rest of one's days."

Her confidence drained away. His scorn was entirely without remorse. "I think I'd prefer an apology to your empty wit."

Impenetrable, the dark eyes glanced back at her. "You really didn't like it?"

"Which? The wit or your noble restraint?" She stood up. "I would say one was as superficial as the other. Your Highness, I must go home now."

"But you have suffered a shock. You thought me a lunatic."

"I still do."

The brass planets trembled under his fingers strong, square-knuckled, with perfectly groomed fingernails. Penny thrust her own hands behind her skirt, then deliberately pulled them out again. What did it matter if he saw they were neither quite clean nor well-groomed?

He glanced up at the painting above the mantel. "The first earl. My great-grandfather on my father's side. There was no madness in his family. Indeed, he looks the very picture of stolid English propriety. Of course, appearances can be deceiving. He was a well-known drunkard, though kind as a baby in his cups. You will stay for brandy. It will settle your nerves. It did his."

Hysteria still threatened just below the surface. To hear him talk so calmly of his great-grandfather! It was such a bizarre discontinuity after one had been terrorized and abducted. Infuriatingly, the residue of tears gave her the strongest desire to sneeze and she was afraid the sneeze might mutate into laughter. Inglorious, humiliating laughter. Beneath the dignity of Miss Penelope Lindsey of Rascall St. Mary, who, after all, was a capable, respected anchor in her community.

She jerked out the handkerchief. "You won't find any brandy. The house has lain empty for years, with just a handful of staff. I've never seen it under anything but dust sheets. However, Mrs. Butteridge, the housekeeper, might have tea."

He walked immediately toward the bellpull, leaving the brass moon tumbling about the earth. "Then I shall order it."

Behind him, the door banged open. Nicholas turned so fast Penny thought she saw the flash of a knife in his hand. If so, it was immediately gone. In a flurry of aprons and waving cleaning cloths, like an upturned laundry basket, a plump woman burst into the room. The distinctly harassed-looking soldier at her heels was the balding man with the scar who'd been lighting the candles.

Mrs. Butteridge: English, ordinary and sensible—a lambent center of sanity in all the madness.

"Miss Lindsey!" she cried. "Oh, Lord bless my soul! An army has taken over the house. Came in without so much as a please or thank you. They're in the kitchen taking the chickens Mr. Butteridge and I planned for our supper and raiding the pantry for bread. They said they would kill a goose. They've turned out horses in Upper Meadow and made Lizzie make up the bed in the best bedchamber. They're all foreign, miss, and don't speak a Christian word, but for this one here—" She thrust a stubby finger at the soldier, who stared at the ceiling, his scar throbbing. "And one other."

"Mrs. Butteridge? You will forgive our rude invasion," Nicholas said impassively. "We thought the house empty. No one meant to alarm you."

The housekeeper turned to him. "And who might you be, sir? To barge into an English home to steal my chickens?" She glanced back at Penny and her round face crumpled. "What have you done to Miss Lindsey? Oh, you brute! You heathen gypsy!" She surged toward the prince, fist upraised. Obviously that flickering impression of a knife had been a trick of the candlelight. Nicholas made no move to save himself, but the soldier grasped Mrs. Butteridge by the arm. The housekeeper glared at her captor. "Heathen, outlandish ways," she said. "And look at *your* face! Getting scarred up like a mountebank!"

Penny sneezed into the royal handkerchief, giggles and hiccups at war in her throat.

"Major Baron von Gerhard's scar is a mark of honor from a duel," Nicholas said.

His handkerchief ripped apart in Penny's hands. She was afraid she might choke. She thrust one half of the ruined silk over her mouth. Stifled, hysterical mirth shook her shoulders. She fought for control, but her breathing was broken by gasps.

"But you . . . are gaining bruises . . . instead of scars—"

He grinned at her and bowed. "Of course, as crown prince, I was never risked in duels."

The housekeeper stared. Her chin trembled.

"It's all right, Mrs. Butteridge." Penny wiped away her tears on what was left of his exquisite handkerchief. "Against all expectations, Lord Evenlode has come home."

The major released the housekeeper and bowed. "Madam, you have the honor to address His Royal Highness, Grand Duke Nicholas Alexander of Glarien, who in England is also Earl of Evenlode, Viscount Saxlingham and master of this house. A grand duke's person is sacred. To violate it means death."

"Death!" Mrs. Butteridge paled.

The soldier grinned. "By hanging. Your life is in His Highness's palm, along with everything else here. The chickens, madam, are already his."

She crumpled like a deflating balloon. "Grand Duke! Lord Evenlode! Oh, bless my soul! I didn't know, I'm sure. Your Royal Highness! But these men have the house in an uproar searching for brandy. I declare it's put me all at sixes and sevens. There's only myself and Butteridge and the girl Lizzie. We don't keep spirituous liquor."

"Then fetch tea," the prince said. "You have tea?" Mrs. Butteridge nodded and sank, clutching her apron. His smile was entirely reassuring. "You can cook?"

"Just plain English cooking, Your Royal Highness."

"Then prepare a meal and we will forget this small misunderstanding." His voice promised a world of interest and support. "Plain English cooking is exactly to our taste."

Backing away with an odd bobbing curtsey at each step, the housekeeper fled the room.

The soldier remained. Nicholas waved his hand. "Miss Lindsey, this is Major Baron Friedrich von Gerhard, captain of my personal bodyguard, known as Fritz to his friends. Major, this is Miss Penelope Lindsey who lives with her mother in the village." The prince then spoke to the major in Glarisch. "The lady's striking appearance is not to be mentioned. You will ensure secrecy and privacy. She will stay here. Take care of the details."

The soldier bowed, clicked his heels, and left.

Nicholas stared into the fireplace. He stood absolutely still, an almost inhuman stillness. His lean shadow, multiplied by each candle and flickering flame, moved in intricate patterns of light and shade across the room. Nothing moved but the leaping shadows and the slow tilt and weave of the spheres still wavering on the brass planetarium.

"I didn't know you were a grand duke when I struck you," Penny said. "Will you hang me?"

"I don't imagine I have the jurisdiction to do so in England."

The last hints of her laughter died in her throat. She gazed at him, appalled. "You might do so at home?"

He looked around, as if startled. "No, of course not. Miss Lindsey, we have things to discuss—"

She'd had enough. There would be plenty to discuss when he found out about the hedgehogs and the cows and the orangery, and she had enough grievances—a lifetime of grievances—of her own. It would give her great pleasure to throw them in his face and see how he liked that, but she couldn't face any more. She was uncomfortably bruised and disheveled. She'd like a bath and she'd like half an hour of ordinary, sane company and a little time to plan what to do about his sudden return.

"It could be a charming conversation, I admit," she said. "For example, I am wondering whether your face will turn black and blue like a speckled hen from my assault on your sacred person. However, I shan't stay to find out. I'm going home."

She stood up.

"Sit down," he said without looking at her. "You won't be allowed to leave."

Her legs folded. A faint panic began to flutter somewhere underneath her bodice. "Don't be absurd. My mother will already be alarmed. When I don't arrive home, she'll rouse the whole village. This is England. You cannot keep me here."

He walked back across the room to face her. He might not have a scar, but he moved like a swordsman, lightly and with lethal intent. "There aren't many advantages to being royal, Miss Lindsey, but when I tell Major von Gerhard that you are my guest, he will obey."

"Fiddlesticks! Unfortunately for your privacy, I speak Glarisch."

He spun away from her and dropped onto the couch. The black eyes showed nothing but an intense concentration. "Ah! I guessed as much."

"It was another clue I should have recognized right away, though I didn't quite register it at the time. While your English is perfect because you grew up in England, you spoke to the horses in Glarisch, didn't you? As you just spoke to the major. You said nothing to him about imprisonment."

"I didn't have to." He leaned back and tossed his feet onto an arm of the couch. Black shadow dancers wavered, swirling and spinning, where the hair fell forward over his forehead.

"Oh, good heavens! Will you attack me if I walk out? Earlier I thought you had a knife."

"I do." In the next moment, it was in his hand. Penny didn't know where he'd pulled it from, but flames were reflected up and down a long, narrow blade. Terror leaped fully formed into her throat.

"For God's sake," he said. "Don't look so alarmed. I'm more likely to be the victim, not the perpetrator, of assassination." The flame-bright blade spun in his fingers. A moment later it stood, handle upright, quivering in the pile of the carpet next to her chair. "There. My knife is closer now to your reach than mine. But you can't go home."

This was worse than anything she'd ever imagined: mad princes with knives. "Mrs. Butteridge will raise the alarm."

He settled more comfortably into the cushions. "You think so?"

"I suppose not. She's your employee. You charmed her and your major has put the fear of God into her." She stood up again. "But my mother—"

"Your mother won't suffer a moment's anxiety. Fritz will take a message that will reassure her completely."

"How kind of him! I assume all your men follow their own philanthropic instincts?"

"They follow orders. Obviously, any local concerns about you must be assuaged so no alarm is raised. I told the major to take care of the details and he will do so, including the Butteridges and your mother—and the vicar and the local tinkers and the innkeeper, if necessary. You are quite safe here."

The colors swirled together in the blue-and-rose carpet. Gilt boomed and sparkled on the walls. His words slid into a disordered jumble, reminding her of the bewildering confusion of horses and madness. When a monarch was insane, how far would his followers go? What had happened when Ivan the Terrible issued his orders? Only in England was the poor lunatic king safely taken care of, while his son became Prince Regent and Parliament ruled the land.

She walked away from the sight of his powerful, elegant form on the couch, as if the movement of her feet on the carpet could drown out the clamor of apprehension. "But why? What is the danger?" At the fireplace she turned back to look at him. "Is this how you live at home?"

"Home?" He put both hands behind his head and stared at the ceiling. "This place was my home once."

"This is England. But you were afraid, weren't you? At old Rascall Manor? You were afraid we were going to be attacked or that some trap waited there? Good heavens! Such Gothic nonsense doesn't happen here."

"No, of course not," he said.

"Then why must I stay?"

He seemed entirely relaxed now, the supple mouth merely willful, his fingers curled over each tender palm. "I am scintillatingly aware that your appearance cannot be a coincidence. Nor, I imagine, can your lack of the customary awe in my august royal presence. Now you tell me you speak Glarisch. I believe I have guessed, but I must know exactly who you are."

Of course. Of course, he was curious. That was all. Of course, he wondered who she was, and this abrupt, commanding manner was probably the normal thing for a prince. He'd even disarmed himself to reassure her. Her demon of panic shrank like a child's imagined imp of darkness under the wardrobe at night. "And then will you allow me to leave?"

"That depends a great deal on your answer."

Penny stared up at the portrait of the first earl. "Very well. If it is all to come out anyway, it might as well be now. Lindsey is my mother's maiden name. Twenty-four years ago she was a governess to the royal house of Glarien. Your mother secured the post for her. I don't suppose you remember. You would have been three years old when she left. Twelve months later Prince Frederick of Alvia—your neighbor and relative—seduced her."

"Prince Frederick was no blood relative of mine. His brother married my grandfather's sister, that's all."

His calm was infuriating. That completely unruffled relaxation and command. "I don't know anything about my father and I've made it a point not to care. Don't royal families constantly marry their cousins like a bunch of prize pigs? When my mother was found to be with child, she was sent home to England in disgrace. Yet she taught me my father's tongue in case he ever came for me. He never did."

"He died. Do you hold that against him?"

"In the meantime he abandoned her and refused to acknowledge me. In English tradition, royal bastards were honored and accepted. Not apparently in your part of the world."

"Come and sit down," he said. "You make me dizzy standing there with all your accusations."

As if her feet belonged to someone else, she crossed the

room and sat on the chair. "I make you dizzy! For heaven's sake, you have offered me no apology, no explanation."

"While you have just offered me yours: You have royal blood. You resent it, but you never forget it." He laid one hand over his eyes. His nails shone on elegant, deadly fingers. "Does anyone besides your mother know your true circumstances?"

"No one living—except Mama's closest relatives in Staffordshire. Why? She always told everyone here she was widowed."

"Then no one will guess what I intend—"

What I intend. Like a startled cat, she felt both guarded and alert.

Someone rapped on the door. "Enter," Nicholas said.

The major came in with a tea tray, set it down on the low table in front of her, bowed, and left the room. A large dog with a silver coat and brown eyes had trotted in behind him.

Grand Duke Nicholas said nothing, but the dog went straight to him and lay down at his feet. In the profound silence a clock ticked quietly. The fire occasionally thudded or hissed as a log fell. His knife and the brass planetarium were each perfectly still now, with no further vibration of insulted metal.

Penny sat looking stiffly at the tea tray. Small tendrils of steam escaped from the spout. Her face shone in the silver pot like a distorted pear, making her nose seem enormous. Her hair was a rat's nest. The dog watched her steadily.

"Oh, this is ridiculous," she said at last. "I will take tea, if Your Highness insists."

He dropped his hand from his eyes and looked at her. "Good."

"Would you care to partake of some tea?"

"No."

"Then what do you want?"

"I don't wish to upset you . . ." he began.

The teacups were a delicate bone china with small patterns of flowers. "Your Royal Highness, I have experienced a wider range of emotions in the last half hour than I would wish on an enemy in a lifetime."

"Then prepare for another insult to your mental equilibrium," he said dryly. "Here."

He reached into an inside pocket on his jacket and produced a small metal case. With a flick of a wrist he tossed it onto her lap. Then his fingers dropped to stroke the dog's head.

The two halves fit together neatly like the covers of a book. The case was richly tooled and decorated with gilt. No, not gilt. Solid gold. The little rose on the front no doubt shone with real diamonds and rubies. Penny unhooked the clasp to reveal a miniature portrait.

A young woman. Her red hair was caught up under a pearl diadem. Her shoulders sloped into a foam of white lace. A heavy diamond necklace encircled her throat. She had wide hazel eyes and a blunt nose. Apart from the diamonds and the pearls and the delicate white lace—apart from the fact that this woman with her redder hair somehow looked beautiful—Penny was looking at a portrait of herself.

"Her Royal Highness Princess Sophia, crown princess of Alvia and my intended bride," Nicholas said. "Through her mother she's my second cousin, second in line to the crown of Glarien. Your father, Prince Frederick, was a younger brother of her father, the present Duke Michael of Alvia. Thus you are Princess Sophia's bastard cousin. You might be her twin."

Penny felt blank with shock. All those silences after her mother had seen the wedding announcement! Mama knew the relationship, of course, but she couldn't have known of this uncanny, sickening resemblance.

"So you are trying to tell me you mistook me for her at the ruins. I see. Mother doesn't talk much about Glarien, or about my father." She stared at him. He seemed shuttered, the black eyes reflecting black darkness, giving nothing away. "There was always gossip in the village about Princess Anna and her family—how you were all gypsies and dissolute rakes and the scandal of Europe. I've always known my father must have been like that, too. Dashing and wild and thoughtless, without a shred of conscience. Is that unfair?"

"All that is just fairy tales. None of it makes or breaks nations. Alvia is less than a principality, it's merely a speck on the map, but a speck with some of the richest mines in Europe. Everyone wants it—"

"Including you? This is why you're marrying Princess Sophia? For mines?"

He lay entirely supine now, feet crossed at the ankles. Yet something about the graceful line of arm and thigh and boot thrummed with energy, a pent-up tension like a hovering hawk. "Glarien has mines of its own."

"Poor princess! So you will take all the mines under your personal control."

"There's nothing personal about it. Two nations will marry in London in a month, an exercise in royal pageantry, vital to diplomacy. Now Napoleon is gone, the temptation exists for more powerful neighbors to carve up Glarien and Alvia and take the mines for themselves, but no one wants the unholy squabble that would result. And worse, by an old treaty, if Sophia's father dies without a living male descendent, Alvia will be absorbed by France. So the princess must have a son. Thus the marriage."

"Which will unite both countries and create a new independent state under the benevolent protection of the great powers, so producing the desired stability in the Alps. The newspaper explained it."

"Then you understand the importance of this. Britain wants it. Prussia and the Tsar have agreed. That's why the wedding must take place in London, while the Allied sovereigns are in England. We shall do more than exchange rings. We shall secure treaty terms, as well."

Penny sipped at her tea. "Why are you telling me this?"

"Because you must understand how serious the situation is. How serious I am." He closed his eyes, his expression blank. "Miss Lindsey. There is royal blood in your veins. Whether you like it or not, that has just determined your fate."

"Because I look like my cousin?"

His glance was almost pitying. She had thought him both old and young. There was nothing young or innocent about him now. "The likeness is uncanny."

"Yes, I see. That does rather account for your madness at Rascall Manor."

"Listen carefully. Princess Sophia has been kidnapped by my enemies. They will say she refuses me. When it is publicly discovered, the marriage will be canceled. I will not allow that to happen." The depth of cynicism in his eyes was more ancient now than the gaze of an adder about to bite. "With a little grooming and new clothes, you could become her. You speak Glarisch. No one except your mother's family and myself knows of your connection to the royal house of Alvia, but your extraordinary appearance will put you in danger, if you remain in the village now that I'm here. The solution is obvious. You will help me avert chaos, Miss Lindsey, by standing in for the princess at my wedding."

Penny spilled tea into her saucer, but she forced herself not to leap to her feet, not to let her teacup smash melodramatically on the carpet. The dog lurched up, staring at her, then lay down again at a gesture from Nicholas.

She covered her shock with a bubble of laughter. "What? You cannot be serious! It's absurd!"

"Stand with me in front of the Allied leaders and take vows for Sophia. Diplomacy will be satisfied, my enemies confounded."

It was too unreal to grasp. "Take vows? My life is here in Rascall St. Mary. I've never been to London."

"Then take this chance. Afterward, you may come home to the village and live out your days in all the obscurity you wish."

The tea sloshed in the saucer. She couldn't seem to keep it still. "But I don't want my life to change."

"It has already changed. I am here. I cannot be denied."

"How could I learn to act like a princess?"

"I will teach you."

"It's lunatic! Impossible!"

He was on his feet—a blur of movement as if the hawk stooped on its prey. The dog didn't move. "Oh, for God's sake! I have never been more coldly, appallingly sane—and I have already weighed the odds."

Penny wanted to wrap her hands over her head as she'd done

with the horses. "It's not even worth discussing. It's madness. I will not do it."

"You don't have a choice. But don't you admit to even a moment's temptation? Princess for a day, Miss Lindsey! A masquerade, bolder than you've ever dreamed. A chance to make a difference to the fate of nations. Imagine the gowns and jewels you will wear, the chance to see a royal world from the inside. The Prince Regent and the Tsar will bow over your hand."

Her alarm only intensified at the thought. "I'd be exposed instantly."

"Nonsense. Sophia isn't known outside Alvia. Her family won't be in attendance. No one will guess; it's too audacious and outrageous. Do it, Miss Lindsey. Do it for yourself, not for me. Life casts few enough chances. When one this splendid offers, grasp it!"

"Oh, goodness! You may be the absolute ruler of a petty principality in central Europe and used to such things, but I'm an Englishwoman of very ordinary habits. How could I choose something so insane? I'm not in the least tempted."

He strode away to a side table and took up two exquisite vases, one in each hand. Penny thought they were Greek, one in red and black, the other black and white, each covered with small leaping figures.

"Life is a madman's throw, anyway. We toss dice and wait for the outcome, all the time knowing that a fiendish fate might tip the table or decide to give our opponent a straight run of sixes. That I might lose doesn't keep me out of the game."

"But the risk! I cannot do it and I won't."

His intensity sparked, like a thundercloud. "It is all risk. This is hardly what I would have wished, for God's sake! Everything will depend on you—the keys to a kingdom like so much candy in the hands of a child. Will you try the sweetmeats or the sugared plums first? These are stakes you can't even imagine. Decide on a whim and a people fall into destruction."

"The image is insane," she said. "No one ever ruled according to the whim of the moment, like choosing a sweet."

Suddenly he smiled. That wicked, charming smile, like a boy's inviting her to share in harmless mischief. "Oh, no? Then you don't know the history of our part of the world—yours and mine. Your blood is tainted, too. Do you think you can hide it behind prim Englishness and country common sense?" He held out his hands, one delicate vase in each fist, the tendons of his wrists stark in the candlelight. "In thirty seconds, I shall drop one of these. Whichever you choose. Which is it to be, left or right?"

Penny leaped up. "Stop! Why should I choose? I shall forget you ever proposed something so mad and go home."

"Now that I have told you about Sophia, I can't let you go, can I? Her disappearance must obviously be kept secret." He spoke gently as if humoring an infant. "Choose. Do you like this red and black better? It's Achilles, I think, sulking in his tent. Or the white on black? The figures seem to be racing in frenzy under an evil moon—the rites of Bacchus?"

"For heaven's sake!" Frantic tears pricked at her eyelids. "They're very ancient, priceless. Stop it!"

"Do you want war?" He lifted the red-and-black vase and looked at it critically. "Achilles with his bronze helmet? Or does the lure of madness haunt your blood?" The tumbling figures of the bacchanal danced under his long fingers as he waved the white vase. "The maenads: mad women who raced, they say, through the nights of ancient Greece, wild with wine, ready to devour men in an orgiastic fury." He held out both vases. "Choose!"

She dropped back to her chair and covered her eyes. "You cannot make me!"

"Ten seconds," he said.

"I can't choose!"

There was a slight click. Penny looked up. Both vessels sat unharmed on their table.

"Of course not," he said. "How could you? But be honest. Search your feelings and tell me: At the moment when you thought I might drop the red one, what did you feel? A tiny disappointment or a minute shred of hope? Then the white? If you are honest enough, you'll find a slight difference in your immediate reaction. That minuscule difference will tell you which you liked best. Without your conscious volition, you'd already made a choice."

"Is this how you hold your subjects?" Penny asked. "In the palm of your hand, facing imminent destruction if they can't guess your whim? Their emotions your playground? I see your dog does nothing without your permission."

He glanced at the animal and his expression softened. "Meet Her Highness, Alessandrina von der Moritzburg." The dog sat and held up a paw. "She's a purebred Glarian wolfhound from the royal kennels. It's her nature to be obedient to princes. I call her Quest."

Penny took the paw and shook it. "Quest?"

The dog lay down and put her head on her paws.

"Alessandrina's kennel name was Sukey. Though we speak Glarisch, our royal titles are German. *Die Suche* means the search or quest. It's a pun."

She felt lost. "Then all this is a jest?"

He walked back to the couch and once again stretched out full length. "Oh, no, Miss Lindsey, this is real. Control and understanding of others are my duty and my fate. So which was it? Red or white? Search your heart. You aren't a country mouse, are you? You were shocked by my demand that you impersonate Sophia for a day, but somewhere you also felt a small tingle of excitement."

"I did not!"

He grinned with open raillery. "Don't deny it. I've already recognized your courage and audacity and wit. Your father was one of the wild gypsy princes. You may not carry his name, but you carry his blood. The bacchanal was your preference, wasn't it? To run naked under a full moon and make sacrifice of your virginity?"

The dangerous temptation was simply to laugh with him. She choked it down. "Your Royal Highness, you've been away far too long. England is too cold—"

"For sacrifice or for madness?" The smile lingered at the corners of his sensuous lips. "To impersonate a princess for a day is simpler and more pleasant than either."

"It's out of the question," she said. "I won't do it. You can't make me."

"Yes, I can."

He closed his eyes and lay still—a fallen angel, shadows and flames. Tail tip wagging just a little, Quest looked up at Penny.

Her blood pounded crazily in her veins. He didn't know her. He was asking something impossible. She'd spent her twenty-two years enclosed by the ordinary routines of Rascall St. Mary—except for her one great mistake, which had surely taught her never again to gamble her future on a whim! Especially when the temptation was offered by a man like this, a man who made her blood spin in warm eddies, who made her wonder what it would have been like if he had seized her out there at the ruins and pressed his mouth over hers. Oh, Lord! Foolish thoughts!

She was a lady of no beauty, illegitimate birth and no fortune. Marriage was out of the question. She'd decided long ago she didn't care. Men had stopped looking at her in that way several years ago. Or, at least, if they did look at her at all, they soon gave up their heavy-handed flirtation when she opened her mouth and they learned her real interests. Apparently male appreciation and female sense were mutually exclusive. Especially when the female was usually rather rumpled and had no dowry whatsoever. How on earth could she pretend to be a princess?

Yet for a moment—just a split second—had she been excited at the thought, as the prince had said? Did the flicker of temptation dance and tease? It was all madness. He couldn't imprison her. This was England. Her mother knew the local magistrate. People in the village wouldn't stand for any such nonsense. She couldn't really be in danger from his enemies. Grand Duke Nicholas had misjudged and his threats were empty. She would refuse and that would be an end of it.

Quest pricked her ears at a small rap at the door. Major Baron von Gerhard bowed in the open doorway. The smell of roast chicken and hot bread spiraled tantalizingly in the air. Penny realized she'd missed her supper. Yet she had no intention of eating this prince's food.

As von Gerhard crossed the room to the couch Penny stood up and walked past him to the doorway. "Major, pray tell His Royal Highness that I cannot help him. I'm going home now. You may assure him that I shan't repeat anything he has told me."

She stepped forward into the hall. Perhaps she could just walk out? Two other men in green uniforms snapped to attention. One of them laid his hand on the hilt of his sword. She backed up again.

The major strode back to her and took her elbow. "Madam, Grand Duke Nicholas is asleep."

"He can't be asleep."

He spoke softly in her ear. "His Royal Highness has barely slept in weeks. Supper is waiting for you in the dining room."

She looked back at the shadowed face, the scandalous lashes, the disdainful mouth relaxed in a curve like a five-year-old boy's. Asleep. The mad prince was asleep, his outlandish dog keeping faithful watch beside him.

"Major, I don't care for supper. I would appreciate an escort home now."

The scar writhed as he smiled at her, though his blue eyes were kind. "Miss Lindsey, the Grand Duke has received my oath of allegiance. I obey only his orders." His grip tightened just a little on her sleeve. "A bedroom has been prepared."

And she had thought hysteria inappropriate? Penny attempted the dignity of a princess. "Under lock and key?"

He nodded, perfectly serious. "For the sake of Glarien, in irons if necessary."

She felt she ought to fight and shout and confront them all: mad prince, mad major, the other trained men who kept Grand Duke Nicholas safe. Yet it was obviously absurd that they could keep her indefinitely against her will. No doubt she would be rescued in the morning. Penny glanced back as the major steered her from the room. The prince was lying on the couch, dark wraith of a fallen angel. She had neither the nerve nor the heart to wake him.

Three

*T*he door crashed open. Something flickered at the edge of her
awareness like a necromancer as her dream dissolved. She'd
been dreaming about a place she'd never seen: Glarien, country
of black forests and ancient castles, rank with wicked secrets.
Wild horsemen thundering through green valleys beneath towering white peaks. Was it really like that?

Penny sat up. She was in bed, in her own nightgown, in a
huge canopied bed with blue velvet hangings. But not at home
in Clumper Cottage. She was in one of the grand guest bedrooms at Rascall Hall. Locked in. The major had escorted her
up here last night and handed her a small bag. Her mother had
packed an overnight case and sent it back with him. Nothing
else could have demonstrated so absolutely the power Grand
Duke Nicholas had suddenly acquired over her life. Even her
mother had acquiesced in whatever story they'd told her. Why?
She couldn't be forced into agreeing to the prince's mad
scheme.

A folding screen sat close to the foot of the bed. Protection
against drafts, but completely hiding the door from her view.
She'd left her dress and robe hanging there last night and her
small case on a chair beside it. Her mother's case, in truth. A
bag that had once gone to Glarien and back.

A man's boots thudded across the floor. Penny clutched the covers to her chin and wriggled back against the pillows.

Nicholas strode around the screen and up to the bed. "A man named Jeb Hardacre was in my stable yard with a cart. He said he'd come for the hedgehogs. Would you be kind enough to tell me what the devil is going on?"

"Your Highness, I'm not dressed. You are in my *bedroom!*"

"You are as charming, Miss Lindsey, as a rumpled chick in the nest. I trust you slept well? It is morning."

He smiled.

His smile was for something delectable and rich, like cream. As if she had stared too long, too close at a fire, a hot wave ran through her blood. Her heart seemed to dive and swoop. She wanted to press both hands over it to keep it in place.

He walked to the window and wrenched aside the drapes. It was barely dawn. Powerful shoulders flexed as he flung up the sash. Cool air flowed inside, carrying a froth of birdsong: blackbirds and thrushes calling up the day.

Penny shivered. "It isn't decent for you to come in here like this. I am most uncomfortable. Please leave!"

He turned to look at her. The dark gaze seemed fathomless, filled with secrets, but promising mischief and delight. "Good Lord! You are better covered than any lady at a ball. Nothing is visible but a plait of hair and a great deal of white linen. Why were you carrying a basket of hedgehogs at the manor last night?"

She felt flushed and awkward, at a complete disadvantage. "They are wild creatures, belonging to no one."

"Ha! And a fig for the laws against poaching! You were trespassing in a ruin that belongs to me and stealing my hedgehogs. Even in England, where you apparently wink at striking monarchs, theft is a hanging offense." His voice carried honey and silk, warmed by that charming, playful smile. A deception. For steel rang quite clearly beneath. "What the devil do you do with the creatures?"

So it was all going to come out. He was bound to be awkward about it. "I tame them," she said. "They go to Covent Garden in London and are sold as pets. Hedgehogs eat insects. They help get rid of vermin in town."

He moved across the room, studying paintings and ornaments. "A remarkably odd hobby for a lady!"

"It is not a hobby," she said icily. "I do it for the money. Count them the payment of a debt, if you like. Don't you think Glarien owes me that?"

"Owes you?" He seemed genuinely surprised. "Why? Your existence wasn't entirely unknown to me, though I never expected to meet you. I knew Frederick had fathered a child with an English governess when he was a visitor in Moritzburg. I just didn't know the details. This morning I found out."

The casual words threatened. The steel had a lethal edge. "How?"

"I have visited your mother."

A prickle of hair rose on the back of her neck. "My mother! This early? You got her out of bed, too?"

"She was up, waiting for me. Fritz told her last night I would come. How do you suppose she has survived all these years? Who do you think paid for the cottage and allowance? She lives on my charity. It seems I even own her home. Clumper Cottage, where you were born and raised, is mine. Did you know that?"

A chasm yawned, dark with frightful possibilities. The twitter and rustle outside soared. She felt ill, almost faint. "You are threatening to turn us out on the streets?"

"I don't know. When your father died, your keep fell to the royal house of Glarien, because my mother found out about it and took up the duty. On her death, the responsibility for you both fell to me."

"Not a personal responsibility."

He walked back to the window and stood there, gazing out. Gold stained his profile, like a painting of a saint. "I have never given you a moment's thought before today. Secretaries took care of it, as a petty expense on the royal purse. I have a country to run."

She bunched the covers in both hands, the luxurious satin and embroidered linen. "Do you run it as well as you run Rascall Hall? Or as generously as you have provided for my mother? She has barely enough to live in any dignity at all. If I didn't do what I can, she'd go without basic necessities."

"Nonsense. The allowance is ample." He strode back to the screen and grasped her dressing gown.

"What can you know about that?"

"Your mother has never complained."

"She'd die on the rack before she'd ask! Don't you understand that ordinary people have dignity?"

He tossed her robe on the bed, the poor thin cotton evidence enough—if this man had any shred of sensitivity—of how hard she and her mother struggled. "It's not my business to know minutiae. I have a staff to take care of details."

"Then tell your staff to let Jeb Hardacre have the hedgehogs."

"Too late. I sent the man about his business." He turned to walk out of the room. "Get up and get dressed. I have ordered you a bath."

Her left arm jammed as Penny struggled into her robe. She had to pull it half off to try again. The frequently darned cotton ripped. Not caring, she thrust her arm inside the torn garment and tugged the remains about her shoulders. Clambering from the bed, she stormed up behind him and grasped his sleeve.

"Wait!"

He spun about, the dark hair tumbled over his forehead, his gaze hot and unreadable as it focused on her fingers clenched on his jacket. "You will take your hand from my arm."

Penny jerked back as if he had burned her with a hot iron. "Oh, of course. The sacred person."

"No one—ever—touches me without my express permission."

"More royal prerogative? You didn't hesitate to seize me! Now you sent Jeb away empty-handed? What about the hedgehogs?"

He closed the door and leaned back on the panels. A small pulse throbbed at the corner of his mouth. "I set them free last night."

She tried to tie the sash. It had worked itself into a maddening knot. "That's a whole week of work ruined! Why?"

His eyes were midnight in a dark wood, thick with mysteries. "I didn't like to see them caged."

"The hedgehogs don't come to any harm at Covent Garden. They live far longer in London than they would in the wild. They're pampered and treated well. They're pets!"

"No longer. No more wild things will be captured here."

Wrapping both arms about her body, she turned and began to pace, that hot gaze burning into her back. "You have no idea, have you? You don't care in the least how ordinary people live, or that the payments sent my mother are so petty and mean. So you own our cottage! Along with palaces and castles and acres of estates. You live in luxury and waste. You have handkerchiefs that cost a month's salary. You have a picture of your bride in a case worth a king's ransom. You've never gone without anything. You snap your fingers and get whatever you want—"

"Not always," he interrupted.

She stopped and turned to face him. The floor was icy on her bare feet. Penny lifted one foot to rub the sole against the ankle of the other. "When did you ever want something and not get it?" she demanded. "Ever?"

The dawn light smoothed over his cheeks, softening the haughty line of nose and chin, smudging the black hair to soot. He was impossibly, dangerously handsome.

"Right now," he said dryly. "I want you."

Cold air poured from the open window. Penny hopped to the other foot and rubbed her freezing toes on her shin. "Then you're right, Your High-and-Mightiness," she said. "I'm the one thing you can't have!"

His own words moved and sank, only to surface with another meaning. *I want you.* She was disheveled and angry. Her hair hung in a long plait down her back, not neat, not glossy—a lion's mane of disordered golden straggles, fuzzy where she'd slept on it. Her blunt nose was pink at the tip and she'd narrowed her eyes, hiding the changeable green behind two rows of stubby blond lashes. Now she was bouncing from one foot to the other like a demented parrot, clad in a torn dressing gown and a capacious white cotton nightdress, and berating him.

There was nothing seductive in her looks or manner, yet his attention concentrated on that one thought:

I want you.

The rush of arousal was so sudden and unexpected, it caught him entirely off guard. Blood sang and muscles tightened. His senses were absolutely, gloriously alert. The tousled scents of sleep and wildness and woman teased his nostrils. Her naked toes were even and straight with nails like pearls, her delectable ankles curved like a cherub's. The nightgown billowed about her knees, swishing against her legs as she hopped back and forth. Tiny golden hairs sparkled on her wrists. The bones of her fingers clutching the robe were clear and hostile. Her throat was a column of animosity. Yet the imagined taste of her, dog rose and woodland, flooded his mouth.

The one thing you can't have!

Distress beat at him. Desire was only another punishment and another weakness, always to be resisted, whatever the cost. But now it pummeled and demanded, mocking his resolution.

His gaze met hers. Hot color swept over her round cheeks and flooded into her hairline. She spun about and clambered back on the bed. Cotton stretched enticingly over female curves. The ragged hem revealed a flash of ankles and dirty pink soles. Her nipples thrust noticeably against the front of her robe as she backed up against the pillows and crossed her arms over her round breasts. His body roared its response.

"Leave!" she said. "I don't care if you're Ivan the Terrible and Suleiman the Magnificent all rolled into one. Get out!"

He swallowed hard, shaken to the core. How could he allow such base feelings when so much was at stake? Old fears moved and shifted, taunting: *devil's spawn!*

"We'll continue this discussion over breakfast. Come down when you're ready." The words sounded cold and hollow in his empty mouth.

With a formal court bow, he saluted her and left the room.

He thought perhaps she wouldn't come at all. The eggs hardened, turned to cork and had to be tossed out. The fresh rolls steamed and cooled, then toughened in their basket. He had it all removed and made fresh every half hour. His stomach growled its complaint. After the fourth breakfast had been thrown away, she came into the room.

She hesitated in the doorway. Her face shone with scrubbing and she'd washed her hair. It was still a little damp, wrapped clumsily in two plaits about her head. Her mother must have sent a fresh frock, for she was wearing a plain yellow muslin, cut high at the neck with long sleeves. Modest, ordinary, not particularly flattering, very English.

Nicholas stood and waited, stiff and formal at the head of the table. He'd buried his shame and desire beneath hard logical analysis, clinging to reason. He knew what he had to do, what Carl might be planning. This woman must help him, but there need not—*must* not—be anything personal or intimate in it. She was absurd, with her hedgehogs and her English manners. The kind of woman who normally would never enter his life, in spite of her own royal blood.

Penny looked at him for a long minute, then walked steadily across the carpet and sat down on the chair Alexis pulled out for her. Her eyelids were red, the skin a little blotchy on her cheeks.

"I am sorry if I am causing you distress," he said. "I must persuade you to help me."

She glanced at the boy. "With an audience?"

"We can talk freely in English. Alexis only speaks Glarisch, German and French." He waved his hand toward the sideboard. "What would you like?"

"I would like to go home," she said. "I don't care for breakfast."

"I would never insist a lady eat when she's inclined otherwise, but I hoped you might be tempted." He smiled, the practiced smile of the court, the smile meant to charm and reassure. "There's no magic potion in this food. Eating it commits you to nothing. It's just a meal."

He sat down and nodded to Alexis: Alexander Gregor, Erbgraf von Kindangen—the youngest of the men he had brought from the *Royal Swan*—a boy with a bright fluff of hair like dandelion petals.

The silver lid of a serving dish on the sideboard sparked sunshine as the boy lifted it.

Fragrant steam rose from the scrambled eggs inside. Soft and fluffy. The boy served the eggs onto two plates, then added a slice of ham and a spoonful of curried chicken to each one. The scents mingled and teased. Mrs. Butteridge must be a good cook.

Alexis set the plates on the table.

Nicholas broke open a hot, fresh roll and took a small pat of butter. Yes, Mrs. Butteridge could definitely cook. The yellow knob melted and slid on the feathery white surface. The eggs fell apart softly under silver knife and fork. The curry was spiced and hot.

Her eyes were as green as a mallard's feathers, watching him. She did not touch her food.

Without tasting any of it, the eggs and meat steaming and fragrant in front of him, Nicholas set down his knife and fork and leaned back, crossing his arms over his chest. After a lifetime of ladies falling over themselves to please him, it was rather interesting to face one who was so determined to be hostile. "You're not hungry?"

"Major Baron von Gerhard told me. You had Mrs. Butteridge cook you four breakfasts and you threw them all away."

He leaned back, his mouth soft with saliva, his throat craving food. "That was your fault. I wanted the breakfast hot and fresh for you."

"*My* fault? All that waste!"

"Even a grand duke can't eat if his guest doesn't join him. But if you don't want it—"

He signaled Alexis. The boy stepped up to the table to whisk away the untouched plates. The tiniest gesture to remind her who held the power in this house, *his* house.

"You really don't understand, do you?" she asked scornfully. "You really don't know what it means to go hungry. You have just thrown away four breakfasts and you sent Jeb Hardacre away without his week's living. He has eight children who depend on the sale of those hedgehogs."

"How does it help him if you go without breakfast? You want

this one thrown away, too? Not that I care. Mrs. Butteridge will cook another."

Her chair scraped as she stood up, pushing away from the table as if forced to move. "I cannot sit here and eat with you. I cannot stay here—"

His attention was riveted on her turned throat and the twists of blond hair. Her dress fit badly, bunched clumsily at the neckline. "Why not?"

She began to pace, the yellow fabric swaying from the high waistline. "I think I must be honest about this." A small pulse beat in her throat. "You were looking at me. In the bedroom. As you were just looking at that food. As if I were something you were hungry for. Can you deny it?"

The shame moved and taunted: *Can you deny it?* "I didn't intend to make you uncomfortable."

Her hand brushed the top of each chair back as she strode down the length of the table. At the end she stopped and turned to face him. "And then . . . I thought about the way you seized me at Rascall Manor and the way you behaved afterward. I thought about it most of the night, for I didn't sleep much. I'm not a fool. I couldn't think you were serious about my impersonating Princess Sophia at your wedding, but I can see that—" She hesitated again. "I am better to just say it, I suppose. You have a reputation. All of you. The princes of Glarien and Alvia. I can see that it might be a thrill to you to—"

He wanted to be gentle, but the word came out like a curse. "What?"

Her chin snapped up. "To dally with a woman who looks like your intended bride. Of course, I'm a commoner and illegitimate, so you might simply think I'm fair game. I don't have powerful connections, though my mother knows most of the gentry around here. But I'm not pretty—"

She broke off as he leaped up and strode around the table. Alexis stared at the ceiling, his face a little flushed. Nicholas ignored him and snatched up a large linen napkin. He took Penny by both arms.

"Not pretty! Why do you say that?" Standing behind her, a hand on each shoulder, he turned her to face a long mirror set into the wall. "Now, Miss Lindsey. Be careful. If you insist you're not pretty, it's an insult to Sophia, isn't it?"

He had meant it to be light, teasing. Then he saw himself in the mirror: a dark, forbidding contrast to her blond hair and tawny eyes. His gypsy venality and her English innocence. Was that how she saw him? Of course not. His corruption and shame were too deeply buried. No one would ever look deeply enough into his eyes or his heart to see it smoldering there. Meanwhile he had to go just far enough to tempt her, as he hoped he had tempted her last night, so she would help him.

She blushed, just a little, a faint glow in her cheeks. He draped the white linen so it covered the homely yellow cotton.

"Sophia often wears white," he said.

His fingertips lay lightly on each of her shoulders. He moved his hands over the small, tender hollows above her collarbone, the strong lines of her neck, up her jawline and past her ear-lobes, until he framed her face in both palms. He touched softly, aware of the fragile bones of her cheeks, her delicate, small ears, and even more deeply of his own pulse quickening and leaping in response. *Be careful!* But he needed to tantalize her and he had absolute faith in his own control.

He smoothed the heavy plaits away from her temples.

"Her hair is more like this. Swept up." He let his voice coax. "You're right. 'Pretty' isn't the word. Try 'lovely, beautiful, a princess.' You would be exquisite in diamonds."

Her eyes widened in the mirror. Morning light sparkled and quivered. *Dear God, it is true,* he thought suddenly. *She is beautiful. Has no one ever told her that?*

She trembled under his hands, a small tremor passing beneath the soft skin and springy hair. "Don't," she whispered. "Don't do that!"

Be careful! He released her and walked back to his chair. Sweet, singing sensation burned on his fingertips. Did he fool himself that he could touch her without consequences? "So what is your concern, Miss Lindsey?"

She tore the napkin from her shoulders and tossed it on the tablecloth. "I would be ridiculous in diamonds! I don't flatter myself that you are suddenly taken with my charms, so it can indeed only be my resemblance to Sophia that sparks your interest. In which case, you think to gain some twisted, perverted pleasure in the seduction of your bride's cousin."

It stopped him dead. He was incredulous. "You think I'm keeping you here in order to *ravish* you?" A tendril of temper uncurled. He had been so careful! For what? For this?

High color made her eyes brilliant. "Yes. That's exactly what I think. Nothing else makes much sense, does it? Why else would you carry me back here and imprison me? You can't expect me to believe all that nonsense about somebody kidnapping the princess."

"Nevertheless, it's true," he said brutally. "But, for God's sake, if I'd wanted to deflower you, you wouldn't have come down this morning still virgin."

"But I am—" She hesitated and started again. "But at the manor—you can't have thought I was Princess Sophia. How could you think I was royal?"

No one, not even Fritz, knew about his migraines—how they could shatter his vision. He stared down at his knuckles gripping the chair rail. Irritation tunneled beneath his court manners. He was getting bloody hungry. "I admit it seems like a madness. But that is what I thought. I carried you back here under the delusion there was danger. I do not want your cherished virtue. I came into your bedroom this morning only because of the urgency of what we must do, not because I desire you."

"It didn't seem that way," she said stubbornly. "And it didn't seem that way just now, with your fingers on my face."

A rush of self-disgust roared into vehemence and bitterness. "By God! Don't you understand? I'm concerned with something so damned wretched that dalliance with a prickly, stubborn virgin is the last thing on my mind. You'll be as safe with me as a novice in a nunnery. I need you to help me. I do not intend to ruin you. I have no personal interest in you whatsoever."

She stood in silence for a moment. Then suddenly she gave a wry smile. A deeply buried humor shone for a moment in her eyes, as if she enjoyed some secret joke at her own expense. Nothing could have surprised him more. "Oh, dear. Well, then.

I think you have told me the truth, after all. In which case, I've just made a rather complete fool of myself. Of course you wouldn't feel such things about me, though I suppose you must about my cousin. But I'm not a royal princess and I can't pretend to be one, and that's the truth, too."

The truth! He had never felt such things about Sophia. It was one of the greatest attractions of the marriage. "Miss Lindsey, please! Sit down and eat breakfast."

"Send it to Jeb Hardacre's family. I don't want it."

"Would you eat, if you knew he has food?"

"I suppose so. Yes." Her straight eyebrows contracted. "Does that seem so very strange to you?"

He ignored the implied insult. "No, it shows you are open to compromise. Pray sit and join me, Miss Lindsey. I've already given Hardacre compensation for his disappointment over the hedgehogs. He can buy his own breakfast. He can buy his whole damned family breakfast for weeks."

"Oh." She gave a small laugh. "Noblesse oblige? How very noble and how very obliging. It's a start, I admit. But you really need to convince me why you deserve the throne of Glarien."

"Deserve?" Anger sprang into full leaf. "I do not have to justify my destiny to you. Just believe this: the alternative is worse."

She had dimples. They danced into her cheeks. "Than you? You turned up here like an avenging angel. You have threatened and browbeaten me from the moment we met. Good heavens, what a splendid prince!"

Prince of devils! Ragged gypsy! With an effort of will, he reined in his distress and tried to state the simple facts. "Miss Lindsey, a throne is at stake. Like much royal history, this is a tale of cousins. Glarien and Alvia both allow daughters to inherit. My cousin Sophia is the only heir to Alvia and she's popular, unassailable. My claim to Glarien is through my mother, daughter to the last ruling grand duke."

"But Princess Sophia is your heir, also?"

"There's someone closer: Count Carl Zanich. He is the only son of a cousin of my mother's. It is usually a mistake for royalty to have cousins. My grandfather should have had them all strangled, like a Turkish sultan. Carl objects that I am half English. He will challenge my right, if he can, before I am crowned this autumn. I will not allow that to happen."

"But I thought you were the ruler already?"

"I inherited when my grandfather died last month, as was his wish. But until my coronation and the oath of allegiance from the nobles, the crown still twists a little in the wind. Thanks to popular feeling about Sophia, it all depends on my wedding."

"Then it seems rather foolish to come to London to wed." She was folding the napkin, smoothing it carefully with each fold.

"For God's sake, leave that! A princess lets the servants do such things."

She looked up, her hands frozen in place. "Is Princess Sophia in love with you?"

He was startled into the truth, even if it came out with a sarcastic twist. "Miss Lindsey, we're talking about a royal marriage. No."

"But she prefers you to this Carl? Why doesn't he just seize the throne while you're out of the country?"

"He must publicly discredit me and persuade Sophia to marry him first, or it would create civil war, the intervention of British and Allied troops, and very likely an attempt by Austria to seize Glarien for herself. No one can hold the throne without the support of the Allies. I *must* marry Sophia in London."

She walked back along the row of chairs. "You really want this, don't you? But how can you rule a country if you don't care about ordinary people?" She stopped and waved both hands. "So you pay Jeb Hardacre in gold. What a grand gesture! How splendid! How generous! That buys this week's food and the next, but what about next year and the year after that? To replace a man's livelihood with charity is a way to turn him into a sot or a villain."

"I cannot have the local population running about Rascall Hall as if they own it. It's my land. Jeb Hardacre has no right to make a living from it. But I will not discuss it further unless you sit down."

At his signal Alexis set her plate back on the table and held her chair for her. She shrugged like a lioness hounded by flies, but with a quick smile to the boy, she sat down and shook out her napkin. "I think he has every right. Your father stole most of this estate from the village to start with. He had the people's common woods and fields enclosed by Act of Parliament in 1772." She took a roll and tore it in two with a quick, angry twist of both wrists.

With relief, Nicholas sat down and picked up his own knife and fork. The food filled his mouth with savory fragrance and sent its comforting message into his blood. It was none of her damn business, of course, whether he had ever gone hungry.

"Long before either of us was born," he said.

She tore into the bread with neat, even teeth, like a squirrel biting a nut. "So? Without rights to the grazing and firewood, no one in Rascall St. Mary can make a decent living, unless the estate provides it. At least your father did that. You haven't. You've done nothing with it. You'd have let this land go to ruin."

"I've had other commitments."

She attacked her eggs. "But it is your responsibility."

"One it would seem you have taken over, and without my permission. What exactly is the extent of your activities on my land?"

Curried chicken disappeared down her throat. She scrubbed her mouth on her napkin, then crushed it and threw it on the table. "Very well. You are bound to find out anyway. Those cows decorate your lawns because I told Tom Robertson to do it. The geese are Widow Blackwood's and she can't afford to have your men butcher them without payment. John Pence's sheep graze the lower pastures by the stream. The whole village is growing vegetables in your kitchen garden. We have started to reclaim the orangery and the orchards—after all, we thought you'd never come back here. We send shipments to Norwich market every week."

"Are you getting rich at my expense?"

She gulped some tea. "Rich! No one is getting rich. Our operations are necessarily rather small scale. I didn't dare attract the attention of anyone who might inform your steward. He lives very nicely in London, presumably on the salary you send him, and never comes here. The rents from the tenant farms are sent to him there. As far as I know he has never spent a penny on repairs or responded to the tenants' concerns. Was that your intention?"

All this was petty, insignificant, compared with what he faced. "I have no idea. Rascall Hall isn't important."

Her teacup rattled in her saucer. "Which is simply the most callous thing you've said yet."

He gave her the look he normally reserved for pageboys who'd broken something. "Callous? You have connived with everyone in the village to break the law."

She brushed back a stray wisp of hair. "Oh, for goodness' sake, why not? You weren't using the land. You were too busy playing at being a prince. But you are also Lord Evenlode, and an English county estate is a lot more than a playground for aristocrats. Rascall Hall is the center of the local economy—or should be. It's your responsibility and you don't care."

She meant it to hurt and it did. He had been born here. Once he had loved every last acre. Yet it was still completely trivial. How could he possibly have given personal attention to his English estates? "My wedding must go forward as planned. Afterward, I'll never see this place again. I can't care about it!"

She pushed some spoons about on the tablecloth. "So what will you do now? Make Tom Robertson sell off his cows and tell the village they can't grow food for their children any longer? That would certainly be in keeping with your reputation."

The enormity of what he had to deal with broke in spume like the ocean's edge. Currents running, waves crashing, cliffs crumbling into the water, while she fretted and worried about grains of sand. Rage exploded into full flower.

"I have told you what I face here and what I must do. What you must do to help me. Absolute secrecy is essential. These people can't continue—*you* can't continue—as usual while I'm here! How can I take more than a passing interest in your Robertsons and Hardacres? Tens of thousands of people in the Alps depend on me!"

The blunt nose and narrowed eyes denounced him. "Yet you have absolute power over the villagers and over my mother. Are you trying to blackmail me with their security?"

"That's rather implied by the situation, isn't it?"

China and silverware clattered as she leaped to her feet. "Then there is nothing more to be said. You're wasting your time to detain me here. If I try to leave now, will you have this boy restrain me?" She glanced at Alexis, standing, face blank, by the sideboard.

Nicholas snapped his fingers. Alexis bowed and fled the room.

He slammed his hand on the table. Silverware rattled. "Sit down."

She sat immediately. Everyone leaped to his orders. It was essential they do so, always. Yet he hated to see this woman in her rumpled yellow dress forced to respond to his whim like a soldier, when his own desires embodied such messy, contradictory demands.

"That's the basic power structure of our situation. I have tried to pay you the compliment of the truth, for God's sake. Please don't try to involve me in your untidy passions, Miss Lindsey."

She stared at him, her tawny eyes glinting green. "But why on earth should I care about you? You threatened force last night. You tried a little charm this morning. You are rather good, I think, with the iron fist in the velvet glove, though you've not bothered to hide the steel very much, have you? It's completely unconscionable!"

"Miss Lindsey, I need your help. For God's sake, I haven't tried to charm you. Instead I've allowed you to see how desperate I am. I will go to any lengths to ensure my wedding takes place."

"Even threats!"

Her stubbornness infuriated him. "How can I rule without steel? Your resemblance to Sophia has brought you into my world, whether you like it or not. What if my cousin's friends see you and try to use you against me? I'm offering you my protection from that."

"I can go away," she said.

He took a deep breath. How could she understand the danger? He smiled, trying to reassure. "I've also tried to show you what an adventure you could have. Don't you understand? It's meant as a compliment. The heart of any negotiation is to recognize each person's goals and interests. You have something I need to use—your likeness to Sophia. I have something you want—power over the lives of the villagers."

"No," she said. "You have it all wrong. I don't want power."

"Yes, you do. You're a reformer. You're annoyed that I will interfere with all your little schemes. I cannot have the villagers making free with my estate, though I don't intend them to suffer because I'm here. But I need you to impersonate Sophia in London and I will do whatever it takes."

She clenched her fist on her napkin. "If you were a good prince, you would never consider threatening the happiness of your dependents. Besides, even if I agreed, how could I be a princess?" Her chair scraped as she pushed away from the table. She marched up to the sideboard with her plate and set it there. China and silver clattered. "I don't know anything about court behavior."

"I will teach you."

"No!" She shook her head blindly. "It's too much. I won't do it and I must leave now. Let this Carl have the throne! I imagine Princess Sophia went with him willingly rather than be married to you. Will you have your men stop me?"

Silver and glassware winked innocently in the shifting light. Once, when he was twelve, he had smashed a whole set of priceless Glarian crystal and reduced it to shards, making a sea of glass ice, bright and hard on the tablecloth. It hadn't helped at all. Yet the temptation to do the same now sprang strongly into his hands.

He clenched his fists. "I would rather convince you. What will that take? Must I sell your mother's house? Ruin the fortunes of every villager in Rascall St. Mary? Imprison you here until you agree?"

She was white, her nostrils and eyelids outlined in pink.

"You can do all of that, but you cannot make me into a convincing princess unless I'm willing."

Slowly, deliberately, he unclenched his fists and laid his hands flat on the table, pushing aside cutlery and dishes. There was only one card left to play, the wild card he had drawn this morning at Clumper Cottage. Nothing was left now but to see whether it might be a trump after all.

"You are right," he said, staring at the white tablecloth. "In the end, the power is all yours. That's been the case from the beginning. I tried to make you understand the importance of it all and I thought you had more courage and more audacity. I was wrong. For God's sake, go home!"

Four

Penny marched across the park and through the meadows on the old footpath that ran from Rascall Hall to Rascall St. Mary. She resisted the impulse to look back. Of course, no horsemen were in hot pursuit. This was England. She had called the prince's bluff and outfaced his threats. If he tried to retaliate against her mother, he'd only create bad feeling among the local gentry, some of whom had powerful connections. She doubted he'd risk it. The last thing he could afford right now was condemnation from British peers. As for his threats about danger to her from his enemies . . . absurd! Ridiculous!

White clouds chased across the sun and sent shadows scudding through the fields. Blackbirds twittered, fussing in the hedgerow. Green scents sprang fresh as she brushed by bright clumps of buttercups and red campion. Nothing had changed, except that the local people could no longer make free with Rascall Hall. She knew he'd meant that. No powerful person in the neighborhood would blame Lord Evenlode for taking control of his own estate.

The path ended in a small gate set into the brick wall behind the churchyard. She stopped with her hand on the latch and dropped her forehead against the weathered boards. If she had escaped so unscathed, why did her breathing echo the ragged rhythm of her heart?

"Pretty" isn't the word. Try "lovely, beautiful, a princess."

She had almost believed it, hadn't she? For that one split second, seeing herself in the mirror with the white linen draped about her shoulders and his hands cradling her face, lifting her hair away in an illusion of style and beauty, she had almost believed him. How foolish! Surely she had learned long ago the real meaning of a man's flattery!

Yet with painful honesty, Penny faced the question: Had she wanted him to find her attractive? Sensible, practical Penelope Lindsey? She knew she wasn't an antidote, but her looks were ordinary enough. Oh, Lord, it was all a madness!

I have no personal interest in you whatsoever.

Well, that had been the truth and one she was comfortable with. With a wry smile, she turned around and stared up at the sky. Why had she thought for a moment he threatened her virtue? All he'd menaced was her equilibrium and her security, far more important in the circumstances, in any circumstances!

The clouds moved, shredding and reforming, sailing across infinite blue. He would realize he could achieve nothing here and he would go away, back to Glarien to fight his cousin. But what would happen to the villagers, and to her and her mother, if they could no longer steal a little bounty from Rascall Hall? Or if he changed his mind and decided to act on his ultimate warning?

Clumper Cottage, where you were born and raised, is mine. Did you know that?

Yet even if he carried out his threat, defying local opinion, they would manage. Mama's relatives in Staffordshire would take them in. And if it was really true that his presence here somehow endangered her, perhaps she and Mama should go to their cousins for a visit and be safely gone from the neighborhood.

Penny turned and wrenched open the gate. Nothing could make her agree to his plan. She couldn't possibly stay for a month at Rascall Hall, taking lessons in royal deportment, and then go to London to defraud the Tsar of Russia and the Prince Regent.

I thought you had more courage and more audacity.

"I think I have all I need, thank you very much, Your Highness!" she said aloud.

The whole episode was completely unreal, anyway. She had been carried off and imprisoned—a wonderful tale for winter evenings around the fireside. A fantastic absurdity!

She walked quickly through the churchyard and up the lane to Clumper Cottage. The tiny front garden was almost hidden by its holly hedge. In the other direction, the muddy road curved toward the village around the big oak tree at the corner. The little house where she'd been born sat a half mile beyond its closest neighbor, the fine Queen Anne vicarage next to the church. Clumper Cottage, a much older building, had once housed a seventeenth-century inn, but had been converted into a private home some hundred years before.

She pushed open the garden gate. Neat beds of rosemary and lavender scented the path. Beyond them lay patches of mint, parsley and thyme. The sweet, colorful aroma had mingled all her life with the richness of dough and apples, all safely enclosed by the ramparts of deep green English holly, which had always defined and enfolded her world.

The front door creaked as her mother opened it. Sunlight winked on her lace-trimmed cap, twice darned with the tiniest of invisible stitches. Shadow patterns stippled over her elegant nose and cheeks. Penny had not inherited her mother's fine good looks—the small delicate nose and precise jaw, or the silky soft, pale blond hair, mostly hidden by white linen—looks that had attracted the attentions of a prince. Mrs. Lindsey's blue eyes were still as bright as a girl's. Only the tiniest hint of anxiety was betrayed now in her smile.

"My dear girl," she said. "Welcome home! I believe you have had an adventure?"

Penny grinned as she fastened the gate latch. "I've been to fabulous lands, sailed over mythic oceans and climbed the beanstalk with Jack. I've been a guest of a grand duke, no less—our illustrious new Lord Evenlode who's been missing so long—only to find him a caricature of himself."

"Indeed?" There was a marked twinkle in the lovely blue eyes. "And he insisted you become his guest with no other chaperone in the house than Mrs. Butteridge? How very shocking!"

Thyme crushed under her feet on the path. The rosemary bore tiny blue flowers. This was home, where everything was normal and loving and cause for a jest. "I was abducted and imprisoned, Mama, like Persephone hauled squealing into the underworld. Now I come to think of it, I suppose it was rather splendid!"

The lovely smile grew a little wider. "Come in, dear child, and tell me all about it."

They walked together into the small parlor with its view of the herb garden. The very familiarity of the simple tables and chairs, the well-thumbed books and chipped china, brought a rush of comfort. What on earth did she know of palaces and castles? Penny made tea and served them each a cup. Then she poured out the tale of her encounter with Grand Duke Nicholas, embellishing every humorous twist. She held nothing back, except his threats regarding Clumper Cottage and that uncomfortable moment in her bedroom.

"And thus, you see," she ended at last. "I told him how Rascall Hall goes to rack and ruin, while he plays at being a prince. In fact, I gave him quite the noblest of reprimands, I believe."

"Penny, dear! Lord Evenlode *is* a prince."

"Yes, and too high and mighty to give a care for his English inheritance." *Like my father,* Penny thought, *too high and mighty to give a care for the lady he abandoned or the child he forced on her.* "And now it's your turn. How on earth did Major Baron von Gerhard persuade you to pack me an overnight bag? I thought you would come marching up to Rascall Hall to rescue me with pitchforks and scythes. I was expecting Harry Blacksmith, flexing those great boxer's arms of his, crying vengeance on foreign potentates."

Mrs. Lindsey laughed and shook her head. "I knew Fritz in Glarien, twenty-four years ago. He was a good friend to me when I first arrived. He still had some hair then, of course. I knew I could trust him that no harm would come to you."

Penny raised both brows. "Because he's lost some hair? Oh, Mama! But he's Nicholas's man now. He'd do anything the Grand Duke said. And what about you, this morning, dragged out of bed with the rooster? Did Nicholas try charm or threats?"

"Neither. We talked about his mother. When I came back from Glarien, I could speak with Princess Anna in her native language. She was lonely. She didn't fit in very well as Lady Evenlode, I'm afraid. Of course, I'd met her before I went to Europe. It was because of her that I secured a post there to begin with."

"And that's all you talked about?"

"I also knew Nicholas when he was a little boy." Mrs. Lindsey sipped her tea. "I was his governess."

"You were Nicholas's *governess?* Why didn't I know this?" Sheer surprise took her breath away.

"When I came back from Glarien—before you were born—Nicholas was four years old. I taught him his alphabet and numbers. Two years later, his father hired a tutor and I didn't see much of him after that. You were a baby. But I would still visit with the countess occasionally. Sometimes Nicholas would waylay me in the hall and give me an orange."

"An orange?"

Mrs. Lindsey fussed with her teacup. "His most precious possession, I think. Princess Anna took him to the orangery whenever she thought of it. Perhaps it was his only time alone with his mother. Little Nicholas lived for those moments."

"What kind of child was he?" Penny asked, intensely curious.

"Intelligent, sensitive, given to great fits of temper when he couldn't cope with all the demands life put upon him. His father couldn't understand him at all, and his mother—" She glanced back at her daughter, quite serious now. "Listen, Penny dear. Nicholas is very aware of how badly he behaved to you. But you cannot expect him to apologize."

"I suppose royalty never does." Penny set her cup on a table and stood up. She tried to make it sound light, dismissive. *My father's people!* "Why are they called the gypsy princes?"

"I'm not sure anyone knows where they came from originally. They aren't gypsies. Glarisch is a unique tongue. The people of Glarien and Alvia crossed Hungary hundreds of years ago to settle in the Alps. That's why they have a Magyar appreciation for horsemanship—and that exotic edge more staid folk find so appealing."

Penny laughed. "Certainly not the kind of man one expects to meet in Norfolk. The Grand Duke is completely arrogant and amoral. He really doesn't care about Rascall Hall."

"He can't, Penny. It's vital he secure his throne."

She whirled about and stared down at her mother. "You mean he came here this morning and persuaded you? Mama, how could you? Don't tell me you like him?"

"Like is too ordinary a word, my dear. I don't suppose anyone *likes* him. He has too much natural power, and he's a man torn between two cultures, fitting nowhere. Brilliant and gifted people rarely offer simple amiability—"

"It's all that erratic foreign fire, I suppose. Yet I see indulgence in you, Mama. I believe you were bewitched this morning, befuddled by memories of that little boy struggling over his alphabet."

"Nicholas never struggled. He just sat there in the greatest concentration until he'd mastered each lesson. Then he would throw himself on me with a great show of affection at the least word of praise. Poor little boy, he didn't get much of that."

"But what child isn't captivating at that age? How was an English boy granted the throne of Glarien, anyway? Nicholas wasn't expected to inherit, was he?"

Her mother's hands smoothed the shabby striped muslin over her lap. "Indeed not. Princess Anna had an older brother in line for the throne. He was killed when Nicholas was eleven. That's when the boy was taken away."

Penny perched on the window seat. The morning sun shone into the garden, tinting the peeling paint on the dilapidated gate. "I saw him leave from this very window. I remember the fancy carriage and all the outriders and postilions as they went past.

He rode by on his pony several times before that. He looked arrogant and embittered even then."

"How can you make such a judgment? You couldn't have been more than six years old!"

"Younger children are often aware of older ones. Besides, he was going to be the next Lord Evenlode, so I'm sure I was curious."

"Poor boy," Mrs. Lindsey said. "Taken away from everything he knew."

Penny worked at the rusted window latch. "Oh, Mama, really! He'd been raised in the lap of luxury, only to be handed absolute wealth and power on a platter. I reserve my sympathy for his subjects." The window flew open. A blackbird rustled somewhere in the hedge, then launched into liquid song. This was her birthplace, the only world she'd ever known.

Her mother set down her cup. "He told me what's happened to Sophia and he showed me the portrait. His cousin Carl intends to steal the throne."

"Why not? Nicholas himself said they were hounds snarling over a bone. Is Alvia's crown hanging in a thornbush ready for the taking, like King Richard's gold circlet after Bosworth Field? Why should we care which prince wins?"

"You forget, Penny. I lived in Glarien."

Penny glanced back into the room, surprised by the sudden sharpness in her mother's voice. "Was the rival cousin your pupil, too?"

Her mother stood and began to gather the teacups. "Carl is twelve years older than Nicholas. He was fifteen when I arrived, too old for a governess. But I knew him. It is *vital* that Nicholas inherit without challenge."

"So you choose the memory of the adorable little boy over the awkward youth? But if Nicholas hadn't been born, wouldn't Carl have been crown prince?"

The teacups clattered in her mother's hands as she set them down on the tray. "Listen to me, Penny! Grand Duke Nicholas isn't used to explaining himself. He's a sovereign. Can't you understand that? But Carl isn't fit to rule."

"Why not?"

Her mother stood in silence for a moment, her expression bleak. "He threatened to kill the children's pets."

Penny gazed at her in horror. "What pets?"

"The rabbits and cats and little Franke's pet stoat. The children I had in my charge at court, Carl threatened to kill their pets for fun, for target practice. If I hadn't stopped him, he would have done it. So he was only fifteen. He was handsome and full of charm, but there was something pernicious in him. It was whispered he'd done something unspeakable—" She bit her lip and looked away. "Servants went missing . . . people left court suddenly, taking their children with them. The old grand duke paid them off, so nothing was said openly. But Carl changed, became ungovernable. One day, in a fit of rage, he beat a horse to death. Do you think Nicholas capable of that?"

Penny collapsed back onto the window seat. She felt lost, lost and afraid, as if she must reach for reassurance, for English fair play. She shook her head, stammering over the words. "No, he spoke to the horses with such a warm—"

"His wolfhound worships him, the way dogs look when they know they are absolutely safe."

Penny looked up. "Quest? He brought her here? He said her name was a pun, a play on words. I think he is in love with her. And he let the hedgehogs go."

Her mother came up to her and took her hands. "What, dear?"

"The hedgehogs for Covent Garden. He said he didn't like to see them caged. He was quite passionate about it—"

A wet droplet fell on her wrist. She looked up. Tears trembled on her mother's eyelashes. Penny leaped to her feet and drew her down onto the window seat.

"Mama! You're on Nicholas's side in this, aren't you? Surely you don't think I should do what he wants?"

Her mother dabbed at her eyes. "Yes, I do."

Penny stood up and paced away, filled with distress. "Even if he loves animals—and I *do* concede that he does—what about people? What if I help him to his throne and he becomes a despot? I don't know that he'd be a good prince. I don't know if his judgment is sound. Our hedgehogs are pampered and petted. They live far longer in London than if they stayed here to be flipped over and devoured by foxes. It's so easy to be senti-mental about animals, isn't it? It's so much harder to care about people, who aren't as innocent or helpless. Because of your memory of him as a boy, you think he wouldn't be cruel? Not wittingly, perhaps. Not deliberately. But a man can be a tyrant just through ignorance and pride."

Her mother looked up. "You could teach him."

She felt as if she'd stumbled into a fine web of fishing lines, with no way out. "No, Mama! Don't even suggest it. He's blind. He didn't even notice how you have struggled with poverty, or care about it."

"He does care, I think, although he does need to learn. Penny, I want you to do this, for Glarien, for your blood. Show Nicholas what you've done at Rascall Hall, show him why it's important. Make him into a better prince and help him to his throne."

"I can't believe I'm hearing this from you, Mama! What about me?"

Mrs. Lindsey stared out at the garden and the dark holly. "Sometimes we have to think of greater things than ourselves. This wedding will keep France and Austria from having to openly squabble about that part of the Alps."

That part of the Alps. It was half of her, too. The imagined fishing lines grew taut—any way she turned, invisible hooks jerked her back. "Did he threaten you? Did he say he'd turn you out of the cottage, if I didn't agree?"

"He didn't even know Clumper Cottage was his, until I told him this morning. All that is taken care of by secretaries. A grand duke can't personally oversee all the dependencies on his purse."

"He said *that* to me, too. He charmed you, didn't he? He came here this morning and charmed you. He knew only you could have a chance of persuading me. Good Lord, it's despi-cable!"

"He did not charm me, Penny. He convinced me. I know Glarien. It's not like England. Everything depends on the char-acter of the ruling prince. I shudder to imagine what civil war would do. Think of the women and children caught in the path of a nation gone mad, tearing itself apart. What about Princess

Sophia, your own cousin, in the hands of a man who would kill a child's pet—?"

Panic began to beat, like a frantic moth caught beneath her ribs. "But how can I impersonate her?" Penny waved her arms as if to encompass all of her small Norfolk world. "I don't know how to greet the Tsar or the Prince Regent. . . . Mama, I have no London manners, let alone royal ones!"

Her mother gazed up at her. A little crease had appeared between her eyebrows. "Yes, my dear, I know." She took a deep breath. "It's another reason why I want you to do this. I think it would be good for you to learn. I'm not worried you'd be found out. You could achieve this masquerade on looks alone—no one gets close enough on these royal occasions to get a good look at the principals. London manners aren't so different from country ones, but a little polish would do you no harm."

"And what would I do with town polish here in Rascall St. Mary?"

Mrs. Lindsey shook her head. "You think you're content to live here in obscurity, but that's my fault. I overreacted to your misadventure seven years ago. I should have taken you to London. You should have had a Season."

"To be displayed on the Marriage Mart? Mama, please! I have neither looks nor fortune, and—" She hesitated, not wanting her mother to think she blamed her.

But the thought was too obvious not to be spoken. "And you are illegitimate. That's my fault, too. As it was my fault to let you bury yourself here after you'd made one mistake."

"But I'm happy here with you. Why can't we go on as we have?"

Her mother wrung a fold of her skirt between her fingers. "I've been selfish, Penny. I've robbed you of your birthright. You ought to know more than village economy and herb gardens. You shouldn't be content with country manners. You ought to know what the rest of the world has to offer, see its glitter and subtlety firsthand, before you stagnate here with me. Your father was a prince."

It was a weapon she hadn't expected her mother to use. Her own royal blood. Penny didn't feel anything but English. Yet it was there, the soft, seductive voice that sometimes haunted her dreams. Half of her belonged somewhere else, somewhere exotic, where a society had stopped two hundred years ago and never quite caught up to the nineteenth century. The hidden, mysterious part of herself that she kept deeply buried, never to be acknowledged or looked at.

Terrified, she lashed out. "And he abandoned both of us! You would put me in the hands of another man just like him?"

Her mother became pale. Suddenly she looked all of her forty-six years. "Your father had no choice. Perhaps if you grow up a little and look more clearly at royal duty, you will see that. I trust Nicholas. The cause is just. You will be safer there than here. What does it cost you? A month at Rascall Hall and a few days in London. To save a throne. To save a kingdom. To save a people from war. I'm surprised you turned him down."

The room blurred. A lump of coal seemed to lodge in her throat. "Mama! I feel betrayed. I thought you'd be on my side!"

Skirts rustled. Warm arms, softly scented with lavender, wrapped about her shoulders. Her mother drew her back to the window seat, where they sat side by side.

"Penny, my dear child! My sensible girl! What's this?"

She laughed and wiped away the tears. "Yes, I know. It's not in the least like me, is it? I shall have to use smelling salts or burnt feathers, and learn to have the vapors gracefully, like Miss Harding up at Nettle Park."

Her mother smiled and offered a handkerchief. The birds had fallen quiet outside. A small breeze rustled the leaves of the ash trees beyond the road. "Listen, Penny. Life offers us few enough opportunities for adventure. You took the first when you were fifteen and nothing but distress came of it. Maybe you can redress the balance now. This is an opportunity for you to do something so much greater than what you've done for Rascall St. Mary. You can live out your provincial, limited days in Norfolk, or you can walk for a day or two on a world stage—"

A blackbird startled out of the hedge, a stray cat in hot pursuit. Penny saw the bird's fear and excitement, the surging, mad dash into the unexamined, open skies, where a hawk might be waiting. The cat sat and licked at its coat, hiding its disappointment behind an assumed indifference.

It was as if her little rush of tears—and her mother's—had washed her clean of all feeling but her usual dry, detached humor. "He said I was a reformer." And that, she thought wryly, was the only real temptation the situation offered.

"He agreed you could to write to me."

"You would leave me alone and unchaperoned with this man for a month, because you knew him when he was a little boy? Mama, really!" A horse clopped by on the road, a neighbor returning home. Penny smiled and waved as if this were a perfectly normal day, as if she could deny forever what had already happened.

Her mother paused at the door, the tea tray in her hands. Her blue eyes were vaguely troubled. "It is my only concern. I trust your common sense and his honor—"

"His honor!" How long had it taken her father? Almost a year? Her mother had been more vulnerable, surely? "He's outrageously handsome, of course. Fortunately I would not think a month enough time to complete a seduction."

Her mother frowned, her eyes clouded with memories. "Do not underestimate the danger, Penny. He's very attractive. He's royal. There's a certain glamour in that—"

As, of course, she knew to her cost. Penny went to her mother and took the tray. "You forget, Mama, I haven't agreed to anything yet."

Penny washed the cups and put away the tea things, unsure why her hands had turned clumsy. For herself, she would never do it. But to assuage that flash of guilt and regret she'd seen in her mother's eyes? A cup slipped and almost smashed against the others. Mama had gone upstairs. Penny knew she was silently weeping, but this time for her own prince, Prince Frederick. A man who had stolen her heart, disgraced her, shamed her, left her with child and them both bereft in the world.

I am here. I cannot be denied. The rush of white-hot anger took Penny entirely by surprise. The appalling arrogance and cruelty of princes! Even her mother had agreed to Nicholas's plans, knowing in the end she must be persuaded. Frantic, she spun about and ran through to the hallway. Jamming her bonnet on her head, she raced from the house.

Pale primrose streaked the sky as Penny marched up the drive to Rascall Hall. She had walked until almost exhausted, pacing through meadows and woods, thinking. The birds were mostly quiet now, except for a blackbird trilling its persistent *pink, pink, pink* somewhere in the shrubbery. The cows were gone. The geese were gone. No villagers gathered firewood. In one day, Grand Duke Nicholas had effectively cleared his estate. Only the Butteridges remained, and they wouldn't even know she was there. Yet her mother had absolute faith in the honor of this grand duke, because she'd known him as a little boy.

Penny stopped at the front of the house and took a deep breath. Rascall Hall sat four square with a tower at each corner. Columns framed the front entry and the stone steps leading up to it. A gracious house, both imposing and cultured, deliberately expressing balance and harmony. The door lay slightly ajar, with no soldiers in sight.

You can live out your provincial, limited days in Norfolk, or you can walk for a day or two on a world stage—

And reform a prince? Only she lay between the villagers and their landlord. Only she looked like her cousin, a princess. She knew where her clear path lay, but she would make this arrogant prince pay at least a small price for it. Penny went up the steps, pushed open the door and stepped inside.

The high ceilings rang with the clang of metal. Men's voices echoed and boomed. She swallowed convulsively as she walked forward, through the archways and antechamber, until she could look into the grand ballroom. Quest wagged her tail when she saw Penny, but she didn't move from her spot against the wall.

The carpet had been rolled up and pushed aside. Four men with swords, clashing and breaking apart, danced backward and forward in strange, quick sidesteps. The strong, springing backs and corded arms shone with moisture. The air was alive and boisterous, broken with the men's labored breathing, cut to rags by the slash of their weapons.

A rush of heat burned her cheeks.

They were *naked!*

Penny looked again. No, not entirely naked! Just stripped from the waist up. The men wore white breeches and stockings.

"Hai!" Nicholas called. "Now, Alexis!"

He lunged forward, beating the youth back across the room, crossing blades, ringing steel. Nicholas was invincible, cast in bronze. Lean shadows leaped and danced as if his own flame moved with him, shimmering over his smooth skin, dying to night where a sprinkling of black hair darkened his chest. Hard breath rasped between white teeth, his hair tumbled about his forehead, but his eyes were lazy, completely relaxed—as his horse had looked dancing in place.

His hand lunged. Steel rang like a bell.

"Sire!" Alexis cried. His blade fell from his hand. The boy bent forward, hands on knees, panting and shaking his head. His back was whip-slim, the white skin faintly scarred.

Nicholas put up his own rapier. He strode to a chair, where he grabbed a towel and mopped at his face and chest. "You are learning well, young man. You'll be a great swordsman." Rubbing the towel over his back, he turned around. "Just watch that left—"

The midnight gaze met Penny's. As if a black curtain descended, the carefree expression disappeared. He barked an order. The other men stopped fighting.

The prince dropped the towel carelessly on the chair and bowed from the waist. His eyes were guarded, but the smile was still lazy, like a cat watching prey. He snapped his fingers. His men gathered their rapiers and left the room by a side door.

"Oh, fiddlesticks!" Her heart seemed to be vaulting hurdles under her bodice. "The last Lord Evenlode used this room for dancing with ladies. I don't see why you and your men can't use it for dancing with each other."

Before he could reply, she spun about and walked away. Not sure where to go, she marched into the blue drawing room. The miniature solar system lay still, the planets dumb on their brass orbits. The Greek vases gleamed innocently on their table. She walked over to them and ran her fingers over one cracked surface. Swords clashed and rang in her memory, where a man moved like Theseus, bull-leaping. Beautiful, lethal, fascinating. She had never, in twenty-two years, seen anything like it.

The door closed behind her. She turned to see Nicholas leaning against it. A clean white shirt hung open at his neck and bloused generously over his arms. The relaxed, carefree look was back in his eyes, confident, at ease with command. Quest waited patiently at his heels.

"Your mother said you would do it."

"Mama also said you would never apologize, even when it was called for." Penny picked up the Achilles vase and pretended to study it. She felt ridiculously hot and uncomfortable. He was tousled and glowing from the exercise, impossibly and undeniably male. "I have agreed to nothing. Would Princess Sophia be discomposed to find you fencing with . . . without shirts?"

"Absolutely. But she wouldn't have shown it. I'll teach you exactly how that's done."

From the corner of her eye, she saw that he was still in stocking feet. No wonder he'd been able to enter the room so silently! "If we can come to an agreement."

His voice cooled. "Really? Of what kind?"

She turned the vase over without seeing it. "I am to teach you to be a better prince. At least that's how Mama put it, though stated nakedly like that it sounds rather presumptuous, doesn't it?"

He crossed his arms over his chest. Quest lay down and put her head on her paws, adoration plain in her brown eyes. "To make another *naked* statement . . . I'm not sure a lady should pay such close attention to that vase."

Penny almost dropped the pottery. In a reflex, she hugged it closer and glanced up at him. "Why not?"

"Because, apart from sword and helmet, Achilles *is* naked. Perhaps you shouldn't embrace him quite so fervently?"

"Well, I've taken the old fellow to heart in all innocence. If you will leave now, I'll set him back on his table and never be any the wiser. Decorum preserved. I did promise my mother that, as well."

"Yes," Nicholas said. A small flame burned in the depths of his eyes as he walked toward her. "I did, too. But do you think to bargain with princes? Faith is ours to make and break as the royal will dictates."

Penny backed up a step, still clutching the vase. "Aren't you also a gentleman?"

His smile teased, dishonest with charm. "Rarely. Especially if you start preaching to me about honor and sin—or nakedness and decorum. I'm about to return to a state of nature to take a plunge in the lake."

The table blocked her retreat. "Why sin? That's the realm of the church."

"You don't think princes have the church in their pockets? How very little you know of history!" He stopped, towering over her, and took the vase from her hands. "Your mother left for Stafford-shire two hours ago. Everyone in the village believes you have gone with her. Your things are in those cases over there. Your mother packed them and gave them to Eric, one of my men."

"No," Penny said. "What if I haven't made any choice yet?"

"But you have." Nicholas held out the vase, resplendent under his beautiful fingers.

He met her eyes and smiled. Achilles slipped from his hand to smash on the floor.

As he walked away Penny stared at the shards—the black and red paint, the broken white edges—and knew she was completely, absolutely, out of her depth.

He paused in the doorway, careless and graceful.

"By the way, that vase was only a cheap replica." A small laugh glimmered in his voice. "My mother broke the original over twenty years ago. She threw it with some force at my fa-ther's head when he refused to chastise me for some small transgression. But that doesn't change the choice you made."

A shadow of danger still curled in his heedless, relaxed hand on the jamb.

"I chose war?"

"Alas, Miss Lindsey, Achilles is shattered, leaving only the bacchanal. You saved the genuine vase—the one that really is Greek—where naked women run wild under a wild moon, ready to tear men limb from limb for the love of Dionysus. Whether consciously or not, you chose the maenads."

Five

Nicholas strode back to the blue drawing room after his swim and change of clothes. He had won as he had known he must. Not because she had been beguiled, but because her mother had convinced her of the nobility of the cause and because Miss Penelope Lindsey was a person of virtue and magnanimity. He ought to feel happier about her acquiescence. She was here, under his control. He had time enough to mold her into what he needed: a replica of her cousin, Princess Sophia. His wedding day was saved. Still, she didn't have any idea of the enormity of her task. It burned and festered that he had entrapped this woman, relying on her integrity at the expense of his own.

An open case lay at her feet. Her ugly yellow dress made a stark contrast to the elegant lines of the large table where she was standing. She was studying something spread out on the surface—books of some kind. Someone had cleaned up the broken remains of Achilles.

She glanced over her shoulder as he came in, and looked him up and down. "Good heavens, what a transformation! It's amazing what a jacket and cravat can do for a man. You are positively intimidating. Your frown would break church spires and send gargoyles screaming into the night. Is that how you rule in Glarien, by sheer black looks?"

He stopped. "Miss Lindsey, we have a great deal—"

She patted the books on the table with one hand. "Yes, we do. You had better look at these. I think it would make a good place to begin. Where is Quest?"

"In the stables. She doesn't like to witness human confrontations."

"Confrontations?"

"We shall begin with my explaining what you must do."

"No," she said. "It's a bargain, remember? Whether you like it or not. For everything you teach me, I teach you something. My mother packed my account books."

Temper crackled. "So, even in the face of what we must do, she still tried—" He took a deep breath and softened his voice. "Do you really expect a grand duke to pore over village ledgers!"

Her mouth set in a stubborn line. "The books are a very good history, I think, of the needs of Rascall St. Mary. Everything you must understand is in here."

He let his tone excoriate. "I don't need to understand anything. *You* need to understand this: In two days my court will arrive from London. Servants, clerks, cooks, grooms, lackeys, gentlemen of the bedchamber and wardrobe and horse. Among them will be men bribed by Carl, spies—"

Her hand jerked across the pages, creasing the paper. *"Spies?* In this house?"

"Of course. Do you think Carl wouldn't penetrate my household? I have certainly breached his. For God's sake! This isn't a game. I'm not just a cipher or figurehead. I have a nation, a people, dependent on me—and now on you. I must explain right away how everything is to be managed."

She faced him as Joan of Arc must have faced her inquisitors: stubborn, brave, fired with higher purpose. The blunt nose had turned a little red at the tip, startling and vulnerable against her white skin. "Then you had better not shout. I grew up without a man in the house, so I'm not used to bluster. If you shout, I won't hear you."

Small tremors exploded in the muscles of his arms. He knew his voice had been cutting and deadly, but he hadn't raised it.

Bluster! Infuriatingly, the temptation roared to shout at her now. Instead, leaving her standing at the table, he turned and left the room. Eric and Ludger snapped to attention at the end of the hallway.

Nicholas leaned his head against the wall and took several deep breaths. It was what he had learned to do as a lad when confronted with a recalcitrant horse. Walk away, regain control, confront the problem from a new perspective. She must understand what they faced, that there was no time for trivialities. Taking another deep breath, he opened the door and went back in.

She still stood like a martyr, hovering over her silly account books, filled with her petty concerns. It was all a madness. How the hell could he make this stubborn Englishwoman into a princess? He softened his stance, as if he approached a wary filly that needed gentling and reassurance, and tried to appeal to reason.

"Miss Lindscy. Please, come and sit down. You are quite safe. But you must accept that your account books are irrelevant to me. We have very little time. In two days this house will be scurrying with people. Most of them mustn't know you are here. We shall have to snatch broken moments of time while I teach you what you have to know. Officials will visit. Rascall Hall will become the Glarian court. If it's discovered what we're doing, the whole plan obviously fails. I must prepare you."

Penny looked down and closed her ledgers. The plaits wrapped about her head like a clumsy coronet. "Yes, I can see all that. But I simply cannot take part in your scheme unless I have some sense that we're equal partners in it." She turned and faced him, as if it took an effort of will to look at him steadily. "Are you deliberately trying to terrify me, or reduce me to trembling hysteria? I'm here partly because I was persuaded my resemblance to the real princess could put me in danger from your cousin Carl. Now I learn his spies will be in this house. How can I possibly be hidden from them?"

He hated this tremulous resistance in the people he must

browbeat. It was an unwelcome corollary of his power. He stepped forward. "Quite simply, if you cooperate."

"These spies—you know who they are?" She walked quickly across the room and sat, folding her hands on her lap. "We don't normally have spies and assassins and such in Rascall St. Mary."

Nicholas dropped into the chair opposite her. "None of those things are cause for fear."

Her tawny eyes fixed on his face. "Are you never afraid?"

"Like a uniform covered in gold braid, it's irksome at first, but later it's just another skin."

She swallowed and studied her nails. "But a cumbersome one, for all that. You can't move freely in it any longer, even if it seems second nature. Has it been very hard being a prince?"

He felt completely astonished. No one ever talked to him directly, or dared ask him such a question. Rocked to the soul, he groped for an answer. "I don't know. It's just what I do, who I am."

She waved her hands with sudden passion. "But you were an English child once, living here in this house. You didn't know you were going to be a grand duke then. Is that boy entirely dead?"

Her candor pierced, as if opening some deeply buried wound. Any number of clever, witty responses came to mind, answers to turn her astute perceptions aside, to protect himself. But the naked truth was more damning than any of them.

"If I did come here seeking my past, there's no more than a whisper, like the scent lingering in a room after my mother had left it. If I turn to look at it, hoping to see something meaningful, there's nothing there but empty air."

"But what of the little boy my mother tutored? You do realize that's another reason I'm here? Because Mama loved you when you were young."

Her direct gaze was an interrogation. He leaned back and deliberately met it with rancor, though something in him began to crave that directness and openness and honesty. Impossible in a prince. An impossible dream of integrity and warmth and simplicity. He covered his unease with well-practiced courtliness.

"Do you want the truth, or do you want me to flatter and beguile? I am much better at the second than the first, of course. Grand dukes rarely indulge in truthfulness."

She didn't seem to understand they were just words, a way to nullify any real approach to the truth. Her honesty was painfully open. "I don't think flattery will work. I need to know, don't you think? I have entered this whole plan far too lightly. I see that now. I'm not sure I can handle royal courts, but I'd better go into it all with my eyes open. You went to see my mother because you knew she'd been fond of you. Was that entirely cynical on your part—to remind her of the little boy you'd once been?"

"I had to do whatever it took to make you come here. You must have recognized that."

"Oh, I did. Yet what she said was still true. My mother doesn't make up things like that. You may think you are altogether ruthless and autocratic and unsparing, but my mother saw something quite different—a capacity for an entirely different kind of greatness."

"Good God! Your mother had sentimental memories and I used the fact without scruple. I am Grand Duke Nicholas of Glarien. Nothing else."

Her eyes were like shadows on winter grass. "You are also Earl of Evenlode."

"Since the days when I lisped over my letters with my governess, my life and my core have been re-formed and remade, as if a trinket were melted down and poured into a new mold. Nothing of the original bauble remains."

"It's still the same metal."

"No, it's not even that." He stood up, driven to pace. The gilt-and-blue room mocked him, a stranger in his own house. "It's tempered and contaminated by impurities in the new mold. The extra hammering beats out the patterns of atoms that held the old metal together. Nothing is left."

"Except the true essence!" Like a dog with a bone, she wouldn't let go. "The original nature of the metal itself can never be broken or destroyed."

The ceiling romped with cherubs and flowers, images of innocence. Nicholas stared up at them, remembering other ceilings, other images in gold and cerulean blue. He suppressed a shudder.

"Don't try to paint a romantic portrait of me, Miss Lindsey! You don't know what I am and you don't need to know—but believe this: I am not that child. If you have come here thinking you can reclaim that English boy, forget any such delusions. I am not a particularly good or admirable man. I am just not my cousin, and I will not see him take Sophia or the throne."

"Well, then. I see." She folded her hands again and looked down at them. "You are telling me I'm wasting my time trying to interest you in Rascall St. Mary? And that, though I believe we have a bargain, you do not agree to your side of it? You would use me, then cast me aside, with no regard to my own wishes?"

"Damnation! Your wishes are petty and immaterial! You have it in your hand to avert civil war. Instead you bring me ledgers with accounts of geese and sheep, or batches of hedgehogs sent to Covent Garden!" He felt trapped. He spun about so quickly she flinched. "Why do you wish to believe well of me? I have one purpose and one destiny. I've said so from the beginning. Rascall Hall means nothing to me."

She gave him a wry smile, indenting dimples in her cheeks, as disarming as any memories of a governess who had once been kind to him. "Very well. I accept that as the truth, though I'm not sure you haven't just done your very best to flatter me, after all. A small offering of the truth can be a deeper flattery than charm and compliments, can't it? The person confided in feels special and important, which obviously I'm not, except that you need me for your wedding day. Who are these spies?"

He quickly strode back to his chair and leaned both hands on its back. "I don't know. I only know that Carl is bound to have secretly planted agents among my staff. I cannot prevent that. I've done the same to him."

"Then no one can be trusted?"

"I trust only the six I brought with me: Fritz von Gerhard, Markos Hentz, Eric, Ludger, Lars and young Alexis Gregor. We occupy this house right now as if it were a hunting box, but that can't last. I'm in England on an official state visit. I should have gone straight to London."

"Instead, you've used your royal prerogative to be eccentric. How can I be concealed in the house?"

Relief swept over him like a wave of warm summer air. She would stay! She would do it! With her full cooperation, how could the scheme possibly fail?

"Come with me."

He turned and strode from the room. Penny remained seated for a moment in the arms of the upright brocade sofa. In spite of everything the prince had said, she still couldn't quite rid her mind of an image of that small boy her mother had come here to teach. A child, lost under these vast gilt ceilings among all this formal furniture, a boy who had loved his governess. His parents hadn't made much time for him. Earls and countesses didn't, presumably, especially when the countess was a princess from Glarien.

Was it just an idle form of comfort to hold on to what her mother had said, so she wouldn't have to confront the reality of the vibrant, threatening man he had become?

"Miss Lindsey?"

Penny looked up. He was standing at the door, holding it ajar for her, shadows and flame, a lock of dark hair fallen forward over his forehead.

"Your Royal Highness," she said. "If this house is to fill up with spies in a few days, then it is imperative I show you now what I've been doing on the estate. If you don't agree, then I'm going home."

To her surprise he smiled. The smile warmed her blood. It made her think of pleasure and sin. "Ah, so the country mouse has sharp teeth after all!"

"The country mouse will certainly bite, if she's caught in the talons of a hawk. We must take a tour of the grounds. Otherwise, no princess."

Sin softened to deception, intensely seductive. "If I agree to this adventure, you will allow the matter to be closed?"

She nodded. Her blood pounded. Her cheeks felt warm. It was her one chance, perhaps, to reach him.

• • •

He followed her from the house through orchards and kitchen gardens, a circuit of several miles. The day died around them, colors fading to shades of gray, trees rustling to sleep as they wrapped themselves in mysterious, dark shadows. The ghost of an English boy ran ahead through the half light, dodging in and out of his mother's roses, the gooseberry patch where he had hidden from his tutor, the hollow oak at the corner of the apple orchard that had been his ship, his castle, his hideaway. All of it had been maintained—held in this perfect re-creation of his past—by the woman who hurried ahead of him, reeling off facts and figures about shipments of vegetables and fruit to Norwich market.

"Mr. Green is still master gardener," she said. "He does it for love, since your father pensioned him off in his will. None of this could have been done without his skill."

Here you are then, lad—the first strawberry of the year! Strawberries in March, forced to fruition by those gnarled brown hands. *See that robin over there, Master Nicholas? He's my friend. I tell him all my secrets.*

What secrets, Mr. Green?

The brown finger tapped against the long nose. *Ah, now, that'd be telling!*

"Grand Duke Nicholas?"

Nicholas looked up. His heart thundered in a foolish panic. She was standing at the door to the orangery.

"How dare you!" he said, striding forward. "How dare you do this!"

The tip of her nose turned bright pink. "Why not? Are you afraid of your own memories?"

She spun about and went inside. He forced himself to follow her. Warm, sweet air absorbed him: damp, fragrant—the scent of oranges and heated tile. He stood for a moment, buffeted by images from the past, and hated her.

The long building swallowed her as she walked to one end. "I love it in here." She ran one hand over the leaves of an orange tree. The windows gleamed, the fire of setting sun reflecting in the small panes, then winking out one by one like snuffed candles. Only the woman stood bathed in red sunlight, where a last beam lit the far end of the building.

"I am reminded of Snow White," he replied brutally, "and death in a glass coffin. I assume your mother told you about this?"

"A coffin? For heaven's sake, this place is the very essence of life and innocence. Don't you think that's why the countess used to bring you here?"

He held his rage leashed, like a mad dog. How dare she talk to him of his mother! "All this is mine. If I wish it gone, that's my prerogative. I can send workmen tomorrow to destroy this whole bloody place, smash glass, rend stone, tear apart trees, let the oranges shrivel and die in a cold English rain."

She looked stubborn. "Brambles would only burst through the rubble. Besides, you don't really wish to destroy it, do you?"

Sunset streamed over her bright hair. She seemed bathed in greenery, an image of fruitfulness, the heavy, ripe satisfaction of the earth, captured inside tall walls of glass. Demeter and Persephone, beckoning with the harvest of life. A craving stirred, deep in his heart, for brightness and sweetness, for oranges filled with juice, for citrus bursting like honey on the tongue, for a woman to assuage the craving in his loins.

This woman.

He looked down at his empty hands and laughed. "No, of course not. It is only the impulse of a child, wanting to obliterate the thing he's denied. My mother liked to give me oranges. Your mother told you that. So, you have shown me and you have distressed me, as you intended. Yet I'm glad Mr. Green still fulfills his heart. I'm glad the orange trees bloom and someone picks the fruit. What did you think? That childhood memories are all sweet, or that I am indifferent now to sensual indulgence?"

He ran his hands over the branches of an orange tree, inhaling the odors, caressing the stems. Her color mounted as she watched him. She turned aside, biting her lip. He plucked a spray of blossom and inhaled the sharp scent, praying she would let it go—let him go.

"Children, certainly, are alive to sensory pleasure," she said.

His defenses shattered like glass, sharp and painful. He walked deliberately toward her, consumed with white rage. "We spoke of princesses sleeping. Do you forget I am a prince? That to awaken with a kiss is one of my roles? I find you more delectable than any of this burgeoning vegetable life. I would like to suck your mouth as if it were a ripe orange. I would like to make you moan with pleasure, here among the warm tiles and overhanging branches. Peel you and savor you. Is that what you want?"

Scarlet flared over her face. Her eyes glittered with sudden tears. "I see I went too far," she said. "I'm sorry."

He opened his hand, scattering crushed petals. "None of it is relevant, except that I don't particularly appreciate attempts to meddle with my soul."

"Obviously not. Alas, that I'm such a natural meddler!"

Her skin bloomed seductively. Her breasts swelled ripe in her bodice. She had no idea what she'd said or why it upset him. She just reacted, as she had reacted in her bedroom and at the breakfast table—the honest responses of the body, female to male, male to female. Shame made him want to cringe, but harsh, hard anger allowed nothing to be held back.

"You burn like a bright flame, Miss Lindsey. However, I am not to be saved by attempts to conjure memories of that child who once lisped here with his mother, or so thoroughly—apparently—charmed his governess. You must also know that royal promises often enough mean nothing."

"I'm sorry," she said again. "Of course, it isn't up to me to try to salvage your humanity."

His pulse beat hard and relentless in his hands and thundered through his heart. Wanting, wanting and sick at the craving. Nothing was left but the desire for cruelty—for punishment—though the pain cut her, too.

"Our relationship has no meaning beyond what I need for my wedding." His words fell like strokes from a lash. "If you attempt to trespass, in spite of what I pledged to your mother, I shan't hesitate to exploit your weaknesses and indulge my own.

It would be degrading, carnal and entirely without respect. Both of us would live to regret it. Shall we go back to the house?"

Rascall Hall was laid out in a rectangle, facing south. Rooms seemed to replicate, making a vast circuit around the central hallway and the ballroom, linked by their arching antechambers. Symmetrical flights of stairs swept away on each side to the next floor.

Penny walked through the rooms in a haze. She had shown Nicholas how she had saved the gardens and the orangery. With a terrifyingly astute perception, he had guessed exactly what she'd hoped for and negated it. Even her vague flutter of desire he had crushed with appalling ruthlessness, making it seem ugly and tainted. A strangling fear clutched her throat: that she had agreed to something monstrous; that she would never be the same again; and that if Nicholas was evil, then evil had a strangely tantalizing allure.

He opened a door. "This was my grandfather's dressing room, with his bedroom above. From that little antechamber beyond, there's a stair that joins the two. I shall use this room as my private study and receive visitors in here."

"Court officials?"

"You need to know whom Sophia will recognize at the wedding and how to acknowledge them—ministers, nobility." Nicholas strode past the desk to indicate a door in the corner. "A screen will be set before this stair door so you can observe them without being seen. It's impossible to tell the difference, but some will be my enemies—spies."

She almost stumbled. She saved herself by clutching on to a brass instrument on a tall stand by the window. Nicholas caught her by the arm and swung her away. She clung to his jacket for a moment to keep her balance, painfully aware of his hard muscles beneath her hand and the rigid rebuff in his manner.

"It's a telescope, isn't it?" She let go of his coat. "How clumsy of me. I'm sorry. Oh, goodness!"

She sank onto a chair feeling as if her mind had fractured into several disassociated pieces. Every time she tried to fit what was happening into something she understood, the prince sidestepped and turned her perceptions into something else. It was as if words and their meanings had separated, as if she might agree to fly on a magic carpet to Timbuktu, or steal the Golden Fleece from the Argonauts. A story, a seduction of fantasies, with no relevance to her real existence or her real self.

His voice seemed to float from some great distance. "Don't be concerned. It is not damaged."

She glanced up. He stood with his back to her, staring down at the telescope. The tension that emanated from him was almost palpable, flames and smoke reaching back to scorch her.

"I don't think I can do this!" she said. "It's like trying to teach a cat to play the piano. You'll get a grand cacophony of notes, but nothing tuneful. Anyone who knows the real princess will realize I'm an impostor right away. I'll be exposed, imprisoned—"

"Nonsense!" Whatever kept him transfixed seemed to evaporate as he glanced around at her. "Even if you are discovered, the fault will be mine. I have forced your cooperation. Your mother's security was threatened. Good God, you'd be the romantic victim of the moment, used by Black Nicholas for his nefarious schemes. No one would blame you."

"Nonetheless, I am still afraid."

He stalked away from the telescope. His back was a single, rigid line of rejection. "Why, for God's sake?"

"Because to read about adventure feels very different from living it," she said.

It was almost night outside, the deep, soft end to the day— the gardens cloaked in shadows. Penny stared at the blackness, silent and deep beyond the glass. Did everything change in the darkness? Did the innocent lawn shift its shape under cover of night and become somewhere dangerous and exotic—a landscape from dreams, where rivers of silver ran uphill into mountain lakes, and forests moved? Of course not. Of course not. It was just an English garden. She glanced back at the prince.

He was watching her intently. "But for you this is an adventure without risk."

"Yet I touched you, didn't I?" She tried to make it light, joking. "The sacred person!"

"It doesn't matter." There was something close to mockery in his voice. Was it directed at her? "Perhaps I may ask for a touch in return." He opened the door in the corner. "Come, I'll show you upstairs."

He hadn't lied. He wasn't that English boy at all. He had repudiated the gardens and the orangery and retaliated for her overtures with brute force. Her mother had been misled. She'd been misled. Grand Duke Nicholas was foreign, alien, and she'd been a fool to agree to his scheme.

Nevertheless, she followed him up the stairs. They led to a large state bedroom, with adjoining dressing rooms, sitting rooms and antechambers. Without another word the prince led her from one to another, silently folding back doors, demonstrating the remarkably up-to-date bathroom his father had installed with its blue-and-white tiles and piped water. Finally he led her back into the bedroom. Penny looked about at the gilt decorations on the walls, the fine eighteenth-century furniture. The huge canopied bed was topped with lions, like the ones over the entry to the stableyard.

"My bedroom," he said. "Chosen for a purpose. There are only two ways into this tower suite: The private stair we just used and the main stair through there." He indicated the doors that let onto the main hallway beyond. "I shall protect the first. One of my bodyguards will sleep in that antechamber to guard the second."

Penny said nothing as he opened a small door to another stairwell and led her up. She felt as if she might be floating, as if her feet were somehow treading six or eight inches off the ground. The stairs wrapped around the inside of the wall. They were obviously in the narrow part of the tower that projected above the roof of the main house. In the small room above his own bedroom, he indicated her cases, sitting at the foot of a narrow bed. A candle had been left burning on a stand beside it.

"You will sleep here," he said. "For the next few days, you may have the freedom of this whole tower, including the bathroom. Meals and hot water will be brought to you whenever you ring, but no one can enter without passing one of my guards. During daylight hours I shall work downstairs. Your modesty may remain undisturbed."

Penny crossed the small room to the outer window and opened it. The wall beneath dropped away into space.

"How very charming," she said. "But I think my hair isn't long enough."

He had walked up to the candle stand, but he spun around and stared at her. "What?"

The lawns and trees slept quietly, perfectly English and safe. Nothing bizarre had happened to the world, unless it had all just shifted back into this illusion of normalcy as soon as she opened the glass. A tawny owl hooted softly, denizen of the familiar night that covered farmyards and softly exhaling chimneys—safe, secure, like a blanket tucked over a sleeping child. The daisies would have closed up their petals. The small nighttime creatures, the hedgehogs, the mice, would be snuffling under hedgerows. Everything was rational and ordinary, except for the man in the room behind her.

"To be Rapunzel in this tower, it would seem I should need some thirty feet or more of hair," she said.

"You don't need to escape." She heard the note of wry amusement in his voice with astonishment. "The prince is already here."

"But you expect me to live in these rooms for a month? In between creeping downstairs to observe your visitors, of course."

He picked up the candle and carried it around the room to light the others on the dresser, desktop and wall sconce. The night outside disappeared into blackness. Penny closed the window to keep out the moths, while his distorted reflection flamed in the glass, mysterious and implacable.

"Why would you want to go out? So you can scrabble in the dirt? We can't have it noticed that Sophia's fingernails appear to have been used as shovels. Spend your time soaking them in the bath."

Penny dropped into a chair and looked ruefully at her hands. "Now I'm thoroughly humiliated. Less intense than fear, but just as painful. You are quite splendid with insults, you know.

Of course, my hands aren't perfect. I work with them. I don't imagine Princess Sophia ever washed a dish or cleaned out a grate in her life."

He set down the candle he'd been holding and turned to her. "Exactly."

She laughed, perhaps from sheer nerves. "Point taken. Very well. Shall I spend my days in torpid languor, like a queen of Araby? Sleep until four o'clock, then spend my nights taking lessons from you in hauteur, five-point court curtseys and the handling of a scepter? What else?"

He looked puzzled for a moment. "What the devil is a five-point curtsey?"

"I don't know. I rather thought you'd tell me."

"When you are a princess, other people curtsey to you."

"Oh. So what do I have to learn?"

"How to be royal." Opposite the window, another small door was cut into the wall. He took a key from his pocket and opened it. "Keep this door locked whenever you're not using it."

"Why?"

"So assassins and cutthroats can't enter, of course. It leads outside—to the roof walk."

The shock hit hard: whiteness and nausea. The room spun. Penny dropped her head forward into both hands.

"You are ill? Can I ring for something?"

The change in his voice saved her. He sounded defenseless suddenly, as if confronted with something he was helpless to mend, something that disturbed him. She looked up. "I told you I was afraid. I don't think I've ever really known what that's like, until now. I don't mean to collapse into palpitations whenever you remind me, but you must see that all this talk of assassination is very new to me."

Several candles blew out as he closed the door and strode across the room to stand over her. Shadows leaped as if he had wings and had opened them in a spread of raven-black feathers. He set the key on the desk.

"You have royal blood." Smoke and the smell of burned wick drifted. "What do you think sustained Princess Elizabeth when she sat at Traitor's Gate in the rain? What gave Empress

Maud the courage to fight King Stephen? What fired Boadicea when she gathered her troops—right here on this very hill—to launch her attack against the might of Rome?"

"Rome won," Penny said. "Boadicea was killed."

"After sacking Colchester and flinging the statue of Claudius in the river. Princess Elizabeth became England's greatest queen. So you feel frightened. Use the sensation as fuel for your courage. That's what Sophia does every day. It is what she's doing now, captured and imprisoned by Carl. So what does fear feel like? Tell me!"

She was floating in strangeness. The indecorous intimacy, the small room, the encircling darkness. She put both hands over her heart, reaching for honesty. "It's a tightness in here, as if I can't catch my breath. And a horrible flutter under my ribs. I think I won't be able to swallow, because I have no moisture in my mouth. Everything's moving too fast. I want to curl up under that bed and hide, but I might be too paralyzed to do it."

He stared down at her, as if genuinely puzzled. "You call that fear?"

"What would you call it?"

He grasped a chair and swung it around, sitting so he straddled it, his hands laid along the back. "I think you have led too sheltered a life, Miss Lindsey, and haven't played enough games. What you describe isn't fear, it's excitement. To have the heart tremble and flutter, men risk a fortune on cards. To have the belly gripe, they face a horse at a fence that's too high. To have the moisture flee their mouths, they visit the wife of a rival in her bedroom while her husband is still in the house. Because at the same time the blood sings, the mind soars and the soul cries out in exhilaration."

She watched his hands, lying lightly on the chair back, the perfectly groomed nails on the long fingers: beautiful, masculine hands. Weakness moved in her, a craving. But if she looked up at his face—at those carved lips and liquid, dark eyes? "You have no idea what games I've played, nor how sheltered I've been. So what does fear feel like? How you felt in the orangery?"

The clean-boned fingers tightened slowly on the gilded

wood. One by one his knuckles shone stark and polished in the candlelight. Then he opened his hands and stood up. He walked to the window. The latch creaked as he turned it. A drift of moths fluttered, clinging to the window frame, then launching erratically as night streamed back into the room. Ghost moths landed on his jacket and hair, fuzzy, fluttering gray-golden petals. A hawk moth bumped, heavy bodied, against his hand. Lappet moths, with their dead-leaf wings and feathered antennae, shriveled and died in the candle flames.

"Fear is a flaying of the senses, until you are laid open and numb, while the soul is peeled from the heart, layer by layer. Horror at the hands of the Four Horsemen laid on your shoulders—the breath of their nags, red, white and black, scouring the flesh from your bones. It yawns like grief, the anguish of the spirit turned loose without bearings. Real fear is an abyss of darkness." He closed the window with a small snap. "What I felt in the orangery was desire."

She sat frozen. "But you are afraid of it?"

He spun about, his gaze like midnight, unreadable. "You owe me a touch, Miss Lindsey."

She thought suddenly of a kiss, of his carved, supple lips pressed against hers. Of her mouth sliding open, soft, soft, under his search. A small flame flared, burning under her skin, as if her very bones knew that she wanted it. She stared at him, thinking of his hands cupping her face in the breakfast room, his threats in a house of glass. "You will not touch my face or hair!" Wild, improper thoughts flooded. "Or below my collar!"

"You do not leave me with much." His voice was wry. "But I agree."

"Why ask for this? Do you think to punish me?"

He took her left hand. "The punishment is mine. That is the truth. Close your eyes."

She felt foolish and vulnerable. Yet as he released her hand she obeyed. Lean fingertips touched just below her hairline and traced down the center of her neck.

It was something she imagined an explorer might do, seeking to map a strange place. Tender and delicate. A man's finger caressing, while her tongue filled with sugar. A gentle, thorough exploration from her nape to the sensitive spot below her ear. A light, sensuous caress over bones and tendons. A soft stroke along her jaw. The sweetness of it melted her. Every hair streamed with hunger. Each nerve ending smiled with the secret smile of the skin. Her throat and the muscles of her neck softened, delicately shivering, to offer a welcome. Transfixed, Penny held her breath while the flicker of fire ran and spread.

"No harm of any kind will come to you here," he said softly. "I swear it. I don't want you to know even apprehension or discomfort. You are safe. This little flutter of emotion has no more substance than the poor moths. Don't be afraid, Miss Lindsey. It is only a game."

Incredulous, stunned, she flung up her hand to force his away, negating that strange, sweet touch, pulling herself back from that molten brink. Did fear dissolve in the face of desire? Had that been his intention? Or did he just deliberately play with her emotions, as his clever fingers had just played on her skin? More important truths burned: He had talked about spies and assassins, of a fraud perpetrated on the monarchs of Europe.

"*Only a game?* How can you say that when you have just spent so much time impressing upon me the exact opposite? Are you trying to tell me to enjoy being afraid? Or that to be a princess is like being a man?"

"Both, if you like." He stared at his fingers as if the impression of her skin might still linger there. "You have courage to spare. When the time comes to act the princess in public, your heart will pound, your stomach will play merry hell with your ribs and the exhilaration will carry you through. You won't make a single mistake."

She stood up to face him, rubbing both hands over her throat. "Is that how you feel on public occasions? Is that what generals do facing their armies? Are you trying to tell me that leadership is all bluff?"

To her immense surprise he looked up and smiled—a warm, secret smile, a smile that reached out like a caress. Shadows fled. Every wall gleamed golden with candlelight, as if he painted the world with brightness and heat. "I said I would teach you to be a princess. I think you've just learned your first lesson, don't you?"

She could not be charmed. She could not let him play arpeggios on her heartstrings. "Your Royal Highness," she said formally. "What else must I know to achieve this impersonation? What about the practical things? I think you had better tell me everything right now."

He walked back to the door that led down to his own bedroom. "It will be simple. Your role in London won't involve that much public exposure until the wedding itself. A few social events and ceremonies. A ride in Hyde Park, perhaps, with the Prince Regent and the Tsar. A horseback inspection of a contingent of—"

The word burst from her before she could stop it. "Horseback?"

The small smile that touched his mouth this time was as fleeting as the honeysuckle-seeking lappet moths spiraling and dying in the candles. "It's just a simple procession."

She whirled about, what was left of her composure completely shredded. "But I can't ride. I can't ride at all. I've never ridden in my life. How could we ever have afforded horses? Huge, lumbering beasts, full of hot breath and danger! You can never tell what they're going to do. I simply cannot ride a horse in Hyde Park. I knew this was all a madness. It cannot be done. I had better pack my bags and leave now. I can go to my mother—"

He remained completely still, but his eyes stopped her in midsentence. "I will teach you to ride."

"No! You cannot teach me to ride. It's impossible. If the princess must ride a horse, then I cannot become her. How can I learn to ride in here?" She indicated the room. "The whole plan is hopeless. I'd better go home now."

"Then have you learned nothing from our conversation so far?" he asked. "I will teach you to be a princess. I will teach you to ride. We can do it under cover of darkness. I shall arrange for security. By God, can't you trust me with anything?"

His black gaze swallowed her. Penny stood still for a moment, trying to quell the tremble deep in her heart. He said it with absolute confidence: *I will teach you to ride.* By itself that certainty could never have persuaded her. Nothing else could have moved her, but this: the annoyance only thinly masked a painful vulnerability; he had called on his forfeit for a touch and not kissed her; and, for a moment in the orangery, she had seen him stripped to his essence, before he had lashed out in retaliation. *Can't you trust me with anything?*

She was still afraid. But if she told him so now, it would be a knife thrust into the heart of a mystery. And it was a mystery she wanted to solve.

"If you can teach pigs to fly," she said.

Six

He had dragged her through the dark, pacing through grasping shadows and the threatening rustle of leaves, hauling her by the hand on the little path where she had once carried back hedgehogs. The great tithe barn by old Rascall Manor was a ruin, long disused, except for the convenient storage of straw, but the walls remained solid. Some of last year's stalks still lay heaped in the corners and had blown in a scattering across the dirt floor. The original floor had been stone, but the expensive square blocks had been robbed to pave the entry at the new house, Rascall Hall.

The broken roof above her head echoed away into vast, gloomy spaces, home to barn swallows and spiderwebs, open to the sky where the stars glittered and the moon drifted, attended by a faithful coterie of clouds. Penny sat on an upturned wheelbarrow as Alexis arrived with one of the horses. Quest lay quietly where Nicholas had told her to stay. The dog's long silver muzzle was pressed against her outstretched paws. Soon it would be dawn. Penny had gone without sleep since the night she had spent in the guest bedroom. Could it have been less than forty-eight hours since she'd been seized by a prince and had her life turned inside out? Her sense of unreality had intensified so deeply she felt nothing at all, only an odd numbness in her hands and feet, as if she floated in ice water.

The prince took the horse's halter and led it into the barn. It was the bay that had bitten her sleeve. Alexis bowed and retreated, leaving man and beast standing together in the moon-barred darkness. The great wooden doors closed with a thud. The horse lifted its head and blew through its nostrils.

"So you believe you are terrified of horses?" Nicholas asked. "This lovely creature, with all his snorts and capriciousness, is nothing but a monster to you?"

Her voice didn't want to work. Her tongue had grown in her mouth, choking. She swallowed and made herself answer, reaching for anything to shrink the dark night down to size. "Not a monster," she said. "Don't be silly. But I do know he's big enough to hurt me."

Nicholas silently stripped off the halter and turned the animal loose. The horse started away and trotted around the open space, tail high, the whites of its eyes gleaming. Its flanks vibrated as it let out a shrill whinny, then it leaped into a gallop and tore around the barn, kicking up its heels, before sliding to a halt and trotting the other way.

Ignoring it, Nicholas strode across the dirt floor and sat down next to Penny.

"His name is Driver. He's a horse with a lot of blood, from the royal stables in Moritzburg. Relax. I just want you to watch him. He's worried. He's been taken away from his friends, the other horses. Now he's abandoned and alone in the dark."

"I don't know why you're doing this," she said. "It's cruel."

"Ah, so you do have some concern for him then? You don't need to. He's a bold horse, though nervous and excitable. He'll manage. His night vision is a great deal better than ours."

As he spoke the horse dropped its nose and grabbed at a shred of straw, before lifting its head and whinnying again.

"That's his other interest," Nicholas said. "Food. A horse is a grazing animal. Grass is his life. Don't you think he's beautiful?"

The horse trotted forward. Then with a violent shake of its head, plunged into another ground-shuddering gallop, mane and tail streaming, flashing through the night like a shooting star. Its shrill squeal stabbed at the moon.

"Only a stone would not think him beautiful," she said. "He's magnificent. I have never thought horses anything other than wonderful to look at, from a distance. But he's so huge! His teeth—"

"Are designed for eating grass." There was a depth of tolerance now in his voice. An ease. As if the presence of the animal brought him some deep peace and relaxation. "For all his strength and beauty, he's just a meal for a predator. He has only one defense against that: to stay with the herd—that's why he calls to them. A horse by himself can't both eat and keep his defenses alert. Alone he can never relax. So he wants to go back to his stablemates. Now, watch."

Nicholas stood up and strode out into the center of the space, the halter rope in his hand. The bay skidded to a halt and turned to face him.

"Well, big fellow!" Nicholas said. "Come here and be comforted." Without hesitation the horse walked up to him. The prince ran a hand down its neck. "Now he feels safe. He's well trained. He's already learned that a man can be an excellent substitute for other horses to provide him with safety and certainty in a dangerous world. So when I gave him the invitation to join me, he accepted."

"But he bit me," Penny said. "He tore my sleeve."

The prince stroked the bay's long face, pushing the forelock aside and rubbing around the base of the ears. The horse leaned into the man's hand, lowering its head in abject surrender. "Only because you invited that instead."

"I did not!"

Nicholas turned his back on the bay. It stood quietly at his shoulder, ears pricked forward. "Yes, you did—in his language. When you cowered and screeched and dropped the basket, you asked him to nip at you."

She was interested, in spite of her fears. Why was this animal so docile with Nicholas when it was obviously bad-tempered by nature? "How?"

"Horses talk with their bodies—and they read what we say

with ours." He turned and gestured. The horse squealed and cavorted, but Nicholas snapped the rope and the bay began trotting in a large circle around him, instantly submissive again.
"They are very concerned to see who'll lead them if there's
trouble. If another horse doesn't offer the right signals, the only
way this fellow can tell who's the leader is to see if he can make
the other give way."

"That's why you make him move now?"

The prince laughed. A genuine, soft, heartfelt laugh. "I
would never let him make *me* move. That would really worry
him! Can't you see the way he's watching me? Look at his face.
His eye is soft and dark. His jaw is relaxed. His ears are alert,
but not alarmed. He's a happy fellow. Driver can trust me to
take care of him."

She almost asked how the animal knew Nicholas was in
charge, but the question died, stupidly, in her throat. Why
should the horse question it, when she did not? Everything
about his relaxed, confident stance proclaimed: *You can trust
me. I offer you infinite wisdom. I offer you succor. I offer you
friendship.* He no longer looked arrogant or proud. Just solid
and reassuring. Her fear began to melt, just a little.

The prince dropped his hand and the horse stopped. Penny
didn't even see the gesture that made the bay walk up to him
again. It stood quietly while Nicholas rubbed at its neck and
said something in Glarisch. When he turned to stride back to
Penny, the bay followed, without halter or lead, like a dog.
Something moved in her. Yet if she closed her eyes, she could
still see that crowd of horses, jostling, pushing, and this animal's large yellow teeth trying to rip flesh from her arm.

"He is only cowed by you," she said. "He would bite anyone
else. He would have trampled me."

His dark eyes remained fixed on her face, impossible to read
in the shifting light. She thought he might even be laughing at
her. "A horse won't step on anything living if he can help it. Not
even your hedgehogs. What happened was your fault."

"*My* fault?"

"He's a naturally dominant horse. When you cowered, he
thought he might have to take charge of the whole situation,

which created a lot of anxiety for him. So he had to make sure. That's why he nipped at you. Not because he is mean, but because he didn't know who was the leader and he needed to find out."

Penny felt miserable, subdued. She could hardly believe the bay standing quietly by Nicholas was the same animal that had come at her with teeth bared. "Then I failed his test miserably, didn't I?"

"You weren't to know, if you've never been around horses."

"What should I have done?" she asked. "What would you do if a horse charged at you like that?"

"No horse would," Nicholas said. "That isn't the invitation I give."

"But I was afraid!"

He turned suddenly and lifted both hands, fingers spread. The horse backed up, snorting, head high. The prince immediately dropped his arms. The bay shook its head and lowered its nose, then stepped forward again.

Nicholas laughed and patted it. "All right, silly fellow," he said.

"Why did you do that?" Penny asked.

"I just reminded him I'm a predator. So are you. Our eyes face forward, like a lion's. Our hands are like claws—especially if we open our fingers as I just did. We eat meat. We hunt and kill grazing animals. I don't want him afraid, only respectful, but if he should ever think that I really am just another horse he can bully, now he knows that he's wrong."

"And that's what I should have done?"

"You should have believed in yourself. He didn't hurt you, did he, even when you provoked him? It was a bluff."

"But I didn't mean to provoke him," Penny said. "I was just minding my own business."

He laughed. "Oh, you provoked him all right! You stood waiting for him with a basket. Then instead of giving him the food he had every right to expect, or telling him to go away and stop being foolish, you collapsed into palpitations. And so you betrayed him. How can you be afraid of horses? Their natural defense is flight. At heart they're all cowards. It's only too easy to make them afraid of us."

"You are telling me I was a fool?"

He turned back to the horse. The bay began circling again, quiet and obedient. "You didn't face a pack of jackals or a pride of lions out for the kill. Only a small herd of grazing animals, flighty and sensitive. Not lions or tigers. Horses!"

"That isn't how it felt. You can't understand. You don't know what it felt like to me."

The bay broke into a canter. "I don't care what it felt like to you. What the devil do you think it felt like for the horses? How can a dumb beast understand our human passions—all our confusing emotions and wild actions? We trap them so they can't flee. With their sensitive awareness, with their natural fear, if we behave unintelligibly to them they can only become more stupid and afraid—or fight desperately and vainly for escape. Only by being calm and confident can we keep them feeling safe. We humans at least owe them that. Think of all the unnatural things we ask of them!"

Driver began to trot, energetic and strong, hooves thudding in the black night. Penny's throat was dry. "Unnatural?"

Nicholas stepped forward. A shaft of moonlight flooded over him. He burned like a flame, upright, lithe, powerful. The line of white shirt, the long legs slipping smoothly down into tall boots, scorched the air, robbing her of breath. The bay skidded to a stop, spun its head toward the man and began to canter in the other direction.

"We ask them to carry us on their backs, when in nature the only creature that springs on a horse's back is a lion. To go across dangerous footing, when to hurt a leg means instant death to a horse in the wild. To let us enclose them in a narrow space, when running is their only natural defense. For God's sake! These noble, sensitive beasts have served our species, suffered for us, died for us, faced guns and cannons for us. The very least we can do in return is treat them with understanding and not confuse them with our own wretched, inadequate emotions."

"I don't think human emotions are necessarily wretched or

inadequate." The bay moved ever faster. It circled the dark space, thundering, throwing up clods of dirt. Nicholas clapped his hands and the horse sprang, kicking out with both hind feet. Penny leaped up. "Why must you work him so hard? Why are you showing me all this?"

Nicholas turned to face her. The bay stopped. "I am trying to teach you that the creature you're afraid of has far more reason to fear you." The horse walked up and stood beside him. "Come here, Miss Lindsey, and make friends with Driver."

The bay was breathing hard, the shining flanks vibrating. It shook its mane and blew through its nostrils. Penny closed her eyes, remembering those teeth, and fabric tearing. "He's too big and . . . and blowing like a steam engine!"

"He won't hurt you," Nicholas said. "This bold, bad fellow is just a big baby. Come. If I ask him to lie down and roll over like a dog, he'll do it. You're completely safe."

As if hypnotized, she walked closer. The horse didn't move. Nicholas laid a hand on its shining neck. "Stand here, next to him, where he can see you. Touch him. He'll like it."

She dragged her feet across the infinity of dark dirt, keeping the man between her and the horse. Nicholas reached out a moonlit palm and took her fingers.

"Here," he said. "Put your hand on his neck. Be confident. Tell him he's a good fellow, beautiful, safe under your command. Tell him with your whole body, with your relaxed shoulders and easy smile. Let the message flow through your skin into his. Believe it. Say it: 'You're safe with me, Driver. I won't let you be afraid.'"

She forced a smile, feeling her hand tremble in Nicholas's grip. "You're safe with me, Driver. I won't let you be afraid."

He set her palm flat on the bay's neck, leaving his own beside it, resting on the glossy coat. The shape of his knuckles, of the veins and tendons, filled her mouth with craving. The certainty and firm reassurance. The tender concern. The beauty of olive skin stretched over strong white bones. Perhaps she had never really seen a man's hand before, never known she ought to marvel at such an intricate work of nature. As she hesitated, he laid his hand over the back of hers.

His palm was warm. The bay coat was warm. Smooth. Impossibly smooth. Under his guidance, she let her hand stroke over the shining, pulsing satin of it, over the hard, flickering muscles. The horse stood like a statue and closed its eyes. Tentatively, her lids pricking with tears, she rubbed over and over again down the flexible, shining neck, as Nicholas directed each caress.

Night breathed quietly, a blanket of darkness. Nicholas released her hand and let her cosset the horse by herself. She wanted to weep, put her head on the bay's shoulder and sob like a child. Her bones had been spun into sugar. Her blood flowed like honey as she balanced on the sweet edge between fear and fascination.

Nicholas reached into a pocket and brought out a piece of carrot. "Put this on your palm. Keep your fingers straight, and let him take it."

She glanced up at him, shadows and flame in the shifting moonlight. Prince of forests and dark places, offering solace. Her heart trembled, stricken from its natural rhythms, skipping into a new beat, deeper and faster, like a tide running into a sea cave. A great lump had formed in her throat, oceans of unshed tears. She took the carrot. The horse reached out gently, snuffling at her hand.

"Here, Driver. I'm sorry if I confused you. I didn't know." Soft lips, slightly prickly whiskers, brushed her palm. Delicately, carefully, the huge horse nosed at the carrot and took it with a sensitive courtesy.

"You are also safe." His hands slipped to hold her by both shoulders. "No lions or tigers will spring onto your back in the night."

Warm breath touched softly on the back of her neck. Lips touched. Firm, warm, kissing softly on the naked skin just above her collar. Penny froze. She didn't dare move or turn around. Her left hand was proffered for the horse, the right still resting on the burning, glorious bay coat. She stood vulnerable, exposed, as shivers of pleasure rippled out from the caress of his lips. She would melt. He would melt her, kissing softly where his fingers had roamed once before. That had been sweet enough. This was spun sugar. A man's mouth gentle, delicate on her nape, as light as a butterfly wing.

Before she could react, Nicholas stepped back.

"Driver was bred in the royal stables. He knows the manners of the court."

"He does?" Her voice shook a little.

"Perhaps he even knows a five-point curtsey. Say thank you to Miss Lindsey for the carrot, Driver."

Black mane flowed like a river. The great muscles and bones roared of animal power. Penny jumped as the bay dropped to one knee in a bow. Nicholas laughed and gestured. The horse scrambled back to its feet and stood four square again. It nodded its head up and down as if it, too, laughed at her. She turned and fled, not stopping until she had reached the safety of the wheelbarrow.

"You expect me to ride him? I can't!"

Nicholas gazed at her, unfathomable, a lithe flame in the night. "Of course not. Ask a horse to trust you, you must be worthy of his trust. Horses are very sensitive to reality. Riding is a conversation between you and your mount. Driver speaks many responsive, elaborate tongues, too subtle for you to learn without confusing him. I'll pick a nice gentle gelding, instead, who won't be worried by your inexperience or misread your anxiety. It's all right."

Once, in a story, a woman had stumbled into fairyland. She had danced forever in brilliant palaces hidden below the earth and thought it merely the frolic of an hour. "How did you learn all this?" Distress made her voice wild. "Who taught you?"

His smile ghosted in the moonlight, like the smile of a hunting fox. "Fritz von Gerhard. It is simply a matter of seeing the world from the horse's point of view. They cannot learn to speak our tongues—though they learn to read our bodies and to fear our whips and spurs. But if we learn to speak their secret languages of the body, we can talk to them in whispers and they'll listen. It's the key to all horsemanship."

He glanced at Quest. The wolfhound immediately stood up and trotted over to him to sit at his heels. There was nothing but trust and love in the dog's brown eyes. "I've led a lot of herds in my time, Miss Lindsey."

He laid her down on a bed of satin and lace, covered in rose petals. He laid her down on a bank of violets, sunny and fragrant. He laid her down in a silver, sparkling stream that ran warm and cold over pebbles of gold. Penny woke with a start and stared into darkness. The sensation of his hands on her body, of her own blood stirring in response, of the broken rhythm of a man's harsh breath in her ear faded to nothingness. She'd been dreaming. Tears pricked at her eyes. She hadn't had that kind of dream for years—a dream of desire. Yet this time it had been imbued with longing for something deeper and more profound than she'd ever known.

She lay in the dark and stared at the window, faintly gray against the black of the room. Dawn would soon break. The birds would be stirring, tuning up for their morning chorus. An odd twitter, a rustle, then one by one, each would join in, until the sun rose in a symphony of birdsong. Yet the night still held sway in deepest silence, in the long, bleak hour before dawn. She felt as if she still watched a horse circling and circling in the night. And a man commanding the animal like a necromancer with his familiar. A man standing quietly in the dark, the horse an extension of his mind, while his silver dog watched faithfully from the shadows.

It wasn't the skill that disturbed her or made her heart contract. Penny turned over and rubbed her cheek into the pillow. It was the simple kindness and understanding for the horse. He'd cared more about the bay's feelings than hers! He could no more hide that generous impulse than hide his own natural beauty. This prince! This man she had thought unfit to rule. She understood nothing, except that she longed to understand.

This bold, bad fellow is just a big baby. . . . He didn't hurt you, did he, even when you provoked him? It was a bluff.

There was a faint twitter outside. A rustle and stirring. Penny climbed from the bed and lit a candle. Still in her nightdress she sat at the desk, where the prince had left the key, and pulled out a sheet of paper. A sharp quill and fresh ink sat ready.

Dear Mama, she wrote. *I miss you more than Scylla would miss Charybdis, were the sea to dry up its whirlpools and leave no shipping for the seizing. I love you more than meat loves salt and know you to be wiser than the Cumaean sibyl. You were right. Our dark prince is indeed an extraordinary man. I just saw him with a horse.*

She stopped and brushed the soft end of the feather over her chin. Why had it seemed so profound, that simple circling in the night and a man who smiled at a horse like a lover? She bent her head back over the paper.

Alas, Mama dear, I cannot describe it. Defiant of anything you would consider decorous, the Grand Duke keeps me imprisoned in a tower (he says it is for my own safety, the wretch), the southwest tower to be precise. Surely nothing could be more suitable for a princess than that. Do you know royalty is a prison? I am sure you do. Princes have less freedom than slaves. Less freedom than birds kept to sing in a cage. Our Grand Duke can have no freedom himself, you see, so he enslaves all those around him, men and horses. How fortunate for me that my sentence is only for a month and then we may be together again in our snug cottage. It will be time to harvest the peas. . . .

It was barely dawn. Nicholas knocked softly at her door. She didn't answer. He turned away and leaned against the wall for a moment, staring at the latch. *I am trying to teach you that the creature you're afraid of has far more reason to fear you.* Was she afraid of him, this bastard daughter of royalty? For he was deeply afraid of her. He knew enough about fear to recognize that.

One after another, moths had been drawn to the candles. One after another they had shriveled and died, caught in the slipstream of heat and warmth rising from the flame, captured by the light that drew them inexorably to destruction. His fingertips remembered the satin flesh of her throat and the quick, hot pulse that beat ever faster under his caress. His mouth remembered the taste of her nape as his soul contracted with longing over her bravery. He had forced himself to stop before his arousal soiled the moment and made it all base.

He tilted his head and stared at the ceiling. It arched in a small curve, embossed with gilt lions' heads. She was more than a candle. She was a pure, bright warmth, bathing the day in beneficence, innocent of its own power to burn. While he, like the ghost moth, was doomed to be a creature of the night. Now, for a month, he must take her away from the daylight so she could learn under cover of night. Take her into his world of shadows and duplicity. Would darkness make her bright flame gutter? Would he send her back to her mother extinguished, only a wraith of smoke?

There was no choice. For him or for her. In spite of what he'd promised, just as he'd warned her, if Glarien required she be sacrificed, then so be it.

He knocked again, more firmly, but silence still flooded the hallway. The Grand Duke of Glarien, Prince of Moritzburg, sovereign lord of countless souls—though not of his own—lifted the latch and went in. She was not in bed. She was slumped in the chair, her bare feet curled against each other like kittens in a basket. Her head, cradled by one wrist, lay on the surface of the little writing desk. Her mouth curved as if she smiled. The red-blond hair roped in its thick plait, following the soft curve of her spine.

She had fallen asleep at the desk. Female and helpless.

Nicholas stood and stared at her, his mouth dry.

Arousal swarmed in his blood. Hot shame and desire clamored in an agony. Was this what the moth felt at the moment of immolation? He closed his hand on the latch, wanting desperately to retreat.

But the air in the room was cold. Her naked feet lay exposed on the floor. Female and helpless in sleep. It was his fault if she was uncomfortable or wretched. His fault. He walked into the room and touched her shoulder. She turned her face deeper into her arm, like a burrowing creature. His heart trembled as he stood with his fingers on the plain white cotton. He felt frozen in time, bewitched by Circe, paralyzed. Nicholas closed his eyes, while voices howled. Above all of them: Carl. Count Carl Zanich, goading and driving. *Go on, Nico! It's your turn now!*

A migraine leaped fully formed into his skull, crashing behind his eye like a gong struck by a giant. He stumbled away to the window and leaned his head on the cold glass, while shudders racked him. He was gasping as if drowning.

Nico! Nico's turn! Devil's spawn!

Blinded by pain he turned to flee. But she sat slumped in the chair, awkward and cold. She would wake up dazed and stiff. Brave Penelope Lindsey, who was frightened of horses, of all things! Jagged lights danced to his right, narrowing his vision. The birdsong outside crashed like cymbals and trumpets, loud and piercing in his suddenly sensitive ears. She was cold. She would wake up cold.

Ignoring the pain, he forced himself to walk silently back to her. He picked her up carefully, as carefully as if she were a newborn foal, and carried her to the bed. She groaned softly, a defenseless little whimper. While the headache thundered and pounded, he adjusted the cotton nightdress over her white ankles and tucked the sheets and blankets about her. Creases marked her cheek where it had pressed against her muslin sleeve, a crosshatch of fine, red embroidery on her pale skin. Her hand lay curled on the pillow. He wanted to kiss all her broken nails and give her hedgehogs, infinite numbers of hedgehogs, and oranges as round and perfect as her breasts, if it would make her happy.

Instead he went to the desk and made himself read what she'd written. *Dear Mama . . . Do you know royalty is a prison?*

Sick with shame he left the room and went downstairs to serve one more day of his life sentence.

She had slept away the day, not sure how she had even climbed into her bed again. Her letter to her mother lay half-written on the desk, so she must have just stumbled back between her sheets and dissolved so quickly into oblivion that she couldn't remember it. When she woke up again, hungry, Alexis appeared with a tray. At last, after another meal, she had received the summons. And the clothes. The boy with the dandelion hair smiled a little shyly as he presented them.

"You will not be offended, ma'am?" he asked formally. "Everything has been washed for you."

It was a pair of breeches, obviously belonging to Alexis himself. All the other men in the house were too tall.

"Where is His Highness?" she asked.

"In his study." The boy shrugged. "Working at something. Grand Duke Nicholas makes lists. He is always working. He said you may use the secret stair."

"You serve him very faithfully," Penny said.

Color washed over the boy's face. "I would give him my life," he said fiercely. "I would die for him. I love him. No one loves him better, not even Major Baron von Gerhard."

The kind of man to inspire worship in his men? Or in this blond boy—who couldn't be more than fifteen?

"Why do you love him so much?"

The yellow head turned away. A muscle clenched in the young jaw, barely in need of shaving. "Grand Duke Nicholas is my sovereign lord."

Something in the boy's devotion almost frightened her. What would happen to Alexis if Nicholas ever proved unworthy of such trust?

The gentle gelding was white. Its name was Willow. Penny felt magically alive, as if she'd stepped from her ordinary life into a new dawn in a new land—supremely, agonizingly happy. The air smelled of dust and old straw, earthy, innocuous smells. Willow made an odd grunting noise, trotting around her in circles. In the great shadowed barn, Nicholas had showed her how to move the horse away, how to make it come to her, with small movements of her body. It was terrifyingly simple. It made her feel glorious, triumphant. To see the soft brown eye watching her with adoration, like a pet. To see all that massive muscle and bone responding to her wish from a distance.

She didn't even have to touch the horse to control it! She could fly. She could turn turnips into roses with a wave of her hand. Had Jack felt this way, waking in the enchanted meadows at the top of the beanstalk? Had Rapunzel known this when—freed from her cumbersome hair—she had run away laughing into the marvelous forest?

"He's doing it!" She laughed in delight as Nicholas told her to step forward as he'd shown her, to turn the horse to go the other way in its circle. "He's doing it! He trusts me!"

The prince was standing, in shirtsleeves, boots and breeches, at the side of the hall, leaning casually against an upright with his arms crossed over his chest. Quest sat beside him, tongue lolling, her intelligent brown eyes watching woman and horse.

"Then be worthy of his confidence," he said. "Put the halter on him."

The bright bubble collapsed. Penny turned and looked at him. "Oh, I can't! I don't know how."

From the corner of her eye, she saw the white gelding stop, then drop its nose to snuffle about on the floor. It picked up a long stalk of straw and looked at her, with the end of the yellow strand hanging comically from the side of its mouth.

"If you don't do something new, how are you going to learn it?" he asked scornfully. "Look at that poor fellow! You've abandoned him!"

He spoke to the wolfhound. Quest trotted away and came back with the halter in her mouth. Nicholas thrust the halter into Penny's hands and sent Quest to fetch a brush.

"Now, walk up to Willow and tell him with your body how happy you are to see him, what a pleasure it is to run into each other like this on such a beautiful evening. Go on. You can do it."

The thread of straw lay still, drooping. The horse watched her, then shook its head, causing its long mane to flop about. The straw disappeared.

Penny walked carefully up to the horse. It did not shy away or bare its teeth. It just stood, a picture of docility. When she held out the halter, the horse put its nose into the loop of leather to let her fasten the straps over the top of its head. She fumbled, unsure, but Willow waited. When she had finished, Nicholas walked up and quietly made adjustments, showing her how the fit should be, then he held out the brush, slightly damp from the dog's mouth.

"This is how horses make friends, in mutual grooming. Brush him like this and he'll be your friend for life."

In firm, sure strokes, Nicholas brushed the horse's coat. Penny stepped back and watched. White coat, white fabric. The horse breathed quietly into the gathering dusk while the man worked, muscles flexing and contracting visibly under the fine shirt. Horse and man, beautiful creatures. She blushed and looked away.

"Your turn," Nicholas said, holding out the brush.

Unsure how the animal would react, she dabbed at its coat with the bristles. The horse flinched. The prince laughed. "He doesn't want to be tickled by a fly. He wants to be massaged. You won't hurt him. Put your back into it."

She brushed more firmly, standing close, leaning her free hand on Willow's broad back as he had done. Nicholas watched her. She hadn't demurred, apparently, at donning Alexis's shirt and breeches. It was common enough, of course, for females to first learn to ride astride, but they were usually children at the time. He'd thought she would make silly objections. It made him foolishly pleased that she had not. The shoes were her own. Sensible, country shoes. Her hair was wrapped in its coronet about her head.

He dropped the lead rope and stepped back. Willow stood completely relaxed. Penelope brushed down the horse's shoulder and front legs. The shirt and breeches fit a little awkwardly, stretched too tightly over her female curves, then hanging loose where she lacked the boy's muscle. Mortified at his own shamelessness, he watched the ebb and flow of fabric over her shoulders and breasts and buttocks, and knew he was like a kingfisher watching for fish, hungry.

When she leaped back suddenly, she almost bumped into him. In a reflex, Nicholas caught her elbows in both hands. He immediately released her, despising himself for what he'd been doing, watching her in that travesty of craving.

"Oh!" she said. "Oh, dear!" She giggled.

Willow stood absolutely quiet, almost asleep. The horse's eyelids lay half closed, shadowing each feathered iris. Its jaw hung slack, making a little cup of its lower lip, prickly with whiskers. The horse had also dropped eighteen inches of dappled pink organ from its sheath. In a slow animal rhythm the tip thudded gently against the round belly.

Penny was scarlet. "Oh, good heavens!"

Nicholas slapped the animal softly on the neck. He felt betrayed, as if the horse had decided to flagrantly make a fool of his desires. "Here now! Wake up, old fellow!"

The horse opened its eyes. The organ slowly drew up and disappeared.

In the ill-fitting shirt, she stood with both hands over her mouth. He didn't know what to say. It seemed a disaster. He picked up the dropped brush and began to work firmly on the horse's off side.

"He was—" She touched the horse on the neck, pushing the mane aside. "Did I invite that?"

"It doesn't matter," he said.

The color still lingered in her face, fiery, like the sunset. "I'm a country girl." She was matter-of-fact, earnest now. "I do know something of—" She stopped and looked away. "I have spoken with Tom Robertson about breeding the cows. I was more surprised than shocked, I think. There isn't any mare around."

"It was just a reflex. He's male—though a gelding."

Suddenly she laughed. "Then rather an indecorous one."

She amazed him. He didn't know any other way to put it. He was amazed by her. He tossed the brush aside. Quest picked it up and carried it to the side of the hall. Penny was here in this out-of-the-way place, female, alone with two males. But at the sign of that primitive, uncontrolled virile urge she only blushed and laughed and said she was surprised. When she had been so concerned about danger and so fervent about fear, didn't this frighten her—the only thing that should? That her soft feminine presence could create such an alarming change in a male?

He took the lead rope and faced her. "It's time you mounted."

She backed up a step. "Now? There's no saddle."

"I want you to sit on him bareback. Just that. I won't let him move. But I want you to learn how freely you can act on a horse—what belongs to you, what belongs to him."

"I don't understand," she said. "Show me. Show me first, then I'll do it."

She stood uneasily, one foot a little behind the other, as he sprang onto the white back. Nicholas dropped the lead rope across the horse's withers.

"This belongs to him," he said, putting one palm on each thigh. "Keep your legs quiet. Only your upper body belongs to you."

With ease, he ran through the exercises that helped young riders learn to sit well on a horse. As Willow stood like a rock, Nicholas showed her how to be free and loose above the hips, while keeping his legs close and still. Later he would teach her the aids—the signals using both body and legs—but first she must learn balance, relaxation and confidence. Reaching and crossing with his hands, his back supple, one movement flowed into another without conscious thought.

"Your turn," he said, sliding to the ground.

He boosted her onto Willow's back. She sat frozen, clutching mane in both hands.

"Let go of the mane," he said.

"I can't! I will fall!" It was a whisper.

"Why would you fall? Do you fear tumbling sideways from your chair at breakfast? Do you think if you don't hold on you will career suddenly from your bed? Let go. Don't move your legs. Let them hang, just as they were."

She opened her fingers and released the mane, one hand at a time.

"Now lift your arms above your head."

She clutched at his shoulder. "I can't."

"Yes, you can."

She did it. One movement at a time. She leaned forward until her forehead touched the animal's mane. With his hand light on her thigh, she leaned back until her braided coronet lay at the top of the white tail. He asked her to relax each time, keeping her legs loose, finding her balance. Through all of it the faithful cob stood quietly, occasionally flicking an ear, while her slender muscles moved under his palm, firing his arousal.

She was soft. Incredibly, enticingly soft. His palm burned

with desire: to know more, to sweep over her thigh and hip and waist to the soft curve of her breasts; to know her belly and dimpled waist; to know what it would mean to be lost and found in the scent and feel of her. This country girl. This bastard daughter of royalty. It was base. If he relaxed his control for one moment, he would be howling with yearning, like a wolf shut out on the moor, a lion lost in the desert, a merman drowned in an ocean, howling his lost soul to the moon.

It grew completely dark. Stars appeared, one by one. Outside, his men quietly kept watch. No one would discover them here, enclosed together intimately in the night, while the false princess allowed an alien being between her legs and surrendered her fear.

"Now," Nicholas said, placing a hand on the small of her back. "You are not to hold on. If you do, it will throw off your balance, which is what riding a horse is all about. When he moves, this is where you must flex, like a little boat lifting and falling with a wave. Supple, comfortable, with your back pliant and your head up, looking ahead to where you're going. Riding is an equilibrium between surrender and tension."

"What an excellent description!"

He dropped his hand. "What do you mean?"

She sat as he had shown her, back straight, legs relaxed. "You take my surrender for granted. You did from the beginning. Yet you aren't really comfortable with it, are you? Tension crackles about you like a thundercloud."

He walked the horse in slow circles. "Why do you say that?"

She was naturally flexible. In the darkness her teeth glimmered as she smiled. "Perhaps horses aren't the only creatures that read what we say with our bodies."

"I don't see Willow flinching from my oncoming storm. What message are you reading that he can ignore?"

She lifted her arms straight out to the sides, keeping her hips flexible and balanced. "I don't know. That you hunt silently and ferociously in the night? I am fortunate you consider me one of your pack, or I might be eaten alive. Yet tonight it seems you are calling very desperately on courage, and I'm not sure why."

"Courage?" He stepped away from the horse's head, walk-

ing backward and holding the lead rope at the end. Once she seemed relaxed and confident, he showed her how to halt and how to make the horse move forward again. She grinned with delight when she found the knack of it.

"Is it because you're constantly in danger? I have tried to imagine it. Living as you must have done. I should hate it. Anonymity is so much kinder. You're always on display, aren't you? So you carry lightning and thunderbolts, ready to hurl them at your enemies. The only thing I don't understand is why you think, when I have capitulated so thoroughly, that I'm one of them."

She halted the horse as he walked up to her. *And what do you think the silent language of your body says to me?* Their eyes met. It was too late to hide his hunger, too late to shield the blaze with iron shutters. As if his fire scorched her, she flinched and jerked, thumping her heels against the gelding's flanks. Willow lurched forward. Nicholas caught Penny's waist in both hands and swung her to the ground, fired with mad desire. Her lips trembled and opened. The straw stacks beckoned. He could take her, like an animal, and no one would stop him. His sex pulsed, turgid, arrogant in its male need, tightened hard against his body. With an intense effort of will, he thrust her away and turned to the horse.

"If you kick him, he'll jump," he said brutally. "Enough for tonight!"

Once again Penny couldn't sleep. Perhaps, now she had launched into this great adventure, she would never sleep peacefully again. She and the prince had walked swiftly back through the dark, Quest trotting at their heels, while Alexis led Willow away, a ghost horse with a ghost boy at its head. A mad exhilaration pounded in her chest. She had ridden a horse! Admittedly, the prince had led her, like a child at the fair. But the burn and stretch in her thighs told her *she* had ridden, making the horse walk and stop with simple movements of her body. And that last moment, when Nicholas had caught her and she had thought—

Penny went to the window and opened it, leaning out to

allow the cool night breeze to wash over her face. *Mama, you were right. This dark prince radiates a powerful physical charm. I feel the danger of it. I know he is perilous. Yet I believe my interest and my curiosity are proof enough against thinking the odd swooping sensation in my heart means anything. And, of course, in your infinite maternal wisdom, you have bound him with an oath—oh, and I am learning to ride a horse!*

Moonlight rippled in the glass, dancing with her own shadowed reflection. She closed her eyes for a moment. In a dark barn a man, limber and pliant, swung and danced on a horse's white back, graceful and certain. He ran his hands down his own thighs, firm square-boned fingers chasing long, hard muscle—an appallingly indecent gesture, a flaunting of masculinity. He walked backward, arms spread like an offering, leading her. *You cannot fall,* the posture said, *I will always be here to catch you.* What a charlatan!

A tawny owl hooted. Its mate replied, sharp and clear in the summer night. Penny opened her eyes and searched the darkness, wondering if she might see the bird drift by on silent wings.

Something moved on the roof.

It was a small sound, a scraping. But it came most definitely from the roof of the house. Penny stepped back and softly closed the window, her heart hammering. Her room lay in darkness. She was already prepared for bed, washed and changed into her long nightdress, and she had blown out her candle several minutes before. On bare feet she crept across the rugs to the door that gave onto the rooftop walk. Bending down she looked through the keyhole.

Nothing but blackness.

She stood up and leaned her head against the panels, her ear pressed to the wood. Faintly she heard the owl hoot again and something bumped on the other side of the door. Something solid and metallic. In a rumble of soft breath, a muttered exhalation, a man cursed.

Cold burned into her lungs as she gasped in a gulp of night air and held it.

The key lay in her desk. The door was locked.

Someone was out there. On the other side.

One silent step at a time she backed away across the room to the door in the corner. Her fingers fumbled on the latch. The stairway curved into silent blackness below. Pressing one hand over her mouth, Penny ran down the stairs and flung open the door at the bottom.

Light flamed, glittering on the ceiling and the rich hangings, the golden lions and the exquisite furnishings of the prince's bedroom. Gilt ridged the tumble of sheets, the pillows carelessly tossed aside, the crumpled coverlet. But the single bright focus of candlelight illuminated two figures near the foot of the bed, caught in a golden tableau against the backdrop of the dark room.

The prince sat at a small table, where the single stand of candles burned. His hair fell forward over his forehead, his eyes smoke shadows where he leaned his face into cupped fingers— the knuckles and lines startlingly beautiful, as if Botticelli had drawn the hand of a saint. A silk dressing gown, heavily embroidered with heraldic symbols and gold thread, lay open at his throat. His skin gleamed, a smooth marble carving of strong neck and collarbones, sensual as satin, against the heavy fabric.

He studied a chessboard.

Facing the prince across the table sat the golden-haired Alexis. As the boy met her gaze he blushed, fiery and awkward. His irises gleamed, as intense as cornflowers, between eyelids rimmed painfully in red. He wore nothing but white shirt and breeches, his feet bare, his wrists raw where they projected from his shirtsleeves. He seemed ungainly and insubstantial, as if caught in a moment of adolescent vulnerability, like the butcher's boy when his voice was breaking. Quest lay under the table at his feet. The tip of her tail moved just a little, a feathered greeting.

The prince dropped his hand and looked up. A tiny fire burned in the black depths of each pupil.

Penny stopped where she was, feeling clumsy and foolish, clutching one hand to the neck of her night rail.

"There's someone up there," she said. "On the roof!"

Seven

"*It's all right, Alexis,*" *Nicholas said gently in Glarisch.* "*Go to* bed."

The boy knocked over some of the chess pieces. He fumbled to set them upright. Nicholas leaned forward and removed the black king from his shaky fingers.

"It's all right," he said again. "Leave them."

Alexis bowed once and fled the room. His bare feet rapped like gnawed bones on the floorboards.

Penny waved her hand awkwardly. "I did not mean—I would not have wished to disturb you. I heard a man. Outside my door."

He sat and looked at her, the fires burning in his eyes, one fist pressed against his mouth.

"I assure you I did hear it," she insisted. "Quite distinctly."

The prince stood, the dressing gown falling in gilt splendor to his feet, and lifted the candlestick. Shadows raced and flared.

"Is reassurance to be my duty tonight?" he asked softly. "You were right to come to me. We'll see who it is, shall we?"

Penny glanced back up the dark stairs to her tower room. "You aren't going to call your guards?"

He walked up to her. "No."

The syllable rang in her ears like the single toll of a bell.

Brushing past her, he ran lightly up the stairs, his dog at his heels. She followed. In her room he listened for a moment. The tawny owl hooted again, a drawn-out mournful cry, as the bird quartered the woods and fields and called to its mate. Penny was gasping for breath, as if she had been carrying firewood or hods of coal too heavy for her.

Nicholas lit four candles. "The key is still in the desk?"

She nodded, then stood dumb as he took out the key and strode to the door, leaving the candles burning. He walked out into the darkness, leaving Quest with Penny. She sat down on the bed, shivering, and ran her hands over the wolfhound's thick coat.

Moments later, the prince reappeared.

He glanced over his shoulder and beckoned to someone behind him. "Come."

A man stepped into the doorway. His hair gleamed red above a green uniform with a gold sash.

"Eric," Nicholas said. "One of my men."

The red-haired man bowed to Penny, his face white and stiff. "I apologize, ma'am, for disturbing you."

"This is guard duty." The prince seemed as remote and cold as the moon. "You understand the penalty?"

The soldier bowed again and clicked his heels together. "Sire!"

"Then remember it!"

Eric stepped back onto the roof walk.

Nicholas closed and locked the door. "He dropped his musket."

Penny pulled the cover from her bed and wrapped it around her shoulders. "How did you know it was one of your men? What if an assassin had crept up and attacked him, then lain in wait for you? When you opened the door you had the candles behind you. You'd have made a perfect target."

The gilt dressing gown flowed, a river of embroidery. "Do you think so?"

All her repressed fear seemed to surface at once, like a pot come to boil. "I know so! Are you a fool? I don't understand

you. You talk about security and guards, then you take mad
risks. You aren't even armed."

He held out both empty hands and looked at them. "It's all
right," he said at last. "I heard the tawny owl. That's the signal
we agreed on."

Penny stared up at him. "What signal?"

He turned his wrists to lay a palm flat on each of her shoulders. Fire seemed to run from his fingers, spiraling down
through her blood. "The owl cry. My men are using the sounds
to communicate. Anyway, if something had been wrong, Quest
would have warned me." He moved his hands to cup her face,
a thumb brushing each cheek. "I am sorry Eric frightened you.
He'll be punished."

She closed her eyes, feeling his fine fingers in her hair and
on her skin, hating what it did to her composure. "No! Don't!
Because of me? No! I couldn't bear it!"

"Hush." He shook his hands, gently moving her head from
side to side. "Open your eyes," he said. "Look at me!"

She could no more have refused him than a mouse can refuse
the summons of the kestrel. She lifted her lids and gazed up at
him.

"He'll be punished because it's a matter of military discipline. It has nothing to do with you."

"But I thought these men were your friends. You fence with
them. You were playing chess with Alexis in your bedroom."

The darkness changed in his eyes, as if smoke spiraled from
a bonfire. He opened his fingers and released her. "Alexis
couldn't sleep. That's all."

He walked away. Quest watched him, but didn't move.

Penny stared at the rigid lines of his back, resilient beneath
the rich robe. "You think you are comfort to sleepless creatures?"

The prince trembled, as if with cold. "Comfort? You might as
well say the grave is comfort for the dead!"

"Then why were you playing chess?"

He spoke slowly and carefully, as if trying to convince her of
something. "Alexis is the heir to a powerful family, important
to Glarien. Chess will train him to think ahead, weigh the con-

sequences of his decisions. It will teach him to master his emotions in order to defeat his enemies."

She groped to understand. "But it's the middle of the night! Earlier you said something about reassurance. I thought you meant you offered some kind of comfort to him."

"He is the Erbgraf von Kindangen—heir to a count. I need to bind his loyalty."

"How very hateful! You let that boy hero-worship you for political expediency, so he'll be staunch and useful to you in the future, but you don't really care about him?"

"I do not wish to discuss Alexis," he said shortly. "It has nothing to do with you."

"I think it has everything to do with me. I'm trying to understand what it means to be royal. Have you never had friends? Even in school?"

"You mean at Harrow? Good God, no! That was six intervals of pure hell. I had to fight daily for my life. English schoolboys don't welcome a foreigner in their midst, especially one who claims to be a prince from some benighted backward nation in Europe and joins them for only one term each year. Anyway, their instincts were entirely correct. I wasn't like them."

"Does it mean you can't care for anybody?"

He was rigid. "I can't care about your feelings or your concerns. Whatever they are, they're not mine. You are accustomed to messy, emotional relationships, with your mother, your women friends, your family—"

"What I feel for my mother isn't *messy!*"

He looked around. "Isn't it? Then what the devil do you think you feel about Alexis or Eric or any of my men? What fuzzy, sentimental judgments do you make about things you know nothing about?"

She pulled up her feet and wrapped her arms about her knees, feeling threatened and vulnerable. "If I'm to impersonate Princess Sophia, you had better teach me. What will happen to Eric?"

"He will suffer the prescribed punishment without complaint."

Penny closed her eyes, remembering. "If you have him flogged, I'm leaving now."

He spun about. "You don't think he should suffer a flogging? How softhearted of you! You are too generous. In any army in Europe, to fall asleep on guard duty usually warrants immediate death by hanging."

She couldn't read what was in his voice. She only knew it was something unholy and dreadful, almost a sarcasm in the face of brutality. Tears squeezed between her lashes. "Please," she said. "That's barbaric!"

"Eric is one of my personal bodyguard. It's not a game or a caprice. I have put your life and my own in his hands." Flames raced and sparkled in the gold threads of his robe. "But you think I should be merciful?"

Penny plucked at a loose thread in her coverlet. Small shivers ran down her spine. "Yes, I do. Of course I do! Isn't mercy a Christian virtue? Why don't you just admonish him and forget it?"

"What about the innocent men who die, because the enemy attacks while the guard sleeps? Is that merciful? Instead you could hang that one man as an example to the rest and his one death might save a thousand lives. An army can't function unless the rules are clear and punishment certain." With thumb and forefinger he snuffed one of the candles.

"So there's no place for mercy?"

Darkness flowed, settling densely in the corners of the room, staining his eyes to pitch. "Soldiers don't march into battle relying on mercy. They rely on the training of the man next to them, backed by the dispassionate justice of their officers. Do you think discipline a matter for individual choice?"

"I don't know. But even an army consists of fallible mortals."

"So it does. But you're no longer a mere mortal, you're a princess. So what would you do?"

"I'm not a princess," she said. "I don't want to be."

He snuffed another candle. A curl of smoke traced through his fingers. "I was seventeen when I took my first command. My leniency was taken for weakness. My troops fell into chaos.

I lost fifty soldiers in a skirmish that should have cost no more than five. Don't talk to me about mercy!"

"But all this—" She waved her hand. "All this is about you, not me. I don't matter!"

His gaze penetrated, almost quizzical. "Do you really believe that?"

She hugged the coverlet more closely about her shoulders. "If Eric's punishment can't be changed and there's never room for pity, why are you asking me?"

He smiled softly, with a wry twist to his lips. "I hoped you could offer an argument to prove everything I just said to be wrong."

Confusion spiraled in her, like the smoke suffusing to nothingness in the cool night. "You want me to convince you to be different? I don't understand."

The light from the remaining candles highlighted his jaw and the flare of his cheekbone. "After that disastrous skirmish, my grandfather had every tenth man in my command flogged, since I couldn't be touched, of course. It was a nice idea, an object lesson in brutality. I watched all of it, though it went on for days. I wanted to be sick, but I wasn't. There is no room for weakness in princes. But I thought you might have a different answer. Isn't there anything you've learned in your simple Norfolk world that would save me from the choices I have to make daily?"

She felt infinitely cold and alone, as if she stared over a precipice into depths of oblivion. "Maybe you could try appealing to your men's pride, instead of using threats of punishment. Perhaps that would work."

"Perhaps it would." The prince picked up one of the remaining candles and used it to light the others, one at a time. "For I learned some other things, too, from my grandfather's wretched display. A flogging breaks something in the man punished. He's generally not much use afterward." His wry smile grew deeper. "If he's hanged, of course, he's no bloody use at all. I abhor waste, you see, Miss Lindsey. I don't have enough men to squander them. So, though my discipline is absolute, I have tried to carve a different path, one based more on respect than brutality."

She watched him in silence as wax ran and dripped, not sure she could breathe.

Nicholas went to the door. He ran his hand over the smooth wood. "My mother would have said this door retains the spirit of the materials used to make it: oak, sacred to the druids; iron, protection against evil. Being steeped in the superstitions of Glarien, she believed doors to be sacred."

Penny buried her face in the coverlet, only half listening to him as the truth burned: *He would have Eric punished because of her.* "You like doors?"

"I most definitely do not like small spaces without them. Eric is not my friend. I cannot treat him with anything but impersonal justice."

She looked up, feeling sick. "So what will you do?"

The prince turned and smiled, a smile of seductive charm. "Eric will muck out the stalls and clean all the other men's boots for a week. He will do it in addition to the rest of his duties. Do you think that's fair?"

Emotion drenched her, tumbled in a floodwater of feelings, battered from relief to anger, indignation to gratitude. She was gasping for breath, blinded by mad tears. "Oh, God!" she said at last. "He will clean *boots?*"

"That is the designated punishment for such minor infractions," the prince said.

Penny leaped up, dragging her bedcover with her. "All along, *this* was his penalty? Cleaning boots? What was all that talk of hangings and floggings? How could you torment me so? Why? What good did it do either of us? You are mad! Mad, vile and dangerous! It's despicable! Were you just playing with my feelings? Deliberately trying to upset me? Why? What have I done to deserve this?"

He glanced down at the latch. His fingers gripped hard on the metal. "I am trying to make you understand. Sophia was bred to all this. I wasn't. I have had to learn. It was a hard enough lesson. But for Her Royal Highness, Princess Sophia of Alvia, such issues are second nature."

She was incredulous. "To be like a princess I must believe myself capable of ordering a flogging or a hanging? Have you done so?"

His eyes answered before he spoke. "When it was necessary. You won't ever discuss such things with anyone, but you must take them into your soul." He tipped back his head, avoiding her gaze. "You have to shed that bloody English innocence, Miss Lindsey. It's there in your eyes. A naive belief in mercy. A tenderhearted faith in human goodness. I want you to understand what Sophia understands. Catch a guard derelict in his duty and the consequences are certain. Every frown or smile creates a wake like a ship in a storm. Remember it. Act on it. Then you will behave like a princess."

Penny dropped the bedcover. "And Alexis? Don't try to tell me you aren't kind to him! It's like reading the silent language of the horses. That boy *was* comforted. He felt secure in your mercy. Why do you try to tell me otherwise?"

"Every door opens and closes on a mystery." He opened the door, the robe swirling in gilt-and-red spirals. "But what I told you was also true."

She spread out her arms. The sleeves of her white cotton nightdress reflected in the windows like the wings of a ghost moth. "Stop! I can't! I don't want to be part of this any longer." The candles flared and guttered as she dropped her hands and moved quickly across the bedroom. "I'm not a princess. I'm Penny Lindsey. I'm just me!"

His eyes seemed to devour her. He snapped his fingers and Quest immediately trotted over to him. "I'm very well aware of that, Miss Lindsey. Good night."

The door closed with a thud behind the prince and his dog. She listened for the small click of the latch at the bottom. Somewhere outside an owl hooted. Penny climbed back into her bed and pulled the covers up over her ears.

Was that how her father had been? Fascinating, imperious, but capable of that sudden warm concern, that flattering, intense concentration of attention? If so, no wonder Mama had fallen so completely under his spell. Had she done it willingly for the sake of those gleaming, golden moments, all the more precious in contrast to the normal hard brilliance of princes? Had she known he would abandon her when he found she was with child? Had she not cared as long as she was part of the game, even for a moment?

That bloody English innocence, Miss Lindsey. It's there in your eyes. A naive belief in mercy. A tenderhearted faith in human goodness.

Yet Alexis had felt safe. She knew it. The comfort of a prince to a boy who woke afraid in the night? Penny closed her eyes. Their two figures had been so intimately haloed in candlelight. At that moment, they had seemed merged in some common bond, some depth of understanding, pawn and king linked in a gambit for checkmate. But, of course, in any opening gambit, it was the pawn that was sacrificed.

Mama, this is the most dreadful mistake. I can't do it. I won't do it. Grand Duke Nicholas is mad.

He had made it! Nicholas leaned back against his door. Quest pressed her nose into his hand. He smoothed his palm over her head and sent her to lie down. She flopped at the foot of his bed, watching him. He closed his eyes, shutting out that female devotion. Triumph and self-loathing warred for his attention, as leaping imps prodded and probed at the souls in purgatory. He had left Penny there in her narrow bed. He had left! But first he had punished her. Oh, dear God! Why did he think it necessary to punish her, when the weakness was all his?

He had touched her face, let his fingertips meet in the soft hair at her nape. If he looked at his hands he would feel that softness again. If he closed his eyes he would see her face, the wide eyes and blunt nose, the tender lips. He could have taken her then. Leaned forward, pressed his mouth onto hers, and demanded surrender. She would have come to him like his wolfhound, unable to disobey. Instead he had opened his fingers and let go. And then he had stripped away something of her innocence after all, because to make her into a princess, he had to smash that kindhearted merriment and replace it with hauteur.

But he craved her just as she was. He craved her warm tenderness. Her feet were as tender as orange blossoms. She had spread out her arms like an angel's wings, thinking she was safe in her drapes of white cotton. Safe in her concern for people she didn't know. Safe in her offering of mercy for a careless soldier, her observations about Alexis.

She understood nothing.

With a violent gesture he launched himself at his bed and flung himself face down on the pillows. Quest buried her nose in her paws. Nicholas muttered prayers for salvation, holding his hands over his ears, but the pain leaped, fully formed, into his skull.

A tentative knock rapped at the outer door. A boy's voice whispered. "Sire?"

"Go away, Alexis," he said. "Go to sleep. We'll find checkmate another time."

He knew despair would pool in the blue eyes beneath the dandelion hair as Alexis replied softly. "Yes, sire."

So the boy would lie shivering and alone for the rest of the night. As Nicholas had done when he'd been that age and thought he'd never get over it. Would he ever get over it? Or would he one day take a rapier, or the ceremonial royal scepter, or just his hunting knife, and wreak revenge on his cousin Carl for everything he'd done? And thus become what his grandfather had intended: a true prince of the blood.

The migraine pushed fingers of nausea through his bones. Howls of anguish ran up and down his spine. Yet his body throbbed with longing, a fire of hunger burning beneath his skin. If he truly were what his ancestors had been, he would go back up those stairs and tear away all that white cotton. He would use her, as was his right. The right of princes to take what they would, where they would—a virgin from her schoolroom, a novice from a nunnery, a bride on her wedding night—and not care if something bright and vulnerable were forever quenched. No prince of Glarien had ever cared what was destroyed in the women who fell into his hands. Why the devil should he try to be different?

Beneath the pounding in his brain, he heard Penny laughing and triumphant on the back of a white gelding. What if that one soul were worth more than all the crowns and kingdoms in Europe? What then?

He pushed himself from the bed and strode to the chessboard, unable to focus, his vision shattered and broken. The pain made him want to retch. One by one he put away the pieces, knights and bishops, pawns and rooks, and snuffed the candles. He ought to try to please her, do something to make amends. He went to the door and wrenched it open. Quest stood up and whined.

He found Fritz on guard duty in the corridor.

"Flowers, Fritz," he said.

Penny woke to warm sunshine. It must be close to midday. Something smelled very sweet, like honey. She opened her eyes. Her room was bursting with color. Every surface overflowed. For a moment she sat and stared at a cornucopia of blossoms. Petals curled, layered in exotic abandon, or clustered like a star burst, or folded around thrusting stamens, rich in pollen. Hothouse flowers, in crystal and silver and porcelain. A treasure. A wealth of beauty. Probably every bloom from every garden and forcing house for miles around.

Who had been forced to go out and find all this? Not Nicholas! He never gave anything of himself. He had tormented her, forced her to remember things she had sworn to forget, then taken her to the edge of despair and almost abandoned her there. How dare he try to make it up to her with flowers! The very excess of it infuriated her.

She slid from her bed and yanked at the bellpull. When Alexis appeared she waved her arms. "Take all this away. Tell Mrs. Butteridge to send it to Jeb Hardacre. He can sell it all in Norwich."

Alexis colored, but he bowed, took a large vase of roses and left. The gilt hair and pink petals made her think of cherubs.

In the sitting room she found a stack of papers left for her. *Grand Duke Nicholas makes lists. He is always working.* His handwriting was neat and tight, the vowels narrow between the sweeping tails of the consonants, as if he had never strayed from the copperplate examples in his schoolboy exercise books, allowing nothing of individuality into his writing.

While Alexis strode back and forth, carrying away flowers, she sat down and studied the pages: lists of facts she needed to know; lists of people with detailed descriptions of each of their relationships to Sophia, their appearance and idiosyncrasies; lists of palaces, dates, events; lists of everything Nicholas knew about the princess's personal tastes and interests. He had written her a primer of Alvian history and a piercingly intelligent summary of the personality of his intended bride. The surprise was how intensely interesting he had made it. *Brilliant and gifted people rarely offer simple amiability.*

The door opened. She looked up to see the prince, his arms full of books. Shadows flowed over his dark hair, staining his eyes. He looked annoyed. "How dare you give such orders to Alexis without my permission!"

She glanced down at the lists he had made for her. "Who put all those flowers in my room without *my* permission?"

"I thought you would like them."

"Did you? A present? How profound! You give the order to some underling: *Flowers!* And they appear."

He hesitated, almost vulnerable. "It was a gift."

She didn't know why she felt she must press the point, why she must attack when it was really such a trivial thing. "Hardly a personal gift from you. You just say the word. Some other poor soul has to do the work, use the power of your name and your purse to force the sale of every flower in the neighborhood. An underling must then place them in my room without waking me. You gave nothing but the order—without expending any of your own energy or effort. It's completely meaningless."

"I'm a prince." His voice burned. "I do not, generally, gather flowers myself. It's my duty to delegate." He strode into the room. "I'm not used to having my orders countermanded, but I regret that you were offended. I did not cut the posies with my own hands for good reason. I was otherwise engaged."

"Really? In making sure Eric put his back into polishing your boots?"

He dropped the books on the table. "No. I was reading your ledgers."

She looked from the unfathomable man to the familiar books. Then she laughed. "I'm amazed. Oh, Lord! You have just very effectively taken the wind out of my sails. You read my ledgers?"

He smiled then, the smile that no doubt made the ladies of the court swoon behind their fans. "Once I began I could hardly put them down. I owe you a debt. The flowers were small recompense for what you have done for Rascall Hall, what you do now for Glarien. Forget them. You have been remarkably competent."

He flipped through the pages, asking searching questions, honing in on the important issues with uncanny keenness. She watched him as she answered, trying to fathom what was happening and wishing it did not make her heart thump like this to have him stand so close. If she moved her hand just slightly, she could touch his lean fingers: sacred, never to be touched—unless he touched first. A man apart, always alone, never to have the solace of offered warmth? Shivers ran down her spine, but they spread and pooled in a fervent longing. Did he know that? Did he deliberately manipulate everything?

"Oh, good heavens," she said. "You liked it, didn't you? All these facts and figures. But what about the people?"

He looked astonished. "What people?"

Penny leaped up and slammed her ledgers closed, thumping her fist on the cover. "The people in here! The reason for all this. You're like a man surveying a meadow, who sees only a hay crop and cares nothing at all for the field mice and cornrails and beetles."

He raised both brows. "Beetles?"

"Yes, why not? Sexton beetles and dorbeetles and ladybirds. Are they beneath your imperial notice?"

"Beetles are food for birds." She thought his eyes even laughed at her. "And have charming enough habits of their own. Dorbeetles clatter prettily at dusk, but their larvae feed on dung. Sexton beetles enjoy carrion. The red-and-black ladybird eats smaller insects live."

His flippant acumen was infuriating. She would be defeated. Defeated and negated by this man. "How do you know all that?"

"I had an excellent tutor and little boys like bugs."

"So you do remember something of it," she said. "You do recall those days spent here in England, before you went to Glarien, before you became a prince."

"Have I ever said otherwise?" He looked down at her hand, still lying clenched on the marbled book cover. "Don't, Miss Lindsey. I'm trying to please you. Don't do this."

He leaned forward and grasped her wrist. With intense concentration he opened her fingers one at a time, smoothing her palm and the back of her hand. She stared at him in confusion, a small terror moving somewhere beneath her ribs, a small fear and a disconcerting stir in her blood. Her heart seemed to struggle, alternately stopping and racing as he focused, rubbing over her palm, massaging the mound at the base of her thumb. He leaned forward and kissed it. Improper. What she had longed for? But this was a piercing, improper intimacy that left her paralyzed.

"The steward in London has been fired," he said at last, releasing her fingers. "I'm trying to fulfill my part of your bargain. I don't mean to cause you distress. You were right about the flowers. They were just an order to Fritz. I don't even know who found them or put them in your room. It was presumptuous."

Tears pricked suddenly. *I am in the wrong!* Penny snatched back her hand and stood up. "No! I was petty about it. I'm sorry. They were beautiful—and if it was Alexis who brought them, I have only hurt him for no reason. I'm sorry."

She stumbled away, leaving him sitting at the table with all her care for Rascall St. Mary spread before him. At the door she looked back. He had dropped his head, his forehead resting on his closed fists, his black hair drifting over her account books. He was absolutely still, except for a tiny, almost imperceptible tremor running over his taut back and shoulders. Like the quiver of a fine horse—like Driver—racing alone and afraid in the dark.

• • •

Long thin veils of high cloud formed a multicolored halo around the moon, pouring pearly light into the barn. Night had closed in around them. A bat flickered past the broken roof. Penny moved in a wash of tiredness, until the prince stopped the horse and walked up to her.

"Enough for tonight," he said.

She slipped from Willow's back and rubbed her thighs. Alexis materialized from the shadows and led the horse away. Nicholas signaled Quest to follow the boy back to the stable.

"Tomorrow my people will arrive from London."

Penny glanced up. "Ah," she said. "The spies."

He seemed clipped and remote. "It will make no difference to our routine, but it will inevitably be noticed that someone is living in my suite. Servants gossip. The grooms will know a horse is being used every night."

She walked across the dirt floor, feeling the sore stretch of muscles, and sat down on the wheelbarrow. "Does it mean an end to these midnight excursions? What do you intend to do?"

"Nothing. They will all leap to the obvious conclusion." He began to pace. "If the need arises, I hope you won't be offended to play the part."

"What part?"

He strode restlessly in and out of barred shadow and moonlight. "The role Alexis already believes. Why Eric thinks you are here, and Lars and Ludger and Markos. Only Fritz knows the truth. The other men haven't seen Princess Sophia in person." He stopped and turned to face her. "How do you think they believe that I use you?"

"Oh," she said, looking away. "You mean they think I'm your mistress? Good heavens! Should I be flattered?"

"It doesn't matter what you feel, only that you do nothing to disrupt that preconception if we are seen."

"Then how unfortunate that my feelings matter to me! Did my mother know of this?" She stood up and walked to the door. "That I should have to pretend to be something that she was: mistress to a prince?"

"Your mother is no fool."

"No. I am the only fool here, it seems. Exactly how far do you intend *this* deception to go?"

"Nowhere, of course. Intimacy isn't possible for me."

Penny hesitated by the huge dilapidated door, oak and iron. "This is not exactly a usual relationship for me either," she said dryly.

He started walking toward her. "I do not usually allow anyone to touch me, nor do I touch them. No one except you has ever spoken to me with such a lack of respect. You don't call me by my title. You don't curtsey to me. I allow it because your father was a prince and because I need you for my wedding. But I don't know how to deal with you. Is this friendship?"

"No," she said. "Friends are people with whom one laughs and shares things, equals. People who care about one another, who can trust each other with the truth, with honesty about their lives and emotions, and know the information is in good hands."

"Ah," he said, stopping again, barred by moonlight, gazing at her. "I have nothing like that to offer a friend."

They walked back to the house in the shifting darkness, the moon a pale pearl above ebony trees. The woods had fallen silent, as if muffled by damp. Penny felt battered and bruised, though it was more of the soul than the body.

Dear Mama: I have decided our dark prince is in dire need of being made human. He hasn't a friend in the world and never had. He made no friends at school, though he was sent to Harrow for brief intervals for six years. He says the other boys tormented him. I can see why. I think he's impossible to understand. Yet when you said he wasn't likable—

Something rustled. The prince moved. Fast. With one hand he grabbed her wrist and spun her behind him against the trunk of a tree. With the other he had already drawn his knife. The breath was knocked from her lungs. She was crushed between the hard bark and the firm pressure of his grip. Penny struggled to control her breathing, trying to listen. Air seemed to roar in and out of her throat, so she put her free hand over her mouth.

If she released all that breath, would she shatter the night and allow catastrophe to overwhelm them?

Silence stretched.

An owl hooted somewhere.

At last a shadowy figure appeared on the path far ahead and signaled with his hand. Nicholas signaled back and sheathed his knife.

"It's all right," he said. "I hope you were not alarmed."

"Alarmed?" She dropped her hand and the breath rushed out, making her voice a hoarse whisper. "What was all that for?"

He smiled. *Smiled!* His lips curved in the moonlight, his eyes soft and dark. "I heard something. A mouse, perhaps. It's nothing."

"Well, it must have been a pretty ferocious mouse. Perhaps the rodents at Rascall Hall have taken to wearing plate armor and carrying maces?"

He was still holding her wrist. Carefully he turned her hand over and raised it to his mouth. He kissed her knuckles. "I'm sorry," he said.

She forced open mockery into her voice. "What? An apology from His High and Mightiness? Good heavens! I *am* flattered. What do you want from me now?"

He gazed down at her fingers lying lightly in his. "Do not ask me what I want."

Penny slipped her hand away and rested it on the rough bark behind her. She tipped back her head and studied the mass of dark leaves overhead, a world of dense woody fragrances, oak leaves and ivy. "A forfeit, Your Royal Highness. I would very much like to know what you want. You've become my task, you know, as much as I am yours."

"Your task?"

She glanced back at him. "Of course. After all, the pawn may survive all eight squares to become a queen in her own right. So, tell me: What do you want?"

Veiled shadows moved, dark on dark as he stepped closer. For a long moment he gazed down in perfect silence. "Then this is what I want," he said in Glarisch. "I want to kiss you. I can't help it. I just want that. To kiss you on the mouth."

Astonishment rooted her to the spot. The moon rode into a small space in the clouds, removing a single veil of darkness, outlining the stark bones of his cheeks. Immediately he glanced away, the turn of his neck like a strong white birch branch in the shifting light.

She looked down, her heart pounding. The night stretched away around them. "I don't know what to say."

His voice rasped, the Glarisch consonants grating. "You asked me what I wanted. I am telling you. Do you think that's easy? I want this. Let me kiss you. Have you never been kissed?" He sounded agonized.

Her heart raced and thumped. The bark was rough under her palms, the tree trunk hard against her spine. She owed him nothing. Certainly not this! Yet a flaring heat in the pit of her stomach made her knees weak. Her thighs trembled and ached. She thought suddenly of her room, filled with flowers, as she tried to make her voice light, joking, and replied in his language, the language of lies. "There was Mr. Wimpole and last year Lord Hitching, under the mistletoe—"

"Twice?" he asked.

"Well, Mr. Wimpole gives me a rather awkward Christmas peck each year at Nettle Park, but then he's a very old friend of my mother's. I don't mind. Lord Hitching, I think, wanted rather more, but I turned aside—"

"Why?"

The memory twisted a little. She tried to laugh. "I don't know. Indeed, he was handsome enough, but I didn't like anything about it. The others thought it was funny, that an earl should trap unfortunate Miss Lindsey under the kissing bough. Miss Harding pouted. I was glad when he made a joke and kissed my hand instead."

"He was a rake?"

"I suppose so. He was certainly very charming, but I thought he was using me to score a point with Miss Harding. It felt most unpleasant."

"That isn't why I want to kiss you."

He sounded desperate. Did he think there were spies out there in the dark trees who must believe she was his mistress? She hesitated. *Every door opens and closes on a mystery.* This wasn't a door she dared open, surely?

Something touched her hand. Paralyzed, she stood absolutely still. It touched again. A paper. A folded paper? She opened her fingers and felt a slip of paper thrust into her palm. In a reflex she clutched it tightly, standing rigid and afraid under the dark oak.

"There was never any mistletoe in Glarien?" she asked.

"I don't have friends." The prince reached down and took her shoulders, forcing her to step forward. "But we are standing under mistletoe now. There is some directly above us."

She craned her neck and looked up. Her palm clenched. *A paper?* Who? Should she tell him? Oh, Lord! Of course not! Whatever it was, the bearer obviously hadn't meant assassination or harm. He must intend her to read it later. Was it a warning . . . for her? Oh, dear Lord help her!

"I don't see any mistletoe," she said, thrusting the paper deep into a pocket.

He pulled her forward another step, into the full gleam of moonlight. The wash of white light brought his face clearly into focus.

Astonished, Penny gazed up into raw, naked vulnerability.

Eight

She knew what it would be like. She knew it in her blood. It would not be like kissing Mr. Wimpole or like those other kisses—heady and misunderstood when she had been just fifteen. It would be torture. Pure, mellifluous torture. *I don't have friends.* The paper burned in her pocket, evidence of betrayal. He reached out one hand and gently touched her hair, then his knuckles brushed her cheek—delicious. Surprisingly, wickedly delicious.

Why did he do this—to her? Why remind her again, when once she had been so determined to forget? His palm smoothed her jaw and cheek, a seeking, reckless touch.

"No," she said, putting up one hand. "Don't! It isn't fair."

He caught her hand in his own and held it. "I believe it is fair. I don't want to hurt you."

"I didn't think your kiss would be painful," she said, trying to tease.

"No, no. Brave Miss Lindsey! You will allow it only because your heart is greater than mine, because you are generous. And even, perhaps, because you would like it, just a little."

She closed her eyes, wondering why her heart felt like breaking. She ought to be firm and sensible and tell him to leave her be. She ought not to kiss a prince who was sworn to his state marriage. A prince who'd made it clear he cared nothing for her feelings. A man who had already stirred forbidden, foolish desires. She knew all that perfectly well as his warm mouth, moving almost tentatively over hers, touched tender lip to tender lip.

His hands smoothed her hair as his mouth caressed. She could imagine nothing sweeter: not blackberries picked ripe from the sunny hedgerow, not honeycomb, not hot sugar on baked apples. Were they both innocent, like children seeking out a new sweetness? Were they both wicked, like the most decadent of rakes and harlots, exploring the ancient, sinister ways of lust? For if he asked, he could lay her down beneath the rustling leaves, spread her skirts and take up her petticoats. If he asked, he could open her bodice, roll down her stockings and let his fingers stray up past her garter, with his mouth following.

And then lust would break loose in a torrent.

Yet it was sweet, sweet, sending her blood in rushing eddies to pool hotly in her groin. Sweet. Passionate. And as warm as love.

Until the kiss grew deeper. And deeper. And she was lost in a deluge of desire.

While all the time the paper lay concealed in her pocket, like a lie.

He shouldn't have done it. He knew with a clear, piercing certainty that he shouldn't have done it. He had not imposed on her before. Not even when his palms burned to slide and explore, not even when his muscles shook with the desire to pull her tightly into his own body. But she had gazed up at him with those wide female eyes, vulnerable and wise, a fine tremble at the corner of her mouth, and his need had overwhelmed him. The need to try something new—something he had never done before—kiss a woman as if he loved her.

He had released her only when both of them had no breath left for life. His lips burned. His body throbbed with longing, shameful and hot. The depraved, sickening need had overcome his desire to spare her, until at last he had kissed her with pure lust, plundering and tasting, stunned by her generosity: that she did not push him away; that she allowed it until he found the strength of will to release her. Yet he only wanted to do it again. Taste her again. Plumb deeper, deeper into the heart of her mystery. Sweet Penny Lindsey, filled with nectar and luminescence like a buttercup.

Ruthlessly, he had suppressed his scorching need, taken her hand and hurried her up through the darkness to the imposing bulk of his childhood home. He wouldn't speak to her. Words would only bring reality crashing back into his life once again. Words he didn't want spoken.

Fritz was waiting in the hall. His scar ran crooked as he bowed. "Sire. We have the boy in the study. He says he was after rabbits. Do you wish to interrogate him yourself?"

Beside him, she flinched. From the corner of his eye he could see she'd turned pale, shocked at Glarian efficiency. Nicholas smiled. The boy who'd been lurking in the shrubbery, waiting. The boy who wouldn't understand Glarisch, but had run away before that devastating kiss had even begun.

"He's a bold lad to hunt my woods and fields," he said. "Let him go."

He could sense her confusion. She thought he hadn't noticed? That he wouldn't be aware of the small, determined creature who waited behind an oak tree in the dark?

"There was a boy?" Her voice was painfully innocent. "Our mouse was a boy?"

"Just someone from the village, no doubt." He quietly signaled Fritz as he smiled down at Penny. "Perhaps I will take a look at this lad for myself. Do you wish to come?"

Her indecision was transparent, her surprise obvious, but at last she shook her head. "I'm glad you will let him go home to his mother. Perhaps I shall go up to bed."

Liar! Not the words, of course, but the omission. So, like everyone else, she would plot against him. Even when he kissed her in a dark wood, even when he put his very soul into that caress, she would take a secret note and hide it from him.

He left the room and waited, deliberately giving her a free rein, waiting to see what she would do. Fritz would already have released the lad, as he had directed using the secret hand language of the Glarian guard. There was a door leading onto the patio from the very next room. She didn't hesitate. She raced up the stairs.

Quietly, he waited. Sure enough, she crept down again. Under her dark cloak, she had changed from her riding clothes into one of her day dresses. The door to the patio clicked shut behind her.

Nicholas followed in absolute silence. The boy was running faster than Penny could walk and had a head start. The two figures flitted through the darkness, down the long ridge across the park and through the meadows to the gate in the wall behind the church. The hinges creaked as she went through, so Nicholas scaled the wall and dropped down into the graveyard like a cat. She hurried away up the path and out through the lych-gate.

The lane slept. The smithy and the schoolteacher's house bulked black at the corner of the village. Beyond them one house sat a little back from the road, tucked in behind ramshackle sheds. A small flame flickered in the window. She crept up to the front and knocked. Jimmy Hardacre, Jeb's youngest lad, opened the door and let her in.

Nicholas stood silently in the dark, watching them through the window. It began to drizzle. He remained absolutely still, though water dripped off the thatch and chill tendrils ran down his face. Behind him the yard started to shine. As puddles collected on the cobbles the dark surface revealed a mysterious watery map. The painted cart in the broken shed was robbed of its colors, like wood long buried in a pond. The only brightness streamed from the small window. The only colors were there, inside, where Jeb Hardacre had set his rushlight on his kitchen table.

Penny draped her long cloak over a chair and sat down. Jimmy was affectionately cuffed by his mother and sent to bed. Jeb lit his pipe, lifting it close to his ruddy face. With exaggerated sucking and blowing, he sent a small tendril of smoke toward the ceiling. The glow of hot tobacco shone like a small red eye in the shadowy room.

Their voices were muffled by thick glass, but Penny said something.

Mrs. Hardacre busied herself at the fireplace where a kettle hung over the coals. Nicholas remembered her. She had been much younger then, of course, but still buxom. Newly married, she had given him apples and scones when he had ridden by on his pony, and flirted and teased with his tutor so warmly the poor man had allowed it. She had spread through the waist, become even more dimpled, but her heart hadn't changed. She set tea in front of Penny, then a plate with scones and jam.

They seemed so warm and familiar with each other, cozy and safe in their English village lives. Jeb and his wife paid Penny an obvious deference, a careful awareness of her status as a lady, yet still they seemed friends, talking quietly at the kitchen table. Did such friends share old jokes about their neighbors? How could they be so easy with each other?

Their voices murmured, too low for Nicholas to make out the words. Jeb jabbed at the air with his pipe in the general direction of Rascall Hall and his wife's voice suddenly boomed as she laughed.

"The lad had no business getting himself caught. I'd have thought after his many nights out after rabbits, he'd have learned to move more quietly by now. To think those soldiers should have nabbed him!"

Penny wrapped both hands about her teacup and stood up, moving closer to the window. "You mustn't let any of your boys poach at the Hall, Mrs. Hardacre. Indeed, I beg you will not. The Grand Duke was in an indulgent mood tonight, I think. But perhaps another—"

She turned away to move back to her chair. Jeb knocked his pipe against the chimney breast. Their voices dropped, again too low to understand.

The drizzle thickened. The yard became darker, shrouded under ever-thickening clouds. The glimmer of the painted cart faded to pitch. Penny was gazing at Jeb Hardacre with an expression of pure, open astonishment. She asked a question, which he answered. Then Mrs. Hardacre said something and Penny launched into some long explanation, waving her hands, very serious now.

Jeb stood up and scratched his head. His gruff voice rang clear for a moment. "Well, I'll be! Did you ever hear the like?"

Nicholas turned away. Raindrops fell from darkness to darkness through the bright beam streaming from the window. Beyond the sparkling water everything else had turned black—even after the rain stopped, when the door opened and Penny stepped out.

"Now, now," he heard her murmur to herself. "It's only Rascall St. Mary."

He followed her back up the lane. This time she walked rapidly past the church, head bowed, past the vicarage and the great oak at the corner. She hurried along beside the holly hedge and opened the gate to Clumper Cottage. Moments later she had pulled a key from a ledge under the porch roof and gone inside.

She felt breathless and suddenly foolish, bolting home like a rabbit to its burrow. Fumbling for the tinderbox on the hall table she struck a spark and lit a candle. Carrying it in one hand she walked through to the front room, empty of her mother's presence.

Dear Mama, I let him kiss me, thinking he was sad. A foolish, foolish thing. I know you warned me. But now it's worse. Now I have learned he is not at all what I thought—what he deliberately led me to believe. I am deceived, Mama! Desperately! Why did you never tell me that a courtier is all deception?

She took the note out of her pocket and spread it on the table. She had read it immediately once the prince left her alone, before she'd slipped out in pursuit of young Jimmy. *Miss Lindsey, If yore in trubble or need help, just say. Just tell my boy Jim what brings this. Jeb Hardacre.*

The door creaked as it swung open behind her. She shrieked, a small breathless shriek, like a bat. The darkness outside streamed into the room.

"May I come in?" Nicholas asked.

Penny dropped into her mother's chair as if she'd been knocked down, and yet relief flooded in: a bright, warm relief. Even a mad, bad grand duke was better than a stranger, and she wanted to see him. She just hadn't thought to confront him quite so soon, and the implications of his being here burrowed and tunneled under her thoughts like moles.

"Oh, I suppose so," she said. "You have already invaded my life, so why not my home?"

"Your home, but my house," he said, as if reminding himself rather than her.

He seemed to fill the small room, too tall, dominating the neat, female spaces. He was wet, his hair damp, his shoulders black with moisture.

"You followed me? From Rascall Hall?" She hated it, the surprise and the dawning realization. "You knew about the note? How?"

"I saw young Jimmy hand it to you." He smiled, drawing all the candlelight to his face. "He was waiting for us."

"So that's why you sent Quest with Alexis earlier, so she wouldn't give Jimmy away? And that, I suppose, is why you kissed me—because you knew Jimmy was waiting and you wanted to let him contact me secretly. You cold-blooded monster!" Penny held out the slip of paper. "Here. Read it, if you like. The Hardacres knew I hadn't gone with my mother. Jeb's brother works in Norwich and saw her catch the stage without me. They were worried. Mrs. Butteridge was acting oddly, they thought. They sent Jimmy to the Hall to see if I was there."

"He has been haunting the place for two days." She digested the import of this while he read the note, then held it in the candle flame until it curled and burned. "What did you tell them?"

She felt rather like a child caught out in a falsehood, though she told him the truth. "I said I was helping you with the estate, but that—because Mama had been called suddenly away to her cousins—we had all agreed to keep it secret, so there would be no gossip to damage my reputation. It's all I could think of. A lame enough story, but the Hardacres won't question it, thanks to your own machinations. Nor will they tell anyone else."

"Ah." He walked to the bookcase and stared at the titles. "I see."

"When you set Jimmy loose so quickly, I *had* to go in person. Otherwise the whole village might have raised an alarm."

Penny stood up and banged her elbow on the chair. Pain shot up her arm.

He turned to her, but instantly dropped his hand and stepped back. "Yes, I knew that. But I had to know what you would tell them."

"Oh, God! It's so hateful! You *planned* it?" Tears pricked as she rubbed her elbow. "You tested me? Why did you take such a risk? If you don't trust me, how can you trust what I just told you? What's the matter with you? You could have confided in me, given me the truth."

He looked genuinely puzzled. "What truth?"

"What Jeb Hardacre just told me! You've made work for the villagers, haven't you? No one is going hungry. In fact, they think you are King Arthur returned to save Rascall St. Mary in her hour of need. You might as well wear armor and carry Excalibur."

"I have plenty of fine armor at home in Glarien, suit after suit of it." His voice was dry, the humor thinly masking that mysterious, deep intelligence.

She stuck doggedly to her point. "That's not what I'm talking about. You've hired men to clear the heath for new pasture. You're making plans to drain Five Acre Bottom—projects I've thought of for years. All the work in the kitchen gardens is to go on, plus a rare sight of hammering and mending on the outbuildings and farms. Mr. Green is to go back to full wages. Jeb thought you'd make a very able lord, for all your foreign airs. Mrs. Hardacre waxed eloquent about what a fine little lad you were once, riding through the village on your pony. They *like* you!"

The dark eyes gazed at her entirely without expression. "That makes you angry? Why? I studied your books. It wasn't hard to see what needed to be done. I have the money. I am doing it."

"You stole my ideas. You used my name to get the villagers' trust, and all the while you didn't trust me." She dropped back to the chair, still cradling her elbow. "Why didn't you just grab Jimmy and let me explain to him? Why did you force me to come back to the village myself? Oh, Lord! You have played me for a complete fool."

"I don't understand why you're angry." He looked down at his wet boots. "I thought you'd be pleased."

As when he'd sent flowers to her room? His bent head was deeply disturbing, as if she had destroyed something. Penny tried to take a deep breath and speak more calmly. "I'm pleased about the work you've created, of course. I'm pleased you're taking responsibility for the estate. But why didn't you tell me? Why test me like this? You've led me to believe I'm in mortal danger, then you deliberately force me to come to Rascall St. Mary in the dark by myself."

"You were not by yourself," he said. "I was there." He indicated the room, the walls flickering in the candlelight. "I am here now. You are quite safe."

"I didn't know that."

He looked up and smiled at her, charming. "You should have guessed it. But if you did not, then you are as brave as I believed you to be."

She glanced away from the bright, melting smile. "Why did that matter?"

"Because you're going to need all your bravery, Miss Lindsey."

"But you manipulated me, even kissed me! I thought—oh, never mind! It was just a way to let Jimmy give me the note without our speaking, wasn't it? You pull strings and the puppets dance exactly as planned. Can't you see how very humiliating that is?"

He pushed damp hair from his forehead. "Yes, I can see that. I shouldn't have done it. But don't think—" He turned and paced across the room. "I wish you wouldn't think so badly of me." He seemed unguarded, uncomfortable. "Miss Lindsey, I can only be what life has trained me to be. I'm not a simple man with simple, straightforward ambitions. I watched you with Jeb Hardacre through the window and thought I longed to trade my life for his. I could be a carter with a buxom wife and eight children—"

"Don't!" she said. "Don't tell me you wish for that! It's too hypocritical."

"I didn't say I wished for it. I only said I could imagine longing for it."

"I don't dare ask again what you wish for, do I?" She tried to fill it with sarcasm, but her hand moved to her mouth, remembering the sweet burn of kissing him. How could a woman quench that fire, once it was lit? Her body craved it. Her soul craved it. The seductive lure of this man's touch.

He ran his fingers idly along the mantel, delicately brushing past the clock and the china. "I wanted to kiss you, because it was you. That's all. Jimmy could have slipped you the note without it. I just wanted it."

"How nice for you, just to take what you want!"

With a crash her mother's little Staffordshire jug hit the hearth and shattered.

"What I want?" For these three words his voice excoriated before he had it back under control. "I concede I am using you. How can I avoid it? Everything in our situation demands it. It's like a marriage of convenience."

"Indeed," she said. "In my observation, the convenience of such a match is always the man's."

"So you think gentlemen exploit and degrade your sex? Is that why you can be easy only with the Hardacres and Robertsons, yeomen and farmers, where you are safe from importunity?"

"I don't know. I only know that you have broken my mother's favorite jug."

He stared down at the pieces. "I'll get her a new one."

The discomfort ran ever deeper, into places of bewilderment and pain. Penny stood up. "Not everything broken can be mended so easily. That jug was a gift from Uncle Horace. How can you replace that?" He stepped aside as she bent down and began picking up the pieces. Her hands shook. "What happens now? Now that you have destroyed what little trust I had in you?"

"It's up to you," he said gravely. "Will you still help Glarien, in spite of me?"

The brown-and-white china was beyond mending. *I wanted to kiss you, because it was you.* She went back to her chair and set the broken jug on the table. He stared at the pieces as if he couldn't imagine consternation at the destruction of something so ordinary.

Folding her hands on her lap, she looked up at him. "I don't know."

"Because men can never be trusted in any marriage of convenience? You might be right." He shrugged and moved a few paces, studying the clock as if seeing it for the first time. "Is that why you never married?"

Burning with agitation, she blurted out the truth. "I *was* married."

For a moment she thought everything on the mantel was in danger: the clock, the vases and candlesticks, the Chelsea shepherdess. But he only raised both hands to his head for a moment, then flung them aside in a furious gesture. His nostrils distended like those of a running horse, pounding through the night.

"What the *devil* do you mean—you were married?"

"It's neither important nor relevant."

"Why didn't I know this? For God's sake! You don't use a married name." He flung the words like an accusation.

"I'm a widow. It . . . the marriage didn't last very long. It seemed simpler to resume my maiden name at the time."

He strode to the window and leaned his head against the glass. "Oh, God! I'm sorry! I'm sorry for your loss. I don't mean to be brutal—"

"It was a long time ago and not a great loss." Which was a lie both so subtle and enormous, she thought the floor might open to swallow her. *Not a great loss!* She made herself glance up at him with a dismissive smile. "Neither condolences nor polite questions are necessary."

He turned his head to look at her, his eyes dark pits. "Oh, God! Why do you tell me this? Don't you realize it's dangerous to tell me this?"

"Dangerous! Why?"

"If you don't know, then you aren't as astute as I took you to be."

Her heart was racing, beating madly. "I cannot see how it makes any difference at all."

He twisted and slid down to sit on the window seat. "I'm talking about temptation." He held out both hands. "Surely you understand? I am tempted. I've been fighting it. This knowledge only makes it harder."

She looked down, trying to keep her voice light. "Are you trying to make me stay here in the cottage? Are you trying to ensure I won't come back to Rascall Hall? I really don't understand why you should do so."

Candlelight caressed his face, the face of a faerie prince lost in a midnight forest. "Because I think I must try to be friends with you. I don't know what else we can do. We're thrust together like this. I've been the agent of it, of course, but it's not truly my choice." He put his hands to his head and leaned forward. "Don't think I want to hurt you! I do not. I do not want to hurt you in any way. But here we are, committed to our marriage of convenience, and I thought we could make it more tolerable if we were friends. . . . If I could learn to be a friend?"

She kept her gaze pinned to her lap, to the pattern of tiny stripes and flowers printed on the fabric of her dress. "I don't know if men and women . . . I don't know if real friendship is possible, in the circumstances."

"Because I kissed you?" He dropped his face into both palms, an elbow on each knee. The lines of his body were piercingly beautiful, firing desire. "Then how can I deal with you? How can you deal with me? I feel like a being from another world, dropped suddenly into this country existence. It's your place, not mine. If I try to treat you as I treat everyone else in my life, I'm bound to cause you pain. I spied on you. I let you be afraid. Nothing I've offered you has been genuine, except . . . except what happened under the mistletoe. I meant that, Penny. I meant it. But I'm afraid of it. Even more afraid now that you tell me you were once married."

The little flowers ran in pairs on each side of the stripes. "Because you thought I was inexperienced. You were wrong. Does it make a difference?"

"It shouldn't, should it? But, of course, it does. Thinking you a virgin . . . it was like a leash on my desires. It made it easier for me." He shuddered.

The small flame danced over the intimate, comfortable spaces: the books and chairs and knickknacks, symbols of her whole life here, her childhood and girlhood. The room she had foolishly run away from when she was fifteen. The room where her mother had held out welcoming, forgiving arms and a warm shoulder to cry on when she returned.

"Have you not had many mistresses?" Penny immediately clapped one hand over her mouth. "Oh, I'm sorry. I'm aghast at my effrontery. You don't have to answer."

His hands were steepled together, his forehead resting on both thumbs. Beautiful, strong-boned hands, hands that might have been painted by Rembrandt, praying.

"No, I will answer. A friend would answer, wouldn't he? The truth is . . . I have never had affairs."

"But I would have thought, in your position—"

"It was always too dangerous. I could never put so much power in the hands of the lady involved. Her family would try to use it to gain influence. Others would be jealous. It's a precarious enough line that I walk every day. To favor one noble lady over another would be disaster."

It was a world she couldn't imagine. Where a prince's sexual favors could sway the destiny of a nation. It made her think of Good Queen Bess, the Virgin Queen, careful with the politics of picking favorites, careful of her own power to destroy peace— and herself—as her cousin Mary Queen of Scots had done. But Elizabeth had been a woman in the sixteenth century. Surely those days were gone?

"But I understand our own Prince Regent—"

"This is England!"

"Oh," Penny said. "Oh, I had never realized. I had thought you must be very experienced."

His laugh was broken. "I'm one of the gypsy princes of Glarien. That reputation precedes me like a trumpeter in a parade. I know how to extract the most political advantage from coquetry at any ball or state occasion. Why would anyone guess?"

"None of the court ladies ever challenged you?"

"Since I was about eighteen, women have done everything, including bribing my guards to let them into my bedchamber, where I have burned with temptation . . . stood and burned as if fire consumed all my limbs . . . while I sent them away without hurt or offense. But I did not dare touch them. Of course, you cannot understand. Why should you understand? And why, in God's name, should I care if you do?"

Her own pain broke and shivered, before dissolving into darkness. Without making any conscious decision, Penny rose from her chair and went to the window seat. She took his hands in hers and pulled them from his face. He looked up, startled. Night flamed in his eyes.

"I think you can kiss a friend," she said. "Without thinking you will ravish her. Especially a friend who wants nothing in the way of political power from you. For heaven's sake. You already did."

She bent down and gently kissed the side of his mouth. Trembling, she kept his fingers in hers and waited.

He'll make a very able lord, Jeb Hardacre had said. *He's a smart man with an eye for what the land needs, especially now he has you to show him, Miss Lindsey.*

He was a lad with a heart of gold, Mrs. Hardacre had said. *He'd have wept over a dead sparrow. He brought his own toys for my little brother when Peter was taken ill with the smallpox and near died of it. I never thought those foreigners could ruin him, and I'm sure I'm right.*

Mad prince. What if I would help Glarien only because it is you? But they *have* ruined you. And I don't know why on earth I should think it my job to see if it's not too late, after all.

He let his fingers lie in hers—smooth, perfect fingers, calloused only where they had held leather reins in a supple, feeling grip. Horseman's fingers. Yet she felt the tension running deeply through the bones and sinews, as if he fought to remain still, struggled not to take advantage of what she had just done.

Her heart began to pound. Her flesh reacted as if he ran his firm hands over her breasts and belly and legs, an intimate flare of longing. She closed her eyes, feeling the weakness and pounding, the intense, growing craving. But his fingers stayed steady, lying lightly in hers, until she thought blue sparks would crackle through the air if he removed them.

"You don't know me," he said. "You don't know what I've done or what I'm capable of doing. Do you think you can teach me that desire can come in increments? I don't think so. I think we must never again be alone like this in the dark. But it will be easier after today."

She stood transfixed, staring down at his ebony hair and broad shoulders, desire racing in her blood. "Will it?"

He glanced up at her and smiled. Her heart leaped in somer-saults—complete, skirts-flying, boots-over-the-head, catapult-ing somersaults.

"My court arrives today. There will always be someone in my rooms, except at night or when I send for you. I have gen-tlemen to dress me and undress me, wash me and shave me. Someone turns down the bed and someone else holds out my dressing gown. Noblemen fight over the honor to put on my slippers or take them off again. Even though only a few repre-sentatives of the noble houses of Glarien are here, they'll be all the more jealous of their privileges. After today, my time is no longer my own."

He slipped one hand over her fingers and carried her palm to his mouth. He kissed it once at the base of the thumb.

She stared down at him in amazement, her palm filled with voluptuous pleasure. "Are you serious? You cannot always command your own time?"

His gaze had turned dark, black smoke in a black storm. "Deadly serious. Come. It is time to go, before it gets light."

You pull strings and the puppets dance exactly as planned. Carefully he had laid out every step of the plan. It had clicked and whirred perfectly, gears turning, wheels spinning, putting every part of the clockwork exactly in place. The people in Ras-call St. Mary would lie down and die before giving out any-thing useful to Carl, anything damaging either to himself or to her. No whisper or word would reach the ears of questioning strangers, however subtle, that Miss Lindsey was living at Rascall Hall so improperly with a grand duke.

He had kissed her—exactly as he'd planned. He had softened her and engaged her loyalty. She thought she cared what happened to him. She thought she could be his friend. She need never know that it was all fake, all lies, that even the truth was a lie for the princes of Glarien.

Did she think he gave work to the villagers simply because it was benevolent? Or that he couldn't control exactly what information left his house? Or that he told her anything without an ulterior motive? The men moved across the chessboard, rooks castled, pieces were taken en passant, the bishop sailed down his diagonal, while the knight leaped the others in a crooked move that had become as natural as breathing. He was rarely beaten at chess.

Yet the queen was the only piece with total freedom of the board and she had secrets of her own. She had been *married!* It hadn't even occurred to him that she might not be a virgin. Did it make his plans more honorable or less so?

The only thing he hadn't planned was his own response. Desire roared, insatiable and devouring. If he closed his eyes he could feel her lips touch the corner of his mouth. After the searing kiss they had exchanged under the oak tree, to not act on that artless invitation had been like a warrior's test of courage—to stand unflinching under fire. Didn't she know how close she had come to being laid down on the floor of her mother's cottage to assuage his ravenous, ignoble desires?

Yet he had not done it. And in spite of all the filthy, nefarious schemes he was forced to pursue, a pain twisted deep in his heart that he might yet hurt that bright English innocence. Innocent, even if she had been married. Innocent enough to offer *him* compassion!

Nine

Penny stood rigid behind the screen, scarcely breathing. She had been doing this every day for three days. Three dull, rainy days, with water trickling down the windows, the light in the house robbed of intensity. Days without a single personal or intimate exchange with the man who had become her fascination.

Her heart beat loudly enough to drown out the ticking clock. Through tiny spaces in the fretwork, she could see his study, with the telescope and desk. The rain had stopped. Early afternoon sunshine streamed in the window, touching flashes of gold on brass, dazzling on the splendor of the medals, stars and crosses on his elaborate uniform. His shoulders and collar were stiff with gold braid. The handle of the ceremonial sword at his hip beamed with jewels: diamonds, sapphires, a single ruby.

Nicholas seemed immensely upright, projecting absolute command. *I do not usually allow anyone to touch me, nor do I touch them. No one except you has ever spoken to me with such a lack of respect.*

Her thoughts whirled and danced like a dorbeetle. He was a ruling grand duke. He had a country to run. She had talked to him as if—oh, Lord! Had she been surprised by his odd changes of mood? Was it strange that he didn't seem to know how to offer friendship? Life and death lay in his palms. Peace or war might result from his whim. Everyone he knew only wanted to use him, for their own power, their own aggrandizement, their own purposes. It was all he had ever known, even from the men closest to him, his bodyguard. Which of them would be loyal to him, if he were not their sovereign?

Could she be different? Could she offer him something else? Were there deeper levels of reform than taking care of fields and woods? She had been touched to the heart by that vulnerable, raw man who had slipped off his mask for a second in her mother's house. She had been moved to her soul by the thought and feel of kissing him. The memory was always there, of those warm lips caressing her open mouth, sweetly enough to drown her.

The thought flared and danced that he wasn't really a rake—not a rake at all—but a man who knew less of the mysteries of the marriage bed than she did. An oddly humbling idea. She felt stunned that when she had offered such an indiscretion as to kiss him again at Clumper Cottage, he had not kissed back, but had shown her his control and his respect, allowing her to relax and feel safe.

Now she saw him at work. A steady procession of British and foreign nobles, ministers and officials, came and went from his private study. Each one revealed nothing but guile. Yet Nicholas prevailed. Flattering, deceiving, manipulative. With his subtle charm, he won concessions for Glarien and hammered out the last details of the marriage treaty, balancing the demands of Russia and Britain—suspicious of Austria and France, but also of each other—with the survival of his nation. Each encounter, each visitor, guaranteed one more link in a chain of security for his tens of thousands of subjects, as long as his marriage went forward as planned.

All of that rested, in the end, on her shoulders—a more humbling thought than any other. So he was showing her, making her understand what it meant to rule. Why else did he insist she witness all this, even when the visitor was not someone Sophia would know? In the ways of court politics, she had been as ignorant and simple as a child.

At last the door closed behind the final visitor for the day. "Come," he said quietly. "You may come out now."

Penny stepped into the study. Warm yellow light glanced off the telescope and dazzled on his gold braid.

"I'm just realizing," she said, "how very rarely I've seen you in sunshine. It is foolish, of course, to feel intimidated by all that military splendor, but I have to admit you are most impressive in all that."

He sat down and put his head in his palms. "Am I?"

His posture disturbed her, his rigid fingers and taut shoulders. "You are ill?"

He dropped his hands and stared straight ahead. "No! It's nothing—a headache. Did you make particular note of the Alvian minister, von Pontiras?"

"How could I not? He reminded me of Uncle Horace the time my great-aunt hatched the moths."

He put his fingers to the right side of his forehead. "What moths?"

Penny did not want to cross the line of sight from the window, so she perched herself on the projecting ledge of the bookcase, leaving her feet dangling in space. "Well, first you must understand what Aunt Horace is like. Here is what Mama just wrote from Staffordshire." She pulled her mother's most recent letter out of her pocket and unfolded it. "'My dearest child,' . . . hmm . . . oh, here it is! 'I was scarcely in the door'—that is my mother, of course—'and not even divested of my gloves and bonnet, when Aunt Horace asked me in those stentorian tones of hers, "Mrs. Lindsey, surely your shoes are a *very* large size?"'"

He dropped his fingers. "Why the devil would your mother's aunt make such a bizarre personal remark?"

"Wait! You'll see. Let me go on . . . ' "I think not, Aunt Horace," I said. "Oh, indeed, I think so!" she replied. "Who makes your shoes? Whoever it is, he must use a great deal of leather, for I declare, you always had very large feet, Mrs. Lindsey. I could not wear *your* shoes." And Aunt Horace put all of us to the blush by pulling her skirts above her ankles to reveal two feet that struck me, as always, as being perfectly normal in size and certainly not smaller than my own.'"

The smallest quirk bent the corner of his mouth. "I'm amazed!"

Penny folded the letter, determined to keep a straight face. "Aunt Horace takes great pride in being an original. She believes she is very dainty, though indeed she is not. Mama and I are always in giggles about it, for Mama is a great deal smaller than her aunt and she most certainly does not have large feet."

"And the moths?"

"It was Christmas. After dinner we repaired to the best parlor, which is hardly ever used. As a child I always longed to play on the horsehair sofa in there, for the leather is hard and shiny—perfect for sliding down the back. Alas, that parlor was completely banned, except on special occasions."

He looked up at her, shielding his eyes. "I was always forbidden to touch anything in this house: that brass solar system in the blue drawing room, this telescope—everything naturally fascinating to a boy. Dear God, why the devil must children be punished for every instinct?"

"Because children break things," she said.

"A little girl would hardly have broken a sofa!"

"No, but by sliding down the back, I'd have offended every rule of proper behavior."

He leaned back and smiled. "So you were all in the parlor. What happened?"

"You must imagine the entire family gathered, everyone sitting as stiff as a poker. Aunt Horace settled herself on the sofa. She pinned me with her darkest gaze and asked me why I *must* wear my hair so my head looked like a split pea. I used to have it parted"—she ran a finger from the center of her forehead across the top of her head—"like this. It was when she got up that it happened."

His smile was broader now, anticipating. "And?"

"She had hatched out a clutch of tiny moths! They were wriggling out of the horsehair exactly where she'd been sitting. The other aunts screamed. My mother laughed. One of the uncles had a choking fit. And Uncle Horace looked just as Count von Pontiras did now: as if fate had finally delivered his one greatest wish, but he couldn't let himself show it."

For a moment, there was absolute silence. Then he began to laugh, a freefall of masculine chuckles, deepening into a roar of pure glee. She had never before seen him laugh without an edge of cynicism. She dropped her mother's letter as she joined in, holding her hands over her ribs. The memory of that Christmas, the memory of all those Christmases, being told she looked like a split pea, being told her feet were too big—agonizingly painful to a young girl—moved her laughter into undignified roars, until she ached and wept.

The gold braid blurred. He caught her by the waist, pulling her forward into his arms. She landed against him with a thump. He buried his face in her hair, his rumbling laughter tickling her ears and neck, as he tucked her head into his chest and muffled her giggles in his gold sash. He could barely speak for laughing, his chest shaking, his hands careful and tender.

"Oh, hush! Hush! Someone will hear us. Dear, blessed Penelope! Dear God, I think I might die!"

She clung to him, warm and secure in his embrace. Between renewed fits of giggles she managed to blurt out her only coherent thought. "F—F—Fiddlesticks! No one ever died from laughing."

He set her away, just a little, and put his forefinger over her mouth. "Didn't they? I thought there for a moment that I might."

She gazed up at him and choked back her merriment. He seemed somber suddenly, yet a small lamp had been lit—far, far away in the depths of his eyes. He dropped his fingers and looked at them, as if the mark of her lips might have branded him.

"But perhaps someone new could be born by laughing," she said.

His hands moved on her back. She saw the change in his gaze, like smoke wavering in a breeze, saw the question and the moment of uncertainty burning in their black depths. Without a word, she opened her lips as his mouth touched hers and gave him her answer.

She had been first kissed once, seven long years ago, and thought that it meant the sun and the moon were being laid at her feet. She knew better now. Yet the sun blazed. Brilliant, life-giving, making daises open their petals and sunflowers turn their faces in seeking adoration. While all the time the moon slid and slipped from new moon to full, shading with subtle gradations of sensation, and making all humans fools. A kiss that was more than exciting, a kiss sublime in its wickedness and passion and innocence. And if women ran naked in orgiastic frenzy under a full moon, thinking to offer worship to the gods, she would willingly, willingly run with them.

He released her at last, breathless, then lifted her by the waist to set her back on the bookcase. Like a flame in dry timber, he strode away across the room, pressing one bent knuckle to his mouth. Penny sat on her perch, holding on with both hands, for she was liquid. Her bones were all liquid, molten and aching for him.

"I think," she said at last, as winded as a runner. "I think someone new could most definitely be born out of laughter."

He crossed to the telescope and touched the brass stand. Perhaps he was trembling, but perhaps it was just the fineness of the instrument, delicately poised to view the wonders of the heavens, that made the metal vibrate like a plucked string.

He sounded so sincere she could hardly make out his soft words. "Penny, don't say that!"

"Why not?"

He spun about and indicated the room, the house, with a wave of one hand. "This place makes me unsure who I am. I feel caught, like a hooked fish out of water, gasping for air. Perhaps you have triumphed, so the memory of my mother and my nurses and my governess—your mother—seep into my mind around the edges."

"I'm sure they do," she said. "There's nothing wrong with that."

The sunlight created halos of light around his medals and gold epaulets, leaving him dark, intense, once again. "But when I go back to Glarien, Schloss Moritzburg will reclaim me. My destiny is there. Mine and Sophia's. Promise me you won't for-get that. Promise me you won't be charmed or think you can reform me. My soul was bargained away long ago. It's no longer mine to give name to. Promise me, Penny!"

She couldn't answer. Her blood still swam lazily. She didn't want warnings or reminders. She didn't want to be wise or sensible any longer. She wanted to dance with Dionysus, with the Greek women, under a wild moon and make sacrifice of her virginity. Except that she had already sacrificed it long ago to a man who hadn't loved her, and maenads—as often as not—tore their lovers to pieces.

Someone knocked on the door.

Penny dived off the ledge and caught her foot in her skirt. She went flying onto the rug as the knock sounded again. She grabbed her mother's letter, curled up her feet, and tucked herself under Nicholas's desk. In one fluid movement he pulled the half-cloak from his shoulders and draped it so she couldn't be seen.

"Yes?" he said.

It was Alexis, deferential and compliant. "Sire, did you wish to dictate notes on today's meetings?"

Penny put her hand over her mouth. Of course it didn't matter if Alexis knew she was in the room, but she had no intention of crawling out from under the prince's desk while the boy was there. As soon as Nicholas sent him away, she could emerge with at least a little dignity.

He did not. The prince sat down in his chair and began to dictate. Penny was curled up against his foot. She had a wonderful view of his gold tassels. Each strand was interwoven with red silk, spiraling up to the knot. The knots made tiny lions' heads. Beautiful craftsmanship, days of labor, to make tassels for a prince's boots. She wanted to touch the soft leather, lay her head against it and surrender.

Instead she curled so she wouldn't touch him. She had a cramp in the back of her neck. Her legs and left arm went to sleep. Yet the longer she lay there, the more impossible to ignominiously emerge. There had once been an English prince drowned in a butt of Malmsey wine, the Duke of Gloucester— Richard the Third's brother? *I will pickle him,* she thought, and had to suppress a renewed fit of giggles.

She forgot her discomfort as she began to listen. Whatever Nicholas was telling Alexis, it was not an accurate account of what had transpired in his meetings that day. Conversations were subtly altered, outcomes twisted. She tried to think of what that implied, but the discomfort in her muscles began to turn into pain.

When the boy left at last, she was too stiff to move. Nicholas bent down and peered at her. "Comfortable?"

"Oh, I rather like it under here, Your Royal Highness. A most agreeable nook. A spider has taken up residence already, but he doesn't seem to mind company."

"He doesn't?" The tassels disappeared as he dropped to both knees and looked under the desk.

Penny dropped her head backward and pushed herself out of the small space until she lay flat on her back. "I shall never be able to walk again. My hands are full of pins and needles. Why on earth didn't you send Alexis away and let me escape?"

The sun cast copper highlights in his dark hair. "I thought you would guess. I wanted you to hear— oh, bloody hell!"

She looked up at him, puzzled. "Guess what?"

Smoke stirred deep in his black eyes as if embers began to smolder. "Ah, Penny, you made me laugh and got rid of my headache."

"These headaches? They are severe, aren't they? You have them often?"

He glanced away. "Yes, though no one but you knows. Sometimes my vision fills with bright lights and I think the pain will fell me. Fortunately, it hasn't yet. A sad weakness in a prince."

"But one you can admit to a friend?" Yet she thought he had turned the conversation, that he had been about to say something else.

She stretched and sat up. They were face-to-face on the rug. He had only to lean forward a few inches to kiss her again. She felt molten and foolish, wanting it, wanting him to lay his hand on her cheek, wanting him to act on the passion she saw blazing in his eyes. She was willing. Willing to kiss away his headaches and his troubles, willing to kiss away all caution and good sense. The moment quaked, like an aspen leaf vibrating in an unseen wind—and then the hurricane struck.

He leaped up, to stalk violently away from her. "This is a mistake. A dreadful mistake. Go away now! Go!"

She struggled to her feet. "Why?"

He whirled on her like a swordsman about to strike. "Go! We cannot be friends. We don't need any more personal contact whatsoever. Nothing but disaster can come out of this. Haven't you realized by now? I am entirely duplicitous and dishonorable. For God's sake! Get out!"

"What about my lessons?"

He put both hands to his head as if in torment. "You need nothing more from me! Fritz can give you riding lessons. You can observe me in here without our talking. When you take your place as Sophia, her ladies will show you what to do. I'll tell you which ones you can trust. Everything else you can learn without me."

She felt awkward and lost. "But I thought I was to learn royal deportment and manners from you?"

"You've already learned everything you need." He pointed toward the door in a gesture of pure imperialism. Sun blazed on the medals ranked on his chest. "Get out! Now! I have had enough!"

Her blood burned. On legs too weak to carry a sensible person, she fled back to her room. She had only once in her life done anything as remotely foolish as this, when she was fifteen. But surely what had overwhelmed her as a girl, could be safely handled by a woman of two-and-twenty? Except that she had gone too far, pushed too hard, and he wouldn't let her in any longer.

She pulled out a sheet of writing paper. Tears blurred for a moment. Brushing them away, she dipped her pen in the inkwell.

Dear Mama. I am in disgrace and will take my lessons from his men from now on. Our dark Nicholas almost became human, just for a moment, and then I believe he was terrified of it. Yet I think perhaps I begin to understand the crack in our desperate prince's black armor. He's lonely. Horribly, dread-

fully lonely. And afraid, I think, of friendship. Was my father as lonely as that? She scratched through the last line, then scored it out over and over until she'd ruined the paper.

The knock at her door made her crumple it into a ball.

It was only Alexis. The blond boy stood uncertainly in her doorway. He was carrying the telescope from the study downstairs. Quest stood at his heels.

"Grand Duke Nicholas said I was to bring this, ma'am."

"Good Lord! His telescope? For me, why?"

"To look at the stars."

"And Quest?"

"His Royal Highness said she might be a companion for you, if you would like."

Penny held out her hand and the wolfhound trotted up to her. The silver fur was soft and warm. Alexis set the instrument down by the window.

She gestured at the telescope. "Do you know how it works?" She felt embarrassed to be so ignorant in front of the youth. "Can you show me?"

"If you wish, ma'am," he replied stiffly.

Penny watched as he turned knobs, then did it herself, bending to peer through the long tube. As she straightened up she caught sight of his reflection in the brass. The dandelion hair glowed like a halo. Like a mockery of the open curiosity in the simple, raw gaze of the butcher's boy, his eyes spoke of juvenile need, but beneath it lay something aware, furtive, uncomfortable. His eyes met hers and he looked down, as if deeply ashamed. Something in the strange mixture of innocence and adulteration touched her to the heart.

"You have a sweetheart at home in Glarien?" she asked gently.

The boy blushed scarlet and shook his head, then turned to go, fleeing like Mercury. The door clicked shut behind him. Penny sat for a long time looking at the telescope, rubbing Quest's coat while the dog thumped her tail on the floor. Alexis was just about the age Penny had been when she had run away to get married. It was meant to be an age of innocence. An age when one still believed in dreams. Yet the boy had looked at her with the knowing, ancient eyes of Merkie Maggie, the fallen woman who haunted the Norwich marketplace and mumbled in her cups about corruption.

Nicholas sat at his desk and smoothed out the crumpled paper. Every day he went through her rubbish. He read every one of her letters before it was sent. It made him wretched with shame, but he could hardly delegate the task. He had learned nothing, except that Penny Lindsey had a perceptive, generous heart. He had sent her away, shouted at her, to save her from himself and she had written nothing but concern to her mother.

He's lonely. Horribly, dreadfully lonely. And afraid, I think, of friendship. Was my father as lonely as that?

He waited for the pounding in his blood to subside. There was nothing he could offer her that was not intensely selfish and ignoble. That he had given in to his desire for even a moment was a weakness so shameful it made him shudder. He was a ghost moth, beating in vain at the glass of a closed window, desperately attracted by the unattainable warmth inside. Only Princess Sophia could accept him as he was. Penny was a pawn, taken en passant. Yet he craved her. He'd been a fool, an abject, blundering fool.

If he closed his eyes he would see her again as she lay, weak and soft from laughter, on his carpet, ready to offer forgiveness and solace. He'd knelt down beside her. He'd already kissed her. He knew she had already known a man, a husband. And he had wanted to annihilate himself in his lust. His erection had pulsed with pleasurable anticipation. His hands had ached to possess every delicate rounded shape, every scented curve, all the secrets of her body. Yet he wanted to do it with tenderness, with humble supplication, and lay his heart in her hands. And that made him a fool, a buffoon of fate, to think that any prince of Glarien could offer such a thing without harm.

So she must take her riding lessons from Fritz and study everything else she needed to know from the notes he wrote out for her daily. She could observe silently behind the screen. He didn't need to see her privately ever again. Quest could keep her company, if she was lonely. Soon it would be time to intercept Sophia's carriage and place Penny directly into the masquerade. After the wedding, when it was all over, his duty would claim him entirely—to balance on a tightrope forever, so his nation did not descend into chaos.

All he had to do was survive each day, one at a time—knowing she was there in his study, knowing she slept in the room above his—without sinking to his knees and begging her to forgive him, or begging her to let him into her bed. In the meantime, he would not let her witness again what he was doing with Alexis. He didn't want her to know quite how easily and willingly he could stoop to the gutter.

In his neat, controlled handwriting Nicholas had filled several pages: *Sophia makes a small study of astronomy and likes to patronize the sciences. The principal planets are Mercury, Venus, the Earth, Mars, Jupiter, Saturn and the Georgium Sidus, discovered by Dr. Herschel in Bath. Jupiter has four moons, Saturn seven, the Georgium Sidus six. Though nearly as large as Jupiter, the Georgium Sidus can never be seen without a telescope. Also discovered within the last ten years, are the following very small bodies: Ceres, Pallas, Juno and Vesta.*

While she lived quietly here in Norfolk, great discoveries were happening in the outside world. She had read about them in the newspapers, but what did it mean to move in such circles, to be able to influence such events? Penny knew the principal planets, of course, but she had never trained a fine telescope on them in a clear summer sky. The surface of the moon was a revelation seen through the lens. If she had felt small and insignificant before, now she felt infinitesimal, and lonely enough to weep for sorrow. Did her cousin, the real Princess Sophia, gaze on that same moon from a prison somewhere in Glarien and feel the same way?

Mama, I am still banished, she had written. *But he sends me his Glarian wolfhound for company. Quest is, I admit, comforting.* Nicholas set down the letter and cursed. Might he jeopardize the whole venture because of his fear of her? He closed his eyes. He did not give her riding lessons, but he imagined her progress as Fritz put her through her paces. He did not teach her, but his mind filled with images of her as he wrote out what he thought she must learn. She would be asleep now in the room above, with her blond plait fuzzy on the pillow. Warm, curled, female, her intelligence and wit lost in dreams.

To be Rapunzel in this tower, it would seem I should need some thirty feet or more of hair.

The door clicked open. He looked up. She was standing at the foot of her tower stairs, Quest at her heels. Her hair parted in the middle—*a split pea.* God, how cruel!

"I did listen," she said, "for some time, to be sure you were alone. I don't see any gaggle of courtiers, so I assume you may receive me?"

His body responded before he could prevent it—the rush of obstinate male desire, firing in the groin and in the palms of his hands. She was wrapped in her dressing gown. Her blond plait fell over her left shoulder. Her arms were crossed over her breasts. She was gazing at him as if defying him to notice.

"What do you want?" he said brutally.

"I want to know why you have been deceiving me about the horses."

She stepped into the room and closed the door behind her. Quest lay down, watching them both. "Major Baron von Gerhard didn't mean to give anything away," she said. "It is entirely my fault. I made him tell me. I've been gathering my courage to confront you about this, so I had to come down right away, before I lost my nerve. But before I go on, I want your word he will not be punished."

He felt astonished, as vulnerable as any captive. "Fritz? You have it. What did he tell you?"

Penny took a deep breath. "Princess Sophia is a superb horsewoman, isn't she? As good as you. I cannot possibly learn to ride that well in a few weeks, can I?"

His fists clenched over her letter. "No, you can't."

She bit her lip and glanced away. "How long would it take—just to be truly competent?"

"I don't know. A year or two, perhaps."

"And to learn to ride as you can—or like von Gerhard or any

of the others? To make a horse do what you did that first day at
Rascall Manor, when you made your mount dance and rear on
command?"

"Oh, God! A lifetime! Since you didn't start as a child, you
might never catch up." She had been right to extract his
promise that Fritz wouldn't be punished. He'd like to put his
old friend on the rack for this!

"So I cannot appear on horseback in London, not if Princess
Sophia's an accomplished horsewoman. That was a lie. Another
lie."

Shame curled like a snake in his belly. "It won't matter. You
may ride in a carriage. The story is that Sophia's been ill. If
she's convalescing, it will make a convenient excuse for all
kinds of things—riding, dancing, anything of the sort."

"Dancing?" Her voice caught. "Of course! She must dance
like an angel. It wasn't even worth the time to try to teach me
that, was it? I should have made a complete fool of myself."
She walked straight toward him, her bare feet soft on the floor.
"I think I hate you. I've worked so hard. It was a triumph for me
to think I could learn to ride. Now I have to know that even
those hours and hours with Willow were all a cheat and a deception. Oh, God! You're truly despicable!"

"I tried to warn you." His heart leaped, his body yearned for
her, and she hated him.

"I want to hurt you." She stopped and clenched her fists. "I
have never wanted to hurt anyone like this, except—"

He slid her letter underneath some other papers and stood up.
"Except whom?"

"Major William Sanders. The man who seduced me away
from my home when I was fifteen and married me."

He felt helpless and incredulous, standing before her while
she berated him. "Your *husband*? You hated him? Why?"

"Because he married me thinking I had money. He carried
me off to Scotland and wed me at a blacksmith's shop. I was
flattered and thrilled. I thought he loved me. I thought it was a
great adventure. When I found out his interest was entirely mer-
cenary, it broke my heart. It didn't take long before he made me
hate him. Now you have done it again. You have seduced me

away from my home with the promise of a great adventure. And now you have made me hate you."

"Because of the *horses*?"

She flung her hands wide. Quest crawled away to hide under the bed. "Yes, yes! Because of the horses! Don't you understand? I was so proud of what I'd done. I thought I could conquer the world. Now I know anyone seeing me on horseback can tell right away I'm a beginner. I feel betrayed and belittled. If I can't trust you even in this, I cannot go to London and be a princess at your wedding. You have just lost a kingdom over a horseshoe nail, Your Royal Highness."

She sat down in the chair where Alexis played chess. The candlelight shone steadily. Her eyelids were swollen, her face wet.

"You don't even know what you've learned!" he said. "Stay there!"

He raced up the stairs to her room and caught up her shirt, shoes and riding breeches. For a moment he stood with her clothes in his hands and trembled like a man with a fever. Her scent lingered in the room. The bed lay rumpled. The telescope and his notes on the planets had been well used. He desired all of it: her essence, her body and her sharp, bright mind. All of it must be forever denied.

When he came down she was still sitting at the table, one hand over her eyes, Quest pressed against her legs. She had not even moved the top sheet covering her letter to her mother. Her integrity was absolute. To pry into someone else's papers was simply impossible for her. While he, of course, must pry into everything.

"Put these on!" He thrust the clothes at her. "I'll wait for you."

She looked up. "Why?"

"You and I are going to the stables."

She wiped her cheek on the cuff of her nightgown. The white fabric fell back, revealing the rounded, blue-veined flesh of her wrist. A sharp wave of craving spun down his spine. His mouth burned with the desire to press his lips onto hers and burn away her tears. His hands ached to open her dressing gown and her nightdress and to stroke the long, sweet lines of her body. His sex reverberated with carnal need: hot, urgent and male.

"Now?" she asked.

"For God's sake, obey me! Or must I dress you myself?"

They walked through the dark in absolute silence. After petting Quest and reassuring her, he'd left the dog in his bedroom. Then he'd left Penny in the barn and gone to fetch a horse. Just as she began to wonder if he would ever return, bay fire burst through the doorway and flashed from wall to wall, whinnying and snorting. It was not Willow. He had brought Driver, the big, bad fellow, instead. He must have ridden the horse bareback, for Nicholas hung a bridle on the wall before tossing a halter to Penny.

The prince leaned against the door and folded his arms. "Go on," he said. "Go out there and tell him to stop all that nonsense."

The horse turned at the far wall and came thundering back through the shadows. She waited for the prince to offer reassurance, to say he was there to back her up, to make sure nothing went wrong. Instead he turned to leave.

"Why? How will that help me learn to ride like Princess Sophia?"

The door closed with a thud. Penny ran after him and almost tripped over the lead rope. Behind her the horse raced, frightened and alone, crying out in shrill, vibrating cries that it was cut off from the herd, abandoned without a leader. She watched for a while, remembering that desperate, crushing feeling when this same horse had galloped down on her and torn her sleeve with its teeth. Teeth designed for eating grass. Teeth that had taken a carrot from her hand gently, with courtesy.

She marched out into the center of the space. The horse dived past her and squealed, bursting again into a shattering gallop, then bucked, kicking out violently at nothing.

For all his strength and beauty, he's just a meal for a predator.

"Here now!" She snapped the rope. "Behave yourself!"

The bay skidded to a halt and turned to her, eyes wary, as if offering a challenge. She took a deep breath. The bay shook its head and made a little lunge at her. Heart hammering, she stepped forward, meeting the challenge with one of her own, and drove the horse away. It burst into another gallop, throwing its head high, so she snapped the rope and kept it going, driving until the black eye became suddenly soft and attentive. Immediately she stepped back, as Nicholas had shown her, and allowed the horse to stop. The sleek bay head dropped, jaw relaxed.

The next time she asked the bay to move forward, it trotted calmly in a circle. She let it trot on for a while, then she invited the horse to rest again. Driver stopped and turned to her, expression meek. Without hesitation she walked up to the horse and put the halter on its head.

She ran her hand down the black mane. "What am I to do, big fellow? Am I to be just his puppet, to be arrayed for one day in a wedding dress and then discarded? He really makes fools of both of us, you know."

The horse blew softly as if to say, *What else did you expect?*

"You aren't afraid of horses any longer, are you?" the prince asked.

She turned to see him standing in the doorway.

"No, but neither can I ride a horse like this, can I?"

"Maybe you never will." He walked forward and took the rope from her hand. "That doesn't matter. You made him submit to you. That is what you've learned. Do you understand now?"

"Understand what? What does this change?"

He rubbed the horse's black nose. Driver stood relaxed, almost asleep, under the steady stroking. Nicholas looked up, his expression lost in shadows. "I didn't know any other way to make you confident enough. Command a horse and you can command a room—or a kingdom. Attitude is all that matters. The horses have taught you how to be royal."

She backed away a few more paces to indicate the huge, empty space where she had circled and trotted on faithful Willow. "So all this wasn't really about riding at all?"

"No. Though I thought you might like it, all the same."

At the wheelbarrow, she sat down, not sure her legs would hold her any longer. "And that was beyond you to explain to begin with? You couldn't trust me with that information? *I want you to learn to be more commanding, and here's how we'll do it.* You couldn't just have said that?"

He ran his hand down Driver's neck, again and again. "No, I could not. It wouldn't have worked as well."

She bent forward, glad of the intimate, protective darkness. "Why do you dislike me so much? What have I done?"

The horse shied and took a moment to calm again. "*Dislike* you?"

"Your deceptions are like the layers of ice in a winter pond. If one crystalline film melts in the afternoon sunshine, the layers beneath it make sure the surface freezes over again at night. We strove for friendship. You rejected it. Since then I have been at a loss. How can I help you with your frozen, rigid world? You give me the night sky to study, distant stars that shine without warmth. My world, the daytime fields and the haymaking and the harvest, you have stolen and taken away. Can't you give anything back? Must you treat me like an enemy?"

He was absolutely still now, the horse quiet and attentive at his shoulder. "I don't think of you as an enemy."

"I know you're more than this ice prince. I know you could slip onto Driver's back right now and make him dance with you like a village girl on May Day. You can do that only out of love, not because it's a cold, hard skill learned in the dark. So why do you shut me out?"

He looked down. "I didn't think . . . This is not what I intended. I can't have you believe that I hate you."

"Then why act like it!"

Nicholas strode away, then came back with the bridle. The horse dropped its head and took the bit. The prince vaulted onto the dark back, dropping his fingers down to her.

"I am sorry I have nothing to give you. Perhaps Driver has."

"How?"

"Come. Trust me. Give me your hand."

She burned with resentment. "I don't know those subtler languages and never will. You said so."

He still held out his hand, steadily gazing down at her. At last she placed her palm in his. A moment later she was sitting on the bay's broad back, her legs hanging in front of Nicholas's.

"Just sit there and relax," Nicholas said. "I'll talk to him for both of us."

Unlike Willow's short gaits, Driver's stride ate the darkness, peeled away dust, even at a walk. Nicholas's thighs flexed. The horse began to trot. She was forced to lean against the prince, fitting her back against his body as her hips rocked with his. Muscles flowed powerfully: a pirouette; the pounding trot done almost in place; a rocking canter, dancing from one foreleg to the other at each stride; another pirouette. The horse moved with profound symmetry and force, its animal power channeled into beauty.

It wasn't a conversation. It was music. Powerful, primitive music, underlain with a drumbeat rhythm. Thrust, *thud,* rock into a new balance, a new melody, every movement smooth as silk. She must flow with it or distract the horse. Yet it was erotic, charged, appallingly indecent. Nicholas's lean thighs cradled hers. His body fit the curves of her spine. His breath seared her ear. His arms held her enclosed as his lean fingers talked their mysteries through the reins. His heartbeat pulsed through her veins.

Her bones and muscles melted, her skin sang—at one with this animal and this man, singing new songs in a sensuous new music of the blood.

Her soul roared its awareness.

When Driver stopped at last, she sat in silence, stunned, unable to contain the fine tremble that ran in little waves over her skin. Pure bodily pleasure.

Nicholas patted the horse on the neck, then swung her to the ground, before slipping down himself. The simple movement pierced her to the heart. All the beauty and power of the man, contained, adept, as controlled as his horse. A work of nature, trained into perfection.

She wrapped her arms over her breasts as her dreams roared into consciousness, dreams of love and a dark lover, and herself surrendering into ecstasy.

"That was wonderful," she whispered. "Wonderful. Thank you."

He stared into the horse's dark eye, the line of his back limber in the moonlight, as he removed the bridle and replaced it with the halter. He looked like a man facing devastation, as if he fought some intense struggle with himself.

"It was Driver's gift," he said bitterly.

She retreated, stung to tears and driven to hide them. His obvious regret poisoned any last strains of the music. "Of course. I would never mistake any of your strange overtures for personal kindness."

"Has no man ever been kind to you?"

"What a very odd question, coming from you!"

He strode away to hang the bridle on the wall. Driver stood quietly and waited. "Tell me about your first wedding. How did this man reach you when you were only fifteen?"

She was grateful to break the moment, to return to the matter-of-fact. "Oh, good Lord! The militia was stationed near Norwich. Though I was too young to attend, the officers were invited to the local assemblies and dances. Someone told Major William Sanders that my father had been an Alvian prince. Careless gossip from Aunt Horace, perhaps. She was staying with us at the time. William haunted the village until he met me. He seemed inexpressibly handsome and dashing. He persuaded me to meet him secretly, in the churchyard and at the old manor. Your estates were my playground, you see. Mama had no idea."

He walked back to the horse. "When I was a lad, I thought the manor seemed a good place for courtship."

"Not quite what you were thinking when you met me there, though, was it?"

"Good God. I don't know what I was thinking. I had a headache. Go on." The bay blew softly, hypnotized by his fingers, stroking over and over.

"There's not much more to tell. William was sent to a regiment stationed in Scotland. He convinced me to run away with him. We dashed off across the border and were married. At first it seemed wonderful, a dream. He was attentive and gallant—

until he found out I didn't have any money. Furious, he had one of his men flogged over something really petty—"

"Ah, so that is how you knew about such a thing!"

"Yes. That's when I realized he was cruel, but it was too late to undo our marriage. One evening in a fit of temper he stormed away and started drinking. There was a brawl. He was killed. So there I was, married and widowed within a few weeks. I came home and pretended it had never happened. He thought I would make him rich. He seduced me with kisses and flattery. He never loved me."

"And so you cannot—" He stopped and took a deep breath. "You cannot believe that any man could love you?"

She wanted a jest, a lighthearted escape, though the words came out cracked, spoken over her shoulder as she retreated again to the wheelbarrow. "It wouldn't do either of us much good for me to believe it right now, would it?"

He opened his hand and dropped the rope. Driver stood absolutely still, watching him. Nicholas walked away, leaving the horse standing, as if tied to the ground. Without a word he strode to the doorway. Penny sat in the dark and waited, her heart in her mouth. The bay didn't move, standing rooted to the spot, as if the prince had cast a spell.

Suddenly the horse whinnied. Penny leaped to her feet. Nicholas stood in the shifting light with his arms filled. For a moment she thought he brought hay for the horse. Then he stepped forward into the moonlight. Flowers. Wildflowers. Campion and stitchwort and buttercups. Common fumitory, charlock, clover. Meadowsweet, hawkweed. The ragged, simple flowers of the countryside.

"I gathered these earlier while you worked with Driver. Everything I could find. Shall I admit they're the first flowers I've ever picked with my own hands?" He dropped them in her lap, then pulled out a strand of clover and fed it to the horse, his back to her. "You ask if everything I give you is false. If everything I say is a game. It might be. There isn't any way for you to tell, of course."

The white campion petals lay open to attract moths. He had

gathered the flowers himself. For her. "You did this secretly? What else have you hidden from me?"

Nicholas turned. The horse stood like a statue at his back. "What do you want to know?"

A soft, earthy scent rose from the wildflowers, plants without artifice. "To prove that you aren't lying to me now? There isn't any question that can reveal such a thing."

He gestured and said something in Glarisch. The horse folded its legs. At another whisper Driver rolled to lie, hooves outstretched, on its side. The magnificent head lay flat on the dirt, the black mane flowing like shadow. All that power and beauty instantly submissive to the whim of the man. Mysterious tears burned.

Nicholas turned back to her. "Try me."

"Then tell me the truth about Alexis."

With another gesture, Driver scrambled back up. Nicholas led the horse to the side of the hall and tied it to a post. Then he paced away, in and out of the shadowed spaces, before coming back to stand over her. The flowers drifted in her lap.

"You want to know why I feed Alexis false reports on my meetings. Why I keep him close by me. Why it matters what Alexis thinks. There isn't any reason you shouldn't know. In fact, I wanted you to observe how it worked. I thought you might have guessed by now."

Penny stared up at him. "Guessed what?"

"That Alexis is working for my cousin Carl, of course."

She clutched at the stems, fuzzy and coarse. "Oh, God! He told me he loves you!"

"Perhaps he does. It doesn't matter."

She thought he skirted the edge of the issue, that even a truth this devastating wasn't everything, or what was most important. "And what else is the matter with Alexis?"

"That's rather his own business, don't you think?"

Shamed, she looked away. "How do you know he's spying for Carl? Are you sure?"

"I've never asked him, if that's what you mean. I assume it. He came to me from Carl's household. Why else would my cousin have let him go, except in exchange for a promise of treason? I make it as easy for Alexis as I can."

"So this is why you keep him by you? This is why he can't sleep at night? Poor boy!" She looked up at him through a glaze of tears, the wildflowers wilting in her hands. "He *does* love you! Yet he must still betray you? Oh, dear God!"

"It doesn't matter," Nicholas said again. "Most of the people who think they love me betray me in the end."

Ten

Did she think it would be different now? Had she thought they'd reached a new understanding? The wildflowers died, though Penny had brought them back to her room and put them in water. In two days, the sad remains were taken away, and the dry, scattered petals were swept up.

After the night with Driver, the night she had learned how Nicholas used Alexis, the night the prince had talked obliquely about love, he'd barely spoken to her again. She'd stood pinned behind the screen to listen to more meetings, more deceptions. By now Count Carl Zanich must know Nicholas kept a woman secreted in his rooms, though Alexis couldn't tell him she looked like Princess Sophia. Instead, the boy fed Carl false information about people and politics, not knowing that Nicholas used him for such purposes without scruple.

If she'd been innocent about the reality of power, the reality of princes, that innocence was flayed from her now.

There was only one brief encounter. He'd seemed harassed, distant—explaining some point of protocol, avoiding the personal—so why had she gnawed at him, worrying him, like a dog with a bone?

How can you tell me now that Alexis is a spy? she had asked.

❧ *171* ❧

You said these six were the only men you could trust, your personal bodyguard.

I trust Alexis to do exactly what I expect him to do, he'd replied. *It's the same thing.*

But it was not the same thing! It made that intimacy, those midnight games of chess, seem incomprehensible, except for a man who in truth had no heart.

So how could he show her how deep love could be, even between a man and a horse? An animal whose only defense was flight made to lie down on its side in the presence of a man, a predator. It was an unimaginable level of trust. *Ask a horse to trust you, you must be worthy of his trust. Horses are very sensitive to reality.*

A week later Nicholas announced that his household was removing to London. Penny didn't know how he'd laid his plans. She only knew that the message had come to her in the middle of a lesson from Major Baron von Gerhard: *Be ready to leave after midnight.*

The rest of his court packed up and left that day. Nicholas went with them. Penny had scrawled the last hasty letter to her mother: *Mama, the adventure begins in earnest now. We go to London. I won't be able to write—*

There was barely time to feel nervous—until she found herself alone in the carriage.

The seat rocked as the horses trotted on, moving south. Fritz von Gerhard rode on the box with the driver. Norfolk turned into Suffolk. She slept and woke randomly, at intervals, as the wheels rolled, bypassing Stowmarket and Ipswich on back lanes. They avoided the bustle of Colchester—where Queen Boadicea had defeated the Roman Ninth Legion—though the carriage window blinds still remained closed.

As she'd retired every night to her room in the tower to restless dreams of a lover—taking her gently in his arms, caressing her neck and her waist and her breasts, sighing his male breath into her mouth—she dreamed. She reached for him in her dreams, felt the hard column of his arms, the thrust between her legs, and imagined a pleasure more sweet than devotion or gillyflowers. Then, after he convulsed against her and spilled his seed deep in her womb, the pleasure turned to despair as he pulled away and cursed her. *They told me your father was a prince. I need money.*

In her dream she wept openly, only to wake to the lonely interior of the coach, glad that no one could witness her mad dreaming.

That last personal encounter with Nicholas spun around and around in her mind.

Thoughts whirled—her own words: *If I am to do this thing in London for you, in spite of everything you told me about what you're doing with Alexis, I want us to be friends. Otherwise it'll be intolerable for both of us. Can you do that?*

He had gazed at her like a drowning man. *I don't know.*

If it were not for what she'd promised, what she now believed would happen to Glarien if the plan failed, she would have walked out and gone to Staffordshire, where Aunt Horace could criticize her feet and her hair before taking her into the bosom of her loving family. It would have been base cowardice to do so, cowardice in the face of her own burgeoning feelings. So instead she had persisted, making the prince face her until he agreed, driven to try to understand him, tormented by the thought of him gathering wildflowers for her in the dark.

You still deceive me. Can you deny that? Can you replace all that manipulation and artifice with genuine trust and humor and honesty, as a friend might expect?

You have my word to try, he had said, and with that she'd had to be content.

By the time they reached the coast it was late afternoon.

Even though she was dressed in her breeches, the major kept her bundled in her long cloak as he helped her into a small boat. Silent, burly boatmen strove on each side, rowing south. The broad estuary of the Thames glowed like molten silver, seawater and freshwater mingling, breaking in ice-green waves over the oars. No one spoke. It was a journey from a dream, deeper and deeper into the heart of a faerie realm, where reality could be left behind and the dreamer delved through her own mind like a diver clefting down through deep water.

At last the boat nosed between reeds. The bow bumped up against a small wooden jetty, hulking in the gathering darkness. Von Gerhard stepped out and offered his hand. Penny reached for it, stepping up onto the gunnel. The boat ducked. Her fingers closed on air. With a sickening splash, she fell into the water.

Gasping, she grabbed for the slimy wooden piers. Before she could sink much past her waist, the major grabbed her collar and dragged her unceremoniously onto the jetty. Water splashed over his coat, wetting him, too. He took her arm as she squelched along a narrow, muddy path into Kent. A second carriage was waiting.

As she and the major approached, the door opened and a familiar, haunting voice said, "Ah, the ocean delivers Aphrodite on a scallop shell, accompanied by a rather grizzled Triton, from their golden palace at the bottom of the sea. In spite of that, I did not expect you *both* to be wet."

Penny gazed up at Nicholas, water soaking through to her skin, and laughed. So he was trying!

"It was hard to leave our watery home without bringing a little seaweed still attached," she said. "What on earth are you doing here, Your Royal Highness?"

Nicholas reached down a hand and helped her into the carriage. "I'm the other aspect of Poseidon: I bring horses."

"I'm not surprised that you choose to talk to me only in riddles, after we have barely spoken in person these two weeks. Where is Quest?"

"In London."

"Which, I am sure, bodes ill." She took a deep breath as the carriage jolted forward. "Should I be flattered that you're here in person?"

"No, you should indeed be troubled." He grinned. "After all, I'm the vampire Grand Duke of Glarien, trailing darkness and disquiet."

"Prince of bats and horses?"

"Of whatever is secret and silent. Princess Sophia's carriages have stopped at a certain inn. One lady is claiming to be her and another lady waits exclusively on her. These two females must be extracted and you must be inserted in the impostor's place."

"One impostor for another. It's rather charming, really."

He was gazing out of the carriage window where trees and houses dodged in and out of the moonlight. "It may not be charming at all. It may even be a trap. I wouldn't send you into it alone."

"Now you've done it!" She clutched at the strap as the carriage jolted. "Like strange noises in the night, that terrifies me!"

He glanced back at her, shadows and ice flames. "I thought you might appreciate familiar company, even if it's mine."

You have my word to try. "So what happens at this inn?"

"Assuming all goes according to plan, when you awake in the morning, you may ask for your ladies Gerta and Beatrice. They are immensely loyal to Sophia and being trusted with the facts."

Lists and lists of names, each carefully described, in that neat, tight handwriting. She knew exactly what these ladies looked like, their complete histories and tastes. "Then I cannot fail?"

Moonlight washed over his cheek and jaw as he smiled at her, the smile that overturned apple carts. "By definition, everything royalty does is right. Just remember that, brave Penelope."

"So no one will know I'm not the real princess?"

"No one except Carl, of course."

The carriage lurched again, skipping over a rut. Her heart lurched with it, slipping and sliding, only to leap up again with a thump. "Oh, dear God! You never mentioned this. You never mention anything. I'm led blindfolded from one sickening revelation to another. Carl will be in London?"

"Of course. Surely you realized that?"

"I did not realize it. He'll expose me!"

To her immense surprise he took her hand. "No. Hush! It's all right. He cannot possibly expose you once you're accepted by the Tsar and the Prince Regent. What can he say? 'This is not the real Sophia. I know, because I have her captive at Burg Zanich?' "

"But if he sees me before that—"

The carriage stopped. A horseman materialized out of the darkness, slipped from his mount and stepped up to the door. Nicholas leaned out and talked to him for a few minutes. Penny caught only a glimpse of dark hair and a smooth, neat skull, like a seal's, but the pale eyes in the handsome face were remarkably shrewd and intelligent.

The coach started forward as the prince leaned back in his seat. The horseman fell in behind them. "Lucas," Nicholas said. "One of my men. Everything is on track. Take courage, Princess."

"This Lucas is a spy?"

"He's a prince. Glarien is rotten with royalty. I try whenever possible to keep them in my employ."

"*A prince?* He, too, is close to the throne? You trust him?"

"I trust him." He looked back at her. "Dear God, I've never seen anything less like a boy in my life. Sit still."

She sat like a statue as he coiled her hair in both hands, pinned it on top of her head, and jammed on her cap. She closed her eyes to avoid the smoke and snow curling in his. The smell of burned cork made her wrinkle her nose as he smudged his finger over her jaw and upper lip to make a little shadow. His thumb smoothed firmly over each eyebrow. She wanted him to keep caressing, to smooth down her cheek and touch the corner of her mouth.

"There," he said, his voice chafing. "Don't lose the cap and we can enter the inn like any other travelers. Gerta will come down to fetch you. Meanwhile, my men will extract the undesirable ladies from the princess's bedroom. No one will suspect a thing."

Penny looked down at her hands. She wanted to lay her head on his shoulder and beg him. *No, protect me from this, take me in your arms and tell me it's no longer necessary.* Instead she said, in a perfect imitation of the butcher boy's broad Norfolk accent, "Can I have an ale when we get there, then, sire?"

•　•　•　•

It was very late when they arrived at the inn. Penny climbed from the carriage and clumped in through the back door after Nicholas, her shoes still sodden. Lucas slipped ahead of them and disappeared. At the end of the hallway, the door opened. A tall, strikingly handsome man smiled at the little party like a wolf. Powerfully built, lean and well muscled, he approached forty, perhaps, though there was no gray in his thick, dark hair.

Nicholas stopped dead. Penny almost bumped into him.

"Why, if it isn't pretty cousin Nico!" the man said in Glarisch. "Do you come racing to meet your bride, like your English King Henry the Eighth romantically rushing to the side of Anne of Cleves?"

"Love is mad," Nicholas said. "Anne of Cleves was Henry's Flemish mare—only one step better than calling her a cow. He divorced her as soon as he could. That isn't what I intend with the lovely Sophia."

"I shudder to think what you intend with the lovely Sophia." The man glanced around Nicholas at Penny, who had shrunk as far back into the shadows as she dared. "A boy? Don't tell me you brought Alexis? How very unoriginal!"

"Dear me!" Nicholas walked forward, forcing the older man to step aside. "If *you* cannot tell Alexis from any other boy in the dark, then who can? But why delay here in the doorway? Come, let us repair to the parlor. Perhaps you will take wine with me to toast my upcoming nuptials?"

"With pleasure," the man replied. "Though who am I to delay you, when the bride so eagerly awaits you upstairs? Of course, I had no idea things had gone so far between you. I'm rather touched to think this might be a love match, after all."

"A love match?" Nicholas asked. "Now it's your turn to be quaint. I have received word the princess is indisposed. Inconvenient, dear Carl, to say the least. But your concern for her does you credit."

Penny thought she might choke. Cousin Carl. Count Carl Zanich. Oh, dear Lord! She studied her shoes as if the secret of the Gordian knot were tied there. What on earth did Nicholas want her to do? She shuffled along behind them as the men strode across the taproom. The light was brighter. Suppose Carl took one good look at her and saw the resemblance to Sophia? And what did it mean—that Carl was here, at this inn, as if waiting for Nicholas?

"Chasms of dastardly possibilities yawn," Nicholas said suddenly.

Penny realized she had heard nothing of what Carl had just said. She looked around the room. A few travelers sat at tables, eating or drinking, or warming their feet by the fire. It all seemed very English and safe, a fashionable posting house just south of London, where a princess had commanded most of the rooms for her suite.

"So your spies didn't know I was here?" Carl asked. "Inefficient of you! Mine tell me you have been secretly enjoying the favors of a woman in Norfolk—so piquant and refreshing! My lips are sealed on the subject, of course. It would not do to upset Sophia at such a delicate moment."

"Then I beg you will say nothing to her," Nicholas replied. "For the sake of all our sensibilities."

"Alas," Carl said. "She is as sick as a cat at a wake and remains retired, even to me. Women are fickle creatures. Perhaps she believes it's bad luck for the groom to see the bride before the wedding."

Nicholas turned and snapped his fingers under Penny's nose. "You are gaping, lad! Go, see to our rooms."

Having no idea where to go or what to do, Penny bowed, hiding her face, and mumbled, "Yes, sire."

She turned and marched away across the room toward the hallway leading to the stairs.

Carl's voice floated over her shoulder. "A damned awkward youth, Nico! Seems to have been dipped in a river. Can't you do better than that? Or may I offer you my own services for the night?" His voice became deeply mocking, cruel. "For old times' sake?"

Penny glanced back.

"A good prince lives only to serve his loyal subjects." Nicholas gazed at him steadily, but his voice vibrated like a harp string. "I am at your disposal, cousin."

A hand caught her by the elbow. She looked up into the features of the man she had glimpsed earlier: Lucas, of the pale, intelligent eyes and dark hair. A prince and a spy. Handsome, young, smiling.

"You did well," he said. "Come with me."

"I thought Gerta was to fetch me?"

"Gerta waits upstairs. Come."

She followed him up a flight of stairs, as if following a reverie deeper into sleep. It was intensely quiet in the corridors. Silence dozed under archways and glazed candelabra with serenity. Lucas moved like a cat.

"You knew Carl was here?" she whispered.

His smile was charming, open. "Of course. Did the Grand Duke neglect to mention it?"

The shock was quickly followed by tremors of fury, yet they died away to leave her feeling numb. So his promise had been just another lie. He could not—or would not—confide in her. He still didn't know how to be friend. She had agreed to all this, but she was in over her head, just a pawn for a prince who had opened a gambit with a kingdom at stake. She tried to think through the implications, the subtleties of the game Nicholas played with his cousin.

"Won't Carl find out what we're doing? Won't he expect his impostor to keep in touch with him?"

Lucas touched her cheek briefly as he lifted away her cap. "Carl has no idea Nicholas knows Sophia's been kidnapped. He won't want Nicholas to discover what he's done, so it's in his best interests to get the Grand Duke away from here as quickly as possible. Nicholas has the same motives, of course—he doesn't want Carl to find out about you. I imagine they are riding together to London at this moment."

"And Carl's impostor?"

Candlelight silhouetted the seal-slick hair. "The woman who's been pretending to be the princess is on her way back to Glarien as we speak, trussed like a chicken with her lady-in-waiting, under the guard of Major Baron von Gerhard. Gerta has uncovered her methods of contacting Carl and can replicate them. Unless we bungle badly, he won't know."

"But what if Carl already knows about me?"

The spy grinned. "Then Fritz already lies slaughtered, and I'm about to face death—unless you think I'm also in Carl's pay? Of course, after tonight, false messages are easy enough for either side to send. Neither Nicholas nor Carl can be sure of the outcome of this encounter, until it's too late. Are you ready, ma'am?"

He pushed open a door.

London was delirious, caught in the rapture of celebrating victory. The Tsar was the man of the moment. The subtle insults traded between His Russian Imperial Highness and the Prince Regent were grounds for endless speculation and delight. The wild Cossacks, camped in Hyde Park, fascinated the beau monde, who rode out every day to observe these odd guests. There were fireworks in the parks and a riot of drinking and merriment in the streets. The fortunes of two small principalities—even with a royal wedding in the offing—were a minor event, a sideshow. Grand Duke Nicholas of Glarien was a mere embellishment, until they saw him.

It gave Nicholas a certain sour amusement when society hostesses, professing themselves ravished by his wit and charm, suddenly fell over themselves in their rush to make his acquaintance. Invitations, some discreet, some less so, arrived daily. What a sad thing that his bride remained secluded, recovering from her indisposition and the fatigues of travel! How fortunate that Count Carl Zanich was here to offer his own charm and support!

The entire Glarian and Alvian parties stayed at Rivaulx House, the London house of a marquess who was absent from home, but happy to put his property at the government's disposal. The large mansion sat in its own grounds off Piccadilly, where the gardens created an oasis of serenity in the heart of London. It was a beautiful house, yet the rooms seemed oddly cold and unused. The bed dominated the grand bedroom. Its canopy was topped with coronets at each corner, dignified with gilt strawberry leaves and alternating silver balls. Nicholas hardly noticed it. Instead he stood for some time and stared at a painting on the wall. In a long valley filled with storm-driven waters, a white horse galloped away toward distant moors, running free under the glowering sky.

A handful of rooms had been locked, including the music room and the marquess's private study. Otherwise, the great house, with its two wings flanking the public rooms at the center, was entirely at their disposal. The supposed Princess Sophia and her ladies took one wing, Nicholas and his entourage the other. Count Carl Zanich, his cousin, was of course offered a suite of his own. Yet Sophia remained secluded, claiming a wretched cold. Nicholas sent her presents every day, the little gifts purchased by his secretary in Glarien, and hoped it really was Penny who was amused by them.

With only three days left until the wedding, the line of carriages stretched all along Pall Mall and Cockspur Street. The Prince Regent was hosting a reception at Carlton House. Nicholas wasn't surprised when the Tsar sought him out for a moment's private conversation.

"We hear it rumored," Tsar Alexander said in his perfect court French, "that Princess Sophia might refuse to come here tonight, as she has refused all her invitations thus far. It begins to look like a direct affront to the Allied sovereigns. We are concerned."

"Refuse, sir?" Nicholas smiled. "I hope not. It would begin to look as if she plans to repudiate our wedding. If she does that, of course, I must renounce my claim to Glarien, for we could no longer fulfill our treaty obligations."

Carl wandered over to them and bowed deeply to the ruler of all the Russias.

"Count Zanich!" the Tsar said. "Your grand duke talks of resigning his throne if a woman proves fickle. Does that strike you as foolhardy?"

"Sir, the love of His Royal Highness's loyal subjects would never allow him to pursue such a desperate course," Carl replied.

"And my less-than-loyal subjects?" Nicholas asked. "What would they feel if Alvia abandoned me?"

"I cannot tell, sire." Carl could barely contain the gloating smile at the corner of his mouth. "I cannot speak for such men."

Nicholas put his hand on Carl's shoulder, over the heavy braid and thick fabric of his colonel's uniform. Carl was ringing like a bell, thrumming with anticipation. "Then how lucky I am to have such supporters."

Tsar Alexander smiled. With his unique blend of shrewdness and sentimentality, he was obviously impressed. The rumors were already circulating. Sophia could not attend, because she had not even come to London. She repudiated the wedding. Nicholas would be destroyed. London hostesses professed themselves devastated, while secretly planning to offer whatever solace the young grand duke might accept. Carl would already have approached the Tsar's representatives, dropped hints around Whitehall, shown himself ready to step into the breach. Politicians had started to formulate the necessary plans to control central Europe and put Glarien and Alvia in the hands of a better man.

The tightrope.

Nicholas had walked out into space on a thin wire, and still Princess Sophia refused to show her face. Did Penny stay in her rooms and quake, too afraid now the time had arrived? Was she truly ill? Or had she determined he was not worth saving and had she decided to escape all his machinations and return to her mother? Why should she risk herself for Glarien? Why should she risk herself for him? He had given her nothing, even if he had given her everything he had.

Or was Penny lost and Fritz lost? Had the unthinkable happened and had Lucas betrayed him, after all?

Carl clapped his left palm hard over Nicholas's hand. "I am yours to the death, sire," he said. "As I have been yours since you first arrived in Glarien. What were you—ten years old? A brave lad!"

"I was eleven." Nicholas shrugged off Carl's grip. "And it was you, Count Zanich, who taught me everything I needed to know about bravery."

There was a small rustle near the door. The Tsar turned. "Grand Duke Nicholas, perhaps your faith in your bride is not misplaced! The evening is to be graced, after all." His pink face broke into a beaming smile. "Indeed, indeed! Princess Sophia of Alvia!"

Nicholas stepped to the Tsar's side, where he could see her clearly. Her hair shone a pure red-gold under a tiara of diamonds and sapphires. Her neck and shoulders rose defiantly from a froth of white lace, embroidered with a fortune in seed pearls. More pearls and diamonds ran up and down the long fall of her skirts, forming a maze of little lions and swans over the train, entwined symbols of Glarien and Alvia. Her silk-and-ivory fan was encrusted with jeweled love knots. A blue sash, pinned with diamonds at the shoulder, marked her as royalty. With her ladies behind her, she paused for a moment to let her gaze sweep over the crowd, regal, imperious, a glance to make stallions fawn and brave men kneel at her feet.

His heart soared like a skylark as the crowd parted to allow her to proceed. She moved forward, smiling and speaking graciously to everyone she ought to recognize: von Pontiras, the Glarian nobles who had visited her court, the men from Alvia who were her loyal subjects.

Beside Nicholas, his rival for the throne staggered like a man suddenly struck from behind, the urbane charm stripped from his face.

"Count Zanich?" Nicholas asked. "You are ill?"

Carl rubbed one hand over his face. "No, no," he muttered. "I am quite well. Quite well. Surprise quickly becomes delight. The princess appears to have recovered."

Penny knew she would never forget it. The sensuous rub of exquisite silk petticoats, the weight of priceless jewels on her skirts, the odd feel of the tiara in her hair. A simple pleasure in the luxurious beauty of the most exquisite fabrics. *Princess for a day, Miss Lindsey! A masquerade, bolder than you've ever dreamed. A chance to make a difference to the fate of nations. Imagine the gowns and jewels you will wear, the chance to see a royal world from the inside.*

Yet wasn't this her birthright, too? Her father had been a prince. She had been trained for this role by a grand duke.

Though, of course, Nicholas had left out almost everything that mattered. As well as experimenting to dye her hair exactly the right shade, Lady Beatrice and Sophia's old nurse, Gerta, had been forced to give her an intense course of lessons in all those aspects of a princess's life that Nicholas had overlooked.

Nicholas was impossibly handsome in a brilliant court uniform, sparkling with decorations and ribbons, the collar thrusting high under his jaw. He stood in a small group with a tall man she knew must be the Tsar of Russia. Next to them, his face a mask of fury, Count Carl Zanich, the only man here who knew without question that she was an impostor, smiled like a death mask.

She opened her fan in the gesture Lady Beatrice had taken two days to teach. Fluttering it in front of her face she walked up to the three men and gave each of them the exactly correct shade of courtesy, while one after another bowed over her hand.

When the time comes to act the princess in public, your heart will pound, your stomach will play merry hell with your ribs and the exhilaration will carry you through.

Her heart leaped as Nicholas kissed the back of her knuckles. She met his eyes for a moment. Darkness and flame hovered in their depths, yet he smiled at her with the warmth of summer. *Whatever happens now,* the smile said, *thank you for this.*

Count Zanich bowed stiffly. She waited, staring at him. The moment stretched. Would he denounce her? Or was even he unsure for a moment?

Nicholas glanced at his cousin. "Why, Carl! You seem thunderstruck."

"I think we entertain a fantasy," Carl said.

The Tsar took her hand. "A fantasy of beauty! So lovely a lady should reside only in fairyland. Madam, it is Russia's turn to be thunderstruck."

"And Alvia's to be flattered." Penny coughed delicately behind her fan. "Alas, my voice is still a little strained. I quite lost it for some days. Your kindness, sir, takes away what little breath I have left."

Tsar Alexander began to beam like a child. "I have it! Russia shall give you away. Your father cannot be here, so Russia shall do it." He turned to Nicholas. "What is arranged? The Tsar must be more than a guest. Russia will honor this wedding. Russia will play the father."

Nicholas bowed. "The honor overwhelms us, sir."

"Then I shall lead this lady into the church," Alexander said. "This wedding has my blessing. My blessing and my countenance. For I can see it is a love match as well as a boon to our new peace in Europe."

Penny raised her fan to cover her blush. A love match! Her first had resulted in a hurried wedding in front of a Scottish innkeeper. Her second would have the Tsar of Russia to attend her. Yet neither wedding was destined to lead to a marriage. At the end, there was only Clumper Cottage and a life that had once contented her.

"The boy!" Carl blurted. "Good God, the boy at the inn!"

She snapped her fan and looked at him as if he were a beetle. "Do you refer to the lad Grand Duke Nicholas sent me for a pageboy, Count? Alas, he was so homesick for Glarien, I sent him home with one of my ladies who pined for her husband—I believe you know the lady. Indeed, I am sure that you do. Major Baron Friedrich von Gerhard escorts the party. Pray, do not trouble yourself about the boy, Count Zanich."

The Tsar put a hand to his heavily beribboned breast. "Page-boys need discipline, madam, but your soft heart does you credit."

"As does Count Zanich's concern," she said, smiling. "He is forever attentive. Indeed, when he came to Alvia six years ago and my father honored him with the gift of a rare stallion, he sent us back a foal each year."

"A fine bay, as I recall," Carl said.

"No, indeed, Count. A spotted horse! And every foal you sent back to us had spots as well."

"Two similar horses were sent to us at St. Petersburg," the Tsar said. "How could you forget, Count?"

"Count Zanich hides his generosity behind humility, sir," she said. "A loyal man."

"The princess flatters," Carl replied. "I am glad the foals pleased. Yet you looked changed, madam."

"I am changed." She fluttered the fan. "Isn't every woman changed by the love of the man she is about to marry? Alas, that I am such a bad traveler! I fear I have caused you all a great deal of unwarranted concern."

The Tsar offered his arm. "You will walk with me, madam?"

She gave him the exactly correct small salutation and folded her fan with a flick of her wrist. "I shall have my bridegroom for the rest of my life. Only for this one night might I have the honor of the company of His Imperial Majesty, Emperor of all the Russias. I accept with the greatest pleasure."

With her heart singing like a meadow pipit, soaring up and down in shrill delirium, Penny laid her gloved fingers on the Tsar's sleeve and walked away with him. Flirtation and politics made rather odd conversational gambits when wedded together, rather like eating sweet amber pudding with anchovy sauce, but that's when she learned why Nicholas's lessons had been vital, after all.

Carl turned to Nicholas with fury plain on his features.

"Don't stab me here," Nicholas said calmly. "It might create a scandal."

"Good God! Perhaps I should stab her!"

"It would make things damned awkward for both of us, if the princess dies in London with the sovereigns of Europe to witness it. We could hardly expect her to later rise from the dead, and I rather fear France would instantly claim Alvia."

The handsome face contorted. "Who the devil is she?"

"I have no idea what you mean," Nicholas replied. "She is Princess Sophia, and I shall marry her on Saturday. How fortunate the Tsar has taken such a liking to her! Makes things so much easier, don't you think?"

"Damn you! You did it at the inn. This woman is your whore from Norfolk!"

"No," Nicholas said. "The woman who is now on her way back to Glarien in the care of Fritz von Gerhard is your whore from Burg Zanich. Shall we go and play a game of hazard with the Prince Regent?"

"Your fat friend?" Carl asked.

"Fat, certainly," Nicholas said. "And friend, of course. It would appear that I am surrounded by friends after all."

The Carlton House grounds stretched almost the entire length of The Mall, beginning not far from Horseguards Parade and running behind St. James's Park until the Prince Regent's gardens bordered those behind Marlborough House. The trees and shrubbery shone with lanterns and tiny bells that chimed in the small breeze. Penny was handed from the Tsar to Lord Trent, from Lord Trent to the Duke of Rutley, until the names began to blur. After one glimpse of him deep in conversation with a German prince, she looked in vain for Nicholas.

In the gardens, where the throng of guests had gathered to watch a fireworks display, she was able to slip away for a few moments and stand by herself in the dark.

She didn't believe she had erred once. Not even when the Duke of Rutley said he'd seen her as an infant when he'd stopped in Alvia twenty years before. She'd remembered the names of Sophia's governesses and the details of her childhood. Sophia's father, the ailing Duke Michael, she imagined as clearly as if she knew him. After all, he was her uncle.

"Do you think you can get away with this?" A hand grasped her by the wrist and pulled her further back into the shrubbery. "Don't scream or act the fool," the voice continued. "That *would* give the game away."

"Cousin Carl?" she said. "May I call you cousin? We are loosely related, I suppose, through my mother."

"Don't bother any longer, sweetheart," Carl said. "You don't need to pretend with me."

He dragged her a few more steps. Fireworks hissed and burst far above her head. The Prince Regent's guests applauded. In the sudden burst of red and green light, Carl's face was lit like a demon's.

"You wish to tell me something?" Penny asked. "I can't imagine what. You cannot expose me without incriminating yourself."

He stared down at her, studying her features. "I wish to look at you. Do you think Nicholas has trumped me? Perhaps he has. But I have a few cards left up my sleeve. Assassination is one."

She concentrated on keeping her voice steady, as she had learned to stay steady and calm with the horses. "If a public funeral is held here in London, you could never produce the real Sophia. France would claim Alvia, then Austria would seize Glarien. They would never back down because you claimed there was a true princess jailed in your castle. You would lose everything."

He grinned and chucked her crudely under the chin. It was a gesture filled with contempt and brutality. Penny flinched, but Carl only laughed.

"But what if I were to assassinate my pretty cousin Nicholas?"

Eleven

More fireworks exploded in a burst of white embers, as if the stars were torn from their moorings and rained down to earth. *Ceres, Pallas, Juno and Vesta.* Fruitfulness, war, queen of heaven, and Vesta—who was Vesta? It only mattered because it had all been written in his handwriting. The neat, tight letters ranked one after another on the careful sheets.

"You think you could succeed undetected?" she asked, while her heart shattered in long trails of white lights. "Surely if Nicholas died in suspicious circumstances, Princess Sophia would never marry you?"

Carl laughed again. "You're in love with him! Sad. Has he bedded you?"

She snapped open the fan. "How dare you ask such a thing!"

The handsome face filled with pleasure. "No, he has not. And, like all women, you think it only his noble sensibilities. I'm charmed. What has he told you? That he's a virgin?" A Catherine wheel began to whir and shriek, sending showers of red sparks through the trees. "My dear Miss—what should I call you?"

"Call me Sophia," she said. "Why do you think Grand Duke Nicholas should have told me any such thing?"

"Obviously you were Nico's woman in Norfolk. You know that Alexis spies for me?"

She felt sick. *Carl threatened to kill their pets for fun, for target practice.* "It does not concern me."

"In this case, Alexis rather missed the point." He reached out to caress the lace over her breast, running his nails past the lions and swans picked out in seed pearls. "He told me you existed. But he didn't find out who you were, and, of course, he didn't know the remarkable resemblance. Do you think I should punish the boy? Or do you think Nicholas's patronage is punishment enough?"

"Don't touch me."

He grinned. "You're a virgin? Better and better. I admit, I did wonder."

His hand ran up to touch the skin of her throat. He rested his palm there, the thumb and forefinger pressing just under her jaw. "You believed he was a man of twenty-seven who'd never known the pleasures of the flesh and the thought fascinated you, didn't it? I know women, Miss Sophia. I know you. I know your weaknesses. You can hardly blame me if I intend to exploit them."

She grasped his wrist, but she was pinned against a bush, unable to escape. "Why are you telling me all this?"

"Because whatever he told you, Nicholas is experienced in sensual gratification. I'm sure he had his reasons for lying to you. He lies to everyone. He was a sneak, even as a boy. I imagine it amuses him, manipulating you in his little schemes. He and I will laugh about it later. You poor deluded creature."

Rockets charged up over the trees, wailing. Far away the crowd gasped and applauded as they burst and rained sighing sparkles back to earth.

The grip at her throat disappeared.

Penny opened her eyes to find she was alone. Shaking, she put her hand over her mouth. A gypsy prince had once glowered down at her by the ruins of a medieval manor: *I didn't think Carl knew. Though he has reached into every other crevice of my soul and tried to pollute it, I thought this one memory at least was inviolate.*

She felt polluted, sick.

What was the truth? How could she possibly know? *If you have come here thinking you can reclaim that English boy, forget any such delusions. I am not a particularly good or admirable man.* She had plunged unwittingly into layers of intrigue, her narrow Norfolk domain shattered by the scope of this new world. Could she adjust? Everything she had ever known seemed petty compared with this.

"Why are you hiding here?" a voice asked gently. "You are splendid, magnificent, royal. I lay my heart at your feet." Penny glanced up. Nicholas grinned down at her, a bright, open smile filled with jubilation. Slowly the smile dissolved. "Oh, damnation!" He leaned his head against the trunk of a tree, dark eyes searching the night sky. *"Carl!"*

"Yes," she said. "Carl. You might have told me he would be at the inn. You knew, of course."

His fists clenched. "I knew."

Stars winked far above their heads. The fireworks had stopped. The scent of gunpowder mingled oddly with the damp, woodsy odors of the garden. "You might have warned me that he would go, literally, for the jugular."

He spun around to face her. "He cannot harm you. He would lose everything if he did."

"Another promise?" Penny glanced away. "You are a man filled with empty promises and a damnable ability to trust the wrong people. Who was Vesta?"

He was caught off guard. *"Vesta?* Goddess of fire. She was worshipped in temples with the burning of an eternal flame. Why?"

"Oh, of course! The vestal virgins. Trusted with tending a fire forever; their only reward a pledge of chastity—and death if they broke it. I'm sorry you can't trust me. I'm sorry you can't see that it would be better if I were forewarned about things. I'm sorry that I ever believed for one moment that you might be a friend. But I will let the Tsar give me away at your wedding, so the world knows Glarien and Alvia are joined in sacred union. After that, I'm glad I shall never see you again."

He stood like a moth stabbed through the thorax with a biologist's pin: rigid, wings spread, sensitive antennae forever stilled. "Good," he said. "It is better so. You will go back to Rascall St. Mary and pick up the reins of your life. I've created a fund in your name. You and your mother will never want for anything."

She tried to push past him. "Damn you! Do you think I do this for financial reward?"

He shuddered. "I can't bear it either!" With both hands he took her by the arms. "We could kindle a fire, you and I, that would roar to the heavens and burn away all of Carl's abomination. But there's a nation waiting and a princess locked in a tower. Fritz and Lucas will find her. They *must* find her. And I must go back to her. Do you understand?"

"Why didn't you warn me about Carl? When I realized he had waited for us at that inn, I was terrified. Now he traps me under the nose of the Prince Regent and the Tsar to let me know just how foul he is. Why can't you explain anything?"

Agony roared in the depths of his eyes. The torture of St. Catherine, broken on the wheel. "I didn't want you corrupted by this. He will not dare to harm you."

"No, he says he will harm you," Penny said.

"And you believed him?"

She wanted only to get away, to try to think. "I don't know what to believe. In a few days it won't matter, will it?"

"Yet it has mattered." He reached out one hand to touch her cheek, fleetingly, gently. "I met you."

The elegant long fingers caught her chin and lifted it. For a moment he searched her eyes. Penny gazed back, her blood pounding, but he pulled away and left her.

It was not possible to keep secrets in any royal household. Penny realized, little by little, that most of Sophia's ladies had guessed the truth within days. Lady Beatrice, one by one, explained to them. The ladies were immediately determined to support the masquerade, for their loyalty was all for Princess Sophia, and Carl was universally disliked.

Yet the ice on which Penny skated felt thinner and thinner. It made her breathless and cold, as if she were to swoop and whirl with the Tsar of Russia, the Prussians, the British, on an endless frozen lake. She took carriage rides in Hyde Park. She attended ceremonies and balls. Nicholas was remote and courteous without offering another private word, though he always appeared whenever she needed public support. And all of London swooned to please him.

Penny watched it. The glittering, artificial world of the beau monde. A world of assignations and flirtation, where lords openly kept mistresses. And their wives—only a little more discreetly—took other lords for lovers. If Nicholas wished it, he could spend the days before his wedding in a succession of welcoming beds. Yet he had told her he had never known a mistress and she had believed it. So why did she also believe Carl? *Grand Duke Nicholas is experienced in sensual gratification.*

She lay awake in her wing of Rivaulx House. He had created a fund for her. After the wedding, he expected her to go back to her quiet life in Norfolk. Yet Carl had spoken of assassination, and she thought he had meant it. She tried to put herself in Carl's place. What would she do now if a throne were her goal?

Oh, God! She sat up, her hands flailing in the dark. Oh, God! Slipping from the bed, she grabbed a robe. Not the torn cotton from her real life, but a silk and lace concoction, embroidered with swans. On tiptoe she crept across the room and opened the door. Lady Beatrice snored gently in her bed in the anteroom. Gerta mumbled and turned over, but didn't wake. Penny stole across the carpet and opened the door into the corridor.

A man sat slumped in a chair, his chin dropped forward onto his chest. *In any army in Europe, to fall asleep on guard duty usually warrants immediate death by hanging.* A guard, asleep. *Eric will muck out the stalls and clean all the other men's boots for a week. He will do it in addition to the rest of his duties. Do you think that's fair?*

She stopped, stunned by the compassion of it. Whatever else he might be, Nicholas was trying to carve a new path and bring enlightenment to the country that had formed Carl. For that, she must help him. But was she a deluded creature to break her heart and pine for her dark prince for the rest of her life?

Rivaulx House slumbered peacefully. She moved silently

down corridors and through public rooms to the wing where Nicholas slept. A few candles had been left to burn, casting a soft, flickering glow over the furnishings and plaster. At the end of the corridor leading to the marquess's state bedroom, she stopped and listened. Lost in the empty, echoing hallways, someone wept. The sound was muffled and intermittent, as if the weeper tried to stifle his grief. The sound of a child who did not want to be caught shedding tears.

In the corridor, pacing quietly up and down, Eric and Ludger guarded the prince's bedroom and ignored the sound. Penny flattened herself against the wall and watched them. Should she march up to these men and tell them to stand aside, she wished to go to the prince in the night? She was a fool. Nicholas, master of chess, would have analyzed and predicted every one of Carl's moves. He had no intention of letting himself get killed. So he hardly needed a warning from her. Yet she wished fervently that he would discuss it with her, that he had discussed everything with her from the beginning. Instead he acted alone, directing the play, while she was just one more lowly player.

The sobbing stopped. The handful of candles burned steadily. Shadows wavered in doorways and alcoves, filling dark empty spaces at the far ends of the hall. Penny turned to retrace her steps and bumped into Alexis. The boy trembled, his gaze slipping away from her. His hair shone like a baby chick's down.

"Alexis, for heaven's sake! What's the matter?"

The bloodshot blue eyes glanced up. "It is nothing, madam."

"Nonsense. It is something. Can you tell no one?"

He rubbed the back of one hand over his nose like a village boy and shook his head.

She grasped his arm and pulled him back along the corridor, opening the door into the first room behind her, stepping backward into a black space filled with faint gray shadows, the smudged gleam of furniture in moonlight. "Alexis, I know you don't sleep, that you weep sometimes in the night. What is it?"

He shook his head.

"Then you and I are going to march out into that corridor, ask

Eric and Ludger to step aside and make the Grand Duke explain all this to me."

"No need for such drastic measures," a voice said from the shadows. "Even princes may creep about in the dark."

She let go of Alexis. Nicholas sat on the windowsill, the dark wash of night sky black on black behind him. He slipped from his perch and crossed the room to the door. Flint snapped on steel. Candles flared. A harpsichord sat with the lid up, as if the musician had just risen and walked out.

Penny glanced about. A violin lay on a small table nearby. "The music room? I thought it was locked."

Nicholas smiled. "It was. Therefore it made a good trysting place."

Alexis had snapped to attention. Nicholas nodded to him and the boy fled. The prince closed the door behind him.

She marched across the carpet and sat down on a sofa near the harp. "Ah. Trysts in the night? Who were the trysters?"

The prince stood quietly, arms folded over his chest. He was dressed in dark trousers and black shirt, his hair tousled. "There were several trysts," he said. "The first was between Alexis and my cousin. I put a stop to it."

"He was taking more secrets to Carl?"

Nicholas watched the candle flame as if craving it. "You told me you wanted me to explain things to you. I said I wanted to keep you from certain kinds of knowledge. You may accept that something unpleasant has been averted, or you may know the details. If you insist, I will tell you."

"Tell me," she said. "I'm tired of moving in the dark."

Light and shadow dwelled peacefully enough on his face and on the dark shirt and high collar, yet a windstorm roared in his eyes. "Very well," he said at last. "I will do it, because I trust your integrity and your compassion absolutely. But I would rather not. After all, the price for biting into the apple of knowledge is expulsion from paradise."

"I was stolen from the Garden of Eden the day I met you," she said. "Your attempts to keep me unsullied are absurd. Why does Alexis sometimes weep as if his heart would break?"

He glanced restlessly at the tall windows, graceful and elegant in their arched alcoves. "Penny, your world isn't mine. I have tried to save Alexis. I believe I'm succeeding. Being in this house with Carl makes it more difficult for him, that's all."

"Why?" she asked. "Why must you talk in riddles? I'm not a child. I ran away to be married when I was fifteen and learned then that life isn't a fairy tale. I see a boy whose loyalties are torn, perhaps, but I believed him when he told me he loved you."

Nicholas vibrated like a powerful horse held back by a checkrein. If the rein were to snap, would he explode into violence? "Alexis might think so. I don't know. I don't know what that would mean. I don't talk to him about such things. I just try to let him know that his dignity is inviolate with me, that the boundaries of his world are within his control, that he is safe."

"Safe from what?"

He paced, striding to the window and back. "Alexis was taken to Burg Zanich when he was five years old. His father had died. His grandfather wanted him trained in a more vigorous household, one where he would learn the requirements of greatness. Where better than at Carl's little court in the mountains—manly, robust, yet intimately involved with all the subtleties and intrigues of the throne? When I was that age, I was worming my way into your mother's generous heart. She gave me nothing but love and tenderness. Alexis received something quite different. It went on for seven or eight years, until I was able to extricate him."

"Carl was cruel?"

He said nothing for a moment, then dropped the words like stones. "Carl is—Carl is an able administrator, an excellent soldier. He is a brilliant man in many ways. But it is my cousin's nature to be brutal to children."

That whip-slim back, bent over a dropped sword. The faint scars on the white skin. "Alexis was beaten?"

"Among other, more imaginative, things."

She began to shake. Hideous, deep shudders. "How did you know what was happening? Did Alexis tell you?" He shook his head. "Then how did you know?"

He stopped and rested his palms on the window molding,

dropping his forehead to the glass. A tremor ran up and down his spine. "It's my business to know everything. How can I rule Glarien if I don't know what's going on? As soon as I could, I took Alexis into my own household. The price didn't matter. When Carl demanded the boy see him tonight, I put a stop to it. Alexis has been recovering."

"But he can't sleep?"

"He has nightmares. When that happens, we play chess. Nothing has to be said. I am keeping him safe, Penny. It's all right."

She shook her head and discovered her own tears. Her mouth and chin were damp with salt moisture. "What were you doing here in this dark room?"

"It was private. I intercepted Alexis and brought him in here. He is old enough now, I think, to understand deeper layers of complexity. Of his own free will he confessed he was spying. He thought he ought to be punished for it. Perhaps he was going to let Carl punish him. Now he knows that nothing he has done has betrayed me."

"You could have told him before," Penny said.

"No, I could not. He had to believe what he was sending was true. I, too, was trained partly by Carl. I told you that if you insisted, you would learn about foulness. Now you have."

It was a world alien to her, unimaginably distant from her Norfolk life. Yet her own father—

"So Alexis doesn't matter any longer, now the wedding is to go forward?"

Nicholas spun from the window, his eyes stark. "Do you think I can step aside and let Carl marry Sophia? Let Carl have absolute control of boys like Alexis?"

"I understand," she said. "And I see it was better for the confession to come from him."

"I thought so. I have tried to balance the needs of this boy with the needs of a nation. On occasion the nation had to win, though I've tried to make it up to Alexis in other ways. Now I have just balanced the needs of that nation against your need to understand. You just won."

"I am flattered," she said bitterly.

"You are in shock. I wish to God you had not found Alexis tonight. If you wish to abandon the masquerade and go home now, I shan't blame you."

Penny closed her eyes. She had seen them together, prince and boy. She had known there was something they shared and not guessed the nature of it. But Nicholas wasn't cruel, while Carl—

"I'm surprised you haven't killed him," she said.

"Carl?" He smiled as if trying to offer comfort. "I'm a sovereign prince. No one would stop me. But what kind of monarch takes the lives of his personal enemies? What would happen if I once gave in to that temptation?"

"Yes, I can see that. But you are tempted?"

"Good God! I am tempted daily. The enticement to destroy him lives like a burn in my right hand. Do the ends justify the means? I don't know. Sometimes I have to believe so, or I couldn't live with myself. I practice diplomacy, a form of lying. I manage my men, a form of manipulation. I've invaded and taken over your life, a form of despotism. I've had to believe it was necessary. But I have never taken a life or ordered a life taken—not even Carl's—for any expediency."

She didn't know what to offer him, how to show him what she felt. All that was left was to let him move into something abstract, something away from the personal. "Yet kings have done so and history might have thought them right."

He moved again, walking restlessly about the room. "Don't play temptress, Penny!"

She leaned forward, pressing her hands over her forehead. "It's the great question always, isn't it? Good men cannot stand by and watch evil triumph, but if I must become like my enemy in order to destroy him, then my enemy has won."

His voice warmed. "I have to respect the fact that Carl didn't kill me. When I first arrived in Glarien, it would have been easy. An accident, a sickness. Children are easy to dispose of. He punished me. He hated my existence. But he didn't murder me."

"Though you stood between him and a crown—like Richard

the Third and the little princes in the Tower? Richard was also a celebrated soldier, an honest administrator."

"Who believed anything was justified for the security of England? Certainly, he knew he would make a great king and that for a child to sit on the throne invited disaster. Yet when the princes were murdered, there was disaster anyway and he lost his crown on Bosworth Field."

"In a thornbush," she said. "So you don't believe Richard was simply an evil man?"

"We'll never know, will we? History has been written by the victors. I think it likely he was a excellent leader for his time, who gave way to this one overwhelmingly evil temptation and paid very bitterly for it. I'm trying to pick the right path, Penny. I didn't want this sovereignty. I would have been content to live out my days at Rascall Hall. But I cannot kill the man who refrained from murdering me when he had the chance."

"Why did you tell me you were not a good man?"

He was gazing down at the violin. He touched the bow gently. The horsehair was frayed, long disused. "Because it is true."

"I would beg to differ," Penny said gently. "But what I think doesn't matter. I will stand with you and speak vows for Sophia. The rest, I imagine, you have already planned in your capable way. Then we shall never see each other again."

He looked up. Her heart leaped, running hard like a fugitive. Though it couldn't make any difference. Nicholas would spend the rest of his life with the princess. There would be no role for Penny Lindsey after the wedding.

Surf pounded in her dream, crashing and retreating from a distant shore. On a warm bed of sand she lay enraptured by her lover. Her breasts ached, her blood ran fire. He touched and caressed, his mouth warm and smooth, his hands firm and graceful. In long, sure strokes he outlined her flank and the curve of her waist, over and over. Dark eyes filled with smoke smiled down into hers as he bent to kiss her. Moaning, desperate, ravished, the surf boomed ever closer. She sank her fingers into his lean shoulders, opening her legs for him, longing for the hard thrust and slide of his desire. *Nicholas! Nicholas!*

"Madam," a female voice said as the shutters crashed open. "It is morning. Lady Beatrice has the list of your engagements for the day."

She struggled awake. Her ladies-in-waiting stood ready. Like the prince, she would be bathed and dressed by others' hands, petted and prodded to meet their expectations of royalty. A prison. For Nicholas, a life sentence.

The day passed in a blur of diamonds and sunshine. A carriage ride in the park. An inspection of her little Alvian bodyguard. An afternoon reception at St. James's Palace. An evening at some huge ball. She nodded and smiled brightly to everyone, even Nicholas, even Carl. The note was waiting when she returned to Rivaulx House. It was almost dawn. In one more day she would marry her dark prince.

She read the few sentences over and over. *I have a proposition, Miss Sophia,* the note read. *If you wish the wedding to go forward as planned, don't go to Nico with this. After your breakfast. In the library. You may bring an escort, if you wish—Zanich.*

She thought it through as carefully as she could. Carl had nothing to gain by harming her. The library was close to her own suite. The house was filled with her allies. If she screamed, guards would come running. She could bring Gerta and Lady Beatrice to witness. She would have only a few minutes between breakfast and her first engagement. Very probably he only meant to try to frighten her, or win her loyalty away from Nicholas with more foul stories about him. It was better to face him and let him know she could not be cowed. Yet she feared and mistrusted the very idea of another private conversation with Carl.

Carl was sitting in a large leather chair near the fireplace when she came into the library. He did not stand up. Penny marched across the long room. Gerta and Lady Beatrice hovered behind her.

He grinned, handsome as Casanova. "Your faithful ladies may linger by the door. What I have to say is best kept private."

She waved the women away and sat down, absurdly comforted by the sight of them waiting patiently on the other side of the room. Gerta was as solid and irrefutable as Mrs. Butteridge. Lady Beatrice was loyal and elegant in her court dress for the day.

"If you wish to malign the Grand Duke," Penny said quietly, "by all means, go ahead. I shall listen carefully, but nothing you say can make any difference."

Carl flicked open a snuffbox. "Sweetheart, you are delicious. Why should I disparage poor Nico? No, I am here to tell you something else: Von Pontiras will assassinate my cousin during the wedding."

Her hands clenched on the arms of her chair. Penny closed her eyes. *Nicholas!* Carl could not denounce her, but what would happen if he succeeded in killing the prince? Yet this made no sense. "Von Pontiras, the Alvian minister? Why?"

The snuffbox vibrated a little in his hands. Inside the lid was a painting of cherubs. "Because I have his wife in my control. If he does not do as we have arranged, I will be forced to send orders for her demise. Sad, but necessary."

Penny felt ill, as if cold, stiff hands clutched at her stomach. Yet she had stood day after day behind a screen and witnessed Nicholas in his role as prince. To achieve his ends he prevaricated, manipulated, hid the truth. He did it because that was how the world worked, the real world where a naive plunge into self-righteous virtue could have appalling consequences.

She answered in the calm, dispassionate voice of a princess. "So Nicholas dies. You return in triumph to Glarien. And Sophia refuses you. Obviously she refuses you, or you'd have disposed of Nicholas before now. You cannot force her, because the minute she appeared in public—and she would eventually have to appear in public—she would appeal to her father, Duke Michael. Your schemes are totally empty."

He took a pinch of snuff and touched each nostril delicately with a handkerchief. "Well, they *were* a little empty, yes. Which is why I have Sophia secreted. It bought me some time. In time, I shall persuade her it is best for her to marry me. Duke Michael is frail—his death is also only a matter of time. But now I see new possibilities. You have created them."

She made herself relax, moving her hands casually into her lap. "How?"

The carved lips smiled as if inviting her to share a wonderful joke. "If Nico is assassinated by von Pontiras, a loyal servant of Sophia's, it would put her in an awkward position, don't you think? Everyone must assume it's by her orders. What could you do? There you are, standing at the altar next to a corpse. If you expose your masquerade, I could make things very ugly for you. Alas, Nico will no longer be there to protect you. So you would continue to play princess."

"I would not," she said.

"Not willingly, perhaps. And rather a desperate measure. However, if Nico is assassinated, what else could you do? The grieving Glarian court will be in disarray. If it is known at that moment that the real princess isn't there, she could quite convincingly be shown to be complicit in the murder, while I am absolutely innocent. I have already laid the groundwork, sweetheart. Thus for the sake of the real Sophia, you would repudiate von Pontiras and offer to make up for the dastardly deed of your own official by marrying me for the sake of peace. It will work."

It bought me some time. She must buy time! Penny looked up, forcing indifference into her voice. "Why not allow the wedding to go forward? If you can persuade Princess Sophia to take you willingly, you can murder Nicholas later. I would already be out of the picture and you could step in to comfort the grieving widow. An assassination in London would raise more questions, create more chaos, than a quiet murder in your own homeland."

He smiled, drumming fingers on the arm of his chair. "Ah, I see Nico has been training you well. Your argument almost convinces me. Indeed, my desires take on the flavor of a whim. Nevertheless, von Pontiras will kill Nicholas tomorrow, unless you do as I ask. I must secure your cooperation, you see, and I thought the promise of assassination might be enough to move you."

Haughty. The look of a woman prepared to order a flogging, if necessary. "How do I know he won't do it anyway?"

"I will give you an order rescinding the one about his wife. You can deliver it to von Pontiras yourself."

She hid fear, as she had hidden it from Driver, thundering past her in the dark barn. "Why do you think it would matter to me? I only help Grand Duke Nicholas for money."

One elegant fingernail tapped on the lid of the snuffbox. "A lie, sweetheart. The thought of Nico's death sent cold fingers down your spine. I know you. I know your type. You're in love. You will sacrifice anything for him, won't you? Recognizing that gave me the idea. Besides, fail me—or tell Nico about this—and von Pontiras's wife dies."

She closed her eyes, remembering lists of names in a neat, controlled hand. Von Pontiras and his wife had been married twelve years. They had three young children. It was reputed to be a love match. She must tell Nicholas and let him find a way out.

"It will not work. I shall not go along with it."

He leaned forward, eyes fixed like a pointer sighting prey. "Yes, you will. For the sake of Countess von Pontiras. Tell Nico and she dies—don't believe for one moment I won't know. I will make Alexis come here and tell me."

The thin ice she had been skating on cracked. "What do you want me to do?"

Carl stood up and adjusted his coat. "Indulge a little fancy of mine, that's all." He grinned down at her. "My tastes are eclectic. It has driven me almost to distraction that I cannot touch Sophia. Think about it! I kidnapped her. I keep her imprisoned. But I cannot touch her."

Ice fractured under her feet with the cold water waiting. Frozen wastelands poisoned. "Certainly she will hardly marry you, if you rape her first." Her voice clinked like icicles breaking.

The snuffbox dropped into her lap. "Rape? My dear creature! How crude. I much prefer willing partners. However, you are her double. As an added benefit, you are untouched by Nico. It's so delightful. So, you will come to my bed tonight, the night before the wedding. If you don't, I will destroy Nicholas tomorrow."

The ice fractured. Freezing water buffeted, driving the air from her lungs. She panted for a breath, for the clean bright air, while dark green water closed over her head. "I don't understand," she said at last. "Why should I trust you? How will forcing me to your bed help you win Glarien or the hand of the princess? What part does it play in any scheme for victory?"

He leaned over her chair, handsome, smiling. "None, sweetheart. That comes later. I don't do this for the throne. I do it for pleasure. A small revenge for being deprived of Alexis. Let Nico stand at the altar with a woman who has just come from my bed. Then I won't kill him, because I want to see his face when he discovers it."

"He won't care," she said, drowning, freezing, in an arctic ocean.

"Oh, he'll care," Carl said. "He'll care, especially when I tell him what it was like."

She didn't know where she found the strength to stand, but she stood and faced him, his snuffbox clenched in one fist. "Alas, you are such a bad judge of character, Count. All you had to do was offer me enough money. You could simply have paid me to stay away tomorrow. So much more direct. Instead you have just confirmed my resolution to help Nicholas to his throne. I hope one night of debauchery with me is worth that."

She stared at him until he stepped aside. With her ladies following, she swept from the room. She made it all the way to her own suite, before she sat down, shaking uncontrollably.

"What is it?" Gerta asked gently.

Penny shook her head. How could she tell them, these kindly, wholesome women? *Carl wishes to hurt me, because he thinks he can use that to cause Nicholas pain. If I give in, I play right into his hands. If I do not, then Alexis suffers and the mother of three children—*

Lady Beatrice gave her a glass of wine. Penny tried to take it, but discovered she was still holding Carl's snuffbox, the one with the cherubs. Why had he given it to her? She opened the lid and found out. A painting, especially commissioned, obviously. Not cherubs. Little boys.

"I cannot go out right now," she said as choking nausea rose.

"I am ill. Pray send my regrets to Grand Duke Nicholas and the Tsar."

Gerta picked up the snuffbox and took it away.

It felt like cowardice. A paralyzing, wretched cowardice. Penny forced herself to dress and make several of her state appearances that afternoon. She even managed to return to her room and let the women lace her into a fabulous ball gown. Thousands of tiny silver-dyed feathers, stitched with diamonds, formed the body and wings of a swan stretched over the skirt. All the Allied leaders, the Prince Regent, the Tsar, the Prussians and Germans, were coming to Rivaulx House for a grand state reception. It would last almost until morning and then she would change into her wedding dress.

If she did not visit Carl in the meantime, von Pontiras would kill the bridegroom at the altar. The cowardice was that she couldn't seem to think about it or plan any strategy. She didn't dare tell Nicholas, in case Carl somehow found out and made Alexis pay a hideous price for it. *I have already laid the groundwork, sweetheart.* She was out of her depth, in a house full of spies. She felt as if she had drowned in deep waters. The ice had creaked and wailed as it closed finally over her head. She had vague thoughts that perhaps when she had Carl alone—when she had the chance—she could stab him, then confess the whole scheme.

But she didn't know what would happen to Nicholas if she did it.

Meanwhile, the sacrifice of one night was hardly so great, if it brought about the marriage and secured the prince on his throne. Women throughout history had bedded men they feared and hated when necessary. Afterward, she could cope. And Nicholas would be free to secure his destiny.

Yet she felt there was some great flaw in it all, that if she were better at chess she would be able to see the moves and countermoves and where they might lead. Instead, she tormented herself trying to think of a way out and saw none.

For the sake of Countess von Pontiras. Tell Nico and she dies.

Twelve

The reception flowed into several rooms, one leading from another. Rivaulx House glittered and echoed. Plaster swags on the walls mimicked the ladies' rich drapery. Chandeliers repeated the reflections of diamonds and rubies, silver and gold. There was dancing somewhere and a supper laid out in a room nearby. In alcoves and on balconies, groups of musicians played softly, the melodies from one room overlapping with the airs from another. Guests circulated, in a steady milling of hot, decorated bodies, from one group to the next. Royalty, nobility, ministers, officials.

If a revolutionary put gunpowder in the basement of Rivaulx House tonight, Nicholas thought wryly, he could rid most of Europe of her leadership at one blow. Of course, he had arranged to have the basements well guarded.

He found Penny at last in the largest room near the front of the house. He stopped and watched her as she chatted with the guests. Her ball gown drifted and fluttered like a bird's wing, elegant, graceful, intensely alluring. A diamond tiara sat in her hair, which was slightly redder than its natural color. She smiled as the Tsar joined her, nodding and listening intently, flattering and regal, a princess with her equals.

Before he could go up to her, the Prince Regent seized him

by the sleeve and dragged him away toward the wine table, filling his ears with a long tale about the latest paintings he had managed to secure for his collection. Penny turned a little and saw them. With a small, distracted frown, she twisted away.

Candlelight and diamonds danced together. He remembered her hair in a rough flaxen braid. He remembered her in a torn cotton dressing gown, berating him. The desire burned in him still, just as fiercely, like a forest fire crackling and consuming its way through dense trees, a roar of need, lit constantly by the brilliant flare of hot flame. Princes before him had torn apart kingdoms, destroyed nations, to follow the lure of that blaze. Helen of Troy, Anne Boleyn, Cleopatra, Queen Guinevere. How could he allow Penny Lindsey of Rascall St. Mary to have that on her conscience?

"You do agree, sir?" The Prince Regent thrust the point home with a jab of his wineglass. "Sir?"

Nicholas smiled. "Your keen analysis, sir, as usual leaves your listeners in awe."

He hoped the hell it made sense. The Prince Regent grinned, apparently satisfied, just as Lady Beatrice came up to join them. Several more minutes of wine and witticisms passed, before Nicholas was able to walk her into a corridor and confront her alone.

"She met with Carl this morning," Lady Beatrice said without preamble. "She came away very shaken, profoundly upset."

"You have no idea what transpired?"

"None at all, except he gave her this snuffbox."

Nicholas took it and flipped open the lid. A wall of dread imprisoned him for a moment, then he thrust the snuffbox deep into an inner pocket. In the next instant, white-hot rage flared. At his hip he wore an elaborate sword, part of his uniform. He saw himself draw it, saw the blade plunge into Carl's chest, saw his enemy fall ashen-faced to the floor while the company gasped and cried out. How would English law deal with a foreign prince who murdered one of his own subjects on British soil? Was murder merely a social lapse for a sovereign?

How much worse the temptation, when it might win him everything he desired! He could probably kill Carl and escape any personal punishment. It might cost him Sophia and the throne, but if Carl were dead, he wouldn't want the throne. He could retire to the country with Penny Lindsey—except he couldn't live with her or with himself, if he were a murderer.

If he gave in to this desire—the desire to take a life—then, like Richard of England, life, soul and crown might as well be torn apart in a thornbush. He was a living embodiment of the state—of law and justice. Only if a court could find Carl guilty, only if there were evidence of a crime, could his cousin be condemned to death.

Yet he knew something foul was in the air. He had watched Penny laugh over her fan at something the Tsar said, but what he had seen was her terror, so thinly masked he thought Alexander of Russia must offer to help her to a seat. Instead the Tsar had said something else and she had acted the princess, unconcerned, happy about her wedding in the morning. Then she had frowned when Nicholas had thought to join her. He had found it hard to approach her—even find her in the multitude of rooms—all evening. So she was avoiding him. Why? Was she afraid of someone's reaction if they were seen together, if she were seen talking to her fiancé tonight?

He thanked Lady Beatrice and let her go, then leaned against the wall for a moment, staring into space. Knights leaped, bishops sailed down diagonals, rooks crashed along rank and file, sweeping away pawns until they checkmated the king. So what would Carl plan to cause Nicholas the most pain? What diabolical catastrophe could Carl precipitate this evening to create the most advantage for himself? And how the devil would it involve Penny?

"There you are, sir! Where the devil has your bride got to? Haven't seen her in an hour or more." It was plump George, the Prince Regent.

Nicholas bowed his head. "Perhaps she has run away with one of your English dandies, sir. How can we mere princes compete?"

George laughed, then glanced at a clock visible on the mantel in the next room, flanked by candelabra of gold and backed by a huge gilt-rimmed mirror. "Two o'clock!" he exclaimed.

"You have an appointment, sir? Perhaps an invitation from my cousin?"

The Prince Regent looked back at him. "Devil of a guess, sir! Count Zanich invited me upstairs to his suite—says he brought a most unusual form of ore with him from Glarien. Going to take Lord Trent and a few stuffy lords from the Foreign Office. Show them what your mines are producing these days—why we must secure this marriage, what? The count said anytime after two would suit him, before he retires. You will come along, sir? A moment of peace away from the ladies?"

"I have seen a great many samples of ore, sir." Nicholas bowed from the waist. "And I am never tired of the ladies." He winked. "If you will excuse me?"

He walked casually away from the Prince Regent, pressing back through the throng, passing along corridors, avoiding eye-contact, until he reached the servants' stairway. Out of sight of the company, he raced up the stairs two and three at a time and tore down the hallways leading to Carl's suite. Pray God it was not too late!

Penny folded her fan and set it on a chair. Her hands felt clumsy, as if they belonged to someone else. She had fortified herself with two extra glasses of wine. Carefully she peeled back her gloves, taking the tip of each finger and wiggling it free.

"I usually have more fastidious tastes," Carl said. "Yet it's rather amusing to think of violating a woman who brings with her the undeniable stench of the byre. Take off the dress, sweetheart. Let me see what a peasant looks like in her shift."

Carl lounged comfortably on the bed, watching her through a quizzing glass. His dark hair was deliberately tousled, elegantly framing his handsome face. He had already shed his jacket and waistcoat and kicked away his shoes. Penny draped her gloves over the back of the chair, carefully arranging the fingers, folding the arms along their delicate seams. A frantic madness careened about her heart, making her blood race in giddy torrents, yet her hands were steady and resolute, smoothing the white gloves.

"I often wallow about in cow pies," she said. "It's what comes of tramping about in the country. But before we discuss the delightful caprice of raping a commoner, I would like proof that what you told me is correct: that von Pontiras intends assassination tomorrow, if I do not rescue his wife by my heroism tonight."

"Ah, the assassination!"

"How do I know you won't go through with it anyway?"

"Perhaps I would rather be kingmaker than king. The man who can destroy the monarch controls the throne."

Sounds from the reception filtered up through the house. Music, laughter and incessant talk. Men who directed the future of Europe: laying plans over wine, between dances, with a casual word in passing. It was a world she had never thought about, never imagined. "You'll never control him."

"I already do. I control Sophia. She's being kept secluded, with no idea of her whereabouts or her captors. When the time comes, I shall deliver her. She'll be grateful to me, her gallant rescuer."

"I'm surprised Nicholas hasn't killed you. It would be no more than stepping on a worm."

Carl laughed. "Alas, my dear, I could never quite stamp out his finer scruples. He won't kill me because he can. He's afraid of what murder without consequences might make him. As if it mattered. He's ruined at the core."

She wouldn't discuss Nicholas with this man. "You have the princess imprisoned in a dungeon?"

"My dear! Do you take me for a barbarian? She inhabits an elegant room with a view of the sky. Of course, she is a real princess. Sophia would never have come here like this. You do realize that you have just betrayed the dregs of the barnyard in your blood?"

"Then I might as well leave," Penny said.

He laughed again. "And let Countess von Pontiras die? Perhaps it would be amusing, after all, to dabble in the gutter and taste the charms of the impostor."

"Alas, I cannot remove this dress by myself. It laces down the back."

He patted the covers with one hand. "It doesn't matter. I can do it for you, if you will only come here like a good girl and sit down."

"Proof," Penny said. "Perhaps all this talk of assassination is a farrago of nonsense."

A small pile of papers lay on the table next to him. He flipped the pages. "Here is your proof, but I think you must pay me for it first. Naked and willing, with your legs open. When I am satiated, you may have the reprieve for Countess von Ponti-ras, and I shall not send for Alexis."

Nausea rose in a wave, with panic a spume on the breakers. She wanted to run from the room. She couldn't go through with it! *Though Alexis would do anything for Nicholas. Even this! Why can't I?*

She took a step toward the bed. *I can. I can. I can do even this for his sake.*

"Countess von Pontiras?" a voice said from the shadows. "Why should she need a reprieve? She has just arrived in London, children in tow, for the wedding, safely guarded by my men and under my protection."

Penny's knees simply folded. It seemed absurd, when the voice belonged to Nicholas. But in billows of white feathers she sank to the floor, light-headed. "Oh, good heavens! Like Leda, I seem to have surrendered to swansdown."

Nicholas walked forward into the light. He moved like a dancer, lethal and lovely, his drawn sword shining. "Like Penelope," he said. "You are a tower of strength and your silken web weaves succor to lost princes."

She mustn't faint! "But Penelope undid her weaving every night to avoid her importunate suitors."

"Meanwhile," Carl said dryly. "She had deceitfully made them an empty promise. What's this, Nico? Can't you see you're being cuckolded even before you are married?"

"Nonsense," Nicholas said, his footsteps soft on the carpet. "Sophia is as true as Penelope, who waited twenty years for Odysseus to return."

Stocking feet thudded to the floor as Carl rolled from the bed. Nicholas moved even faster. Light sprang from the blade.

The tip wavered almost delicately at Carl's throat as he was forced to sit down again. With the other hand the prince leafed through some papers beside the bed.

"Ah," Nicholas said. "Your threats to von Pontiras. Alas, he'd have made the devil of an assassin."

"By coming here," Carl said, "you have secured his wife's death and thus you have just sealed this pretty child's fate. Von Pontiras will know whom to blame. Like a Greek tragedy, we shall find ourselves surrounded by the corpses of women."

"Really?" Nicholas said. "Then how fortunate we are that von Pontiras came to me—as you knew he would. But, of course, none of that was what truly enthralled you, was it?"

Carl grinned, obviously unafraid. "No, the reward was the thought of rutting your whore for you, since you are incapable."

The blade pricked. A single bead of blood ran onto Carl's white shirt. Penny sat as if paralyzed and watched the concentration on Nicholas's face. The tiniest of movements would result in death.

"Oh, dear," Nicholas said. "You seem to have nicked yourself shaving."

Carl continued to stare at him, as if daring the prince to press another three or four inches. "Nor do you have the nerve to drive that blade home, my sweet, cowardly Nico."

Tension emanated from the lean back and determined wrist. The blade shivered as Nicholas smiled. "You almost make me believe you want to die, cousin. But you will not succeed in making me kill you—though I admit I crave it as Tantalus craved food. Sophia, my dear brave girl, get up and collect your gloves and fan. Carl is expecting company."

"Company?" she said.

His sword moved just a little, forcing Carl to tilt up his chin. Nicholas was pale. A fine sheen of sweat glossed his features. "The Prince Regent and a gaggle of British peers are on their way here right now. A pretty plan, Carl! Did you think that if they found you in bed with Sophia, they would demand the wedding be canceled? Is a scandal about sex enough to change the fate of nations? Or should I become what you have tried so hard to make me, and let them find your corpse? A bold gamble. Either outcome would probably cost me my throne. Do you trust that I care enough about Glarien not to act?"

The grin faded. Carl sat rigid, gazing up at the prince. The tiny trickle had stopped, but the blade remained steady, pressed against his throat. Nicholas was poised like an executioner, his face white.

Penny scrambled to her feet and grabbed her gloves and fan from the chair.

"The Tsar is a sentimentalist," Nicholas went on. "He believes in love. Prinny's heart is as soft as butter, and he has a rather natural abhorrence of state marriages. Perhaps they would indeed suggest I step aside, if they discovered Sophia would rather have you. What else would they think, when the news rocked the house that she'd been found in your bed? Diabolical, Carl, but not clever enough. Lord Trent and his friends in the Foreign Office have harder hearts and harder heads. And if you close your fingers on that knife, you will die, devil take my finer scruples."

Penny saw it then, the dagger lying close to Carl's right hand, half hidden by a pillow. Amazed at her own temerity, she walked up to the bed and removed it.

"I had thought about stabbing you myself," she said. "But I wasn't sure where to get a blade. How considerate of you to provide one!"

Nicholas looked at her and his tension disintegrated. Color came back to his face as he winked. "Thank you, Sophia. Shall we leave, before Russia and Britain discover more than one in Carl's bedchamber?" He nodded to a door at the side of the room. "That way! George approaches like Athena, bearing martial splendor in his wake. I'm not in the mood to meet all that glitter in the hallway."

Penny hurried to the door and opened it. She was in a small, dark dressing room, lit only by moonlight washing in the window. A moment later, Nicholas joined her and sheathed his sword. She heard Carl stumble from the bed as the door to the corridor opened, but Nicholas stood for a moment staring at the window, his head tipped back against the wall. He swallowed convulsively, his hands clenched at his sides.

The Prince Regent boomed out a greeting. "Brought wine, sir! Good God, sir, cut yourself shaving?"

Silently, Nicholas supported Penny by the waist and pulled her with him to another door. He said nothing as he led her along hallways. Markos and Ludger said nothing as they snapped to attention. The prince and his future bride arrived with perfect secrecy in his bedroom. With a click, he snapped the lock shut behind them.

Quest lay beside the bed. She lifted her head and stared at them, the tip of her tail wagging softly.

Penny began to shake. Still in silence, Nicholas pulled her to his chest and held her. His uniform clanked with decorations, so he cradled her head in his hand, stroking her cheek. "Hush," he said. "It's all right."

She felt absurdly cherished, cocooned in tenderness. The ice in her veins melted. Tears flooded, taking her by surprise. Gulping and snuffling, Penny clung to his strength. He waited, holding her, until she stopped sobbing, then he picked her up and carried her to the sofa by the fireplace. He set her down, poured a glass of wine, and held it out. Penny took it in shaking fingers.

"Why did you do it?" His voice grated, as if he choked back something else he wanted to say.

The heady aroma filled her mouth. *I did it for you!* She swallowed. "I didn't think there was a choice. Von Pontiras—he came to you?"

Nicholas squatted beside Quest to stroke her head. "No. But I do have his family in my protection. It's my duty to guard the helpless and forestall trouble. That von Pontiras loves his wife so much obviously made him vulnerable to Carl's manipulation. So I took some simple precautions, and I have informed von Pontiras of them. There won't be any assassination attempt. Carl just wanted you found in his bed."

She shuddered. "He had a knife under his pillow. Would he have used it on me?"

"To intimidate you, perhaps, if you lost your nerve. He wanted to punish you for helping me, and he wanted to make sure I would feel humiliation over it."

The memory of Nicholas's tender, strong hand on her cheek burned. She wanted him to stroke her as he stroked Quest, not reveal more layers of his hateful intrigues. "Would it have wrecked Allied support for the wedding?"

"Perhaps. I don't know."

"Then I was a fool to go to his room. I played right into his plan to destroy you. Oh, God! It didn't occur to me that he'd have such a direct political motive."

He stood up and moved away, rigid and implacable in his gold braid and medals. "Why should it? I'm sure he set you up very thoroughly."

The wine warmed and soothed. She gulped it down, then re-filled her glass from the bottle he'd left beside her. "I'm sorry. I'm not as practiced in all this as you are."

He turned to her almost fiercely. "I didn't want you to be. Dear God! For that alone, Carl almost died."

His distress unnerved her: the fine vibration in his hands, the attempt to control the passion in his voice. "Surely Carl didn't want you to kill him?"

The braid on his court uniform gleamed. The dog pressed herself against his legs, but he gestured and she trotted over to Penny. The silver coat felt rough and warm. Penny buried her face in Quest's ruff, while the wolfhound licked her hands.

Nicholas stood and watched them. "He wanted me to be tempted. As I was. By God, I almost did it!"

"He is your subject," she said. "Who would punish you?"

He strode across the carpet to stand over her, vibrating in every muscle. Thinly leashed power flowed from him, like a dark horse flashing its defiance in a dark barn. Quest whined softly and nosed him. He rubbed her ears and the dog fell silent.

"Exactly. No one. Which is why I must not. I can never indulge in personal revenge. But I did not plan that you should pay this price!"

"Oh, I don't know," she said, looking up at him. "It's been rather fun, wearing diamonds."

He touched her hair, tentatively. Quest lay down and put her paws over her nose, her limpid gaze fixed on his face. "Penny, I'm sorry. I'm sorry I forced you into all this. Alas, I don't really like you in diamonds." Carefully he lifted away the tiara and set it beside the half-empty wine bottle. "I would rather have you in your own ugly cotton, with your hair in a plait and your nose scarlet at the tip as you scolded me. Why don't you berate me? I deserve it."

Penny bit her lip and glanced away. The delicate touch of his fingers at her temple made her want to weep again like a lost child. "Because it's only a show, all of this. It's as if I stepped through a doorway into fairyland. In fact, I thought for a changeling I was doing rather well!"

His mouth quirked in a wry grin. "Too damned well! I hate it!"

She closed her eyes, craving his caresses as his lean fingers moved down her cheek. "Then what about you in all your gold braid and decorations?"

The subtle touch stopped. "What?"

"Look at you in all that! That military splendor! It's like a decorated room: drapes held back by gold cord, diamond chandeliers, everything gilt and baroque finery."

He stepped back and stared down at her. "I hate it, as well."

With quick, violent movements, he unpinned his sash and decorations. Stars and crosses dropped like children's toys to the floor. He peeled off the military jacket and tossed it to a chair, where it slid crookedly, like a discarded doll. With a few snaps and twists he unbuckled his sword belt and threw aside the weapon. Piece by piece he stripped off all the glory and splendor, until he stood before her in shirt and trousers. With long, elegant fingers he pulled off his cravat and dropped it, rubbing the other hand over the back of his neck. The floor was littered with the insignia of his rank, leaving the man blazing with his own inner brilliance.

"Stand up," he said. "I can't bear you in all that either: swansdown and pearls—a wicked shell to attract Carl. I don't want this to happen to you." Her tears swam, burning her eyes as he reached down both hands and pulled her to her feet. "Open your fingers!"

She let her hands relax as he pulled off her rings: Sophia's rings, diamonds and sapphires, one of them the engagement ring a grand duke had given a princess. He unpinned the jeweled star holding the royal blue sash across her breasts. He tossed them all aside, a fortune in jewels clattering onto the table, rings clinking into her empty wineglass, ringing against the tiara. Quest dived under the couch.

"Turn around," he ordered.

With the same lethal focus he unclasped her diamond necklace, then began unlacing her ball gown down the back. In a haze of heat, she let him do it. His fingers feathered step by step down her spine. The touch burned through her corset and shift. At last the swansdown and pearls slithered to the floor, to drift at her feet in mounds of white feathers. With deft fingers he pulled the pins out of her hair and braided it into a loose plait along her spine, working with feverish concentration.

"That's better," he said at last. "Now you look more like Penny Lindsey. This is how I want to remember you."

She knew she was blushing, but she laughed. Somewhere in the room Dionysus laughed with her, urging the bacchanal. It seemed uproariously funny. "You want to remember me in my shift?"

"In your shift," he said. "Angry with me or laughing at me. I will remember you like that till I die."

Her laugh died like a sigh in the wind, swallowed into a great well of sadness. The tears pricked again and she shivered. "Oh, Nicholas, we're both such lonely creatures, you and I."

"We are all alone forever," he said. "I've never expected anything else."

His lips touched her nape with a warm, soft caress. Tension and heat flowed from his mouth, from his hands at her shoulders, his fingertips just touching bare flesh. Penny shivered, yet her blood burned. Swansdown pooled at the hem of her petticoat. *We are all alone forever?* She couldn't bear it to be true! Carved griffins grinned at her from the corner posts, gilt coronets smiled on the great state bed of a marquessate. Somewhere across Europe Nicholas had a bed more magnificent than this, the bed of a grand duke, the highest rank he could hope to attain. His bedroom. His lonely bed.

It beckoned like a siren.

I don't suppose anyone likes him. He has too much natural power and he's a man torn between two cultures, fitting nowhere. Brilliant and gifted people rarely offer simple amiability.

She turned around, trailing sprinklings of swansdown, put her arms about his waist, and laid her head against his shoulder. It fit there as if nature had carved out a cushion for her troubles. Beneath her questing palms his spine was supple and strong, his back lean and hard. He felt glorious. Desire flared between her legs and filled her mouth with honey. Her breasts crushed into his chest, aching for his touch.

His intaken breath was harsh and short. He stood absolutely still in her arms, leaving his own hanging at his sides. She snuggled closer, running her hands up his back. His arousal reared against her belly, the hard, urgent response of a man. Feeling dazed, she ran one palm over the enticing bulge in the fabric of his breeches. For a single moment, they stood together, locked in place. He was a grand duke, a prince, sovereign ruler of a nation. In her arms she felt only the man, brilliant and tortured, on fire for her.

A fine, high tension sang in his muscles as he took her by both shoulders and set her away from him, pushing her back to the couch. "Penny," he said gently. "This is the wine, that's all. It's my fault."

She put her face in her hands. "You don't want me?"

He strode away, kicking aside his discarded finery. "God! How can you ask it? *Want* you? When you sit there in your shift like the Lorelei! I'm demented with wanting you."

Swansdown glistened. Penny reached for her discarded dress, shivering. "I want you, too," she whispered. "As you said, just the wine. Men and women shouldn't get undressed in bedrooms together, should they?"

He tore the coverlet from the bed. "Not when the man feels as I do."

"But you aren't a man. You're a grand duke." Pearls and feathers crushed in the palms of her hands. She had touched him! Felt that leaping male power under her palm. Foolishly she craved it. The glamour of a prince? Or the vulnerability of the man?

He strode back to her and wrapped the cover about her shoulders, tucking it over her knees and back. "Penny, beloved, I want you. I want you so badly I think I might burst. But you're fuzzy with wine and distress. You aren't thinking clearly."

She looked down, biting her lip. "How can you live with all this control? Doesn't it eat you alive? What happens when the curb breaks?"

Quest crawled out, whining slightly. Nicholas touched the silver head, stroking his fingers over her coat. The hound pressed into his legs, the wolf eyes half closed.

"I can control my actions. Unfortunately, I can't control my feelings—"

"So the ice prince admits to having feelings?" she said bitterly. "Then prides himself on negating them!"

Restlessly he turned and began to pace. Long, lithe strides devoured the carpet. Quest trotted beside him, staring up into his face. "Isn't this what you wanted from me? A display of messy sentiment? In the orangery? In Clumper Cottage? You wanted me to admit to human failings, human weaknesses. Good God! Do you think I'm so graceless?"

"I think you pride yourself on being more than mortal, like clockwork. You crave efficiency and order, but it's all just a shell of spines, like a hedgehog—"

"To protect the weak underbelly from foxes? I'm only too aware of the power of human emotion. Who do you think we gypsy princes are? Who do you think Carl is? We have a reputation throughout Europe: princes driven by their appetites, eschewing control and civil boundaries, with the wealth and power to take what they want. I will not be like them. I will not, Penny! Do not try to tempt me!"

"What of *my* temptation?" she asked. "Do you think only of yourself?"

He spun so fast that Quest sat down. "Penny, beloved—oh, God! I'm thinking only of you."

"Why?"

"Because of what happened after you told me about your uncle Horace."

She hugged the coverlet. "When we laughed together, and you sent me away? What are you talking about?"

"I wanted you before that, of course, with the urgent desire of a man's body. It didn't feel anything like clockwork. It led me to kiss you. It led me to dream about you. Now I lie awake every night and imagine you there." He pointed to the marquess's bed. "On that mattress. Every night. I hunger and burn for you. Nothing assuages it. Does that shock you?"

Oh, Lord, she had imagined and dreamed of him, too! She swallowed. Be careful what you ask for, her mother had said often enough. Be sure it's really what you want before you make the bargain final. A princess and a nation are waiting for him. After tomorrow, he has no place for you in his life.

"I don't know." Hadn't William fired her with desires by letting her know how much he wanted her? "Don't men have such thoughts all the time?"

He held out his hand and Quest bounded up to him. Man and dog flowed, white shirt, silver fur, athletic and lithe. "I've never felt it like this before. This unsettling leap and plunge in the blood—the way I notice every last thing about you: each hair a strand of desire; the sensible way your thumb fits your hand; the music of listening to your breath, as if breathing were some kind of miracle."

She tried to diminish it. "Well, it is, isn't it? A miracle. Breathing, that is."

He stared down at Quest. "Ah, but then something else happened that day in my study, something far more unfortunate. I wasn't sure how to deal with it. I misjudged how you would react when I tried to put distance between us. I should have realized. . . . It's impossible, of course. No doubt it's just an infatuation and will pass."

Her breath had caught somewhere underneath her ribs, driving an intense pain through her heart. "What do you mean?"

"As I said, it's impossible." He looked up at her and gave her a half smile, infinitely amused, infinitely sad. "I'm in love with you—ridiculous, isn't it?"

It's impossible. Why had she played with fire? *Ridiculous, isn't it?* If he knew how she felt, how much more impossible for him!

"You'll get over it," she said at last.

The smile widened, as if a deep appreciation for his own frailty spread only the most wicked amusement. "Is that all you have to say when a man bares his bloody soul and admits his absurdity?"

"I think you're in pain," she said, fighting the odd strangling panic. "I don't believe love is meant to be painful."

"No, of course not. Love is meant to be comfortable and safe, like Jeb Hardacre and his wife snoring before the kitchen fire. That is not what I feel about you." He laughed with obvious bravado. "This is a madness. I want to enter your skin. I want to discover your very essence—why you're so enthralling and mysterious to me. I cannot allow any of it."

Love isn't meant to be painful? "So you can't bear my company?"

"Obviously, I must root out this lunacy now. My only consolation is that this madness is mine alone. Meanwhile, rest assured I shall never speak of this again."

His sincerity rang clear as a bell. For one moment the temptation yawned, the primrose path: *I have fallen in love with you, too. I fell in love with you when I was a child and I saw you ride by like a boy prince from a fairy tale. I have lied all my life, if I ever said I felt anything different.*

She stood up, shedding swansdown, and folded the coverlet. "I would like you to know I am honored. I am honored by your feelings." She felt awkward and cold.

"I love you enough to do nothing about it." He turned away. "I should not have told you. I'm sorry. Sophia and I will rule together. I'll have Ludger take you back to your room."

Quest lay down and stared after him as Nicholas walked to the painting of the white horse and studied it. He stood in silence as Penny gathered her jewelry, thrusting the rings back on her fingers, gripping the tiara as if it were paste. Then he grinned at her again, a sudden flash of humor, intelligent and reckless.

"It is a madness, isn't it? After all, we're to be married in the morning."

The sun shone brilliantly on the carriages. Bells rang. People cheered. But it was just one more amusement in this summer of entertainment and not that many Londoners cared very much about two obscure principalities in the Alps. Penny walked up the aisle in a haze of sunbeams and glitter. Nicholas waited for her dressed in white silk, blazing with gold and state decorations. She thought madly that he was encased in polish, a symbol of the exquisite, designed only to intimidate.

Yet he smiled, his eyes dark, as she came up on the arm of the Tsar. She wondered if women could die of desire. An ignoble envy curled beneath her longing, envy for the cousin she had never met, the woman who would truly take this man to have and to hold for life, the real Princess Sophia.

Ceremonies and celebrations took most of the day, until at last the bridal party returned to Rivaulx House. Triumphant. Successful. Count Carl Zanich had sadly been taken ill and could not attend the wedding breakfast—a meal that kept its traditional name even though it was served in late afternoon. The festivities continued into the evening. Penny watched Nicholas move among the crowd in his white silk, flamboyant with jewels, like a prince holding a glass slipper. Yet he vibrated with energy: more resonant, more powerful than any fairy-tale Prince Charming.

So what on earth was going to happen at midnight? The wedding had taken place, the play had been presented. Did the players turn into pumpkins and white mice and just go home when the clock struck twelve? Back to Rascall St. Mary to gather hedgehogs for Jeb Hardacre for the rest of her life? Penny had no idea what Nicholas planned next, an omission so glaring she thought she must have been mad not to think about it before. She caught his eye and he winked at her, just as a contingent of court ladies surrounded her and bustled her from the room.

"Gerta!" she whispered. "What now?"

"Why, the wedding bed, ma'am. The nobility must publicly

witness the bedding of bride and groom to make sure the marriage is consummated."

It was Alexis who delivered the message, slipping her a paper note as she left the room with her ladies. The note burned in her hand until she was at last able to open it:

Swan bride, you believe yourself triumphant. But on this happiest of days, think for one moment what he is really like. Ask him what he and I did together after you were smuggled into that inn—your affectionate cousin, Zanich.

Thirteen

*N*icholas watched her go, safely surrounded by her ladies. They would peel away the wedding gown with its layers of exquisite lace. They would dress her in sheer white silk. They would comb her hair down around her breasts. They would place her in his bed. He would go to her, assisted by his gentlemen, the nobility of Glarien and Alvia, in a ritual at least five hundred years old. He would go to her, wait until the courtiers had retired, and, in spite of the yearning that was consuming his soul, he would leave her untouched.

The room smelled strongly of roses. Masses of white blossoms covered every surface. They gleamed like fresh snow in the candlelight. His bare feet crushed more white petals strewn across the floor. He wore nothing but an embroidered gilt dressing gown, the buttons set with rubies. In a distant past this ritual had been accompanied by jests and ribaldry. Now the nobles filed solemnly behind him, looking slightly uncomfortable. No one would stare directly at the bride, and they would leave before witnessing him performing his royal duty. It was 1814, after all, not the Middle Ages.

Penny sat propped up by pillows, her hair rippling down to her waist. The bedcovers were folded back. The thin silk of her nightgown was decorated with swags of white lace and ropes of pearls. Ribbons encrusted with more pearls wove in an elaborate web over her shoulders and under her breasts. The sheer fabric revealed shadowed nipples. She was a little flustered and pink, her eyes enormous as she surveyed the men arrayed at the foot of her bed. And then she glanced away, biting her lip.

He did not have to look over his shoulder to know that Carl had entered.

"A blessing for fruitfulness, sire." Carl knelt at Nicholas's feet and kissed the hem of his robe.

Nicholas smiled. "And bounty for Glarien and Alvia. We are twice blessed."

Carl rose and smiled back. "May I claim my prerogative as the heir soon to be displaced? As is traditional, we all contribute to this happy occasion."

"Hardly necessary, Zanich," murmured one of the counts. "The princess—"

Carl turned to him. "You did not take your turn at the ceremonial disrobing, sir?"

"By all means," Nicholas said, holding out his arms. "The last piece is yours, cousin, since the final act is mine."

With unnecessary brutality, Carl wrenched off the dressing gown. The courtiers discreetly looked away. Nicholas kept his eyes on Penny's. *Take courage, beloved!* Yet his cock rose to stand hard and proud, mocking him. Stark naked he walked to the bed. Then he turned to the assembled nobility.

"An auspicious day for Glarien and Alvia, sirs. I thank you."

Without a word they bowed and hurried from the room. Only Carl lingered for a moment on the threshold.

"Think yourself lucky, Princess," he said. "There was a time we'd have inspected you, too. As for Nicholas, I already know just how pretty he is."

The door closed with a click.

"Hmm," Penny said. Her cheeks were fiery, her eyes brilliant as she looked up at him. "They have taken away your dressing gown. How are you supposed to clothe yourself now? With rose petals?" She waved her hand, gallant and brave. "They have covered the sheets with them, too. A bit messy, but very sweet smelling."

Nicholas sat on the edge of the bed and put a pillow over his lap. "So I see. I'm sorry about all this. Tradition. Everyone gets to remove an article of clothing, which they can keep, of course, with any attached small jewels. Royal largesse. Graf Linstein claimed the honor of my shirt, Erbprinz von Rorschia my left stocking and the diamond garter that came with it. I'm damned if I remember who took off the right one. But Carl, as my cousin, was within his rights to demand my dressing gown. With all those bloody jewels, it's worth a king's ransom."

She glanced up at him under her lashes. His blood surged.

"I thought he might strangle you with the belt."

He kept the pillow pressed firmly over his sex. Heat burned there, demanding resolution, filling him with shame. "Too many witnesses."

Short wisps of golden hair curled at her temple. The blunt nose was a little pink at the tip. He wanted to kiss it. "What did he mean about inspecting me, too?"

He kept his voice light, joking. "At one time, the grand duke's bride was also disrobed before the courtiers. To make sure she had no blemish, I suppose, though I think it was probably just prurient interest thinly disguised as a necessity for the state. My ancestors thought of women as chattel."

She leaned forward and grasped the bedcovers, which had been folded at the bottom of the bed. Silk slid sensuously across her curved flesh as she stretched. The pillow grew hotter.

"Well, thank goodness that's over with," she said. "I have a vial of chicken blood."

He looked at his own hand, at the dark hair sprinkled on his rugged arm. Her wrists were so smooth and round, delectable, female. His mouth filled with craving. His sex swelled and vibrated. "Chicken blood?"

She pulled the covers up under her chin and grinned at him. "Yes, Gerta thought we should stain the sheets with it in the morning. I'm supposed to be your virgin bride. Of course, she gave me rather a lot. We could make it look as if murder had been committed instead, if you like."

He forced himself to look away from her. Across the room a white horse raced up a painted valley to freedom. He tried to concentrate on the threatening storm, the wind-whipped trees. "Alas," he said. "I'm sworn away from murder. What else would you like?"

"Are you sure you dare ask that?" Her voice teased.

Like the horse, he was all muscle and bone, the practical, unrefined knitting together of any man's body, hard and unyielding. It revolted him. Only the woman in the bed behind him was soft. Soft breasts where infants could be suckled. Soft arms and legs, round and smooth. Soft female belly and a throat like a sugar confection. An ache spread along his sinews. His blood surged back and forth through his veins, like a pounding tide. But his arousal must be denied. Always, always, the howling need must be denied—until Sophia. Until the real princess and the necessity to make her a son. And perhaps, after all of it, he would fail at that yet.

"I owe you a kingdom," he said simply. "What would you like in exchange?"

"May I have anything?"

He must not think about Penny! Was that painting a real place? If so, it was nothing like Glarien with its glacier-ridden peaks and rolling green valleys. This was open moor, somewhere in the north of England, perhaps.

"Anything you like," he said.

"Then I ask for what you have no intention of giving."

He looked back at her and his body responded faster than his distressed mind. "What?"

She tugged at the embroidered ties at the neck of her nightdress. The hair over her breasts was caught in the ribbons. His gaze riveted there on the playful curves, ripe with pearls. Her face was flushed like a sunrise and her breath was coming too fast.

"I want you to make love to me," she said. "That is what I want in exchange for a kingdom."

Desire surged, hot and urgent, braying its demands. *Would she be silken and cool—balm to his disordered blood? Or would he melt in her? Run molten into her essence, like silver from a crucible?* Desperately he sought to shield himself from the enormity of what she had just asked, while awareness thundered in his veins.

"Ah," he said at last, though he fought against bitterness. "So in the orangery the flaying of Nicholas had barely begun?"

She pushed her hands through her hair. The red-gold strands caught in a veil over her round wrists. "Stop it! Don't try to defend yourself against me with cleverness or sarcasm. I want more than a memory of intrigue and danger to take with me from my adventure. I want a memory of you. No one will ever know. If the desire and the prompting is mine, you aren't forsworn."

His arousal thrust, rearing hard against the pillow. "To ask for what can neither be granted kindly nor refused politely is hardly fair."

"I'm not a virgin," she said. "You will leave no torn maidenhead behind, nor a child. It's too close to my monthly courses for that. Gerta told me so."

"Gerta?"

"Yes, Sophia's nurse. Perhaps she thought it was natural that you and I would consummate this marriage tonight. I received a great deal of practical advice along with the chicken blood. Perhaps Gerta doesn't want a man who has never known a woman to clumsily deflower her princess?"

Astonishment rose and burst like bubbles in champagne, heady and mad, while his blood pounded through his veins. "Is that what you think? Oh, dear God!"

Her eyes were green as glass. "You said last night that you loved me. Did you lie about that, too?"

"No. That was the truth. You sear my soul, beloved. It doesn't make any difference." The words seemed to echo and resound. *I'm in love with you.*

"It makes all the difference in the world, Nicholas. I would rather like it, I think, to have a man touch me who thought that he loved me."

He envisioned himself suddenly racing from the room stark naked with his rage blossoming in his hands. The astonished courtiers, the shattering of months of diplomacy, Carl's triumph. He struggled to regain control. Would she say the same to a ghost moth who claimed he loved the candle? *I would like you to visit me, moth, and taste my flame!* Yet if it was better for the candle, the moth would die willingly. She didn't know what he'd done. She thought he had never known a woman.

"Penny, beloved. Don't ask this!"

The bedcovers rustled. She laid her head against his naked back and put her arms about his waist to catch his hands in her own. He looked down at them for a moment. Practical, female hands, smooth now from daily ministrations of lemon juice and wool. Beautiful hands, tender and innocent. His own lay dark and hard beneath them, the square knuckles ostentatious. He had calluses from handling so many sets of reins, riding so many horses—the horses who had taught him how to conquer rage and be sensitive to things unspoken, to vulnerability and heartbreaking courage—the horses who also embodied nobility without avarice.

"I must ask it," she said. "Don't deny me. I couldn't bear it. I know this is right." Her voice caught and broke in a little laugh. "After all, we are married."

"I don't know—" He broke off, looking away, groping for what he could say. "I don't know how."

Her hair rubbed soft on his shoulder. Silk caressed his skin. Her breasts crushed sweetly into his spine. "I don't know how either. Do you think I learned very much from William? Only mechanics. I don't know how to do it with love and this burning desire that refuses to be denied. It's what I want. It's what you want. So let's find out together, you and I. A wedding gift!"

He knew his will was strong enough to refuse her, in spite of his howling body. He knew there would be a price for both of them, if he gave in. He knew he would be forsworn, breaking his pledge to her mother, his childhood governess, a woman to whom he owed a debt as great as life. He knew he risked his own precarious balance, that whatever the outcome of this, the tightrope might jerk away beneath him, leaving him hurled unsupported through space.

Yet if he denied her now, he might as well strike his knife into her heart. Brave Penny Lindsey, who had just reached the eighth square to become a queen, had just checkmated him. So he must give her what she thought she wanted. She wouldn't know it was an act, a play elaborately written and directed, by a man who loved her enough not to let her perceive the truth. But what if—in spite of everything—his touch defiled her?

Devil's spawn! It's Nico's turn now!

A shudder rippled through his muscles. Penny knew a moment of pure terror. "Do you not desire me?" she asked.

"I desire you."

The simple words rang with conviction. She smoothed her hand up his arm, over tendon and muscle, delectable to touch.

"You think to forego your desire in order to protect me," she said. "You think to protect me from you, from what you have done and what you think your past makes you. That is foolishness. Love washes everything clean."

"Penny, you want me to forget who I am? Forget what the past owes, the future demands? I'm a prince. I'm committed to Glarien, to Sophia. There's nothing I can give you."

"No," she said. "I'm asking for a moment out of time. Tonight. Now. No consequences. Just our adventure reaching its natural culmination, so I can go back to Norfolk knowing that at least once in my lifetime a man found me worthy of loving, just for myself. Anyway, you'll get cold, wearing nothing but a pillow. At least get into bed."

He laughed. The laughter was poisoned. Yet he turned to her.

She held back the covers and he slipped in beside her. She caught a glimpse of his arousal, rearing proudly from the dark hair between his legs. The power of a man, potent and beautiful. He pushed the hair back from her forehead. The simple gesture felt wonderful, tender and deferential. He ran a long strand through his fingers and took it to his lips. Gazing into her eyes, he kissed her hair and smiled.

"Then the decision is made. For God help me if I can deny you any longer."

She tugged him down and kissed his mouth. She couldn't bear it that he thought he was not a good man. She couldn't bear it that he'd always been used, as if he were assaulted daily by vampires, that no one ever gave him anything back. She wanted to give him something precious and unique, the most valuable thing she possessed, to show him how worthy of love she believed him to be. She had nothing at all that she valued, except her heart.

She twisted in his arms and thought the carved griffin on the post winked as he rolled over her, taking command.

He took her face in both hands to kiss her again.

Her mouth opened under his. The kiss changed.

He kissed deeper, with a strangely innocent fervor, ripe with promise. His hands strayed over her face, his fingers seeking, tentative. As she melted beneath him she heard herself moan. He broke the kiss and looked down at her. His dark eyes devoured, hot and hungry.

Long fingers moved through her hair. Delicate, tender, delicious. She touched his naked skin, the hard, superbly honed back, the lean shoulders and muscled arms. He was a revelation to her palms, as if she discovered intense beauty for the first time in her life, as if she'd never marveled at anything in nature before, as if she were newborn. He stroked her flank reverently through her thin gown, sending delicious tremors down her spine. His hands caressed and set flames. His palms worshiped and pampered.

"Penny, you are inexpressibly lovely. Do you like me to touch you like this?"

She arched her back. "If I were a cat, I'd be purring. I want to bring you pleasure, Nicholas. I want us both to find succor."

"Succor?" he asked. "Is that what this is?"

She laughed weakly, gazing into his eyes. "I'm not sure I care, as long as it's you."

"Then may we have this bizarre nightdress off?"

"Yes, if you can only figure out how to untie it."

He propped his head on one hand, assessing her with a grave indulgence. "You aren't embarrassed to have me look at you?"

"Not if you would like it."

"I would like it very much, though you may be modestly covered with rose petals, instead."

She felt no shyness, though not even William had seen her entirely unclothed. "Naked seems more honest. I want honesty, Nicholas."

A small shadow clouded his eyes for a moment, spiraling into dark smoke, but he smiled. His clever fingers crooked in the pearl ribbons, pulling them away, one at a time. A catch and drag as each loop surrendered and her skin fired beneath his touch. *Brilliant and gifted!*

She knelt and let him open the silk all the way down the front. He sat back and looked at her. Her instinct was to cover herself with her hands. She resisted it, though his gaze felt like a touch, intimate and penetrating.

"You are more beautiful than I imagined." His voice was light, a gentle caress. "And, yes, I imagined! Nakedness suits you."

She looked down, knowing her cheeks flamed. "I always thought my breasts weren't big enough. They don't make a very provocative swell in an evening gown."

He raised his brows, deliberately mocking. "Oh, yes, they do! They make a very provocative swell without one, too. But you are shy, after all, honest Penelope. Don't move!"

She sat perfectly still as he gathered white petals from the bed. With intense concentration he set them in patterns on her skin, necklaces of sweet scent. The petals caught and drifted, staying on her shoulders and the upper curve of her breasts, then tumbling from the tips. Her nipples rose under his touch as her blood pooled hotly between her legs.

"Ah," he said, with a small secret smile, "the petals will stay better now."

He swept up another handful and set them one at a time on her hair and her cheeks. Rose scent tingled. She sneezed. Petals exploded from her skin to catch in the black hair dusting his chest. She reached out to gather them, wanting to dress him in roses, too.

"The sacred person," he said with a small smile, catching her hand. "Not to be touched." The flame burned darker in his eyes. "Let me be the one to touch you. Let it all be my gift, beloved."

He reached for her, pulling her forward to kiss her again. Penny unfolded her legs so she straddled him, her breasts against his chest. With infinite restraint he laid her back, still kissing.

"You are dressed in roses," he said gravely. "It's time to undress you again. Lie still."

She lay still, breath rasping, as he removed the petals one by one. He took one foot in his hand. Carefully he rubbed over her instep and ankle, as if he found the curves and bones intensely intriguing. His hands drifted higher, up to her knee, careful, with deliberate restraint. She was melting, melting, becoming helpless under his palms, flowing and melding into a new mold, her skin a moth's wing of sensation, her bones a song of liquid gold. Her lids closed over eyes swimming with moisture as he rubbed over her thighs and belly. Her hands surrendered, the fingers opening helplessly, as his thumbs caressed the inside of her elbows and the soft swell of her palm.

"Oh, God," he said with a half laugh. "I'm dying, Penny."

"I would like it," she whispered, opening her eyes and smiling at him. "I want you."

"How?"

She gestured. "That bit fits inside this bit."

He laughed as he rubbed his penis over her belly, but the laughter died as the heavy tip found her. "Ah! Don't move now, or I'll explode."

"You're meant to explode," she said, frowning deliberately.

"It'd be damned clumsy if I did so right now. Penny, dear God, you are exquisite!"

She felt the stretch as he entered, sliding on her moisture, making her want to sigh aloud. Holding her breath, she waited for him to find his equilibrium. He shook for a moment like a ship's sail in a storm, then he began to move.

Once she had been flattered and beguiled into wedlock. The mysteries of the marriage bed had proved pleasant and interesting. It had all been made meaningless and sour when she had found out why William had wanted her. This time she had beguiled a prince into reopening those mysteries. Otherwise she would never know them again, and she wanted him to know them at least once with gentleness and humor and kindness. Because he had been damaged somehow, hurt in ways she couldn't imagine. Because he had a cousin named Carl who suggested ugly, dreadful things she didn't want to understand.

And because, sick with love, she couldn't help herself any longer.

So she offered everything she knew of sensitivity and tenderness, letting herself respond to his touch with abandon, holding nothing back. Open to his exploration, vulnerable to the depth of her being—and the result was exquisite, exquisite, moving her too profoundly to fathom, opening an ache of longing and intensity in her heart.

What had she wanted in return? To capture a man's soul? To break down all his defenses and see him open and vulnerable to her? Instead, concentration rode him like a blind force. All his brilliance focused, as if this were another game, another strategy he must win. Clever, imaginative, stretching the boundaries of sensuality, playing at passion, he thrust hard when she wanted it and slow when she wanted that. Sensations built and swelled, until she cried out. The climax caught her by surprise, rocking her into astonishment and rapture and exhaustion.

When he rolled away from her, she was ringing like a bell, filled with melodies she had never known, captured from the high glittering snows of the Alps—and taken breathless into darkness, so velvety and deep she knew something clandestine and secret still dwelled there. For Nicholas, her dark prince, sensitive and brilliant—who had told her he loved her—had given her only his body and nothing else.

He slept, the sheet wrapped half over him. Penny studied him for a long time, the carved face and powerful limbs. He might not have taken mistresses, but he was indeed not innocent. He was too clever and aware for that. She thought he had used every ounce of his courage and strength just to maintain his control—because he wanted to spare her? Her heart contracted. He had played her like a master, moved her to her soul. So why did she think, after all, that it hadn't been quite honest?

Honesty?

How much had she risked by not telling him how she felt? She knew she was loved, by her mother and the villagers, even by Aunt Horace, for all her foolish tongue. She had treasured it that this man had told her he loved her. But Nicholas lay beside her bereft. Was that what kept him still hidden from her? Had anyone in over twenty years ever told him he deserved to be loved—for himself and not because he was royal? She had thought to save him by not telling him how deeply, madly, she was in love with him. Now it seemed a dreadful cruelty. His black lashes cast shadows like the fringe of yew trees at the churchyard. Penny blew out the candles, plunging the room into darkness.

In the morning, I will tell him, she thought. *I will let him know—*

Nicholas lay absolutely still, holding on to the raging, foul feelings, pretending sleep. At last she lay back and doused the candle flame. She began to breathe deeply and evenly. He pushed up on one elbow and looked at her—beautiful, silver in the moonlight, with a small smile at the corner of her mouth. She couldn't possibly have guessed at the truth, but he thought he had satisfied her. He had just invented it as he'd gone along, acting out what he thought she might like, trying to offer her tenderness and homage, acting the hardest part of his life. So she wouldn't know. So she wouldn't know what he really was. He had entered her with restraint, ridden her with restraint, holding on desperately, like a man on the rack.

He swung his feet from the bed and walked to the window. The moon sailed pale and pure over London. Shudders began to convulse down his back, then his legs. He buried his face in the curtains and let the rage swell and roar. The rage and disgust. The white-hot nausea and repulsion. When he straightened up at last, his face contorted with tears, the curtains were damp, but the deep wracking sobs had retreated back into their familiar haunts, a black pit of despair and hatred. All that Carl had left him.

Penny woke to sunshine and a room filled with people. Nicholas stood in a new dressing gown in front of the fireplace. He nodded and all the gentlemen filed out of the room after him, leaving her surrounded by ladies. Gerta reached down and helped her from the bed. When the sheet was pulled back,

Penny saw the trace of blood. Chicken blood. All of Europe would know Glarien had consummated its treaty with virginal Alvia. So Nicholas had created this little lie in the bed they had shared together, and she would have no chance to tell him how she felt.

Lady Beatrice let her know what would happen next. Everything was being packed. The two courts were returning to Europe. Nicholas would have her smuggled away and returned to Rascall St. Mary. A pain like a wound settled around her heart. She hadn't told him. Her dark prince, loved for one night, then never again to be part of her life. He would go back to Glarien, to the legitimate princess. Penny Lindsey, bastard cousin of his real bride, he would never see again. Suddenly she was glad he didn't know how she felt. It was better for him, obviously, not to think he had broken her heart.

Her coach left that night for the docks. The *Royal Swan* was moored below London, ready to sail back to the Continent and send the royal contingent up the Rhine to the Alps. When they reached the mouth of the Thames, she would be smuggled off in a small boat, her duty finished. The pain intensified, the pain and the longing. If only she could wave a magic wand and re-make the world!

The deck of the ship was a mass of sailors, standing at attention beneath nets of rigging. Nicholas was nowhere to be seen, but Count Zanich came forward to greet her, arms outstretched. He caught her gloved fingers in his own and kissed her on both cheeks.

"The Grand Duke is in his cabin, refusing everyone," he whispered in her ear. "He doesn't want to see you again. But I have a new plan: What if Nicholas dies *and* Sophia dies—and you and I rule together? It's not ideal, but it might answer."

Shocked numb, she removed her fingers from his, groping for control. "You would murder the princess?"

His smile was urbane, charming. "When she learns what Nico did with you last night, she might kill herself. She believes that she loves him. Women commonly do. Tragic, really."

"Why on earth should you care? Because no woman would ever believe she loved you?"

He stepped aside as she strode past, head high. Her ladies showed her to a tiny cabin. Penny sat down on the bed. Once they were off the coast of Suffolk she would be sent home. Nicholas would remain on this ship with Carl. Which left both the prince and the real princess within reach of that murderous intent, and Penny Lindsey unprotected in Rascall St. Mary. She could be kidnapped and taken to Glarien to play out her masquerade for the rest of her life. Of course, it would probably be a very short life.

But if she remained in the royal party, publicly seen throughout the journey, Carl would gain nothing by harming Nicholas or the princess. So she must play her part until the real Sophia was rescued. But—after last night—would Nicholas agree?

The ship moved. The thud of sailors' feet rang clearly. Whistles piped and ropes creaked through pulleys, followed at long last by the crack and boom of unfurling sails. It was pitch night when she was escorted from her cabin by a determined sailor. In the inky sea below the ship, a small boat bobbed on the swell.

The pain sank and twisted. After what he had done—what she had made him do in a bed full of roses—he didn't even want to say goodbye?

The sailor began to hoist her over the edge.

"Gently," said a man's voice.

A dog stood behind him, faintly wagging her silver tail.

"Nicholas!" Penny felt suddenly faint. She put out her hand and he caught it.

He bent over her fingers and kissed them. "Be brave, Penelope. You have been a light in my life, beloved."

"I think I must stay!" she blurted. "Carl—"

"No," he said. "You must go."

He nodded to the sailor, who picked her up bodily and carried her down the ladder.

The boat cast off, six men straining at the oars, Belgian boatmen, joking and cursing in their own tongue. Two Glarian soldiers had been sent to escort her. One was the red-haired Eric. The other was a boy with hair that blazed white in the moonlight when he took off his soft cap: Alexis.

"You told me once that you loved him," she whispered to him in Glarisch. "Do you love him enough to disobey his orders?"

Alexis stared at her.

"Listen," she said. "I can do nothing without your help, yours and Eric's. Until the real princess is found, Nicholas and I are safe only if we're together."

It took cajoling and tears, but at last the boy nodded. The red-headed man listened also. He obviously hated Carl.

When they arrived on the shore, the boatmen waited while Eric and Alexis escorted Penny to the waiting carriage. She changed quickly into the boy's outer clothes—trousers, jacket, the soft cap. The empty carriage trotted away. She and Eric walked openly back to the boat. The moon slid behind a dense bank of cloud, as if conspiring to assist her. Alexis, wearing only his underwear, slipped into the cold ocean. He would swim to the ship and climb aboard secretly, while Penny marched onto the *Royal Swan* in his place. Once there, they would switch once again—she would be hidden like a smuggler, while Alexis reappeared as himself.

Penny Lindsey would go to Glarien with her dark prince after all, though she wouldn't let him find out until it was too late to send her back.

Quest whined. Nicholas touched the silver ruff and quieted her. Penny was gone. His destiny had arrived: to be prince of devils forever. If he closed his eyes he could see and feel her. Soft, sweet flesh and the scent of roses. Himself hard for her, pulsing with ungovernable hunger and an overwhelming desire for nullity, extinction. He craved it with a mad, buried howling. It obsessed him.

He hated the feeling.

Like St. Augustine, he had been tormented for years by visions of beautiful women. He had awoken sweating in the night, racked by white-hot anger. He had practiced to gain control over his body. Yet he hated that driving need. The need that had once made him smash crystal and break furniture, until Fritz von Gerhard had used the horses to teach him how to contain his rage. The noble, honest horses, who were so easily made afraid.

Lucas and Fritz would have rescued the real princess by now, though Carl would be kept from discovering it. As soon as the *Royal Swan* touched port, he would leave the ship and take Carl with him. From now on, Carl must be watched twenty-four hours a day. As Penny would be watched in the invincible net of security he had thrown around Rascall St. Mary—until he and the real Sophia were crowned together in Moritzburg, and Penny was no longer in danger.

This other feeling, this fragile bloom that he called love for Penny Lindsey, the ache and pain in his heart, the tenderness that had enabled him to make love with her when she asked it, he would force away from consciousness, until it died in the dark from neglect.

Crammed into the princess's tiny cabin, Penny had thought she'd make plans—enlist Gerta and Beatrice, decide when to tell Nicholas. Instead, she was seasick. Horribly, wretchedly seasick, every breath contaminated with nausea. Gerta appeared with basins and cold cloths, Beatrice clucked and tried to make her sip wine, while Penny asked aloud if they would please let her die. At last the ship's sickening plunge calmed to a round roll. The *Royal Swan* had made landfall.

Heavily veiled, still shaky and weak, she finally came up on deck. The royal party was transferring to the boats that would take them up the Rhine. Nicholas and Carl were nowhere to be seen. She would have to wait till she could find a way to approach Nicholas alone, or send him a private message. A royal prince, surrounded by his court.

A few hours later, hidden in the middle of a gaggle of ladies, Penny was helped onto the princess's barge. Everyone believed Princess Sophia was a poor traveler—a part she was playing only too well! Exhausted, she curled up on the silk bed and went to sleep. The river gently rolled by.

She awoke to see Gerta nervously twisting her hands. "I have ill news, madam."

Oh, God! Nicholas! "The Grand Duke—?"

Gerta shook her head. "Grand Duke Nicholas and Count Zanich are not on the barges. They took horses this morning and rode off with a handful of men—all expert horsemen. A hunting party, they called it, but in truth they're riding hard straight to Glarien."

Penny pushed herself from the bed. "His personal bodyguard? Fritz, Eric, Alexis—?"

"They've all gone, madam, all except Alexis."

Should she laugh or cry? Somehow she must catch up with Nicholas, before Carl took some dreadful revenge on him and the real Sophia. So she didn't know the way. So Penny Lindsey had never done anything so physically daring in her life. What did that matter? She had Alexis to help her.

Fourteen

*R*ain *beat at the tiny leaded windows. Nicholas watched the* drops wrinkling and running on the glass. The weather had finally forced him to take shelter at the Wild Hart inn in this small village several days past Frauenfeld. The soft, rolling valleys had given way to ever steeper roads as the Grand Duke's party followed the wild rushing of a little river. The Glarian border was within reach, once they climbed the high slopes of the Erhabenhorn and crossed the St. Cyriakus Pass.

Penny would be at home now, safely back in Clumper Cottage with her mother, working with the new steward, making Rascall Hall prosperous. If he closed his eyes he could see her, encased in light at a kitchen table, encased in glee as she learned to ride a horse. If he closed his eyes he could see her, encased in nothing but her own hair and trailing patterns of white petals.

It was a pain so intense he felt ill.

The wolfhound pushed at his legs. "I'm a foolish man, Quest," he said, crouching down and rubbing his face in her fur. "A foolish, wicked man."

The royal barge would be moving slowly up the Rhine, with Lady Beatrice and Gerta now prolonging the farce that Carl, ironically, had started: Princess Sophia was a bad traveler and preferred to remain secluded. Meanwhile Lucas and Fritz would have the real princess secreted in their prearranged hiding place. When the Alvian party transferred to carriages to follow him over this long road into their Alpine kingdom, Sophia would join them. Then Grand Duke Nicholas and his bride could return in triumph to Moritzburg to their coronation next month. He would give her a son. France would lose any hope of gaining Alvia. Glarien would remain independent. He and Sophia could grant the people a free constitution and let their sovereignty fade into benevolence.

A perfect plan and an infinitely empty future.

Quest sat down as someone rapped at his door. Nicholas called permission to enter. *Oak sacred to the druids, iron to scare away the wee folk.* Markos Hentz held up a man who swayed in the hallway—Lucas. Eric and Ludger ran away past them, swords drawn.

"Ah," Nicholas said. "Count Zanich is gone?"

Markos nodded, face white. "Taking several of your courtiers with him. Lars was on watch. He's dead. A kick from a horse, but it was no accident."

To fall asleep on guard duty usually warrants immediate death. . . . Nicholas swallowed the sudden deep rage of grief. *Lars!* Lars, the fuzzy brown-haired soldier from Harzburg. "For God's sake, help Lucas sit down."

The spy folded to a chair, his seal-slick head plastered with rain. Blood oozed from a tear in his coat. Markos poured a glass of brandy and handed it to him.

Lucas took the glass and gulped. "We failed, sire." A little color returned to his pale skin. "We couldn't secure Princess Sophia. She wasn't at Burg Zanich." He set down the glass to wring one hand over his face. "We can't even find out where she is. Meanwhile, though Fritz has done as you told him, rumors are rife in Glarien."

Markos cut away Lucas's torn coat. He stopped the wound with a wad of cravats.

"Rumors about Sophia, the wedding?" Nicholas asked.

"The old tales. Half the population is calling for Carl to rule in your stead."

"So my cousin has kept his agents busy? The people believe Sophia was forced to the match and they want my blood for it? I'm not surprised."

Lucas grimaced. "Your Highness foresaw this?"

"Of course. But I had to go to London to secure the support of the Allied powers. If Carl tries a military coup now, he'll face the armies of half of Europe."

The spy swallowed the rest of his brandy. Blood soaked steadily through the pads. "Nothing so obvious, sire. Your cousin's men have secured the St. Cyriakus Pass. I barely made it through. If you attempt to cross it, you'll be killed."

Water gurgled in the gutters, washing in rivulets across the cobbles. The sky pressed pitch black into the empty inn yard. Nicholas set his saddle on the back of a stout nag, a mount built for tough travel in the mountains. Under the broad stable overhang, flambeaux sizzled, spitting and hissing. He had dispatched messages, cast a net of new strategy—one so full of danger Lucas had begged him not to try it. The Glarisch-speaking peoples were to be ruled by phantoms, while their grand duke groped for an impossible balance on a tightrope that ran ever thinner into a shadowed future.

Picking up his saddlebags, he glanced up at the walls of the Wild Hart inn. A light burned in his room, where Lucas bit down on a cloth as Markos dug out the bullet. Did Carl think he had checkmate—Sophia still imprisoned, his rival lying trapped outside the borders or about to walk into an ambush in the pass? Nicholas smiled grimly. The knight had always been his favorite piece, leaping over the other men in a surprise move. Fritz and a loyal army were camped near Moritzburg. If he could secretly reach them and gain control of the capital, he might outwit Carl yet.

Of course, if Quest disappeared, it would immediately raise suspicion, so she must stay with Lucas. In spite of the risk, in spite of the thin odds, Nicholas would make this journey alone. Eric would tell the rest of the court—the nobles who'd stayed loyal and those of Carl's agents who remained behind to spy on him—that the Grand Duke was taken ill and could see no one.

Lucas would take his place, as Lady Beatrice's woman imper-sonated Sophia on the Rhine barge now that Penny was back in Norfolk.

Ah, Penny, are you sleeping? Do you lie awake and gaze at the moon? Or does it rain in Norfolk, too? Rain on Clumper Cottage and Rascall Hall, on the cows and the vegetables and the orangery? I am mad with grief, beloved!

Nicholas tied on his saddlebags and led the horse out of its stall, a packhorse tied to its tail. Princes should never love. Not places. And especially not people. Yet he loved her. Penny Lindsey of Rascall St. Mary. He would never love any other woman as long as he lived. Thank God the world conspired to protect her from him!

He tightened his girth, just as two nags trotted into the yard. Nicholas watched from the shadows. The riders were just boys. One dismounted and grabbed the bit of the other horse. His boots splashed. The second rider peered about through the rain, swaying in the saddle. Their mounts stood with heads drooping, ears plastered flat, coats soaked to steel gray. The first boy tilted his head, looked up at his companion, and said something. Yel-low light shone on his face for a moment: *Alexis!*

Nicholas strode three long paces and grabbed the second rider before she fell. Alexis snapped to attention, blushing scar-let under his cap of yellow hair.

"Put the nags away," Nicholas shouted. "And stay out of my sight!"

Alexis saluted and obeyed.

Penny stumbled into his chest, chill and wet. The blunt nose dripped water beneath her soggy braids. She was dressed like a boy, but he would know her anywhere, even here in a black night not far from the snow-topped roof of the world, even here, where catastrophe roared from the sky. He hauled her into the shelter of an empty stall and thrust her up against the wooden partition. Her hat was a shapeless mass of wet felt. It wadded in his hand as he tore it away. The packhorse pulled back, startled.

The thunderous roar of rain bellowed of disaster and madness. "So what the devil is this? Lodona, the nymph changed into a river?"

"I had to come," she said stubbornly. "I would not have been safe in Norfolk and if I'm here I can prevent—" She shivered as if unsure. It incensed him, maddened him, broke his heart. "Carl intends to murder Sophia and assassinate you."

"Good," Nicholas replied. "Then we shall have perfect balance in the world, for I intend to murder you."

She steamed and quavered in the shifting light. Her mouth shone pink. He wanted to kiss her. Thrust her up against the manger and kiss her cold, wet mouth until the heat of it burned away the night and conquered the roaring rain. Thrust her down in the straw and tear away the ugly male clothes. Thrust into her warm, female body. Alas that it would be nothing but a vicious rutting, heartless and hot, to be wept over afterward in an orgy of self-loathing.

"You're a monster," she said, rubbing water from her face. "I've just ridden across Europe to find you and now you threaten me with death. What will you do with my body? Bury it in the midden?"

Water stubbled her lashes and plastered her clothes to her skin. She had laid catastrophe directly into his hands. He had wanted her safe at Rascall St. Mary as he faced his destiny. He had faced that future with iron determination. Now his craving roared like a fiend. And the dreadful knowledge ran deep, deeper than fear—the queen had once again swept unexpectedly across the board, but this time he must checkmate, whatever the cost. She was here. He would use her. He *must* use her. And break his oath to himself. He had no other choice left, but was his love at least enough to keep her heart whole while he did it?

He pulled off her wet coat, wrenching her arms from the sleeves. Her shirt was soaked, molded to her breasts. His gaze caught there for a moment, beyond his control to prevent. She was as lovely as any nymph from myth doomed trying to escape the embraces of Pan.

"The midden? Beloved, I can think of far more enticing things to do with your body than that." He let his voice excoriate her. "But alas, we don't have time. I'm happily embroiled in a coup. Now, thanks to this merry little plotting of yours, I have to deal with you, as well."

Her chin quavered. "A coup? Count Zanich?"

He wrapped his own, drier coat about her shoulders. "Lucas couldn't find Sophia, so Carl still has her. He won't harm her, any more than he will harm you—though it was a bloody close call, wasn't it? Suppose my cousin had looked down from a window just now? Alexis deserves to be beaten for this."

Penny hunched into his coat and looked away. "I'm not frightened by your attempts to be nasty, and you can hardly punish Alexis for my transgressions."

"I would stretch him on the rack and paint his treacherous little soul with pain, except that I know the fault is yours. So what the *hell* made you come after me?"

"Carl would have kidnapped me in Norfolk and brought me here anyway."

I should make you wail for me, beloved, as I have wailed for you! Lain awake at night and bayed to the moon like a mad dog! Did you think I wouldn't have protected you, even across oceans?

"No, he would not," he said. "I had secured your safety, and your mother's, even Aunt Horace's. Alas, by some insane oversight, I had not planned that Alexis—and Eric—would disobey my direct orders."

She looked back at him. "Good Lord! You will stretch Eric, as well?"

He touched his lips to the curve of her neck and tasted her pulse, rapid and hot, beneath the veil of rainwater. Rage and anguish made his voice silken. "On second thought, I think I'll reserve the rack for you."

She burned in his hands like a flame. "Oh. In that case, if you would be kind enough to unhand me, I'll just sit down right here in the straw and weep."

"No." His mouth moved up her neck. She tasted of iron-rich mountains and horses. "I have a more imaginative torture in mind for you than that."

A fine tremble ran beneath his palms as if her limbs sang, but she turned her face aside before he could kiss her mouth. "Then I wish you would tell me before I expire from curiosity."

He opened his hands, like a sailor letting go of a mooring rope. "You are my ruin, Penelope Lindsey. I can't leave you here. I can't send you back to England now and guarantee you'll get there. So I'm going to have to take you with me. I'm sure it's what you intended, but do you think your courage equal to it?"

She met his gaze without flinching. "Where are we going?"

"To hell and not by the high road. As it happens, Carl has already gone, taking several members of my court with him. He left a pretty enough excuse, but he has also left an ambush for me in the St. Cyriakus Pass."

She pushed at the straw with the toe of her boot. "Oh, of course. Spies and assassinations. Then he will take the real Princess Sophia to Moritzburg, once he has left you to rot in the snow. That's why I had to come. Don't you see?"

"I don't want you here."

She looked tired. Her mouth trembled. "No. I gathered that from the way you left me in London. So what are you going to do? Will Your Highness stay here and keep safe?"

"Not at all. His Highness intends to go straight into Glarien."

He stepped aside as she pushed past him, keeping his hands still, not reaching out to her, not catching her to his heart and kissing away her sorrow.

"But you said your cousin holds the pass. If you attempt to cross it, you'll be killed?"

"Perhaps." The rain beat and wailed. "But someone has to rescue Sophia."

She stopped with her hand on the iron ring at the opening to the stall. "I can help. I can continue to play princess, so Carl won't gain anything by hurting her—or you."

A gallant, fine bravery—would it be easily broken? A different tightrope stretched, drawn between protection and need. "Yes," he said. "I'm aware of that."

"So what do you plan?"

He wanted to take her hands, almost as filthy now as when he'd first seen them, gathering hedgehogs. He wanted to enfold them in his and offer her safety and laughter. Instead he leaned against the manger and crossed his arms over his chest. "The Erhabenhorn offers more than one way into Glarien. But I shall not be good company. I did warn you, my sweet, tempting reformer, I am prince of devils now."

"Oh, fiddlesticks," she said. "It's your fault that I'm here. After all, you taught me to ride."

She had once thought adventure would be fun, as in tales of Charlemagne or Lancelot or Jack the Giant Killer. Tales of travel to glorious, strange places, where danger made the heart beat just a little faster, before the book closed in time for tea and toast. Instead she had left the barge with only Alexis for company and found misery: worry, discomfort, bad food, worse beds and the agony of riding day in, day out, in the footsteps of a prince and his men, all of whom had ridden since childhood.

Now she rode after him up a dark track that seemed to go nowhere, a packhorse following behind, their path enclosed by dense trees. The rain pounded and pulsed. Water ran down her neck. Her soaked breeches were slick on the wet saddle. The reins had turned into slippery eels, alive in her hands. She followed a man who had become a complete stranger. *My life and my essence has been reformed and remade, as if a metal trinket were melted down and poured into a new mold. Nothing of the original bauble remains.*

Her every overture was met with an icy, brilliant politeness, the cold wit of a man who played chess with nations. A shell impregnable as steel and just as shining. It seemed incredible that she had shared his bed in a heady song of creativity and passion.

Alexis, in disgrace, had been left behind with Quest. At least the wolfhound had seemed happy to see her. Eric and the other men lingered at the inn, making sure no one knew that Nicholas had ever left. Yet why did he risk this journey without the protection of his bodyguard? She had pleaded and cajoled without success. If Carl's men found them, the outcome was obvious: *What if Sophia dies and Nicholas dies—and you and I rule together? It is not ideal, but it might answer.*

They found shelter in abandoned barns and huts and once in a cave. Nicholas made her rest while he saw to the horses: grooming; taking them to water; hobbling them in choice, sheltered meadows; feeding the grain the packhorse carried along with their own food, extra clothes, and bedding.

He shared bread, cheese and wine with her, breaking food with the elegant fingers that had once placed rose petals on her breasts. He didn't touch her and barely talked to her. It rained for three days—lightly in the mornings, turning to thunderous downpours in the afternoons—while they climbed steadily higher into the Alps, riding as long as it was light with only short breaks for meals and rest. She was wet, day and night. Wet and cold. Her lungs burned in the rarefied atmosphere.

"Am I cleaning boots?" she asked once when they had to dismount and lead their mounts up a slippery staircase of rock. Sharp-edged stones bruised the soles of her feet and rattled away down the slope if she took a careless step. She was gasping for air, each breath searing. "I disobeyed orders. Is this the prescribed punishment?"

He looked back at her. Water streamed over the planes of his face. "Why do you ask?"

"I thought such a chastisement was merciful at the time. Now I think perhaps a flogging would be kinder than all that drawn-out worry over blacking and spit-and-polish."

He gave her a cold, tight smile. "Faster, certainly. Though just as humiliating. However, I'm the one mucking out the horses, so let's just accept that we share in this punishment."

She felt defiant. She wanted to force him to some kind of reckoning. "Why does it have to be a punishment?"

"Because that is the nature of ambition." It was as if he spoke through a wall of steel. "It is also the nature of pilgrimage."

Water ran cold over her face and sent damp trickles inside her collar. "Pilgrimage?"

"We're on slopes of the Erhabenhorn, a mountain sacred to the Almighty. Pilgrims took this route long ago as penance. We'll get shelter at a holy shrine tonight. Shall we go on?"

The rain thinned with the daylight. Black, wet day giving way to a gray, chill twilight. The path had become impossibly steep. Once again, they led the horses.

Nicholas stopped. "Look ahead."

Penny glanced up from the rocky path. A square stone tower rose above them, topped by a pyramidal roof and a cross. Behind the little stone building, the high mountains rose in ranks, but the church still dominated its own knob of rock and the meadow rioting with wildflowers that fringed it. As she watched, a single shaft of white sunlight broke between the clouds, illuminating the building against the bruised backdrop of sheer cliffs and towering heights. Something in the juxtaposition of the massive mountains and the humbleness of the little church filled her with a poignant awe, as if the landscape had been created just to inspire this moment.

"The pilgrim's church of St. Cyriakus, the healer," Nicholas said lightly. "It's barely the size of a henhouse and one thousand years old."

"Why was it built here?"

"Because it faces *Der Drache*—the Dragon—across the valley. The mountains of Glarien boast saints and demons in equal measure. It was believed that a dragon lived curled in those far cliffs. Its tongues of flame roasted several passing travelers, until the saint cursed it and locked it forever in a tomb of rock."

She glanced at him, still and mysterious, her dark prince. "People believe that?"

He grinned. "Of course. Even though St. Cyriakus lived in Rome several hundred years before this church was built, and Glarien—just to spite some of its neighbors—is officially Protestant."

Penny followed him the last few yards to a stone hut built below the church. Nicholas tied and unsaddled the horses. It was always his ritual to take care of their mounts before he rested or ate or washed. She didn't begrudge it. If he would have allowed it, she would have helped him. Instead she sat in an exhausted huddle on the doorstep and watched his lithe back and careful, strong hands and the heartbreaking way he whispered endearments to the animals.

When the door opened behind her, she almost fell.

"Don't be afraid, daughter," a voice said gently.

Penny looked up into the face of an old man wearing a long black robe and a large crucifix. He held a stick in one hand. With the other he felt carefully for the door frame.

"You have come to visit the shrine?" the blind man asked. "So that St. Cyriakus may bless your marriage?"

"My marriage cannot be blessed, Father," Penny said.

A gnarled hand rested gently on her hair. "Every couple who visits this holy place is blessed. At harvest time your children will be weighed in grapes to be given to the poor." He chuckled. "St. Cyriakus will not stint either children or fruit. Let me take your husband's hand."

Nicholas laid his palm in the old man's. The blind eyes closed. "The grand duke's heir is weighed in gold for the poor every St. Cyriakus day. You remember it?"

"I remember it," Nicholas said.

"You never weighed enough as a boy, Your Royal Highness," the priest said, rapping the ground with his stick. "You should have eaten more. Is that why you have done so much good for the people now?" He pinched Nicholas's arm, then groped for his shoulder. "Ah! Ah! You've become a fine man and a fine ruler! But when Princess Sophia has a baby, it'll be a tiny enough measure of St. Cyriakus gold for the people. It'll take them a little while to understand your reforms. Glarians are stubborn."

"Grand Duke Nicholas introduces reforms?" Penny asked.

The old priest chuckled again. "The new grand duke replaces all our old barbarities with kindnesses, daughter. Kneel."

The idyllic scene made her suddenly frantic, but Nicholas caught her hand and pulled her down beside him. They knelt side by side on the wet, rough stones, while the priest laid a hand on each of their heads and began to recite a long blessing. Her fingers were entwined in the strong, sure grip that had soothed the horses. She thought she could feel his heart beat in rhythm with hers, binding her, binding her in this mad marriage to the man she loved and could never have, the man who daily repudiated her. Tears broke and rolled as it began to rain again, gently, a soft beneficence from the heavens to mingle with her weeping and blur it into insignificance.

Their bed was in the church porch, the traditional lodging, apparently, for pilgrims.

"How did he know who you were?" Penny whispered after the old man had gone.

Nicholas stared out across the narrow valley to the peaks. "He did not. He is mad, a mad hermit. It was harmless to humor him."

"What was that about reforms for Glarien? What barbarities did he speak of?"

"I don't know." He rested one hand on the stone wall and leaned his cheek against it. The line of his back and arm was piercingly lovely, a live bulwark against the dying day. "The law codes, perhaps. The way the courts work. The schools and hospitals. The lost franchise."

"What franchise?"

"The people of each town and parish have always elected two representatives to a council that advises the grand duke— until my grandfather refused to call the council and let it all lapse. Any form of government dependent on the qualities of one man is horribly flawed. I am reinstating and expanding the council. Meanwhile, I have abolished the worst excesses of the law code and tried to redress a few of my people's grievances, that's all."

She hugged her blanket close under her chin. The stone floor was unforgiving beneath her hip as she tried to turn over. "I've been a fool, haven't I? From the beginning, when you let me accuse you of not caring about ordinary people, about your subjects, when I berated you about Rascall St. Mary, you had already done all this—instituted changes, begun creating a parliament. Why?"

His voice sounded merely weary. "When I was a child, I was weighed every St. Cyriakus day to determine the largesse given to the poor. What did you say at Rascall Hall? 'To replace a man's livelihood with charity is a way to turn him into a sot or a villain.' I didn't want to weigh more to give the people of Glarien food, I wanted to see them prosperous in their own work and with the dignity to determine their own lives. As soon as my grandfather died, I began what I could. Once I am crowned with Sophia, it can all go ahead."

"Why didn't you tell me?" *He was a lad with a heart of gold,* Mrs. Hardacre had said. *He'd have wept over a dead sparrow. He brought his own toys for my little brother when Peter was taken ill with the smallpox and near died of it.*

"Only another kind of vanity," Nicholas replied. "It seemed better at the time if you didn't think too well of me."

"Oh, God," she said. "You conceited bastard!"

He turned then, but with the light behind him she couldn't see his face, only the powerful lines of his silhouette. Craving moved in her, pooling hot blood in her groin, her longing for his body and his kindnesses almost undermining her.

"I'm as full of self-importance as the next man, obviously, but I don't think it simply conceit to judge when it might be better not to blow one's own horn. The glamour of being royal brings its own shadow—the responsibility not to misuse it. I don't deny conceit. I would deny that it rules me. I would deny that I'm not capable of sometimes making good judgments. For God's sake, I've made plenty of bad ones. The price is always paid in gall. Anyway, you are the bastard, Princess."

"I am the idiot who has let you play me for a tool," she said bitterly. "Good night."

The rain stopped in the night. Thank God. For up here it would soon have turned to snow, even in midsummer. They had ridden on for one more day, barely speaking except for necessities, and slept in a disused hut high up in the Drachenalp. What had that mad old priest surmised? He had blessed their union in a ritual that was at least seven hundred years old.

Penny wouldn't have followed most of the archaic Glarisch with its odd rhythms and distorted vowels. But Nicholas understood. In the sight of God and St. Cyriakus, they were bound for eternity: not the grand duke and the proxy princess as it had been in London, but Nicholas and Penny, man and woman, in a bond that simply couldn't be broken, yet could never be allowed. It helped to be a modern man, he supposed, for whom religion was merely a gloss. Yet a profound disquiet fomented—as if the dragon stirred in its grave of rock—like the guilt and horror of any long-ago pilgrim yearning hopelessly and too late for absolution from mortal sin.

Nicholas stared at the mantled pinnacles guarding the frontiers of Glarien. Dawn light flared in a high wilderness of frost, as if the mountains caught fire. Beneath his feet the small meadow scintillated with flowers. As the rising sun caught each one, petals blazed: the darkest rose pink, lace white, pollen yellow, blue bleeding to purple. A carpet of bloom rioted over the short turf until it fringed away at the edge of the last stands of trees. And beyond them the high Alps, like rows of blushing maidens.

He had first seen this fire of dawn-kissed ice when he was eleven, on that journey to Moritzburg—mountains blazing across the morning horizon beyond the rolling green meadows of the Win Valley. His mother's face had fired with joy at the sight. He'd realized then that she hadn't liked England and had left her husband behind with barely a shrug of regret. His parents had never seen each other again.

Yet regret dogged him now day and night, poisoning his judgment. Regret for Lars, for all the men who had given their lives for him. Blunt, clever Lars would never see the Alps catch fire again. Lars was dead. It was the greatest of his own weaknesses—a potentially fatal weakness in a prince—that Nicholas couldn't bear to have any man die for him.

Now he brought Penny, step by step, with him into the lion's den. If he failed, made one slip, she would fall into Carl's hands while Grand Duke Nicholas became a memory, helpless in death, like the high wind whistling over the ice. Pain reverberated as a bird began to sing, calling a cold, liquid litany across the glaciers. Men died, women suffered, so that princes had power. But if princes failed in their sacred trust, who would rule? The mob? The upstart opportunists who had run France during the Terror?

"I'm stunned," she said behind him. Her voice was still a little bruised with resentment. "I had no idea. No wonder Rascall Hall seems insignificant to you."

He turned. The sun gilded her hair and stained pink across her cheeks. She lifted both hands, as if to catch the bright rays as they broke through the high clouds. Beams of sunshine gathered in her palms like gold. Hunger for that brightness surged through his blood, firing the desire he'd kept banked for days.

She dropped her hands and stared at him, flaming with light, while flowers sprang like shattered rainbows at her feet. He knew his craving must be written on his face, past his strength to control, as hers was written in her dilated eyes and flushed cheeks.

"Flowers," she said. "At least they're not white roses." She turned and strode away.

"Don't run from me," he shouted.

She stopped. "How dare you? How *dare* you? Accuse *me* of running? We've been traveling for days. If this mission fails, I face a far crueler fate than you. Yet, after all we've shared, you treat me like a pariah. *You* are the coward!"

He walked up to her, his control back in place. "Of course. Because I have delayed what has to be said? Very well, I'll say it now. Our wedding night was a mistake—a natural enough moment of weakness when we were both flushed with success. I had no intention of ever seeing you again."

She was rigid. "So it seemed a kindness to leave me with a pretty memory?"

Shame burned like a dark calyx beneath each ridge of bright petals. Desperately he strove for honesty. "It seemed a cruelty to refuse you, certainly."

Penny wrapped her arms about her breasts. "I can't think of anything more hateful, Your Royal Highness. It's like your splendid conceit when you let me think the worst of you. The way you humored me when I said your reform was my mission. 'I serviced your sad little needs out of pity, to do otherwise would have been unkind.' Yes, you put me on the rack! You patronize and humiliate me."

"That isn't the truth."

She spun toward him, the rising sun shining wheat and salmon in her hair. "Then what is?"

He groped for a way to mend it. "The needs were mine, obviously. They were terrible and strong. You were generous."

"But you would never have touched me, if I hadn't asked? Oh, God! What a condescending, odious attitude! A man obsessed with self-control, who admits only that he made one wrong judgment and regrets it. It's hateful! You're hateful!"

As if the face of *Der Drache* cracked open, his passionate anger roared. "When have I ever denied it? Do you want more proof?"

He seized her head in both hands and pressed his mouth over hers. He kissed ruthlessly, forcing her mouth open. She struggled, but he kept kissing—tasting, inhaling, her wheat hair soft in his hands, her breasts crushed against him. It was a deliberate ravishment, brutal and harsh. Yet passion flared. His arousal reared between them and he felt her response. When he opened his hands and let go, her lips were swollen and hot, her nipples erect beneath the boy's shirt.

"Go on," he said. "Strike me! Why not?"

She stepped back, rubbing the back of one hand over her mouth, dawn-stained mountains firing in her dilated eyes. She gave a brave half-laugh, though tears shone on her lashes. "Well, there's the sacred person, for a start. Do you think I deserved that? What for?"

Shame washed through his blood. He was seized with madness. "Because that was honest. That's what I want. I don't want to play games of seduction and subtlety. I want to take you, here in a meadow of flowers with those peaks watching it and the dragon ready to howl flames of triumph. You accuse me of duplicity? Good. Then you are beginning to know me. But don't think I made love to you from pity or with disdain."

The ice-cold peaks glistened, pristine, defiantly shedding mantles of pink-stained cloud. The grazing horses moved awkwardly in their hobbles. The hut behind her revealed, stone by stone, its dilapidated condition as sunbeams searched into every crevice.

"Yet you think you have absolute control? That real yearning cannot move you? And that tenderness is only a sham for you?" She shrugged out of her jacket and tossed it to a rock, then yanked off her boots and stockings so she stood barefoot in the grass.

Craving seized him as if he were caught in the mouth of the monster and shaken. "For God's sake, I don't deny raw desire."

Her breeches were filthy, stained with travel. She bent and tugged them off, leaving her clad only in the boy's shirt, too long for her. His blood roared, pounding through his veins. The ice peaks sparkled, blinding him, scattering crystalline colors over her hair.

He was desperate. "I thought I would never see you again. Can't you understand? How else could I have risked what we did?"

"You said you were in love with me."

"Then I lied!"

She peeled off her shirt. The sun ran over naked flesh: her woman's curves; her small, ripe breasts; her sex hidden and mysterious behind its fuzz of hair. Moisture shone on her eyelashes like pearls, fired with the cold dawn light.

The shirt hung in her hands, partly covering her. "You moved me to my soul that night in London. Each rose petal scorched my skin. I was fired, ecstatic, enraptured, as if you really were Prince Charming and I, Cinderella. Though I thought you held back, held yourself back and safe from me, it was still the loveliest thing that ever happened to me. Why do you want to smash the memory of it—of anything real or intimate we have shared?"

"I do not," he said. "I only want to crush anything it might seem to have promised."

"Yes, I suppose you do." Tears broke and ran, tracing down her cheeks. "Just another manipulation. Everything you do or touch is planned from the start. Everything! When you first kissed me. When you made me ride Driver with you. You deliberately took me to that church, knowing what the priest would say: that he knew you. Why do you deny it?"

"I never saw him in my life before. I did not plan what happened there." It was the truth.

"You knew Carl would insist on the wedding night rituals and you wanted to fulfill them—every part of them—in case there was doubt cast on the marriage. He might have burst in on us, mightn't he? With witnesses. Mightn't he?"

"It had been suggested, during my disrobing earlier." Another truth, intensely painful.

Her lip curled. She was magnificent, unashamed, glorious. "The prince of Glarien could hardly have been found sleeping in the armchair on his wedding night. No, he had better be found rutting with his bride. He could make it a pretty enough affair. After all, he'd planned an exquisite enough campaign of seduction to lead up to it. Afterward she would go back to Norfolk with a tender memory to nurse into her inevitable spinsterhood. How very generous! You even pretended reluctance, so I would ask for it. You bastard!"

"None of that is true." His rampage of desire cracked and shifted. Rage boiled up, refusing to be denied. He strode up to her. "I could have raped you. I still can. I'm a prince of Glarien. I carry the blood of monsters in my veins. My ancestors were vampires. They despoiled their way across Hungary, ravished their way into the Alps."

"As did mine! My father was a prince from Alvia. Have you forgotten? When I was very little, he sent me a doll. I broke it. It's my blood, too. This is my country. I'm not here for you. I'm here to fulfill my birthright." She dropped the shirt.

He tore off his jacket and wrapped it about her, pulling her to his chest. Shivering and hot. "Penny! Beloved! I can't bear it!"

He lowered his head to hers and began kissing again. The sway of her back slid under his palms. She was infinitely beautiful. Rage dissolved, shredding in the face of such pristine loveliness. Perhaps he groaned like a man flogged. Perhaps he bit through his lip to keep from screaming on the rack. For one moment he fought for objectivity, before the hot shivering need overwhelmed him and battered him to the ground, taking her with him.

Her fingers touched his hair and cheek. She ran her palms over his shoulders. Without a word she pushed at his shirt collar, peeling it back, and pressed her mouth to his neck. Dawn light glowed over her shoulders, over her breasts. The nipples stood out hard. Gooseflesh rose on her skin in a wave.

She lay beneath him on his spread jacket, crying. Frantically he kissed away the tears. Frantically he feasted his palms on her chill flesh, then tore at the buttons on the front of his breeches until his cock sprang free. She grabbed at him with shattering bravery, caressing him as if she found him wonderful. In an agony of longing he let her do it, holding himself back, the dread of hurting her swelling and pulsing along with his need.

"Penny, I did not lie," he said. "I did not lie. God help me, I love you."

She caught his jaw in both hands and smiled, wriggling beneath him. Without any subtlety or gentleness he thrust her legs apart. Her moisture and heat enveloped him. He drove into her, fiercely possessive, taking this one woman as he had dreamed of taking her, with absolute abandon. She met him, wrapping her legs over his back, crying out. Her hands slipped into his hair, holding tightly enough to hurt. Laughing wildly he plunged into her heat. Pain and pleasure mingled into ecstasy until the mounting waves of need coalesced into a shouting, turbulent orgasm.

He rolled away, exhausted, then staggered to his feet. He pulled his clothes together, hideously aware that he had taken her naked while he was fully clothed. She curled up on her side, pulling his coat over her breasts. She smiled.

"I think that was honest," she said.

Shame roared. Migraine slammed fully formed into his brain, making his right eye throb and burn. Shattered, dazzling lights danced around his vision like demons.

"It was honest," he said. "It's a disaster for both of us. Don't blame me, Penny, if I tried to lie. I've broken my oath, to your mother and to myself. God forgive me."

He staggered away into the hut, fighting nausea, shaking with terror and remorse. She had no idea. Her mind was still filled with romantic fantasies. He didn't even know how to begin to break them, or if he should break them. In a few more days he would send her back to England. Forever. He could hold on. He must.

She walked into the hut, dressed again. Her shoulders looked fragile in the shadows. She stared at him gravely. "I think you must allow me my own autonomy in this."

He forced himself to ignore the headache. "What do you mean?"

"When you first came to Rascall Hall, I didn't want to help you. I was content enough with my life in the village."

He picked up a halter. "It no longer contents you?"

"I took on a cause. The cause is bigger than Grand Duke Nicholas now. What did you think? That I can trifle with the Tsar and not be contaminated with a new discontent? I'm here to do what I can for Glarien. I know you think you must spare me. I don't give a damn about that. How do we stop Carl? How do we rescue Sophia?"

So she tried to negate what she had just done, what he had just done. She tried to claim nobler ends. Treacherous thoughts moved, unholy temptations.

"I don't know," he said. "Let me explain one small inconvenience. Carl has spread rumors about me. He always did. Now the effort is intensified. It may be that the people will tear me apart as soon as they see me."

"Rumors? What rumors?"

He laughed, unable to hide bitterness. "That I'm decadent, depraved, corrupt. That I am bestial. That I practice the black arts."

She gave a little laugh. "Then I think our cause is doomed. After all, I know perfectly well that you practice the black arts. How else did you achieve what you've done to me?"

Fifteen

*T*hey rode over the high passes of the Streitaxt and the Ochsen-horn on goatherds' tracks, leaving the Erhabenhorn behind: God's mountain cloaked in cloud and mystery. The sun shone from a sky washed clean as blue wool. The air tingled with ice crystals and flowery scents. When the sound of cowbells—and once, human laughter—rang too closely, Nicholas put his horse into the trees or dropped out of sight over a ridge. Penny followed blindly. They met no one and she had no idea where they were going. She only knew she rode with a gaping hole in her heart and the mad tingle of insanity dancing at the edge of her brain. Alas, what had happened to sensible Penny Lindsey?

She had followed a necromancer into fairyland and the price of the journey was his possession of her dreams. The line of his back enthralled her. His fine hands. The intensely masculine strength and grace and mastery. All that beauty dedicated to bedevil her. For he was locked in a deathly silence, as if unable to speak.

She tried once to reach him. Remembering his kisses. Remembering that one night in a bed filled with rose petals. Remembering his fierce passion as he took her in an icy dawn, surrounded by wildflowers. They had stopped for their midday bread and cheese. The bread was stale now, the cheese getting hard. He sat on a rock and divided it, passing her the more generous ration and a cup of wine.

"Why does it seem better to you if I'm not willing?" she asked. "Is a willing woman so terrifying? I want to be honest because I think there's nothing to be gained by pretense."

His eyes filled with pain before he looked away. "My reluctance has nothing to do with that."

With a mad insistence, she stood up and walked into his line of sight. He glanced up at her from fathomless wells of darkness.

She looked at his hands, their startling beauty stained with the honest dirt of caring for the horses. "Perhaps if we pretend to be something, we become it—just for that moment, at least. I pretended to be a princess in London. You pretended to be a lover. For that moment, whatever you intended, that is what happened. Nicholas, it isn't necessary to break my heart, truly. I understand your destiny. I know there's no future for us. I see that your honor forbids you to think you can make me your mistress. But this insistence on silence is driving me mad."

He jerked as if she'd struck him. *"Honor?"* Then as if realizing he had given something away, he smiled. Something in the smile threatened to break her heart. "What do you want me to say?"

"Anything. Anything true. I want to share whatever is killing you now." She sat down and put her head in her hands.

He crossed the few steps that separated them and knelt beside her. Her hands strayed onto his shoulders as he bent her head to fit there, cradled in his arms. Great racking sobs welled up from some dark, hidden pool of despair.

"Penny," he said. "Hush. My silence isn't for you."

"Then what?"

His fingers stroked her hair. The long horseman's fingers, filled with subtle mastery. "I have sorrows other than what I carelessly allowed to develop between us. You don't need to know."

"I must know. I must know what is happening. How can I cope when we reach Moritzburg, if I don't know everything? If

you don't tell me, I'm leaving and may you practice your black
arts on houseflies!"

He pulled her down to him. She slid off the rock to be enfolded in his arms. He cradled her head on his shoulder,
stroking her back. She thought he hesitated, as if reluctant to
speak, then the words came out one at a time, clipped like beads
cut from a string.

"Very well. Here is one. Lars is dead. Carl killed him at the
Wild Hart. It was made to look like an accident."

"Oh, Nicholas." Shock stuck in her throat. Her voice was
raw. "I'm sorry. Why didn't you tell me?"

His fingers touched her hair. "I didn't want you to know."

"Because you loved him?"

Tiny calluses ran rough over her cheek. "Lars? No. He was a
good man. A good soldier. His death fills me with a terrifying
fury. But I didn't love him. Princes cannot afford to care too
much about their men."

Penny pulled away and looked at him. "And a man can't afford not to, for the sake of his own soul. He died for you. Can't
you make space in your own heart for your grief?"

His eyes were shadowed with black smoke. "What the devil
do you mean?"

"I think we must make a shrine for Lars. Something for re-
membrance. What did he like?"

"Plump blondes and apricots." His voice was bitter. "And
beer. The things most men like."

"Apricots? If you hadn't loved him at all, you wouldn't
know that. Let us make him a shrine, up here in these mountains. We'll make it peach and yellow. You have your blade. Cut
some stakes and let us build something—a cross in his memory."

He dropped his head, staring at his hands. "Penny, I'm a
prince, not a carpenter."

"Do you think Lars would care about the quality of the
workmanship?"

Nicholas stood up and strode away. He hacked some
branches off a tree, stripping bark to shape some clumsy sticks
with his knife. She walked away to find flowers, anything or-

ange or yellow, gathering them in big bunches. When she came back, the prince knelt before a small pile of stones. A rough cross jutted up from them. Whatever his lack in skill, he had carved one recognizable word in a flattened place on one stick. *Lars*. She covered the rocks with the blooms.

"You have done it for him, with your own hands," she said. "I think he would like it."

She stared through blurred lashes at the bright sky, while Nicholas knelt by their little shrine and sobbed at last.

The next morning their track began to dive downhill. Below them the broad valley overflowed with heavy mist. Nicholas stopped his horse. Penny rode up beside him. In the distance the mountain peaks soared rank after rank, tipped with dawn light. The mist in the valley made a white eiderdown, fluffed over whatever lay beneath. As they watched, it began to dissolve in layers, like a trifle being eaten by a child. First the whipped cream, then the custard, then the fruit, until finally the child's spoon scraped at cake and jelly and formed them into fantastic shapes.

The top layer had lifted from the ramparts of a castle. A castle from a fairy tale, rich in towers and spires, gargoyles and battlements, the accretion of centuries.

"In 1022," Nicholas said, "a knight called Moritz built a keep to guard the crossing over the Win River. The castle was taken twice by treachery, but in eight hundred years it has never been taken by siege or direct attack."

"That's your capital city?" The mist seemed to froth about the towers, peeling more deeply to reveal high stone walls growing straight from sheer granite cliffs.

"When a bridge was built over the ford, a walled town grew at the foot of the castle rock. The knights of Glarien became counts of Moritzburg—Moritz's castle—then princes. Though we rose to be dukes of Glarien and finally grand dukes, we still hold the title of Winsteg also—the bridge over the Win that started it all."

Church spires and chimneys broke through the shredding mists. Rooftops followed, clustered about the forbidding castle rock. A town full of citizens. How many of them believed their grand duke, with his new reforms and his promise of a parliament, practiced black arts and intended treachery?

"The bridge is still there?"

He glanced back at her and grinned. "The bridge is where we shall stand or fall. I imagine Carl has it well guarded."

He rode forward. As they descended the dizzying track into the valley, the mists burned away before them. Behind them lay a bright day in the high Alps. Large bells rang as the cattle moved to pasture after milking. Perhaps this was the last view she would ever see: the prince riding and the clouds parting in front of him like the Red Sea before Moses, while far beyond him the mountains surrendered their blushing pinks for veils of snow white, like so many brides.

Her heart began to pound as they rode closer. From the heights Moritzburg had seemed insubstantial, like an iced-cake fantasy. From the valley floor the castle rose in a forbidding pile, dominating the town. Without hesitation, Nicholas drove his horse forward. His mount began to trot, then to canter. Penny rode behind him, their packhorse clanking at her heels. A camped army materialized around them as if soldiers had been sown from dragon's teeth. Nicholas rode straight through them, past tents and campfires without a backward glance.

"These are your soldiers?"

His teeth gleamed for a moment through the fog. "All soldiers in Glarien are mine. Even those who think they are loyal to Carl. Don't worry. Fritz is waiting for us in the mist."

Sick with apprehension, Penny followed until Nicholas pulled up before a small cluster of farm buildings. The farmhouse was built from rough stone, but a fire and fresh food waited within. Penny gratefully ate hot soup while Nicholas and Fritz made plans.

"I have four thousand loyal men camped at this end of the valley, sire," Fritz said. "Carl has only a fraction of that in Moritzburg."

"But his men hold the bridge. They'll be nervous. Nervous trigger fingers are dangerous."

"We can take them," Fritz said.

Nicholas smiled. "In 1428 a garrison of ten held the bridge against an army of ten thousand. What you suggest would no doubt be splendid, if brutal."

Fritz looked grim, the scar white. "They hold a good defensive position, of course. There'll be losses on both sides, but we'll win in spite of history."

Penny set down her spoon. Her appetite had gone. "That's what you will do? Storm the bridge?"

"No, Princess. I don't crave civil war." Smoke spiraled in his eyes. "I prefer not to take my own kingdom by force."

The Win River ran fast and furious beside the road, roaring down from the glaciers, cutting a deep ravine. Penny saw the bridge before she focused on how it was built. Beneath a soaring arch the Win thundered into a chasm. At one time a ford must have crossed above the waterfall where the water was shallow, before it made its precipitous plunge. Now the bridge spanned from rock to rock. To fall from the parapets would be a toss to the death a hundred feet below, into a maelstrom of white water. On the other side, the guns on the ramparts of the castle kept the old ford and the bridge in their sights, guarding the town clustered beneath the rock.

A good defensive position.

The bridge was blocked with a mass of men. Their helmets gleamed silver and black in the morning sun like a flock of magpies. Hoisted on gilt rods, two banners waved high above the soldiers. A mass of townspeople hung from windows and outside stairways, watching.

"Those black leather hats make excellent buckets," Nicholas said, "in a pinch. The silver feathers are just for show. A bloody nuisance and impossible for the men to keep in good order. The uniform and banners are those of Zanich, of course. By tradition, Carl may keep a force of his own."

Soldiers. Carl's soldiers blocked the bridge. A flutter of panic disrupted her heartbeat, robbed her mouth of moisture.

Beside her, Nicholas rode a new iron-gray horse with a silver mane. He was encased in a white uniform with flashes of gold braid. An ivory velvet cloak with a yellow silk lining swung from one shoulder. From his ceremonial helmet to his boots he glimmered in precious metals, white silk and black leather. Other than the vivid dark hair and eyes, only the blue sash of royalty and the decorations that covered his chest broke the startling metallic monochrome. A fortune in gold and diamonds for desperate men, even the hilt of his sword was jeweled. At one time, perhaps, such regal splendor might have cowed any crowd. But times had changed—ever since a revolutionary government had cut off the head of a king in Paris.

She had begged and cajoled, even wept. She had not been able to prevent him from doing this. They rode alone. Major Baron von Gerhard and his four thousand men had been left behind at the farmhouse. Fritz had added his own arguments, daring to insist, at one time hammering his gnarled fist on the table. Nicholas had ruthlessly reduced the older man to a red-faced silence.

"No one will stand up to you?" Penny had shouted then. "Well, I will! You may force obedience from your men, but not from me. You will not ride alone to your death!"

He had fixed her with a gaze that burned like coals. "Dear me! Grand Duke Nicholas will do as His Royal Highness damned well wishes. You, madam, will stay here. Perhaps you will burn a candle to St. Cyriakus?"

In the face of his bitter sarcasm she had slumped to a chair and dropped her head into her hands. "St. Cyriakus? Why?"

"The saint made a living driving devils out of princesses." His voice had become surprisingly gentle. "He rescued the daughters of both the emperor of Rome and the king of Persia from their mortifying afflictions. Alas, he was martyred for his trouble, but such is the price of canonization—or of messing with female demons."

"Very well," Penny had said. "If you insist on being a martyr, I'm coming with you."

He'd gazed at her for a moment, his mouth set in a strange small smile. "Obviously I cannot prevent you, short of locking you up. You will be perfectly safe. No one would harm Sophia."

So she rode behind him in the uniform of a captain of his

guard, green and gold, on a white horse the same age as she was.

"You'll need a steady old fellow," Nicholas had said with a hint of humor, "in case there is a mishap, after all."

The Win roared and tumbled. Nicholas urged his mount to a gallop. Penny tore behind him. Stones clattered as the horses raced toward the bridge. Wind whipped at her face. Her horse surged beneath her in a wild, suicidal dash.

I think you have led too sheltered a life, Miss Lindsey, and haven't played enough games. What you describe isn't fear, it's excitement. To have the heart tremble and flutter, men risk a fortune on cards. To have the belly gripe, they face a horse at a fence that's too high. To have the moisture flee their mouths, they visit the wife of a rival in her bedroom while her husband's still in the house. Because at the same time the blood sings, the mind soars, and the soul cries out in exhilaration.

In a mad reversal of everything she believed about herself, she knew she was appalled, terrified and aflame with excitement.

The soldiers on the bridge were armed with muskets. Their faces came clearly into focus, grimacing as they tore into their powder packs and rammed home bullets. Penny wanted to laugh. She had gone through so much! Now she was going to die with her dark prince in a hail of lead.

An officer held up his hand. The muskets rose, barrel mouths gaping. Nicholas tore toward them. Iron-shod hooves rang on the stones as the horse suddenly squatted on its hind legs and skidded to a halt, neck bent gently. Penny's horse stopped automatically behind it.

"When I dismount, take my horse and ride back a little," Nicholas said quietly. *"Do it!"*

He vaulted from the saddle and held out his arms.

"You may not pass," the officer said.

Penny caught his horse's trailing reins. Suddenly she felt dizzy and unreal, as if all this were happening to someone else. They were ringed in loaded musket barrels.

"Do it!"

She led his horse back, her heart thundering. Her excitement dissolved into pure terror.

His spurs clicked on the stones as Nicholas strode steadily toward the massed muskets. Still walking, he unstrapped the sword from his belt. He stopped and laid it reverently on the cobbles.

"The blade of St. Cyriakus," he said. "Containing the saint's finger bone in its hilt." The men gaped over their raised guns. Nicholas began to walk forward again. "I am unarmed."

In a single smooth movement, he unpinned diamonds and gold. They fell with the blue sash and his velvet cloak to the cobbles. No one moved as he shrugged out of his coat. His shirtsleeves shone white in the clear morning light. With one hand he undid the buttons on his embroidered waistcoat and dropped it behind him, striding ever forward.

"You may not pass!" shouted the officer, red-faced beneath his silver-and-black headgear.

Nicholas lifted his arms and wrenched his shirt over his head, to walk steadily—clothed only in breeches and boots—into two hundred musket barrels. His back flexed with each stride, long smooth muscles knitting into the indent of supple spine. Sun slipped over naked skin in a silken caress.

"I am your servant," he said, clear but quiet. "A man, like yourselves. I am also your prince. Who will be the first to shoot me?"

The officer was sweating. "You're an Englishman who lays claim to the throne of Glarien and wants to impose foreign ways on us."

A muttering rose from the men. *Devil, black devil, to fly here over oceans and mountains—on a broomstick—on the back of a black goose—to arrive here on your demon horse without going over the pass of St. Cyriakus.*

Nicholas stopped, with the closest gun barrels only five feet from his naked chest. "It takes a son of Moritzburg to know the high tracks over the Erhabenhorn, the Streitaxt, the Ochsenhorn. Your family has long pastured its goats in the shadow of *Der Drache,* Herr Linn. Your mother's house nestles below the south flanks of the Ochsenhorn, Herr Adler."

Two men stepped back, faces pale, their muskets wavering, though the rumor kept running. *Prince of devils. Black Prince Nicholas.*

"I remember you both," Nicholas said. "Herr Adler reset a shoe on my horse after my cousin and I went hunting from Burg Zanich. Herr Linn held the bridle. It was a job well done. Do you think a future grand duke doesn't remember his subjects?"

"Your Royal Highness gave us each a gold sovereign," one of the men blurted. "You weren't much more than a lad."

"Ay, an English lad," another voice said. *Our Count Zanic has a better claim!*

Nicholas smiled, confident and sure. "It takes a prince of Glarien to make a pilgrimage through God's own mountains. Yet any man is humble at the shrine of St. Cyriakus on the slopes of the Erhabenhorn, where I took my bride for the hermit's blessing. I am yours, soldiers. I am your servant to do with as you will."

He made a sweeping gesture, filled with power and imperiousness, and dropped to one knee.

He's a suitor, Penny thought. *He has wooed. Will he win? Or will they tear him limb from limb like a fox caught by hounds?*

As if choreographed, the rest of the musket barrels wavered. A great shout went up from the soldiers. Surging forward they flung down their weapons and surrounded Nicholas. The officer shouted orders, but the men had broken ranks. Some ran to gather his clothes and jewels. Others raced straight toward Penny. With a thumping, sick heart, she rode forward to meet them, leading Nicholas's horse. *It is all or nothing. The horses have taught you how to be royal.* She closed her eyes for a split second and whispered a quick prayer to the saint who cast demons from women.

"You are in the palm of my hand, daughter!"

Startled, she looked up, but no one was there who could have spoken.

Penny urged her horse to a trot, then a canter. The mob split, running on each side of her. Dropping her reins on her mount's neck for a moment, she tore off her cap and pulled the ribbons from her hair. It uncoiled and fell about her shoulders, flying back behind her as the horse began to gallop.

"The princess!" someone cried. It was taken up on all sides. "Princess Sophia! Princess Sophia!"

The last group of men divided to reveal Nicholas clumsily reclothed in all of his glory. Rough soldiers had played courtier and fought for the chance to hand him his coat or his sash. Carl's soldiers. He grinned up at her, before catching his horse's reins and vaulting into the saddle. With a sweeping gesture, he drew the jeweled sword from the scabbard and held it aloft for a moment so the sun blazed from the steel. He looked exalted, as if an intense communion ran between his face and the brilliant blade.

"Behold, men of Moritzburg, men of Burg Zanich, men of Glarien!" He swept the blade down and sheathed it. His horse spun, pirouetting, until he faced Penny. "My bride! Wed in London before God and the Tsar of all the Russias. Princess Sophia of Alvia, brave and true. Who but a princess of the blood could travel the high mountain passes and outshine the meadows and peaks of the Erhabenhorn in beauty? The hermit blessed her with fruitfulness. She promises you a son for Glarien and brings Alvia as her dowry."

The roar from the crowd became deafening. In a tumult of support, Grand Duke Nicholas and his bride rode into their capital city.

The town with its steep-roofed wooden houses was bigger than it had looked from the farmhouse. Their procession wove past shops and churches, climbing in a meander around the castle rock. At last they approached it from a long tail of granite, where a road had been cut up to the fortress itself. They passed for several hundred yards along a knife edge that had Penny holding her breath lest her horse should slip. *A good defensive position.*

She could easily have been jostled over the edge when they reached the drawbridge, but Nicholas rode tightly beside her where he could catch her horse's reins if necessary. The drawbridge was dropped across a gap of twenty feet where the rock was naturally fissured. Nicholas rode across with Penny, leaving the rabble of soldiers standing and cheering on the road.

"Well," he said. "Welcome home, Your Royal Highness."

She had expected something grim: gaunt stone walls weeping moisture and history; rusting suits of armor and displays of halberds. Instead, inside its ancient walls the castle of the grand dukes of Glarien blazed with gilt-and-white plaster and a cornucopia of paintings. Cerulean blue skies filled with nymphs and cherubs adorned the ceilings. Portraits in gilt frames jostled for space on the walls. The feeling was rich, baroque, and alight with Italian influence. A modern royal palace, nestled like a pearl inside the rough shell of an oyster.

"Glarien is wealthy," Nicholas said in her ear, tossing his cloak to a servant. "Did you notice how many of our craftsmen's shops house goldsmiths?"

Female servants came forward, dropping deep curtseys. Penny was ushered away and taken to a suite several floors above the grand reception rooms. Beyond the hangings of red velvet, the rich tapestries and carpets, she found rooms filled with dresses sent from Alvia, an entire wall of shoes, boxes of jewelry and ribbons, everything that Sophia hadn't taken to London.

The ladies stripped Penny of her riding clothes and enveloped her in a long muslin bathing robe, before helping her into warm water scented with mountain air and wildflowers. She was to have four hours' rest before being summoned to perform her court duties and receive the mayor and elders of Moritzburg in the throne room.

Wrapped at last in a dry robe trimmed with priceless lace and pearls, she dismissed the women and wandered into the princess's bedroom. She stopped before the dressing table. Her uncle, Duke Michael, had sent his daughter some of her personal trinkets. Penny let her fingers stray over them for a moment. Scent bottles, brushes and combs, everything inlaid and exquisite, the little feminine luxuries accorded a princess.

She snapped open the lid of a small case, rich with jewels, knowing exactly what she would find, for she had seen its twin at Rascall Hall. Yet she had to sit down before she could look at it. Her cousin, Princess Sophia, had gazed on this before she set out on her wedding journey, before she had fallen into Carl's hands. It still kept a faint trace of her scent: a miniature of Nicholas.

And now Sophia was lost.

I'm an impostor! I'm borrowing someone else's life. How can I be foolish enough to fall in love with another woman's husband?

"A good enough likeness," he said behind her. "But it doesn't quite capture my more demonic characteristics."

Penny looked up and saw him in the mirror. He had been bathed, like her. His dressing gown was black, embroidered with red lions. Her face suffused with color. For a moment they were both still, as if caught in amber or in a portrait, before he put one hand flat on her shoulder, slipping it under the silk robe. She watched the awareness lighting his eyes as his lean fingers move up her throat, caressing, and the answering comprehension in her own.

"This is wrong." Her voice caught and broke. "It was all wrong, from the beginning."

"Yes, I know," he said.

With both hands he began to peel the white silk away from her shoulders. He bent his head and kissed her skin. In the mirror his dark hair made a startling contrast to the froth of lace.

The fire of his lips burned and weakened her. "Is Vulcan your god?" The words sounded breathy and insubstantial.

He smiled up at her under his long lashes. "Do I make thunderbolts for Jupiter?"

His hands moved down, taking the robe with them so the upper swell of her breasts glimmered in the mirror.

"You melt metals," she said. "You fashion intricate contrivances."

His fingers were lovely in the glass, the edge of his thumb brushing aside fabric to caress her nakedness. With infinite care he released buttons so the robe fell with a sigh to her waist. Penny burned and melted, seeing herself defenseless in his hands, her white skin framed by red lions and black silk, her breasts round and small.

"It is wrong," she said. "And it's my fault."

"I love you," he replied. "Of all the wrongs I might do, even at the risk of my soul, this is the only one that won't be denied." He dropped his head and let his mouth stray over the curve of her shoulder while his hands moved up to stroke her breasts. "Oh, dear God!"

Glowing, fervent chills ran through her blood. His fingers brushed her nipples. She saw them harden, saw the intensity of wonder and admiration in his eyes. Sensation centered in an exquisite throb.

She caught his hand in her own. "Nicholas, it's my fault! I began it. I didn't understand. But this is wrong!"

"It isn't wrong. I *must* risk it! I love you more than my own life."

"And Princess Sophia's life?"

His hands stopped, his skin dark against hers. He gave a wry grin. "Alas, I can never love even you enough to wish Sophia dead."

"That isn't what I meant." She twisted toward him, turning her back on the glass and its lecherous images.

"Isn't it? Your cousin was never real to you before now, was she? She was only a name, a thought, without substance. Now you see her things and realize she's your own blood." He picked up the miniature and looked at it. "Yet Sophia did not care enough about this to take it with her."

"You are *her* husband in the eyes of the world. You can never marry elsewhere. Neither can she."

"Must both of us never love elsewhere—for a lifetime?" He pulled her to her feet. "For a lifetime, Penny! Do you think she and I are married in the eyes of St. Cyriakus? There is only one marriage that's been blessed by a saint, yours and mine." Without subtlety he tore away his robe so he stood naked before her. "I am only a man!"

He strode away, magnificent and commanding, a perfection of bone and muscle. Her mouth went dry. Could she die of desire?

"I am—I have never known—" He turned to her, aroused, splendid. "Penny! For God's sake!" He went to the bed and stared at the sheets. "Perhaps I have toiled, like Vulcan, in underground caverns. Perhaps I have forged monstrous caprices of metal. Like the smith of the gods, I am lame, tarnished. I don't ask that you love me. How can I ask that?"

"I do love you." Was this pain in her heart from its tearing and breaking? "Why else would I have come here? This is what Carl threatened. He said he would kill you and the princess and force me to act as his wife. And now we are tempted! Tempted to forget the real Sophia, tempted to think I might live here with you forever."

Nicholas looked up. A slow smile spread over his face. "Ah, Penny! Even if that *were* the temptation, it isn't possible."

What if Sophia dies . . . ? "We must find her." She felt frantic, afraid she might yet be weak and foolish. "We must find her, and I must go home."

"We'll find her. But what is happening in this room has nothing to do with Sophia. This is you and me. How can you deny me now?"

I am denying you, after insisting we become lovers, now I am denying you. You didn't want me to come here. You wanted me safe in Rascall St. Mary. I came because I am stubborn. Because I was pompous enough to think I could help you. I didn't know—how could I have known?—that you were forged from pure gold.

"Nicholas. Once you tried to teach me about choices, the red or the black. I know what my blood has already decided. But afterward the future is yours—yours and Sophia's—to re-create Glarien."

"This is now," he said. "Come to me, Penny. Let me take something of you with me through the rest of my life."

And you will educate yourself using my body? So when you take Sophia, you will capture and enthrall her from the very first night? As you did me, as you do me, so I dissolve and disintegrate in the face of my desire.

She stood up and walked to him. He caught her in his arms and kissed her. His erection flamed hot against her belly, the imperious royal demand. *Women have never refused kings,* she thought hazily as he laid her down on the bed and began to ravish her with his beauty.

Bliss. Pure unutterable bliss. To touch her. To enter her. To find her hot and willing. Her breasts shaped soft and female in his hands, under his searching mouth, against the skin of his chest. His control shredded before the overwhelming bliss of the plunge, sinking down, down into her molten core. So he failed in this. He could no longer deny it or control it. He risked everything—a kingdom, his soul, his life—for this white-hot blazing moment, and then the next and the next. . . .

She shuddered beneath him, accepting him, stroking her hands over his back and buttocks. He stretched himself, letting her fingers touch him—anywhere, everywhere—taking her mouth with his own, while the sensations built into ecstasy, the blinding, driven male ecstasy. The pleasure was so intense he shouted aloud at his mad culmination. Perhaps this time all would be purified, all his shame burned away.

He rolled away from her, shattered and exhausted, and grabbed for his robe. Penny curled into the sheets as if folding a white rose about herself and stared up at him. She was infinitely precious, infinitely fragile and never to be possessed beyond this. He couldn't have her heart and mind. Even the memory of her body must dissolve and be gone, leaving him bereft and forever married to a stranger. A stranger who looked like her, was as worthy as her, but was not Penny Lindsey.

"I love you," he said. "To touch you is exquisite to me."

Exquisite and dreadful! The pain stirred and the memories. *Your turn, Nico!* Desperate to hide his reaction, he turned and strode away across the room.

"What's wrong?" She looked dreamy, softened by his lovemaking.

He groped for self-control, knowing he still craved what terrified him, knowing he would make love to her again and again. . . . Yet he didn't want his voice to sound as brutal as it did. "Carl was bluffing if he threatened to use you to impersonate Sophia. We have only a couple of weeks before this is all over."

She sat up, clutching the sheet, her eyes dilated. She was beautiful, desirable, maddening. "What do you mean?"

"We're to be crowned in three weeks. Duke Michael, though too frail in health to travel to London, will come here from Alvia for the coronation. You convinced the Tsar and the Prince Regent, but do you think you could fool Sophia's own father? You must be gone by then. Sophia must be found."

She looked down, vulnerable and female. "Oh, I see. Then I'm glad. I'm glad we cannot be tempted past that."

"As soon as Sophia is rescued, you and I will never see each another again."

"Yes, yes. A kingdom depends on it." She glanced up. Her eyes seemed bruised. "Yet you have no idea where she is?"

"I will find her!" His words slashed like the strokes of a whip, because there was no other way he could let them fall. "So I'm using you. I'm making you my harlot. As your father used your mother. Can't you see that? Another prince of Glarien ruins another woman, in a pattern as old as history."

Her breath was coming fast. She swung from the bed, slipping on her robe. Her hair uncurled in a fuzzy mess around her face. Infinitely lovely. "I must be alone for a moment. Outside, in the fresh air!"

He leaned back, unable to move as she wrenched open a small door in the corner of the room. She probably thought it led to a balcony. It did not. It revealed a small flight of stairs, curving in the thickness of the walls, where the castle shed its modern veneer and revealed its Gothic bones.

Nicholas waited, shaking, fighting nausea, before he strode to the foot of the stairs and forced himself to go after her, finally crawling the last section on hands and knees.

The worn stone was cool on her naked feet as she raced up. Arrow-slit windows shed bars of light, below and above them always shadow. At the top she opened a door and stepped out into blazing sunshine. A narrow pavement led between a steep rise of turret roof and the battlements. The walk ended in another door, locked.

She paced the short length, the sun warm on her shoulders.

They had made love, this time at his insistence. It had been so profound, she was shaken to the core. Her breasts felt different, tingling and alive, as if her nipples were aware for the first time. She felt suffused with new life. They had taken no precautions, not even paid attention to the calendar. Without any evidence, she knew it: She had just conceived his child. *Another prince of Glarien ruins another woman, in a pattern as old as history.*

A child. A royal bastard. Whatever happened, if it was true, he must never know. She leaned through one of the square openings between the merlons. The wall beneath made a sheer drop to the roaring waters of the Win, dizzyingly far away. Giddy, she looked up. On the far horizon the mountains blazed around the high, distant peak of the Erhabenhorn. *St. Cyriakus will not stint either children or fruit.* Not even bastards or English peas! So Penny Lindsey must go back to Rascall St. Mary and raise her child and her garden—as if she had never met a prince—as her mother had done.

Your father had no choice. Perhaps if you grow up a little and look more clearly at royal duty, you will see that. Her mother's voice sounded as clearly as if she had been there. Penny dropped her head against the rough edge of the merlon. *Forgive me, Mama, if I have ever judged you or my father. I was indeed a child.*

As her mother had done, she must ask nothing from her dark prince and never regret it.

The door made a slight noise behind her. She looked over her shoulder. Instantly she went to him. "Nicholas! You are ill?"

He was white, his skin clammy. "No." He gave a small half laugh and wiped one hand over his face. "I'm afraid."

She didn't dare touch him. The splendid body, the sculpture of muscles, shook as if he had fever. "What are you afraid of?"

"The hands of the Four Horsemen laid on my shoulders—" He shook his head, grinning.

"Tell me!" she said. "Tell me!"

His grin was a death mask. He clung to the support of the door frame as he sank to his haunches. "I'm afraid, Penny!"

"Tell me!" she said again. "It's easy, when we know we'll never see someone again. Once I took the stagecoach to

Staffordshire. There was a woman traveling the same way. She told me things about her life—intimate things she had never told anyone, but felt safe to tell a stranger. I'm the one person in your life you'll never see again. You can tell me. What are you afraid of?"

"This place," he said. "That stairway. And this place. All high places."

She waved her hand to indicate the short pavement and the battlements. "Here?"

The line of his neck was piercing against the red-and-black robe. He put both hands over his hair and dropped his head. "Here is one place I'm afraid, yes."

"Why?"

"I was eleven years old." His voice rasped. "Carl brought me up here. He made me stand there—on the merlon. Then he took me by the ankles and flung me upside-down over that drop. I remember my cap falling and falling, spiraling away to be lost in the Win. I thought my boots would come off in his hands, so I would follow that hat. It had a feather. It flipped over and over, as if the feather were a single broken wing. I was sick. I hung by my feet, retching. I pissed in my breeches. He held me just long enough that I thought I would die, then—"

He choked, grasping his head. Penny knelt beside him and tried to take his hands, but his fingers were locked. "Nicholas!"

Slowly he dropped his hands and looked up at her. "It's nothing. Nothing. He pulled me back up and told me I was a filthy little coward. I was. I am. I didn't come up here to tell you all that. I came to fetch you. We have a state meeting in an hour."

"You once told me fear was nothing to you—no more than an irksome uniform."

The sun shone on his hair as he leaned his head back and stared at the sky. "I was talking then about peril. I'm not afraid of physical danger."

"I don't understand."

He took one of her hands and kissed it. "Of course not," he said. "How could you?"

Sixteen

Wearing one of the princess's priceless gowns and trailing her train of ladies-in-waiting, Penny walked through the grand reception rooms. Nicholas had drawn maps for her at Rascall Hall. Sophia had been here. It wouldn't do to get lost. Yet her mind felt blank. Oh, God! That dizzying, sickening drop! He had been just a child. *It is my cousin's nature to be brutal to children.*

In full court uniform, with sashes and decorations, Nicholas was waiting for her in an anteroom. Behind him, a huge painting of life-sized figures on horseback filled a wall. One of the horses was perched on its hind feet in a little rear, front hoofs folded. The riders wore gilt and decorations, as if it were a ball.

"It was painted in 1790 or '91," Nicholas said quietly. "Alvia had made a grand state visit. The man on the gray is your father, Prince Frederick. He was engaged to marry a German princess."

Heart pounding, Penny stared at the handsome face. Did she resemble him at all? Perhaps in the wide, blunt nose and something about the mouth. *My father!* "But my mother was here."

"If Duke Michael had no children, Frederick was heir to Alvia. His marriage was important. He had no choice at all. Your mother knew that."

Tears threatened. "Yet they fell in love. It must have been terrible for them."

He held out his arm, so she could place her gloved fingertips on his sleeve. "You've spent your life resenting that he couldn't be a father to you, searching to make amends as you could, but he never married the princess. He died when his horse plunged over a cliff. Sophia became heir."

Prince Frederick stared down, haughty and imperious. A royal prince. Penny put one hand over her belly. *I'm sorry, Papa, that I ever judged you. Sorry. Sorry. I didn't understand. Yet even though I denied it, you thought of me and sent me a doll.*

She choked back the tears and turned to Nicholas with a smile. Perhaps she had grown up at last.

"I'm ready to meet the mayor. Let's go."

Nicholas came to her again in the night and then every night, silently. In silence he lost himself in her body as she lost herself in his. Penny abandoned herself to his lovemaking, frantic, hot, shivering in the dark. If they had not made a child, they would. She was glad. Wildly, madly glad. She would like to have a little boy, just as he had been when her mother was his governess. *Intelligent, sensitive, given to great fits of temper.* And doomed, like her, to grow up without a father. Was it selfish of her not to care?

Every night, when they finished making love, he left immediately. One night she crept after him. He stood at a window in the small anteroom that linked the two royal bedrooms and stared out at the stars. *Ceres, Pallas, Juno and Vesta.*

She stepped through the door. "Nicholas?"

He spun about to face her. Almost imperceptibly, he was shaking. "Penny? Go back to bed."

"What's the matter?"

Streaming moonlight made him demonic, enchanted. His eyes glittered. He drew back his fist and drove it at the window. Glass burst and shattered. "This!"

"You made me face my fear over the horses," she said. "Let me help you."

His upper lip curled in a snarl. Broken glass shivered like shards of ice. "*Help* me? How? With what?"

She groped to understand. "You said you were afraid of heights—"

"Heights! Yes, I did, didn't I? Come, the heights beckon!"

He seized her hand. Dragging her back into her bedroom, he flung open the door in the corner. She slipped and stumbled up the stairs behind him. The little pavement shone silver-gray. The shadows of the merlons yawned in dark pits.

Releasing her hand, he walked to the battlements. "This *place*? Do you think I didn't come here and make myself face it? Over and over again. I climbed up here—" He leaped up onto the wall. "After that time with Carl, every bloody day I climbed up here like this and defied the Win to take me."

Turning about slowly, he held out both arms, his robe flying like black wings behind him.

Penny stood transfixed. Cold terror choked. "Nicholas!"

He stepped down and caught her face in both hands. "And now I have frightened you. I'm sorry. It wasn't the heights that made me reluctant to come up here after you."

"Then why did you lie about it? What was it?"

He grinned as if life were a merry jest, a ball tossed among friends at a fair. "It was what happened afterward, which hardly matters. This matters."

She held on to his hands as he kissed her. Deeply, ravishingly. Kissing until she fell weak in the knees against him, unable to make sense of any of it. She was just another glass globe, carelessly tossed by those clever, juggling fingers, for the amusement of an invisible crowd.

He led her back at last to her bedroom and left her there. Night air streamed in through the broken glass and rustled in his robe as he passed the window in the anteroom. Blood from his broken knuckles still dampened her hands.

The royal procession arrived. Gerta and Lady Beatrice. Alexis and the rest of Nicholas's men. Word had reached the watchers at the St. Cyriakus Pass that the Grand Duke and his bride were already in Moritzburg. The ambush had melted away. The first council was called.

Penny sat in her chair of state and watched Nicholas gather the men to his heart. One by one, prickly nobles and gruff burghers softened to his charm, to his astuteness, to his authority—to the man who had learned to command horses with a thought, yet still leave them noble beasts, full of fire. When a count or a goldsmith proved recalcitrant, Nicholas pinned him in a brilliant, leaping series of moves, like a gambit for checkmate with knights, until the man willingly, laughingly, joined the cause. This was greater than personalities or private hatreds. Grand Duke Nicholas was trying to make Glarien into a constitutional democratic principality.

Her mother had been right: He was a remarkable sovereign.

Penny Lindsey of Rascall St. Mary was entirely irrelevant, except to play her part as a princess. She rode out every day, visiting the people, listening to their concerns. Were they surprised by how much Princess Sophia understood of their everyday lives? It was all she could do to help Nicholas.

Count Zanich trotted up to the castle with a long retinue. He was received with courtesy as befitted a grand duke's heir. No mention was made of the troops at the bridge, or the ambush at the pass—a small misunderstanding of orders, obviously. Nicholas gave him a seat of honor at the council table and Penny watched their careful work begin to fall apart. It was subtly done, a small question planted in another prince's mind about the Grand Duke's motives, a snide offering of sympathy to her. She did her best to deflect it, but she was relieved when Carl announced he must return to Burg Zanich to take care of private business.

His bow was filled with confidence. "I will be back, sire," he said smiling, "for the coronation."

Nicholas had known how it would be, if he once gave in to the temptation. A madness. An obsession. To taste her and explore her. To know her breasts and buttocks and sweet, secret places. To know her eyelids and earlobes and the corners of her mouth.

To know the backs of her knees and the soft curve where her neck joined her shoulder. To worship her. To ravish her. To feel his own potency throbbing and swelling in imperious demand. To make her soften and moan for him, before he drained himself over and over again into her generous body.

Passion consumed him. As he knew that if he once began to revenge himself on Carl, the retaliation would never stop. He had too much vehemence. Reason couldn't save him. He was a prince of Glarien who had abandoned restraint. His mouth overflowed with her scent. His penis knew her moist, velvet embrace. His hands remembered her skin. And she opened her arms to him, opened her legs to him, as if there were no tomorrow.

The punishment waited each time, the inevitable reaction driving him from her bed before she found out. He shook and sobbed in quiet corners, alone in the darkness, and berated himself that the melodrama of it made a cheap mockery of his pain and his passion. Yet if it went on like this, he faced defeat. The vehemence would drive him to madness, to the long drop to the Win, or the wicked edge of his own sword. And then Carl would wreak retribution on Penny.

It was a private meeting. A handful of candles cast long shadows about the small room. No one from the court was there. Only Penny, Nicholas and the remaining five of his personal bodyguard who had first ridden with him into Norfolk: Fritz, Markos, Eric, Ludger and Alexis. Perhaps the ghost of Lars hovered, jealous of the still living.

"We have run out of time," Nicholas said. "Lucas and his men have found no trace of Sophia. Though she's not at Burg Zanich with him, obviously Carl has her. We must retreat, so he will bring her out into the open. We leave Moritzburg."

"Sire!" Fritz said. His face was pale and set, the scar livid. "It's too risky!"

Nicholas paced away to the dark window. "You wish Duke Michael to arrive from Alvia and discover Miss Lindsey? We leave tomorrow and concede the field."

• • •

Dressed in a dashing shako and green dress uniform, Penny rode down the stone causeway, Nicholas beside her, his five bodyguards at his heels. Quest loped alongside the horses, her silver coat shining in the sunlight. A small contingent of nobility and important townsmen rode with them, followed by a sizable troop of Fritz's loyal men.

She knew she must be carrying his child now. She hugged the knowledge to herself, as if that could assuage her broken heart. At some point on this journey, she would be sent secretly back to Norfolk. She would never see Glarien again. She would never see Nicholas again. If only she didn't know where they were going: on a glorious day under a sky of blue silk, they rode to Burg Zanich.

"Like a flock of obedient sheep," Nicholas had said, "we shall trot into the lion's den. Perhaps the lion will be feeling sleepy and only snap at flies."

"And perhaps he's wide awake and will fancy the whole bloody flock for his supper," Fritz had replied.

Nicholas had grinned at his captain. "Oh, I rely on his appetite, but he'll have to catch and shear us first, and you must admit we're a prickly mouthful."

They rode rapidly through rolling valleys, past horse farms and dairies, then climbed out of the Win Valley until Moritzburg was just a fairy-tale confection in the distance. Above them, through thick trees, the peaks glittered. Water rushed and tumbled beside the road, spinning over little waterfalls, carrying ice water to the Win from the high Alps.

The trees thinned as they approached the St. Alban Pass. Quest raced ahead. The horses' hooves rang among sharp stones as they passed long slopes of scree, glittering with mica in the sunshine. Hugging the contours of the mountain, the road twisted and bent so Penny could no longer see the end of the column of troops.

"I realize I'll be sent away long before you reach Carl's castle," she said quietly. "But allow me to be curious. What do you intend to do when you get there?"

Nicholas glanced at her. She was amazed that he was smiling. "I doubt, to be honest, that we'll arrive—" Suddenly he looked ahead. Quest had loped up a slope of scree. "Quest!" The wolfhound stopped for a moment, tongue lolling, and gazed back at her master. *"Quest!"*

Her Highness Alessandrina von der Moritzburg barked, swung her head, and raced away, leaping over rocks, almost disappearing on the lichen-dappled slope. A man sprang from a hiding place, only to fall and tumble as the ground collapsed under his feet.

"Ride!" Nicholas shouted.

With a deafening roar, rocks splintered above them. In a slash of sun-lit fire Nicholas drew his sword and slapped Penny's mount on the rump with the flat of the blade. Her horse bolted, clattering over stones as the entire mountain gave way. Granite scraped and rent in an avalanche of scree, gathering momentum as boulders tumbled, uprooting trees. She flattened herself over her mount's neck, choking as the air filled with sand, deafened as an angry mountain roared thunder in her ears.

Alone, she galloped to safety.

Her horse stopped by itself and dropped its head, flanks heaving. Penny looked up. She was in a small grove of trees. Behind her dust hovered in the air, obscuring the road. There was a deathly, absolute silence. Nicholas had hesitated. Hesitated because Ludger and Markos rode behind him, with some of the nobles and the mayor of Moritzburg. He had looked back to shout another warning.

Oh, God! She stumbled from her horse and knelt down under a pine tree. Oh, God!

Her horse began to crop grass at the side of the silent road. The bit jingled. *That's his other interest, food.*

Oh, God, Nicholas! Dear God, let him survive. Let him only be alive somewhere in the world. I'll never even hope to see him again—I'll live my whole life happily without him—if only he's alive.

Her horse looked up and whinnied. Penny scrambled to her feet. Two dust-covered horsemen rode toward her. Even in their grime, she recognized them: Nicholas and Eric. Her knees gave way. Nicholas vaulted down. The red-haired man dismounted and caught reins as the prince strode up to her.

He caught her by the arms, pulled her up and dragged her back into the trees. His eyes searched her face for a moment—his gaze like a bottomless cavern—then he crushed her mouth with his. She clung to him, crying and kissing. The muscles in his back leaped under her fingers. His hands cradled her head, holding her as if he'd never let go.

"I'm all right," she said at last when they came up for air. "Nicholas, I'm all right."

His lips pressed her hair. "Should I admit that, for a moment, that was all I cared for in the world?" He pulled out a handkerchief and gently wiped dust and tears from her face. "I'd have traded the whole world for your safety."

You, too? I made a bargain with God. Was that wicked? "What happened?"

"Quest scented the man who triggered the ambush. I have trained her to sniff out traps. If she hadn't made him set it off too soon, so only part of the rock slide came down, we'd all have died. She saved our lives."

Penny slid down to sit in the soft duff under the tree—had God taken this price for her bargain? "And now she's dead? Oh, Nicholas!"

More hooves clattered. A man dismounted. Befouled with rock dust, Fritz strode up to them. "Sire, the way is blocked behind us. Markos climbed up where he could see around the bend. The entire side of the mountain has collapsed. Most of the troops are trapped on the other side, but the road is gone—and any bodies."

"How many?"

"Most escaped, but any man caught—"

"Oh, God!" Penny glanced up. "Alexis?"

"He was riding at the back of the troops, ma'am," Fritz said. "I'm sure he survived. On this side, we're all sound: Eric, Markos and myself."

"But not Ludger?" Nicholas leaned back against a tree. His eyes spiraled smoke. "Or some of the burghers of Moritzburg? And a handful of heirs to noble houses? The mayor?"

"We can't be sure, sire."

"You expected something like this?" Penny asked.

He turned to her. The fire had gone out, leaving only blackness. "Oh, yes. But I thought it would be more subtle and limited in target, not quite this bloody extravagant. Carl must be more desperate than we knew."

"Sire, should we dig for bodies?"

He was a prince of Glarien. Able to command, to plan, even in the face of disaster. His voice was clipped and deadly. "Send Markos back. He will have to climb over the rubble and leave his horse here. They're not to waste time digging, except to rescue the wounded. The buried are already dead. Let them lie in peace. The troops are to return to Moritzburg to escort the townsmen still alive."

"And yourself, sire?"

"Markos is to tell them I was killed and that you have taken Princess Sophia on to safety at Burg Zanich. Those are orders."

Penny stared up at him. "Killed?"

"I am ghost enough," he said, smiling down at her. "What can Carl do then, except play out his hand?"

Fritz wiped dust from his face with his sleeve. Fine sand ridged on his scar. "Sire! You cannot do this!"

Nicholas turned on him like a fencer. *"Cannot?"*

The old soldier looked stubborn. "If it's believed you're dead, Carl will seize the throne."

"He will, indeed." Penny expected ire, even royal thunder. But Nicholas's smile was a crevasse in ice. "And Markos's message will make it believed Sophia went to Burg Zanich. Thus, Carl must produce her."

Fritz stared at him, his eyes red-rimmed. "That's madness! You can't risk it! If he does produce her, it'll be somewhere you can't reach her." He thrust one fist into the palm of the other hand. "For God's sake, sire! Once Carl declares himself grand duke, he'll have to make sure your death becomes a reality."

"Good," Nicholas said. "Then we have entered the end game. I am dead. That is an order!"

Fritz clicked his heels and bowed. "Sire!"

Nicholas leaned back against the tree as the old soldier left. He stood in silence for several minutes. Time for Ludger, once again for Lars and also for Quest. Penny gave him time for his own anguish and felt the gaping enormity of her own. The deaths of the men made her feel numb, but Quest's loss burned bright and urgent. Was it wrong to feel so great a grief for a dog, simply because you had loved her?

"You can't send me back yet," she said at last. "Not until you know the outcome of all this. I might yet be of use."

He did not move. "I must send you back to England."

Penny dropped her head forward. "When we know Sophia is safe, then send me away. I don't matter in this, Nicholas. You know that. I know that. Only Glarien matters—and Alvia. Carl cannot be allowed to rule. Not when he would murder all these innocent men—"

She startled as something rustled. Nicholas turned to greet the newcomer. She approached shyly, her tail hanging between her legs, her coat stiff with rock dust.

Quest.

"Well, Princess." His voice caught as he held out one hand to her. "You're a good girl." Quest sat and panted, gazing up at her master, before tentatively reaching up with one paw. Nicholas knelt and put his face against her head. "It's all right, Quest. Good girl."

Penny heard the break and laugh in his voice. Silently she thanked St. Francis, who watches over the animals and makes sure they can outrun falling rocks, and God, who had not yet made her pay for her bargain.

From the St. Alban Pass, Penny had thought she might be able to see all the way into Italy. That was how Nicholas would have sent her home, the way Princess Sophia had traveled from Alvia. But they had left the road below the pass and traveled in single file up a narrow track. Quest trotted ahead of Nicholas. Penny kept her mount's nose close to his horse's tail, while Eric and Fritz rode behind her. He had agreed not to send her to England just yet. Could she tell her heart he was reluctant to let her go?

They camped, building shelters from pine boughs. For warmth, they slept huddled together, wrapped in nothing but their cloaks. Nicholas was silent and withdrawn, the other men grim as they went about the daily business of survival: caring for the horses, preparing food. Often enough, when their track dipped into forest, the men had to hack through deadfall with their swords. Paths around bogs and streams in the high mountain meadows sucked and slurped at the horses' feet. The high glaciers were impassable for the mounts, so they could only hug the edge of the ice.

Four tiny human beings and a dog, insignificant in the wilderness of peaks.

Penny washed and cooked, no longer a princess. Her tall hat had been pressed into service as a bucket. She looked at her hands, grimy from the cooking fire, the nails broken from gathering kindling. The hands of a woman who had lost her heart to her dark prince and couldn't help him in his grief. She had no idea where they were going, or what would happen, now that Nicholas was dead to Glarien.

Two days later, she found out. They had ridden all day. As night closed in they had come up at last to a small building. It reminded her of the stone hut by the chapel to St. Cyriakus, but there was no blind hermit here. Instead, a single man waited, his pale eyes glimmering in the dusk, his hair slick as a seal's.

"Ah, Lucas," Nicholas said as he swung from his horse. "We return from heaven to the underworld."

Inside the hut, a welcome fire burned in a small stove. A lantern cast light over benches, a table with wine and food, a small bed. Nicholas signaled. The men offered Penny a share, then sat down and tore into the fresh bread and cheese that Lucas had set there. She sat on one end of a bench and tried to force herself to eat.

Nicholas leaned back on a chair in the corner and watched. "What news, Lucas?"

"Count Zanich holds the castle at Moritzburg. The garrison has sworn allegiance. So has the nobility. His own troops are there as well. The town is in mourning for the sad death of the mayor, three of its prominent citizens, and the young Count von Forschach—and Grand Duke Nicholas, of course. Carl wept publicly over your loss. It was most affecting. But he says you would wish your remains to stay undisturbed in the bosom of the mountain."

Nicholas watched Eric break off some bread. "So he isn't sure I'm dead?"

Lucas grinned, but there was no amusement in it. "No one actually saw you die."

"And what is being muttered in the marketplaces and behind closed doors?"

"What Carl is paying his men to say: The deaths were your fault; that it was a trap to kill the mayor; that you've always meant harm to the von Forschachs."

Nicholas closed his eyes. "So if I should reappear, miraculously restored from the dead, I would very likely be set upon by a mob and killed by my own people? Poetic! Who else is with Carl in Schloss Moritzburg?"

"Alexis," Lucas said. "The boy is his personal servant, never leaves his side."

A muscle clenched in Nicholas's jaw, but he said nothing.

"And your widow," Lucas went on. "Princess Sophia of Alvia. She looks pale, but she seems composed. I've not been able to speak to her privately."

Indignation was clear on Fritz's features. "The princess *agrees* to marry Zanich?"

Lucas gravely met the major's gaze. Penny wondered what emotion he was hiding behind his calm recital. "Princess Sophia suggests, of her own free will, a wedding as soon as possible. I was there when she announced it to the council. For the sake of Glarien, she will take part in a public betrothal two days from now and the coronation will go forward as planned, with her father in attendance."

"The king is dead," Nicholas said dryly. "Long live the king! I didn't think Carl would be interested in waiting for his bride to mourn her first husband."

Penny gazed at him, the clear profile of the man who had once said he loved her and had now just spent four days acting as if she didn't exist. These men would make plans. She was excluded. In fact, any further role for Penny Lindsey was over. Sophia had been found. A lump formed in her throat, a hideous, betraying lump. Mumbling some excuse, she went outside before they should see her weep.

The moon was coming up, shining white light over a great sharp peak to the north. It almost looked like the Erhabenhorn, but that was impossible, of course. They had traveled for days since they'd last seen it. Footsteps crunched on cold grass.

"We've made a great loop," Nicholas said behind her. "The Win Valley lies below us. If you were to walk five hundred yards up to that ledge, you'd see the lights of my grandfather's castle. Do you think Carl is gazing from my window right now? Or if Sophia wonders what has happened to us?"

She spun about. Moonlight cast exotic shadows over his features. "What are you going to do? Ride into Moritzburg with your men to show everyone you're alive?"

He smiled. "If I can get there without being shot in the back. Carl will have men watching every road—"

"And the bridge, of course! You think he would just shoot you?"

"Anyone could be blamed. Some poor artisan would probably be hanged, drawn and quartered for the crime. Carl has crossed his Rubicon now."

Her legs folded. She sat on the cold, damp grass beside the stream and put her head in her hands.

"It is possible," he said quietly, "that Sophia truly is willing to marry him."

The surge of dreadful, selfish hope made her weak and dizzy. *Come back to Rascall Hall with me. I am carrying your child.* She said nothing, only watched as he walked off a few paces, his boots black among the glimmer of flowers, until tears blurred her vision and she had to look away.

"I'm sure you understand the temptation." His voice was quiet, a supple seduction in the silver night. "To remain dead to Glarien. To simply let Carl win. Could my life be my own? Could I reclaim everything my royal heritage has cost me? Ah, Penny, if you only knew how close I am to saying yes to the devil."

"I know," she said, wiping away the tears. The cold night glistened around her. "But you are known at the courts of Europe. You cannot die here, then reappear anywhere else. Sophia is married to you. If she weds Carl and you're discovered to be alive, you would make her a bigamist, destroy Glarien and Alvia in a stroke. How could you simply disappear?"

"Oh, I could. Anyone can disappear. In South America, New Holland—but unfortunately I think I must attend the upcoming Congress at Vienna." A little glimmer of irony shimmered in his voice. "I've worked pretty hard on the treaty terms Glarien and Alvia need from the great powers. I can hardly trust Carl to carry it out as I would wish, and I doubt if he'll uphold my reforms."

"And Sophia?"

"Sadly, I suspect Sophia would rather not marry Carl, whatever she's said publicly." Water burbled in the stream. A small breeze blew cold off the glaciers. "There's also Alexis."

Penny shivered. "Yes, I know. You can't walk away from it. I didn't think you would. So what will you do? Gather your armies and march into Moritzburg?"

"If I did, how could Sophia let me know what she wants? I must speak to her alone."

"Privately? How can you?"

His hand touched her hair. Penny looked up. Nicholas had gathered white flowers.

"I will do what I must. Eric will take you back to Norfolk. It's an end for us, Penny. Take care of Rascall Hall for me. You taught me more than you know, beloved."

He dropped the flowers on the grass, then turned and walked away. She scrambled to her feet and stared after him, remembering English white campion, petals open in the night to welcome the moths.

Fritz appeared out of the dark and caught her elbow. "He mustn't go, ma'am."

She looked down and bit her lip. "I'm to go back to England."

"His orders, yes." The scar leaped, a shadow in the moonlight, as the old soldier grimaced. "He intends to go to Moritzburg secretly and alone. He'll ride into certain death, unless we stop him." He nodded his head. "He's in the hut."

The major released her arm. Penny marched up to the hut and pushed open the door. *Certain death, certain death.* Nicholas was writing something on a sheet of paper. He looked up.

"Your last will and testament?" she asked.

"Not exactly. Penny, this is our parting. I've written something for you to take with you. Don't read it until you're safely back in Clumper Cottage."

Didn't he hear her heart crack, like the rending of rock on the mountain?

"Nicholas," she said. "There must be one last time." She watched his face as she peeled off her jacket and kicked off her shoes. "Please," she said. "Just once more!"

He stood and backed away from her, nostrils flared like a running horse. "I thought that you loved me," he said. "I had thought, in my weaker, wilder moments, that your love for me might even be as great as mine for you. Will you prove me wrong now?"

The bitter edge in his voice stung. "I love you," she said. "You can't abandon me by dying! My father did that. I won't have it happen again." She wrenched away her belt and yanked her shirt out of her waistband.

The hut was tiny, filled with the heat of the stove. He backed another step, pushing aside a bench. "You cannot prevent me, Penny. You cannot hold me or stop me—"

"I can give you one more memory," she said and cast her shirt aside.

He stared at her as if helpless. She caught one of his hands and laid it on her naked breast.

In a flare of white-hot desire, his mouth met hers. His tongue scorched. Agonizing shivers of yearning made her legs tremble, her arms quiver, as all her blood pooled in her groin. He kissed deeply, passionately, kneading at her nipple with one palm. Penny pushed at his clothes, laughing, shaking, sliding her hands up under his shirt, feeling the keen fire of his muscles under her fingers.

"Bloody hell!" She heard the surrender in it and pushed away her tiny glimmer of guilt and doubt. "I cannot—" Taking her by both arms he set her away, then pointed to the tiny bed. "Sit."

She folded back the blanket and sat on the sheets, weak with longing. Nicholas met her gaze and smiled. She thought she might burn, catch fire and burn, from the flame that blazed in the black depths.

"What does it mean to a man to love a woman?" He unbuckled his sword belt with one hand and dropped his weapon on the table. "Just this leap in the groin?" His jacket already lay open. He shrugged out of it and threw it aside. "Or that he will live all his life without her and yet know he was a better man for having known, even briefly, what he has lost?"

"I don't know," she said. "It doesn't matter. I love you."

His shirt bunched as it slithered over his head. The buttons on his breeches flicked open one by one under rapid fingers as he caught his heel on the crossbar of the table and yanked off one boot, then the other.

"I'd give anything of my own to hear you say that, Penny." His breeches peeled away from the swell of hard, masculine thighs and the clear bulge of his arousal. "But how can I sacrifice a nation for it?"

Her mouth was dry, aching with unshed tears. "For princes, duty is greater than love. It must be. I know. I have always known, as my mother did." *But I love you enough to try and stop you uselessly sacrificing your life in a wild, impetuous gesture!*

He bent to peel off his stockings, then turned to her, erect. She stood up and wrenched off the rest of her clothes, casting them aside in an untidy heap.

"Like Adam and Eve, before they knew they were naked—"

"It was better," he said dryly, "afterward. Once they knew about sin."

The longing shook him, made him helpless, vulnerable, making a fool of his irony. To touch and possess her. Know the silken fire of her skin against his. He thought he might find peace in that first moment when he entered her. In the slide and thrust into oblivion, the world might disappear, along with all duties, all memories, all knowledge and all shame.

Her legs wrapped around his thighs, her hands wandered over his shoulders and back and buttocks, seeking, drawing him close. She was warmth and softness, yielding and open, her nipples hard and dark rubbing against his chest. In the heat of his passion, his heart tore open in tenderness, because she accepted him and said that she loved him and let him assuage his unease in her hot, resplendent embrace.

The exquisite, shuddering rapture concentrated all his attention. White-hot, the release and the voluptuousness, until he lay exhausted beside her without the strength to lift himself away. She clung to him, her face as smooth as a slate wiped clean, her tawny eyes wide in the flickering light. She said nothing, just gazed at him as if trying to fix his features in her memory. His face, his hair, his shoulders, his arms, his chest. As if she would never again in her lifetime know a man.

He pushed her away and stood up. He must escape, before the sickness and the shaking started, before she found out—

"Penny," he said. "I'd like a promise from you."

Her eyes were guileless. "A promise?"

"To marry. Find a good man and marry him. I don't want to think of you alone the rest of your days." *Because you deserve better. Better than me!*

"I thought men were meant to be jealous."

He reached blindly for his clothes, eager to be gone. "I should die of jealousy, but I don't need to know, do I?"

"Don't go, Nicholas!" She put out a hand and caught his arm. "It's no use! I'm not noble enough, nor generous enough!"

Nausea filled his mouth. He wanted only to be outside, away from her, before she saw his shame. "I must go! For God's sake!"

The hut enclosed, choking him. Shaking her off, he strode for the door.

Penny shrugged into her shirt and hugged her arms about her waist. If he didn't escape, she would see what happened next. She would find out and her love would turn to revulsion. He had been mad to allow this one last time in this tiny hut where the walls pressed in on him like this. Nicholas cursed as he shook the latch. The door had been locked on the outside. Rage broke like an avalanche, icy and murderous.

"Bloody hell! What a nice conspiracy of traitors!" He turned and pressed his back against the wooden planks, groping for control. "Even you!"

She pulled on her breeches. "Oak, sacred to the druids. Iron, protection against evil. A door can be a closure as well as an opening. If you go alone to Moritzburg now, you'll die. What use is that?"

He strode to the table and picked up a bench. In a single swing he hurled it at the door. Wood splintered as the bench disintegrated. "Fritz! Open this bloody door!"

The major's voice floated outside. "Sire, you cannot go."

"Cannot!" The hut was stone, without windows. The door solid, banded with iron. The table followed the bench, breaking into splinters.

Penny shrank back on the bed.

He must escape! Now! "Open this bloody door! That's an order, damn you!"

The night returned nothing but silence. Panic welled up like blood from a wound. He must get away from her, before she found out. *Must. Must. Must.* He dropped his head back and howled. Somewhere outside, Quest howled in return. He let his voice wail. Primitive, mad. Prince of devils.

Migraine thundered into his skull, felling him. His vision shrank as the flickering light from the stove sprang into deadly shards of red light, attacking his eyes. Outside, Quest howled again, the primeval cry of her long-lost ancestors, the family she had been bred to hunt and kill. Nicholas let the agony and rage roar from his lungs in response. The walls closed in.

Your turn, Nico! You filthy sniveling coward! Don't you like that?

He would retch. Vomit. Somewhere in his shattered field of view he knew Penny cowered in a corner. Her cheeks shone with dampness.

"You revolt me," he shouted. "What we just did revolts me. I can't keep myself from it, from craving it, but it disgusts me. Is that what you wanted to hear?"

She cowered in the corner, wiping her hand over her face.

Perhaps he was weeping with pain. His right eye seemed to take up an entire half of his skull, bulging like a monster in his brain. He was essentially blind, seeing nothing but shattered, flickering lights, dancing in crazy patterns that leaped and reformed in rhythm with the pounding of blood trapped madly under bone.

"I've known men who crave wine." He was amazed his mouth could still form words. "They try to fight it, because when they give in, they drink until they are stupid, sick, unconscious. Then they hate themselves and swear never to drink again. But they do. They can't help it. Pursuing that moment of pleasure in spite of the nausea and wretchedness afterward. Again and again. That's how I feel. I tried not to give in to it. Now I can't resist you, though after we make love, I am sick. I hate myself. I have to get away!"

Her features melted, her mouth forming a small, sad opening, her gaze blank and dark. Water swam over her face, making her eyelids red and raw. His sword lay on the table. The other temptation. The temptation that beckoned with the irresistible promise of simplicity. Mark Anthony had used it after the battle of Actium, when all was lost, when he couldn't bear humiliation in front of Cleopatra, whom he loved, and Octavius, whom he hated. The simple, welcoming blade, dealer of death.

Instead he went to the stove and wrenched it open. With the small ash shovel he scraped up hot coals and carried them to the door. He piled them on the floor, taking the paper he had been writing on and setting fire to it, adding kindling from the broken furniture. Flames began to lick at the wood, crackling in the quiet night.

"Fritz," he shouted, putting his mouth to the keyhole. "Open this bloody door or I'll burn it down."

The wood begin to char, the air fill with smoke. Behind him she covered her mouth and coughed. Even her fingers were wet. It hurt. Terribly. It hurt him that he had done this to her. Taken a bright, shining spirit of the day and dragged her down, at last, into darkness. Smoke turned her into a wraith.

The door opened.

Fritz stood with Eric and Lucas, swords drawn, their faces eerily lit by the little fire on the threshold. Nicholas reached for a blanket and dropped it over the flames, snuffing them.

"You can't go, sire," Fritz said calmly. "We'll use force if we have to."

Nicholas backed and picked up his own blade. He couldn't focus on those demon faces, wreathed in dying smoke. Under the low ceiling of the room, there wasn't room to swing his sword. But he had one advantage and they all knew it.

Neither Fritz nor Eric nor Lucas would try to kill—he would.

He seized a plank from the broken table and used it as a battering ram, leaping over the ashes of his little fire, driving the point of his sword at Eric. In moments he was outside, thrusting and parrying, fighting three of the best swordsmen in Glarien. He couldn't focus clearly or see what he was doing, so he fought entirely on instinct. Yet the mad, ruthless rage carried him forward like a berserker. Eric cried out and fell to one knee. Fritz had already staggered back against the wall of the hut, his blade dangling uselessly from suddenly limp fingers.

Lucas backed away, smiling, then swung aside and dropped his sword to the ground. No doubt his arm was still weak from his wound. Nicholas ran for the horses. He slashed at the ropes, freeing all of them, caught his own mount by the halter and swung onto its bare back. Without looking back, he galloped away down the mountainside, the other horses following like a wild herd. Quest raced ahead, a silver streak disappearing into the dark night.

His mind filled with flames. Were they enough to burn away the devastation he had left on the face of his lover?

Seventeen

"*Well*," *Penny said. "I don't think that worked quite as you* intended, Major Baron von Gerhard."

She had torn strips from the sheet to bind up the men's wounds. Eric had a slash to one leg and Fritz had been run through in his upper arm. Lucas had taken off at a run after their fleeing dark prince.

Fritz grimaced. "It doesn't do to cross royalty."

"It's treason, isn't it?" Penny asked lightly. "Will he have us hanged and quartered?"

"I'm already bloody quartered." Eric gave a grim smile. "The Grand Duke just about took my damned leg off."

She felt amazingly calm. Absurdly calm. He had said making love to her revolted him, made him sick afterward. He had broken furniture and tried to burn down the hut with them inside. He had ridden away like a madman. So why did she feel so numb? She was almost serene.

"We were wrong. Wrong to try to stop him from rescuing Sophia and Alexis. How will he get into Moritzburg?"

Fritz walked to the bed and sat down, cradling his wounded arm. "There's an old way. The abandoned ford under the bridge. Secret passages. He knows them."

She closed her eyes and thought of that great stone pile

thrusting out of its granite base above the Win. "He's afraid of heights."

The major stared down at the bloodstained rent in his jacket. "I know that."

"These secret ways involve climbing?"

The scar leaped as Fritz looked up. "And worse: They go through some damned small spaces. He's not overly fond of tight spaces either."

Penny waved her hands to indicate the ruined hut. "Like this one? Why tight spaces?"

"He was about twelve," Fritz said. "He went missing. There was uproar. We didn't find him for three days. He was trapped in a disused cellar in the dungeons. It only had a pit opening at the top. He couldn't climb out. He said he'd fallen in."

"But you think—"

"Carl pushed him. I know it. That boy had been there in the dark, with the rats and the damp, for three days without food or water. The old grand duke made him stand at attention until he'd say what had really happened. But Nicholas insisted it was his fault, an accident, so his grandfather punished him."

She sat down, wondering why such horror didn't reach her, why she felt as if she'd been frozen. "Punished him? After three days in a cellar without food? How?"

"Had one of his companions flogged while Nicholas watched—a lad he took lessons with and was fond of."

Something had happened to her stomach. It felt tight, as if it might have turned inside-out. "An innocent boy?"

Eric flexed his leg, testing his bandaged thigh. "Who was the other lad, then?"

The old soldier looked at the redheaded man. "Lucas."

"Lucas?" Penny asked. "Lucas knew Nicholas when they were boys?"

"It's an old friendship," Fritz said. "His Christian name is Franke: Franke Lucas, Fürst von Gramais. Your mother taught him when she was governess here. He's a prince in his own right. After Nicholas and Carl and Sophia, Lucas has a pretty fair claim to the throne of Glarien himself."

Little Franke's pet stoat. The children I had in my charge at court . . . The knot in her stomach had spread to her limbs. They began to shiver, as if trying to untie themselves. *Glarien is rotten with royalty. I try whenever possible to keep them in my employ.*

The shaking became uncontrollable. Penny looked up at Fritz in open terror. "I don't know what's happening to me," she whispered. "I'm think I'm going to be sick!"

Water roared. Nicholas clung close to the damp rock. The Win River tumbled away beneath him, glad of its freedom. He shook his head. Moisture ran from his hair over his already wet face. The migraine had broken. Somewhere on that wild dash off the mountain, the pain had retreated. The shock of cold as he crawled across the old ford had completed the rout. Yet the empty space left in his skull filled with fear that the slightest movement, the wrong thought, could bring it all crashing back again, a pain that might render him helpless.

There had once, long ago, been a chain marking one side of the ford. He had fought hand-to-hand underwater, from one ancient ring to the next, while the force of current battered his body and tore the breath from his collapsing lungs. Now the castle rock loomed above him in the dark, bristling with small clumps of grass and pink flowers, shallowly rooted. Enough to send a man crashing to his death if he made one misstep.

He had fought his own men. He had done his best to kill them. He had deliberately tried to destroy Penny. And he called it duty. Self-disgust was only a sniveling coward's emotional wallow, a pathetic attempt at a conscience. He was devil's spawn, crawling like a cockroach to reclaim his own. He reached up a hand and tested. No earth. No flowers. Just a small projection of rock. Muscles screaming, he hauled himself up, until at last he gripped the iron grating in both hands.

Four hundred years ago this chute had emptied the castle's privies. Now it was a way in, a way that led through cellars and dungeons—dark, closed spaces where he might just go mad once and for all, and never be found. Bracing his feet against the rock face, he worked at the catch. It was rusted and stiff. Dogged, silent, with cold, numb fingers, he hammered at it. It gave way at last and he hauled himself inside. Into the cold, dank tunnel that led up into darkness.

Her Royal Highness, Princess Sophia of Alvia, paced slowly around her chamber. Nicholas was dead. Lit by a single candle, the miniature portrait gazed up from her dressing table. Unbearably handsome, brilliant, terrifying. They had been destined for each other since childhood. She sat down and stared at the painted eyes, the raffish tumble of dark hair. He had found a woman to impersonate her in London. So that kidnapping, her imprisonment in one unknown room after another, had all been for nothing. In the eyes of the world they were already married. And she was already widowed.

He had almost outwitted his enemies. Until now. Nicholas was dead. For the sake of Glarien and Alvia, she must marry Carl, who had rescued her from her mysterious imprisonment. Her father would want it. If she did not have a son before Duke Michael died, France would lay claim to her homeland. Only alliance with Glarien could make Alvia strong enough to survive. She could not be responsible for the ruin and destruction that was bound to result if she did not do her duty.

She would marry Carl. He visited her formally every day, courteous, deferential, and softly—with a painful delicacy—letting her know just how venal Nicholas had been. Carl was her duty. Alas, that she loved someone else!

Something scraped in the hallway, a scratch of claws. She went to the door and listened. For a moment, old tales crowded in, tales that made her hair prickle at the back of her neck. The latch rattled and panted, giving a plaintive whine. Sophia took a deep breath and opened the door. A silver wolfhound slipped into the room past her skirts and lay down at the foot of the bed. The honest brown eyes looked into hers as the dog cocked its head, listening. Sophia sat down and stared at it. For several moments a deep silence stretched, broken only by the steady tick of the clock on the mantel. The dog dropped its head to its paws, with both ears pricked, then everything happened at once.

The wolfhound leaped up, the clock struck midnight, the little door to the battlements flew open and Sophia fainted.

She woke up to see Nicholas sitting beside her on her bed, gently bathing her temples. He smiled, that heartbreakingly charming smile she remembered from their childhood meetings.

"I'm sorry," he said. "I know. Gargoyles come alive and vampires haunt the night. I should have knocked first."

"You are ill?" she asked. "Dear God, you look like a ghost."

He glanced away, as if faintly embarrassed. "Like all the ghouls and specters of the night, I am death warmed over."

"Carl said you *were* dead." She was insanely, madly glad he was here.

"Very nearly."

"I am . . . I'm ecstatic it's not true. But how did you get here?"

"Up the rock and in through the cellars. Moritzburg Castle is full of charmingly narrow secret passageways, one of which, fortunately, leads to the roof. The rest was easy."

Sophia took one of his hands and turned it over in hers. "You're lying, Nicholas."

He glanced down. His palms were bloodied and torn, the knuckles skinned. "Very well. I'm lying. It wasn't easy. I was bloody terrified. There were times I thought I couldn't do it. I was wretchedly sick. Not quite the gallant knight errant come to rescue the fair maiden."

"Why did you pretend to die? Why do you come here now, like this?"

He looked up. His eyes seemed infinitely hollow and black. "To allow you to decide your own future. Do you wish to marry Carl, or would you rather I came miraculously back to life to reclaim you?"

She fumbled awkwardly, letting him take back his hand, the beautiful shape marred with filth and blood. "What do you think? Carl has been very assiduous with tales about you. It only makes me dislike him the more. He hates you, Nicholas. If he finds you here now, you really will die."

"It's a risk." He seemed remote, like a man who has been through five straight days of battle and is still dazed and deafened by the guns. "If he doesn't kill me, will the mob do it for him?"

"I don't know. But here is your answer." She leaned forward and kissed him briefly on the lips. His mouth was cold. He did not respond. "If you've come to save me from marriage to Carl, I'm more than willing, Nicholas, even if he did rescue me."

"Carl? I'm sure it was most touching and gallant. Meanwhile, Lucas wore himself to the bone trying to find you."

She looked down, unable to hide her emotion, yet determined on her duty. "It doesn't matter. Let's be crowned together as planned. Carl had me kidnapped, didn't he? I thought his rescue might be a fake."

"Did he also tell you I had a mistress?"

Sophia nodded. "A poor, benighted peasant girl, he said, who looked like me."

Her heart turned over at the sudden unguarded expression that raced across his features. "Neither benighted nor a peasant. While you lay imprisoned, she led the people directly to her heart, kept their love for you alive. She's your cousin."

"My cousin?"

The wolfhound nosed at his bloodied hand. He began to caress the silver fur in long, loving strokes, ignoring his own obvious discomfort. The brown eyes closed in doggy bliss.

"We both enter this marriage with our hearts already given elsewhere," he said. "It will be as it has always been. I can't offer you anything but an attempt at courtesy and civility, Sophia. I'll do my best to make you happy. I have nothing else. Is that enough?"

She laid her hand tentatively on his sleeve. He let it lie there unheeded. *"My cousin?"*

"I'll tell you in the morning. Until then, do you mind if I lie down and go to sleep?"

Confused, she shook her head. He tugged off damp boots and thrust them under the bed. His torn, filthy jacket and breeches followed, leaving him clad in just shirt and undergarments. Ignoring the princess standing lost beside him, he pulled back the sheets and rolled underneath them. In a few seconds he slept. The dog jumped onto the covers and curled up at his feet.

Sophia looked at them for a moment, then tiptoed into her ante-room to wake Gerta and ask what on earth she should do now.

Penny slogged through the night on foot, Fritz at her side. It had taken arguments and shouting. The redheaded man had been left behind in the ruins of the hut. With the wound to his leg, he couldn't walk. Eric had been supposed to escort her to England. Fritz thought he himself must fulfill that obligation.

"I'm not going yet," Penny had insisted. "I can't. I must see this through. I don't expect to ever again see Grand Duke Nicholas privately, but I must know if he lives and what happens to Alexis. Princess Sophia is my cousin. Anyway, you can't just take off for England. He no longer needs me, but he might need you."

She thought only the last argument had swayed Fritz.

They caught up with Lucas toward dawn. The Prince of Gramais had gathered the horses and tethered them at a small farm. The farmer's wife fed the strangers a large breakfast of cheese curds and bread without asking questions.

"So here we are," Lucas said at last. "A failed spy. A wounded major. And an Englishwoman who looks like a princess. A sorry enough group to take action against Carl and rescue the Grand Duke."

"There's more news from Moritzburg?" Fritz asked.

"Feeling's running high. Rumors abound against Nicholas's memory. It's like an avalanche. It starts with a tiny crack in the snow, then gathers force until it can annihilate forests. The von Forschachs are calling for the funeral to be canceled and replaced with a trial."

"What sense does that make?" Penny asked. "They think he's dead."

Lucas's pale eyes were almost pitying. "The bodies of trai-tors have been exhumed before in order to suffer punishment. Carl is just trying to make sure Nicholas won't live, if he does return."

She shuddered. "Then you think he's doomed?"

His scar writhed as Fritz smiled at her. "I should have taken you away. You sure as hell can't appear in public now. If there are two Princess Sophia's, you might both be burned at the stake."

"Of course," Penny said. "But there's no reason at all why Miss Penelope Lindsey from Rascall St. Mary shouldn't visit Glarien for all these jolly festivities. All I need is a nice English dress and bonnet. The henna has already mostly faded from my hair and I'm sure I can remember how I used to do my plaits. Find me a nice respectable family of British visitors to stay with and no one will question it."

Nicholas woke to a vague rustling. Quest pushed up against him, her tail thumping. He opened his eyes to see Sophia, dressed in some formal gown of white silk, tied with black ribbons and with a black sash tied over the breast. Gerta fussed around her, while Lady Beatrice put final touches to her hair.

Sophia ignored them as she stared down at him. She had redder hair. They had put some kind of rinse in Penny's. The princess had none of that innocence in her wide gaze. Sophia had been raised to rule. "You remind me of Hamlet after he saw the ghost."

"'Tis bitter cold, and I am sick at heart."

"I have a formal reception in half an hour. What do you want us to do?"

He sat up and grinned at Gerta, who frowned at him, before he spoke again to his wife. "Make an excuse, any excuse, to send Alexis up here. Don't warn him what he might find. Just tell him to fetch you a wrap or your gloves. Then carry on as if nothing has changed."

Sophia fingered the black sash. "With your funeral arrangements?"

Nicholas leaned back and stretched. Muscles protested from his ordeal entering the castle. "There won't be any funeral arrangements. There will be a trial. My trial. For treason—and witchcraft, of course. There must be a crime against the soul to justify prosecution of the dead. Like poor King Charles the First of England, I'm about to lose my head—or my corpse is, if they can ever find it."

• • •

The morning of the trial dawned clear and cold. The mist burned slowly off the towers of Moritzburg. Knots of people had gathered in the streets. Buildings smoked vapors, corbels glistened moisture, spires shone in the new sun. Penny couldn't quite make out the feeling of the crowd. Anger burned like a fever, but doubt and confusion created the more obvious cough and splutter.

For the English visitors to Glarien, stopping on their tour of Switzerland and Italy to witness the splendor of the upcoming coronation, it was a little disconcerting to find they were instead to first witness the trial for treason of a dead grand duke, followed by the betrothal of the new one. Apparently, if the dead fellow had been guilty of crimes against God and nature, his marriage would become null and void, so his widow could marry Count Zanich right away. A necessity, really, for a seamless succession. This was hardly the moment to leave Glarien without a crowned sovereign—and one firmly married to Alvia. Funerals had been held the day before for the citizens lost in the rock slide on the way to the St. Alban Pass. Anger had been even more obvious then. Anger and a sullen resentment.

Penny had no idea why she'd been unable to weep, or why she couldn't seem to keep down her food.

As if a bridal veil were drawn aside for a kiss, the mists shredded away into a blue sky. As if witnessing the bride and groom in that public embrace, a sigh whispered up from the crowd. Everyone began to move. Penny lost contact with the English family she was staying with, to be swept with the crowd, up through the twisting streets, up the rock causeway where she had first arrived in the guise of a princess, across the narrow drawbridge, and into the great open space inside the bailey. A platform had been set up before the smaller curtain wall that guarded the inner ward. To let the people hear all the evidence, it was to be an open air trial.

Leading Sophia by the hand, Carl mounted a set of steps and seated her, then himself, in two great chairs of state. Nobles and gentlewomen surrounded them. Was that Alexis—his golden head glimmering in the sun—and Lucas, Prince von Gramais? On Carl's side, supporting him? Her heart turned over. Even more sinister, a contingent of soldiers stood at attention to control the crowd, a garrison wearing the silver plumes of Zanich. Penny was jammed up against the batter, the sloping base of the wall. Confident that her bonnet shielded her face, she squeezed up onto a projecting stone where she could more easily watch the proceedings.

Carl stood up to speak. A man just below Penny began to cough. Several people shushed him. A high-strung tension connected the crowd, straining to hear their new grand duke. Flags whipped in the breeze on the castle towers. Muskets clanked. People sneezed and rumbled. Penny couldn't make out a word Carl was saying.

A translation ran back through the crowd, simplified, passed on from man to man in a diminishing relay. "He says Grand Duke Nicholas practiced black arts. That he bewitched the princess. The rock slide that killed our mayor was his fault. Glarien condemns his memory and enters a new future, as if he had never existed."

With the muttering repetitions a hot wave of anger ran palpably in the still air and the newly burning day. Penny felt faint. The accounts of Carl's speech seemed to break into disjointed fragments, mixed with comments from the people . . . *unnatural acts . . . vicious propensities . . . deserved death . . . cheated us of wreaking our own revenge . . .*

Frantic to know what was really happening, Penny elbowed her way along the base of the wall, closer to the platform. Carl's voice began to ring, until at last she stood where she could hear him clearly.

"It is a great grief to me," he was saying, "that my cousin— my little cousin, Nico—the boy I once loved, should have become a viper in—"

He broke off. The crowd began to sway as if stirred by an invisible hand. A shout went up. . . . then another. *"Nicholas! Grand Duke Nicholas!"*

Nicholas rode alone and bareheaded from the inner courtyard. Sunlight glanced off his brilliant white uniform, dazzled on gold braid, died like a sigh in the black depths of his eyes. The horse was jet black. In a measured, stately dance, it trotted slowly across the cobbles. Complete silence fell. Iron shoes rang on the stones in a cadence that matched the beat of her heart. *Thud, thud, thud.*

With a click and crash, the guard fixed bayonets and presented arms.

The crowd fell back, allowing him to pass, then closed in behind him in a solid wall. Penny climbed farther up the rough stones of the batter. The people seemed locked in step, opening a narrow path then pressing close behind Nicholas, until he stopped his horse at the platform and made it rear, just a little, front hooves folded together.

Carl smiled, pointing at the silent man on the black horse. His eyes narrowed. "Arrest this man! He is—"

Sophia leaped to her feet and strode forward. Her voice was high and clear. "Yes! Nicholas, my beloved husband. Grand Duke of Glarien. Succor to Alvia. Who wed me in London and brought me into my homeland over the sacred passes of the Erhabenhorn, blessed by St. Cyriakus. Escaped from the machinations of this man here—" She pointed to Carl.

"My dear," Carl said. "With his black powers he bewitched you. He even made an evil copy of you." He swept his arm and pointed straight at Penny.

She felt pinned like a butterfly stabbed in a case. Myriad faces spun to look at her. A low murmur ran through the crowd.

Princess Sophia laughed. "Why! It's my own cousin, Miss Penelope Lindsey from England, in *such* an English bonnet. Her father was my dear uncle, Prince Frederick. No evil doings here, Count Zanich, except yours! *You* are the man who would have killed Grand Duke Nicholas. *You* are the man who keeps me a prisoner, who murdered our mayor on the road to your own stronghold, who would undo all our reforms. You, Count Zanich, corrupt the very air of Glarien and steal the souls from her citizens."

The crowd roared. The sound was inhuman, mad. Men surged. Women screamed. With the unstoppable force of an avalanche, people began to push forward. The soldiers wavered. The wall of steel fell as if mowed by a scythe, leaving the platform undefended. Nicholas spun about on his black and shouted an order.

Penny thought she heard a new thunder of hoofbeats, before she was pulled from her perch and lost in the frenzied stampede of a crowd gone mad. Her bonnet was pulled back. The strings chopped up under her chin, choking her. Rough hands wrenched at her hair and dress. Struggling, she went down under a flailing mass of arms and legs. In a reflex she clutched her hands over her belly, over the tiny hidden life that flamed and danced under her heart.

"Look at her hands," his voice said with a hint of amusement. "She's been digging for turnips in that English garden."

She was wrenched upright, her hair fallen loose and tumbled over her face. Someone did indeed look at her fingers and laugh. The roar of the crowd had clearly turned to cheering. *Nicholas! Sophia! Nicholas!*

Penny knew now quite clearly what was making the knot in her insides. Hatred. She hated him. Even when he leaned down from the black horse and took her by the waist, several hands in the crowd helping to lift her into his arms, she hated him. Unable to see anything, crushed against his medals, she hated him as he galloped through the applause, through the curtain wall and into the inner ward, where the gates clanged shut behind them.

His voice whispered so softly in her ear she thought she might be dreaming. "Penny, I can never make recompense for what has happened between us. Know only this: I love you. I shall always love you. Princess Sophia will have only the shell of this prince, for an Englishwoman forever has his heart. I am sorry for it, for both of you deserve better."

He released her to slide in a straggling heap on the stones. The black horse circled, lifting each hoof high in a trot like a dance.

Penny lifted her head to see him nod to Sophia.

"Madam," he said. "You have just given me a kingdom."

"And you've really brought me a cousin?" Silk rustled. Sweet scent enveloped her. Penny looked up into the face she saw every morning in the mirror—the hair a little redder, the

skin more perfect—a vision of herself as she might have been
had she been born beautiful and legitimately royal.

Her heart dived and raced. She scrambled to her feet and
made a five-point curtsey. "Your Royal Highness," she said. "I
am honored."

Nicholas looked at Sophia without visible emotion, almost
as if he were blind. *He is seeing colors,* she thought. *He has a
migraine. Oh, Nicholas!*

"Miss Lindsey wasn't supposed to be here," he said dryly.
"She almost ruined everything. Alexis, well done! You have a
mount ready for Princess Sophia?"

A white horse danced out of the stable led by a groom. A
blood horse, capricious with fire and spirit, a mount Penny
knew she would never be able to handle. Sophia was lifted onto
the saddle and the horse bent its head to her hand, relaxed.

"Come, madam," Nicholas said. "I had to choose between
my cousin and yours, but I trust Lucas has Carl safe by now. We
must reassure our subjects that their future is in good hands and
that they are all safe under the rule of our new laws."

From the outer courtyard rose a cacophony of noise. Side by
side, Sophia and Nicholas rode to face it, an island of calmness
and certainty in a world gone mad. *I had to choose between my
cousin and yours . . .*

In spite of what had happened in the hut, he had chosen her.
She had not really been in danger, not once the people began to
cheer, but he had set aside everything to rescue her from the curious crowd. There was nothing else she could ever ask of him,
now his destiny had arrived.

An Englishwoman forever has his heart.

Alexis took Penny by the elbow. "Ma'am? Please come inside."

"Alexis?" she said. "You still love him, even after all this?"

"Of course," the blond boy said quietly. "Don't you?"

"I am glad you no longer wear your hair so your head looks like
a split pea, Penelope." Her plump form silhouetted against the
Norfolk winter's day outside, Aunt Horace sat down with a

thump on the window seat and pulled off her gloves. "This new style suits you."

"It's the style I've worn for several years now, Aunt Horace," Penny said.

"Oh, you'll no doubt dazzle the local beaux at the Christmas parties again this year. I trust there'll be mistletoe at Nettle Park? It's too bad you always had such very large feet. Are they still growing?"

"No, Aunt Horace," Penny said. "It's not my feet that are growing, it's my belly."

Mrs. Lindsey turned from the doorway, where she was shaking snow from Aunt Horace's cloak before hanging it from the hook in the hall. "We're to have a new addition at Clumper Cottage this spring. Penny is to have a baby."

Aunt Horace gave a small scream, like a mouse caught by an owl. "A *bastard*?"

"Don't be upset, Aunt," Penny said. "Foolish of me, I know, but who on earth would ever marry me, when my feet are so large?"

"We're very happy about it." Mrs. Lindsey came into the room. "This baby's father is also a prince."

Two plump arms reached out. "Penelope, you poor lamb! You poor darling! You have been ravished by one of those wicked gypsies, just like your mother? Come here and tell your aunt Horace all about it."

Penny laughed and shook her head. "I was certainly ravished, Aunt Horace, but I assure you I was a willing participant."

Eyebrows shot up to crease a round forehead. "Then why didn't he marry you?"

"He had to marry someone else," Penny said. "It was a matter of duty. A woman he risked everything to rescue, for the sake of a nation."

Aunt Horace snorted. "I should think if this prince had any nobility at all, he'd have rescued *you*!"

Penny put one hand on her swollen belly. "No, Aunt, it was far more noble in the circumstances for him to rescue the woman he didn't love."

The child kicked. *His* child. She had been making her unborn baby a scrapbook of newspaper clippings. News of Glarien, of His Royal Highness Nicholas Alexander, Grand Duke of Glarien, Fürst von Moritzburg, sovereign prince of Glarien, Harzburg and Winsteg, who had been thought killed, yet had returned unharmed to reclaim his throne and his bride, Princess Sophia of Alvia. Penny had cut out the accounts of the coronation, with Sophia's father, Duke Michael, in attendance. She had filled pages with snippets about the peace and prosperity the new sovereigns were bringing to Glarien.

Only one story had she kept out of the scrapbook. Nicholas had been too late to save Carl, Count Zanich, from the mob. Carl had rallied a small group of loyal men and fought his way free of Lucas's protection to attempt an escape to Burg Zanich. They had not even reached the bridge.

"Carl wasn't the only one who could tell tales," Alexis had said, while escorting Penny back to the English family. "Lucas and his men have been spreading Nicholas's side of the story. After all, the people of Moritzburg have seen him in action for themselves. They wanted the reforms. And Princess Sophia is a goddess to them. The crowd would sway whichever way she pointed. You helped with that, Miss Lindsey—when you went out among the people and listened to their troubles. I only arranged for his uniform and the black horse and to keep him hidden in the castle. Carl was a fool to think he could win popularity by blackening Nicholas's name. The old memories of Carl still dogged him."

So the people had killed Carl. They had dragged him from his horse and beaten him to death. It might even have been Penny's fault. She had created a complication, delayed things, disrupted Nicholas's plans. *Miss Lindsey wasn't supposed to be here.* He had chosen to rescue her, when his intention had been to personally protect Carl—in spite of everything his cousin had done—and deliver him to the law. It frightened her that he could love her enough to save her first, and because of her, he had failed to save Carl. She hadn't spoken with him again. The English family, shocked at her ordeal, had shown her nothing but kindness on the journey home.

Now Nicholas and Sophia ruled with the help of their elected council. Penny would have only this to show her child: head-lines from newspapers, proof that her baby's father was a brilliant sovereign. It was more than she had known of her own father. She wanted her baby to understand. When Nicholas gave Sophia a son, all of his plans would be complete. He didn't know about this other child to be born in the spring in England. Penny put her hand over her belly, determined he never would.

Whatever her own pain, however much she yearned for him, longed for him, loved him with her entire heart and soul, she had Rascall Hall to think about: fuel for the hothouses, pruning in the orchards, a load of grapes to ship to London. Jeb Hardacre would take them. The only things that would never again go to market were hedgehogs, hibernating now over the long winter, and still safe when spring finally arrived.

No more wild things will be captured here.

He wrote every day. Long letters, pouring out all the memories, all the grief. *When I was eleven, I came to Glarien. I had a cousin. His name was Carl.*

Every day he burned them.

My mother used to take me into the orangery. I thought she was a goddess, remote, beautiful, unreachable. An ideal of womanhood. I wanted her to love me. She let me suck those sweet juices and laughed when I spilled them down my chin. Sometimes I saved an orange for my governess, whom I loved. I had a cousin. His name was Carl—

He had to stop and retch in a basin. Sophia came in and gravely handed him a towel.

"It can't go on, Nicholas," she said.

He sat on the bed, watching his hands shake.

I had a cousin. I admired him. I thought I loved him. His name was Carl. He held me off the battlements and afterward—

"Nicholas!"

He looked up and smiled. "We are succeeding, I think, in creating our brave new world in Glarien."

"We're succeeding beyond your wildest expectations. I fear

only that the personal price you're paying is too high." She wet a cloth and held it to his temples. "What do you write every day?"

"Nothing. Something for Penny. No, something for me, I think." The ashes of the last letter glowed dully in the grate. His obsession was to write it all down, every last detail. "It doesn't matter."

Sophia smoothed her hand over his forehead, like a sister. "You have a headache? Nicholas, you can't go on like this. You can't exhaust yourself day after day, doing your duty in public, then collapsing in private. Even your strength will give out eventually."

"You wish me to do my duty in private? I can't."

She blushed a little and turned away. "We must make a son."

"I know you're in love with Lucas, Sophie," he said. "Take him to your bed. Let him make you a son. Who would ever know? His blood is royal, too." He spread his hands on his desk, the hands of a sovereign, stark with purpose, empty of passion. "Penny said something once about King Arthur. Shall I sit at my round table and let Lucas play Lancelot to your Guinevere?"

"If I cannot be shown to be a virgin," Sophia said. "I cannot ask for an annulment."

Quest crawled underneath the bed and whined.

A girl! Penny rocked the pink, squalling bundle in her arms, then guided the rosebud mouth to her nipple. Outside, the early summer breeze whipped about in the garden. The baby rooted blindly for a moment, then fastened on with remarkable strength. A girl. She had named her Sophia. In March Napoleon had escaped Elba, landed back in France and advanced on Paris. King Louis had fled. The Congress in Vienna had suddenly broken up and the diplomats and sovereigns had scattered—including Nicholas, who had been there guarding the interests of Glarien and Alvia as the great powers reshaped the map of Europe. Then news about Glarien had disappeared under the weight of reports from France and Belgium, where the Duke of Wellington gathered armies to fight his old enemy. Meanwhile Penny had given birth to a grand duke's natural daughter and fallen in love once again.

It had been over a year since her dark prince had first seized her when she was gathering hedgehogs. A lifetime of long months since she had last seen him, riding away to pick up the reins of his destiny. *Miss Lindsey wasn't supposed to be here. She almost ruined everything.*

A large droplet fell on the baby's forehead. Sophie opened her mouth in milky bubbles as her little face screwed up in protest. Penny wiped away her tears and the baby started sucking again. Her father had once sent her a doll. Nicholas didn't even know that this little Sophia existed. He didn't need to know. But she would make sure that her baby knew about him.

"Daddy is a great hero," she said to the oblivious little face and the round fist pushing at her breast. "Daddy is wise and good. I hope he thinks so. I hope he believes it. I hope the princess gives him a son, a little half-brother for you, Sophie. I hope my love for you is enough. I didn't think I'd fall in love so deeply with you, you see. Of course, I had no idea that I'd fall in love so deeply with him. I'm a great fool, Sophie. But I love you and your granny loves you, and no harm will ever come to you. You'll be wiser than either of us, you clever little lady. You shall marry an ordinary man, a prince only in your heart."

The guns thundered, hour after hour. Nicholas rode beside Wellington, surveying the progress of the battle. The Allied troops fought before a village called Waterloo in Belgium. The Glarian soldiers, led by Fritz, were being held in reserve. Eric and Alexis waited with them. Alexis had filled out and grown taller, almost a man. His bright hair shone golden in the summer sunshine. Nicholas didn't believe Alexis had nightmares any longer. The youth was in love with the daughter of a count from Alvia. Carl had been buried with all the respect due a prince of the blood. Perhaps Alexis had managed to bury his past with Carl.

As he had? All those letters, pouring out the agony, facing the demons and stripping them of power, one by one. He had written them for Penny, then burned them when it seemed too selfish and cruel to cause her so much pain. Then he had found the pen creating a new resolution on the paper. *I had a cousin. I admired him. His name was Carl—and he, too, was damaged—*

Where had it come from, this compassion for Carl? Compassion? Mercy too hard won, perhaps. But hatred had dissolved into emptiness and from somewhere the emptiness had filled with a new forgiveness. An understanding that had brought him from Glarien.

So he thought—hoped—he had reached a new clarity, but he must still let fate play its hand, in case he had judged incorrectly. If the French triumphed, Glarien would still need him and all of his plans would fall to dust, but if Napoleon was defeated this day, Nicholas need never see the Alps again.

Of course, when Wellington decided to throw the Glarian troops into battle, Nicholas would ride into the thick of the fighting with them. Blind chance might decide in a split second that he would never see England again either. Even if he survived, would she have waited for him?

The redstart fluttered up into the ivy on the ruined walls, calling its alarm. *Twee-tuk-tuk!* Penny glanced up. She had been watching the bold red-tailed male making its little sallies after flying insects, then drop to the ground to hunt for beetles. Its dive for cover startled her. Doves had been calling repeatedly. They too suddenly fell silent. Something rustled, coming around the edge of the old tithe barn.

She stood up, brushing grass from her skirts. Sophie, replete, burped and bathed, slept peacefully at Clumper Cottage with Mrs. Lindsey to watch over her. Penny rarely left her, but sometimes a restless longing forced her outside to stride away across the Rascall Hall estates, faster and more furiously than she could walk carrying a baby. Almost always, those walks brought her here, to the ruins of old Rascall Manor, where she had once collected hedgehogs and learned to ride a horse. The place where she could weep for him, miss him and find the strength to go on for one more day.

Brambles rustled. A spray of dog roses dipped and swayed. A flash of silver fur, then a bright tongue licking her hands.

"Oh, God!" She crouched to throw her arms about the wolfhound's ruff. *"Quest!"*

Eighteen

"*I am here,*" Nicholas said.

Quest sat, vigorously wagging her tail. Penny clutched at her, burying her face in the dog's soft coat, while her breath rushed in and out of her lungs like a storm surge. *Nicholas!*

"I am here." His voice broke in a half laugh. "But this time I can very easily be denied."

Penny gasped for breath. "You fought at Waterloo. I read about it in the newspapers."

"We've won peace for Europe. Napoleon is exiled to St. Helena."

"Yes, I know. That was in the newspapers, too."

He blazed unchanged in the broken sunlight, dapples marking his face, echoing his dark hair and eyes. Shadows and flame, both ancient and innocent, like a forest god.

He glanced about at the ruins. "This is where they told me I'd become crown prince. Where I learned the boundaries of my life had just stretched to infinity, far beyond the twenty-two furlongs that connected my home to the outside world." He reached into an inner pocket. "I've just shrunk them again."

"What do you mean?"

"I brought you something."

He held out a small packet. Penny stared up at his face as she took it. A small tendril of fear for him uncurled along her spine. *Nicholas!*

She unwrapped the brown paper. Something nestled in cotton.

"Sophia told me it was foolish, that I had a whole nation of carvers at my disposal, but I wanted to do it with my own hands." A hint of self-mockery flitted at one corner of his mouth. "It took several months of trying. I'm afraid I ruined quite a few blocks of wood and cut myself a few times—"

The cotton parted to reveal a carving. It was plain, without gilt or paint, whittled from some fine-grained white wood. A horse, running free, about six inches long. A horse much like Willow. The wooden mane and tail streamed in an imaginary wind.

Tears swam, blurring the little horse as if it plunged through waves. "Nicholas! It's beautiful! I don't know what to say."

"I made it for you." Quest sat down by his heels. He laid one hand on the dog's head. "Perhaps I needed an excuse for a second pilgrimage. The first took me up the Erhabenhorn. This one brings me back here."

She waved her hand. "Old Rascall Manor is also a sacred place?"

"Simply because it's where you are. My life only has its deepest meaning because of you. I didn't understand what the heart could feel, until you showed me. You taught me many things. Perhaps one is that there are some things even a prince cannot delegate. That horse is a small enough gift and a paltry enough token of my desires."

A painful lump lodged in her throat, strangling panic. "What are your desires?"

"To love you, to live with you, to marry you. Easy enough to want, of course, but I don't know if it's possible for me, or for you. If—as I suspect—it is not, I can go to London."

Tears swam and choked. "What about Sophia and Glarien?"

The wolfhound rolled onto her back, holding her paws in mute supplication. He rubbed at her belly. "It won't reach the English newspapers until tomorrow, but I've renounced all claim to the throne, my Glarian titles and honors and properties.

I'm publicly stripped of all those stars and crosses and the sword of St. Cyriakus. They let me keep Quest, but not the stables. I have ceded the crown to Sophia."

The line of his back and arm was piercingly beautiful, heartbreaking. "You have *abdicated*? I thought Sophia must have a son—"

He glanced up and smiled. "With the cooperation of Duke Michael of Alvia and the Glarian council and the consent of the Allies in Vienna, our marriage is annulled." His voice was steady, dispassionate. "On the grounds—privately admitted and publicly understood—of my impotence. On the year's anniversary of our nuptials, Sophia was proved to be still virgin." The smile deepened, a flash of brilliant, wry self-derision. "Gerta testified about the chicken blood on our wedding night. It was easy to prove Sophia and I had never consummated our marriage."

It sank in slowly, like a drop of oil splashed on milk. He and Sophia had never—all that passion and potency, none of it had found release with his princess? She felt stunned. "But you're a great ruler. How can you abandon your destiny?"

"My destiny? I don't know. My goals are fulfilled. Glarien has a new constitution. A grand duke—or duchess—with limited jurisdiction, under the guidance of the elected council. It took months of diplomacy to lay all the groundwork with the great powers and win the trust of the people of Glarien. We had to wait for enough stability in Europe before it could be risked. Waterloo has won us that."

Her breath came hard, as if she once again struggled up the slopes of the Erhabenhorn. "You achieved all that, but you have *abdicated*!"

He shrugged as if it were something inconsequential, trivial. "Like Napoleon, I go into exile. I've agreed never to visit Glarien or Alvia again."

She turned the wooden horse in her hands, feeling the careful curves, the strong lines of the back and neck, the delicate nostrils. Her heart hammered and swooped. He had given up everything? His throne, his wife, his men, even his horses?

"Princess Sophia will rule alone?"

Quest sat up as Nicholas walked away a few paces. "She'll marry Lucas. They've been in love for years. Glarien and Alvia will bloom under their rule and she'll no doubt have a son within the year."

It seemed too great to comprehend. An enormity. He had given up a throne—the duty he had unknowingly been born to? It terrified her, that he might have cast himself loose in the world.

"Nicholas, you were always destined for greatness. You would throw it all away?"

He looked up at the overhanging oaks. "Wellington is of the opinion that a British peer will matter more to the future than the figurehead sovereign of a minor principality in the Alps. Glarien is secure in the care of Sophia and Lucas. Now we have peace, Britain promises to remake the world." Sun slipped over his dark hair as he smiled at her. "I'm still Lord Evenlode."

She closed her eyes. *He'll make a very able lord,* Jeb Hardacre had said. *He's a smart man with an eye for what the land needs.* Was it enough for a man of his ability? "You will live at Rascall Hall?"

"No, of course not! I can quite easily fulfill my new responsibilities in London. Are you afraid I've come back to pick up the reins here? I don't expect you to welcome me. You may continue as you always have—before I disrupted your life. The estate is yours to run as you see fit. I've not come this time to force you to choices you don't want to make."

The little wooden horse cavorted bravely. She set it on a broken piece of wall and stared at it—the evidence of months of learning, whittling, cutting himself. "The red or the black? I don't blame you if your duty sometimes made you seem brutal. After all, there were times my interference must have driven you to distraction—"

"Never!" he said fiercely.

Sobs burned, blinding and sore. The wolfhound's rough tongue scorched over her hands. He had given up a throne. *To love you, to live with you, to marry you.* She stood dumb, her mouth full of tears, her hand on the dog's head, knowing the chance was here, now, and would never come again.

"Nicholas, the creature you're afraid of has far more reason to fear you. We hold each other's hearts like two fragile glass spheres. Why do you think you must leave?"

He broke a stem of bindweed from the wall and shredded it. "That last day, after I delivered you from the crowd, I would have sold my soul to the devil to have left Glarien with you. I had you there, on my saddle. No one could have prevented it. Two things stopped me. The first was my duty to those countless souls dependent on my keeping faith: Alexis, Sophia, Lucas, all the citizens of Moritzburg—even Carl. I had to trust you would understand that."

"I understood it."

The pink trumpets drifted, to die in the long grass. "The second reason had to do with myself. Whether my love might only damage you, besmirch you, drag you down to the devil with me. It isn't a question I can answer. I wanted to explain. I wrote you letters."

"I didn't receive them."

"No, I destroyed them unsent." His fists clenched, crushing the remains of the flowers. "They were painful to write. I didn't want you to suffer through all of it with me. You remade me. You showed me what it means to love. Thoughts of you gave me the strength to get through this last year. Should I return bitterness for that?"

"It was not all one-sided," she insisted. "You taught me greater things, expanded my provincial viewpoint, made me see deeper truths. You even gave me a new understanding and love for my father. Don't you know how precious that is?"

He seemed poised on a knife edge. "Not nearly as precious as what you gave me. I love you, Penny. I always will. So how the *hell* could I send you the letters—"

"Love means understanding what the lover must do for his own soul. What do we have to fear from the truth?"

"The truth? Dragged hideously from its dungeon, where it has lain half-starved in the dark? In the hut above Moritzburg, after that last time—" His voice broke, shattered, venomous, the vehemence of a prince of Glarien sending his enemies to the rack. "All those times! The battlements, the broken glass in your anteroom! I tried to burn us both alive! How could you forgive it? I *want* to spend the rest of my life with you. I *want* to lay my heart in your hands. But how can I be sure it isn't my own selfish need crying out for fulfillment, willing to trample you in the process? I couldn't bear that, Penny. I must leave!"

Remembered hoofbeats echoed, thundering in the dark. She raised her voice to drown them out, almost shouting. "Then is this all I'm to have of you? Doubts and burned letters? After I won you a throne? A throne you had the nerve to repudiate! You risked that, yet now you cannot risk love? Whatever pain you suffered, I would not have shirked from sharing it."

He stood pinned against the broken wall, the bindweed reaching tendrils as if to trap him forever, yet his eyes were determined, filled with a deadly finality. "I am the coward. I shrank from it."

"Then you still don't trust that I love you? That love conquers all things? I love you, Nicholas. You must tell me everything. You must write those letters again."

Silence stretched for a moment. He was enfolded in shadows and flame, as if he burned from within. All that determination and fire turned inward, blocking her out.

He swayed as if drunk. "Must I? It was a bitter task, Penny."

She forced disdain into her voice, a deliberate taunting. "Then Carl has triumphed after all. You've let him take your soul with him into hell, where he can gloat over you forever." Her heart pounded madly, without rhythm. "If you would have any honor left, you owe me that explanation and an apology. You cannot leave without it."

"Because you ask, you shall have it." Nicholas smiled with pure bravado, the wicked smile of a gypsy, not to be defeated or outwitted. "Though princes never apologize."

The hallway lay quiet, the walls and floors sleeping beneath erratic beams of afternoon sunshine. Penny followed Nicholas into the study and up the secret stair to his old room. Mrs. Butteridge had kept the house ready, insisting the earl might come back one day. The housekeeper, who—like everyone else he had ever touched—had given her heart to this grand duke.

"You see?" Penny said. "Paper and pens. I shall be in the tower."

Without looking back she opened the little door and climbed the stairs. She felt giddy. She had no idea what she was doing or why she was doing it. What a welcome home! Oh, God! She dropped into the chair at the little desk where she had once written letters to her mother and set the white horse to cavort across the polished surface. *I think perhaps I begin to understand the crack in our desperate prince's black armor. He's lonely. Horribly, dreadfully lonely. And afraid, I think, of friendship. Was my father as lonely as that?*

Oh, Lord, what a smug, judgmental girl she had been!

It was stuffy, so after a few moments she opened the window. Doves cooed in the woods and she thought she heard a song thrush, though it was a bit late in the season for them. A small breeze washed through the gardens. Her mind seemed frozen, a strange disoriented wasteland, aware of her surroundings without being able to give any of it meaning. *There's a robin,* she thought. *And a bullfinch. What's he doing out this time of day? Oh, and there's his pale little wife. Why is the male always more flamboyant? Mr. Green says bullfinches mate for life. Too bad they're so hard on the buds in the orchard. A pair can strip a plum tree in no time.*

She glanced down at her hands and wondered why the backs were damp. She rubbed them over her cheeks and found her face was wet, too. She was crying. Silently and unaware, weeping as if her heart would break. Her breasts ached. Sophie would wake up hungry, looking for her mama. Her granny would have to comfort her with sugar water. Penny had never left her baby for so long before. Her heart contracted as if truly hearing those distressed little wails. She walked back to the chair to sit down, squeezed her eyes shut and put her hands over her ears.

The door opened.

"Here it is," he said. "The truth, blinded and blinking in the sudden light of day. It doesn't hurt as much as it once did. Somehow by writing it over and over, trying to explain it to you, perhaps I at last have explained it to myself."

He stood in the doorway, his hands filled with paper. He walked forward and poured the sheets into her lap.

"And the apology?"

He strode across the little room to stand at the window. "I am sorry for all the wrongs I have done you. I am sorry for the cruelties and the silences. I am sorry I could not tell you what I felt when it mattered, or explain before it was too late. I am sorry to impose on you now, like this. Don't read any of that, if you don't want to. Only know it is offered with a sincere heart, though seared by reluctance, because it is owed. Penny, you think you offer love, when I don't even know if I can survive your forbearance."

She swallowed. "I was very angry with my mother when I came home. Angry that she hadn't told me about my father. Angry that she willingly sacrificed me, her only daughter, for a kingdom. Your kingdom."

He turned. "What do you mean?"

"Mama knew I would fall in love with you. She decided you were more important, that Glarien was more important, and she thought I would survive—or even that loving you would be good for me, force me to grow up. Perhaps I have. I've survived, though it hasn't been easy. But I'm not angry now."

"Except with me?"

Penny shook her head. "No, Nicholas, I'm not angry with you. You see, it isn't that Mama didn't love me, or that she cared so much about the security of an Alpine kingdom, it's that she loved my father more than life. She did it for him, for his memory. I can understand that now. Can you?"

"Your mother was the only person who offered any real love to me when I was little. Then I used her. Is that unforgivable, too?"

"You had important reasons," Penny said. "She was a willing participant. She forgave you long ago. She still loves you, because of the child you once were."

He lapsed into silence, standing rigid with the open day streaming and beckoning beyond his dark head. Penny's body vibrated, shaking with longing for him. Nothing had changed. She didn't need to go through the ordeal of reading what he had written. She already knew it, surely. But she would do it, for his sake, because otherwise he would never believe that she loved him anyway.

Beloved, he had written. *If I could offer myself to you freely, you know I would do it. An hour with you means more to me than a lifetime of power or influence in the world. You think I am lonely. That is true. But the other truth was imprisoned underground because it belonged there. I cannot make a friend without defiling the friendship. I cannot take a lover without taint. I don't know what you have guessed. You think Carl was cruel, that he terrorized a small boy, and the thought of it brings compassion to your generous heart. . . .*

Penny glanced up. Nicholas stood like a man strapped to the triangle, awaiting the whip, head bent, arms spread, hands gripping the window frame, as if he couldn't stand without support. She gulped down salt tears and made herself read on:

The first time was after he held me off the battlements. I was crying. He took me in his arms. He told me what a sniveling little coward I was, then he kissed me. Not the comforting kiss of an older cousin, but the kiss of a lover. As I shook with fear and loathing, he used me—as later he used Alexis. You have known it, of course,

She put down the sheets. She had known it.

"You don't need to read on," he said. "I knew I was cursed from that day. I was sick afterward, as I was sick every time Carl forced himself on me. I wanted to kill him. When I was twelve, I waited for him with a knife. He disarmed me with a simple turn of the wrist, then threw me into a hole in the dungeons. I was there for three days."

In the dark. Without food or water. "Why didn't you tell anyone what was happening?"

"Whom? My mother—a remote, shining goddess of purity? My grandfather? My father in England, ailing and alone here at Rascall Hall, brokenhearted that his princess had left him? I don't think children used in such a way can tell anyone. The shame and guilt they feel is indescribable. I was the crown prince. I was supposed to be strong. I thought the only way I could make it stop was to try harder to please Carl. So I learned to please him, to do everything he wanted."

"You were a child. Carl was twelve years older. Your mother should have seen it. She ought to have known something was wrong. It wasn't your fault."

He flinched as if the whip had been laid on. "Yes." He looked back out at the sky. The bright summer sun washed color over his set, pale face. "It makes no difference now."

She was afraid, terrified. The fear was like grief, like the Four Horsemen of the Apocalypse letting their nags breathe their hot breath down her neck. She tried to read on through her blur of tears, then wiped them away with the back of her hand.

"A princess would use a handkerchief," he said, holding out a square of embroidered linen.

She blew her nose clumsily.

When I was fourteen, Carl told me I was old enough for a woman. . . .

Penny set the letter in her lap and closed her eyes. She could no longer stifle her weeping.

Nicholas took the paper from her hand and crushed it. "I didn't want you to know. I didn't ever want anyone to know. It was ugly and terrifying. Carl and two of his friends demonstrated. The girl cried and struggled, but they gagged her and did it anyway. Then it was my turn."

"I have wondered," Penny said, her mouth bitter with tears. "I have wondered if you were unable, or if you raped her, too. Carl suggested things, you see. He said you'd known women. I've had all these months to think. I surmised something of the kind. But you were a child, Nicholas. It doesn't matter what you did. The fault was Carl's."

"Was it?"

She clutched the damp handkerchief. "Do you blame Alexis for what happened to him?"

"Alexis? No, of course not!" He stared down at the crumpled paper. "No one but you has ever known this. Not Sophia. Not Lucas. None of my men. It was my secret—and Carl's. After it was over, we ate oranges. I behaved, as I remember, with exquisite bravado."

"And those other two men?"

"They each met with an unfortunate end—Carl made sure I witnessed that. It was a quite deliberate campaign of terror. I thought I would die next. Carl orchestrated everything that happened, other women, other cruelties. All the time he took me to his own bed, as well. I hated it. I hated him. A year later I managed to stab him. He claimed it was an accident, though he nearly died. But after four years of using me almost every night, he never touched me again."

Did the truth matter? Why should she think it was critical he not lie to her about this, that he admit all of it, however painful? "Not even at that inn south of London where I first met him and replaced his impostor?"

He spun about. "I would have done even that, had it been necessary for your sake. It wasn't necessary."

She ran one finger over the back of the carved horse. "I didn't quite understand what he was suggesting at the time. It was rather lost among his insinuations about Alexis. He wanted me to believe you and Alexis were lovers. I never did, for indeed, it wasn't something I could even imagine."

"Alexis! Dear God! The boy was always safe with me. I have rather an abhorrence for men's bodies. No, Carl has never touched me, nor I him, since I was fifteen."

She blew her nose again. *Though he has reached into every other crevice of my soul and tried to pollute it, I thought this one memory at least was inviolate.* "He didn't have to. He already thought he had the key to your soul. Carl knew about the orangery here, didn't he?"

"Of course. Oranges were hard to come by in Glarien. I'd poured out all my boyhood secrets to him when I first arrived. How much I missed my father. How I missed Rascall Hall and the simple days here with my mother, before she became entirely the princess. I thought he was a model prince. Someone I could look up to."

"You were eleven years old and you had just lost your father. It was natural you would look for a hero in an older cousin, especially one who seemed so handsome and dashing—"

"Carl had great gifts, Penny. He could have made remarkable

contributions to Glarien. It made it worse. When he was a child, perhaps it happened to him—some man at Burg Zanich, where he was helpless and afraid, or at the Glarian court. My grandfather spread a miasma of cruelty over everything he touched."

Penny opened a drawer in the desk and took out the tinderbox. "You spent a lifetime negating what Carl tried to make you, what your grandfather tried to make you. It's over now. You were a child."

"I knew what I was doing."

"You were younger than Alexis was when you first brought him here. It's a selfish indulgence now to still blame yourself. Carl wanted to destroy you. He was jealous. He hated you. But he didn't win."

Nicholas seemed consumed, the flame flaring in the depths of his dark eyes. "He won. After Carl left court and went back to Burg Zanich, I continued using women without even knowing their names. Professional harlots brought secretly to the castle by a servant of my grandfather's, then paid off and sent away. My grandfather probably thought it was healthy, the rutting of his heir, proving his manhood. I craved it, though every time I was sick afterward. I think my rage might have consumed me—would have consumed me—if it hadn't been for Fritz."

"The major? How?"

His hands were stark, beautiful. "I went off with him in the summers to learn horsemanship. It was the only time I was safe from Carl. We traveled throughout Glarien, over the high mountains and into the deep valleys where the herds were pastured. Fritz was infinitely patient with me. The horses had taught him. You cannot win a horse with anger. A single loss of temper can undo months of careful work. Whenever I became frustrated and rage threatened, I learned to walk away and control it. I stopped using the women. It didn't stop the craving, but it helped the pain. But I knew I was ruined, foul."

"You were wrong," Penny said.

He hesitated. "You haven't had time to think about this—"

She picked up the carving to cradle it. "I've had an infinity of months since last summer. I don't need more time, Nicholas. I love you."

His face contorted. She thought perhaps she had finally, irrevocably, misjudged. That he would simply walk out.

"What Carl did. What you did. It's over," she said. "Burn that letter!" She lit a candle. The flame fluttered in the slight breeze from the window. "I love you, Nicholas. We are blessed by St. Cyriakus. Anything a child does can be forgiven. You've spent enough years in remorse."

He reached out and took the candle, his face streaked by tears. The letter flared for a moment, then crumbled to ash.

"Very well," he said. "It is over. I had better go."

"If you walk out now," Penny said, "then Carl has still won, even beyond the grave. When did you last sleep?"

He smiled like a ghost. "Three nights ago, maybe four."

"And you have a migraine?"

"How did you know?"

"Come downstairs and sleep," she said. "In the morning I shall come for you."

His mouth tilted in a quizzical half-smile. "Come for me?"

"I love you," Penny said. "I shall always love you. Did you think the learning was all yours? Don't you realize what gifts you gave me—how you transformed that pompous, provincial girl you first discovered here? Do you think you have nothing left to give me, or that I have not yearned for you, missed you, needed you, every day? Nicholas, I love you. None of this bitter past matters any longer. I want you to live here with me."

She walked back to Clumper Cottage in a daze. Mrs. Lindsey was marching up and down carrying Sophie and patting the baby's back. Her face lit as she saw Penny come in. "I know," she said. "Nicholas has come back. Fritz is here. He's told me everything."

The major smiled up from the window seat. He looked more grizzled and more tired than she had ever seen him. The scar was livid.

"You know he has abdicated, Mama," Penny said. "You know he has very nearly lost his way."

"Then you'd better find it for him"—Fritz ran one hand over his balding pate and nodded toward the baby—"if that mite's to have a father."

Penny took Sophie in her arms and stared down at the owl-like face, innocent, vulnerable. Her heart swelled. "I had enough love without a father," she said. "But I think Mama was very lonely."

Nicholas woke and rolled almost out of bed before he realized where he was. Rascall Hall. He made himself relax and lie back on the pillows. A great silence stretched through the house, as if everyone else still slept. But there was no one else: no Alexis, no Markos, no Eric, none of his trained men. He was no longer Grand Duke of Glarien. He was only an Englishman, safe in his ancestral home. Through narrowed eyes he stared at the windows. It was early afternoon. The sun was already moving around to the west.

He had told her. She had not turned away in revulsion. She had looked up at him with those tawny eyes and told him she loved him. She wanted them to live together. Oh, God! *Penny!*

He held up his empty hands and looked at them. He craved her. He wanted to feel her, wanted to touch her. With a vague surprise he found nothing but pleasure in the thought. A pure, bright pleasure, uncorrupted by memories. Carefully, like a man probing a sore tooth, he pushed at the concept. All the old feelings were there, labeled and open, but without the power to wound—at least for this moment. He remembered the agony of putting those feelings onto paper. The letters he had written her in Glarien and burned. The account he had forced on her yesterday, bleeding the facts onto the white surface, sitting at the table where he had played chess with Alexis, offering nothing but a dumb presence, never giving the boy an ear for his own pain, never admitting once: *I understand, Alexis. It happened to me, too.*

Until, at last, before Waterloo, he realized that Alexis knew. Perhaps Carl had even told him in the end, and the youth had taken strength from that, after all. Enough strength to deny Carl his desires those last days in Moritzburg.

Had the very fact of voicing his shame been an expiation? It was as if the written word could rob memories of their demonic power. *It's over now. You were a child.* He had always known that, rationally. He had tried to believe it. Why did it make a difference that she had said it?

He pushed himself from the bed and walked naked to the bathroom. Hot water steamed and curled, filling his father's blue-and-white tub. Nicholas lay back in the water and contemplated the future and the past. He owed her his life. If she wanted it, she should have it. That he loved her more than his own soul seemed irrelevant. But if it proved that he was still tainted, after all, then he loved her enough to leave her in freedom.

"It's all right," she said. "It's just me. I've seen you naked before, remember?"

Water splashed as he groped for a towel.

She sat down on a gilt chair. Her blue muslin dress seemed tight across the breasts, as if she had gained weight. Her hands lay loose in her lap, a little red against the blue fabric. "I think we have a difficulty. Fritz is in love with my mother. He wants to marry her."

He laughed. "Yes, I know. He's loved her for twenty-odd years, ever since he first saw her in Glarien. Why is that a difficulty?"

Her eyes blazed as she lifted her head. "Because my mother has said yes, and I don't think they will want me living in Clumper Cottage with them."

"Ah," he said. "I see. Why don't you move into this house?" He waved one hand. "I should like it, I think, after I have gone to London, to know you are here."

"I should not like it by myself." He liked her new plumpness. She looked ripe, bountiful.

"Very well." He rose from the tub and wrapped himself in the towel. "I thought I ought to leave, but my future is in your hands, Penny."

"Would you stay with me then?"

"I want it more than life. But can I have what I want without worse hurt to you?"

She blushed and glanced away. Of course, she couldn't know what he had been thinking, what he had been hoping. He couldn't know himself, unless he tried it. But if he made love to her again and was sick again, then what? The fear of it shook him to the core. Yet his body had already responded to her bright presence, to her ripeness, to the shy welcome in the turn of her head. Bravery had very little to do now with climbing into a castle or facing guns at Waterloo. Courage was only the risk of vulnerability before someone who had the power to crush your heart in the palm of her hand.

"You still think that you love me?" she asked.

"Penny, you hold my soul in your pocket, though very casually, like a handkerchief."

"Not casually," she said. "Carefully, tenderly, with absolute devotion, as you hold mine. Yet if you don't take the risk, you will never know whether your love is enough. Although I know that it is and I know that mine is. I have no fear at all."

He walked up to her and took her chin in his hand. She gazed into his eyes, a fine tremble at the corner of her mouth. Gently he leaned down and kissed her. She reached one hand to the back of his neck and kissed back.

Afternoon lay soft over the room, casting long beams of amber and gold. Nicholas picked her up and carried her to the bed, letting the towel fall. He laid her on the white sheets and peeled off her shoes. Penny bit her lip and said nothing. Slowly he unrolled her stockings, taking them off an inch at a time, kissing her soft thigh and the back of her knee. He was hard, pleasure throbbing in his groin. She saw it and smiled, blushing in the golden light.

"If I have ever been thoughtless—" He stopped and laughed. "No, every time I *was* thoughtless, I would atone for it now."

"No," she said. "There isn't any need for that. Today is a new day. Every day is a new day. Let us be done with repentance. I love you. I haven't stopped. I would never have stopped, even if you had lived out your days in Glarien with Princess Sophia. I love you, Nicholas. You are splendid to me. You always were. You always will be."

He pulled out laces and rubbed buttons out of their buttonholes, so her dress fell away to be discarded. "And you to me," he said.

He caressed slowly, as if exploring a new wonder. The soft pillow and dent of her navel. The tiny bones inside her wrist. The knob and trough of her ankle. The little dimples in her bottom. He felt his body melding to hers, his legs entwining with hers, his arms encircling, holding and feeling. She kissed him. She kissed his mouth and his chest and his hands, wrapping her arms about his back, exchanging touch for touch. Slowly, lazily, as if they had a lifetime to explore each sensation.

Touch merged into touch, skin fused to skin. He wasn't sure where she began and he ended, his mouth, her mouth, his callused palms, her sunny hair. The long slide inside her was only an extension of his seeking hands, her pliant mouth. She moved with him, warmth growing to heat, heat building to a burn. The cleansing flames of carnality, honest and hot, built in his blood like a fire. Pleasure became intensely voluptuous, incinerating doubt. Without restraint he explored and plumbed, laying himself open in absolute trust. *She loves me. I can give her the power to wound me and know she'll not use it.*

She convulsed against him and cried out, her mouth contorting in little gasps. His sex roared its response, pouring out his soul in helpless spasms, deep at the mouth of her womb. He lay defenseless and satiated, while she stroked his hair. He waited, holding his breath, for the revulsion and the nausea.

They didn't come. *They didn't come.* He felt nothing but joy, clear, untrammeled enchantment.

She was only beautiful to him—beautiful, wholesome, loved.

An English summer day flowed past the windows, bathing the world in beneficence. He felt whole and real, as if anything but this had been just a bad dream. He stretched and sat up to look at her. Her hair lay in a fuzzy tangle. The end of her nose was red, because she was weeping a little. She was soft and plump in all the right places. Female. Her breasts were full, blue veined, the nipples engorged and damp.

"Miss Penelope Lindsey," he said. "I love you. Why are you wet?"

She sat up to lay her head on his shoulder and wrap her arms about his waist. She looked dreamy, bathed in sunshine. "It's milk."

The thought hit like a sudden shock of sunshine, flaying a man who has just stepped out of the shade. *"Milk?"*

"I call her Sophie. I hope Princess Sophia will approve. Not every child can say that her father gave up a throne for her."

"You have a baby? *We* have a baby. Oh, my God!"

She let go to smile up at him, a small tentative grin. "Only a prince could be so innocent," she said wickedly. "Babies are often the result of lovemaking, you know. Yet, alas, I want you for myself, because I'm helplessly, passionately, forever in love with you. You don't mind?"

He leaped off the bed and shouted, hollered at the gilt ceiling. *"Mind!"* Naked, without shame or awareness, he began to laugh. "Mind?" Laughed away years of duty and discipline, hearing the sound of his own laughter roaring in his ears. He had made love to her and felt nothing but joy. Joy and a burning, clean flame of passion, reducing shame and regret into insignificant cinders. She loved him, in spite of everything he'd done—*with* everything he'd done. She had given him a daughter. She needed him. She wanted him. She loved him.

"Penny," he said at last. "I'm very happy. I would like to make more babies with you. I would like to try making them every day, several times a day, as often as we can. I would like the rest of our babies to be legitimate—though I swear little Sophie will never know the difference—so we will have to get married right way. You and me, Penelope Lindsey and Nicholas, Lord Evenlode—English peer and the happiest man alive. When can I see her?"

"Now, if you like," she said. "She'll be downstairs by now with Mama and Fritz and Mrs. Butteridge. My mother and her bridegroom walked up from Clumper Cottage with her. I told little Sophie we were already married in the sight of St. Cyriakus and that our union was blessed by the saint. She will know she is special. But I suppose if she has a brother, he might like to be able to lay legitimate claim to his earldom one day. I'd be very honored to marry you."

"Special license," Nicholas said. "Right away."

Epilogue

Dawn glowed outside the window. Soft, pink, promising a glorious summer day. Penny snuggled back into her pillow and let contentment wash over her. A whole year of days—autumn, winter, spring, another summer—had slipped by since she and Nicholas had been married in Norwich. He had made her his countess and himself a force to be reckoned with. How foolish to have thought his talents might go to waste! The Duke of Wellington had been absolutely right.

Nicholas, Earl of Evenlode, had made a brilliant maiden speech in the House of Lords on behalf of the working people of England and never looked back. Not quite the way to endear himself to the ruling clique! Yet they listened. He knew how to convince without offending, how to manipulate when necessary, how to win over both rivals and enemies. The courts of Europe had taught him. Now all that skill was being used to benefit the Hardacres and Robertsons of Britain.

She smiled.

Rascall Hall was an island of prosperity in an England struggling into a new future. She and Nicholas were part of that future, remaking a world in which royalty would be less significant, where seats in Parliament were no longer in the pockets of the privileged, where justice gave every citizen equal dignity. It might take their lifetimes, or longer. Perhaps only a man who had been a sovereign himself could work for that goal with such genius.

She reached for him, only to find his place empty. Quest lay fast asleep, twitching in doggy dreams on her bed near the fireplace. Outside, birds were beginning to sing, but another, more poignant chirping blended with the birdsong.

Beneath that contented little crow, another sound rumbled in the quiet morning sunshine. In the little anteroom that had once been Alexis's bedroom, Nurse snored softly. She was one of the Hardacre girls, buxom, sensible, infinitely kind to children. All the connecting doors in the tower suite stood open—the door from the earl's bedroom into the children's room, and Nurse's door beyond that.

Penny's smile grew wider. She slipped from the bed and shrugged into a robe.

She tiptoed across the carpet and leaned silently against the door jamb. Little Sophie lay deeply asleep, her blond curls like gold coins on the pillow.

In a simple, dark dressing gown over a white nightshirt, Nicholas sat in a chair by the window. Frederick, Viscount Saxlingham, three months old, gurgled and chirped like a blackbird, kicking his feet in his father's arms. The baby turned his face and nuzzled, fists round as currant buns. He began sucking on the collar of Nicholas's nightshirt.

"Hush, now," Nicholas whispered. "You'll wake your mama. Don't say you're hungry already, little fellow?"

Milk leaked from Penny's breasts, but she didn't move.

"You may be the new heir to Rascall Hall, sir," Nicholas said, "but what you don't realize is that your mama needs her sleep. She is the light of my life and the balm of my days. Since the day that I married her, I've been free. Free from a misery I thought would haunt me to the grave. Free from headaches that once almost paralyzed me. I wonder why they say marriage feels like shackles, little Sax? It feels very much like wings to your deliriously happy papa."

The viscount gave up on the nightshirt and thrust his fist in his mouth. The sucking sounds grew louder. Then he threw both fists wide, kicked his heels, and smiled up into Nicholas's eyes. Penny's heart swelled at the new flame that danced in those black depths.

"Your sister Sophie was never this greedy, sir. Are men always the takers? I think sometimes your mama has given me my very soul." The baby's mouth puckered. Nicholas lifted him and gave him one finger. The pink mouth latched immediately onto a knuckle. "What the devil have I really given her? Besides you and that golden-haired sister of yours?"

"Not much, indeed, my lord," Penny said softly. "Only everything I love. Especially your own foolish self." She walked into the room and scooped her new baby from his father's arms. "Well, sweetheart!"

"Is the endearment for me or that moppet, Lady Evenlode?" Nicholas stood and bowed, indicating the chair. "You had better sit down before he pulls you over."

He laid a shawl around her shoulders as Penny settled the baby to nurse, his deeply satisfying tugs pummeling her heart as much as her breast.

Nicholas leaned against the window frame and watched.

"I came in late from London," he said after a moment. "I forgot to give you the best news of all."

"As I recall, you didn't give me any news," Penny said. "In fact, I'm not sure we exchanged more than two words. My memories of what transpired when you arrived home last night are very physical and just a little indelicate. Certainly not to be discussed in the nursery."

He laughed softly. "Oh, I don't know. How else do we make Sophie and Sax some more brothers and sisters?"

It was silly to blush, but she blushed. "And then, as I recall, you fell deeply asleep."

"As you did, wrapped most securely in my arms. Indeed, now that you remind me, it was the most delightful end to a tedious journey and a direct path to blissful dreaming. Are you aware how profound a pleasure that is to me—to fall asleep with you afterward?" His expression moved to pure mischief. "Though not *more* than the pleasure I find with you before we fall asleep. . . ."

Her blush grew deeper, though she laughed. She had thought she'd shared passion with her dark prince before she was married. But now he no longer held anything back, passion had only moved deeper and deeper—an exquisite journey, enhanced by the sensitivity and inventiveness of a man of brilliance, who had shed all his demons forever. She, plain Penny Lindsey of Rascall St. Mary, had fallen into a fairy tale, after all!

She transferred the viscount to the other breast. He rooted for a moment before taking hold, his own dark gaze fixed on his mother.

"You don't ask for my news?" Nicholas asked.

"You've charmed more stuffy lords into supporting your latest reform?"

"Tiny increments, one step at a time. Even Rutley will vote with me on this one. But my news is even better than that."

"Fritz has found you a fine new horse? Mama and I watched him yesterday training that lovely gray mare you brought back from Newmarket. He's very content managing your stable, you know. Rascall Hall will become famous for its horses, thanks to the pair of you."

"I'm lucky to have his help, but that isn't the news either."

Penny glanced up. She would never get used to it, that this man loved her, a man like a forest prince. His smile was open, truly content. "Then out with it, Nicholas! You look like a cat with its paw dipped in cream."

The smile changed, just a little. "Hmm. Quite a thought. The dipping in cream, not the cat. Shall we try it?"

"My lord, you have a lascivious tongue!"

He stepped forward to lift up her plait. He kissed it, then trailed little kisses down the braided length until his mouth touched deliciously on the back of her neck. "Lascivious? I should hope so! An inventive, wicked, hungry, very curious tongue, I trust. Shall we retreat to our room and see what it fancies this morning?"

Penny laughed, bending her head to let him kiss her ear and the side of her throat. "Who am I to deny the fancies of my prince? But first, the news?"

He nibbled her ear, then kissed her cheek, whispering against the corner of her mouth. "Eric has been promoted to captain of Sophia's personal bodyguard. Markos and Ludger have both married, but they still serve the crown. But there's even better news than that."

She closed her eyes for a moment, savoring the sensation of his beautiful hands touching the back of her neck. "But that's splendid! What could be better?"

"Lucas and Sophia have a son, Crown Prince Michael."

Her eyes flew open. "Oh, Nicholas!"

"It worked, Penny. Everything I hoped for. Alvia and Glarien are secure. The festivities in Moritzburg will lift the roof off the castle."

She stood up to lay a newly sleepy Sax in his cradle. "And Alexis?"

"How do you think I learned all this? Alexis is in London. He'll be here tomorrow. He brings us a present."

"Alexis is coming here? Then no wonder you're so happy! But why would we need a present, if we're to see Alexis in person?"

"Why would you think Alexis comes to see us, madam? Fritz and your mama will make a huge fuss of him, too."

She was genuinely puzzled. "The present is for Mama?"

"The present is for Quest."

Penny laughed. "If you're going to tell me that the Erbgraf von Kindangen brings dog bones across Europe for our softhearted mutt, then I'll know the world has gone mad."

He grinned. "Dog bones? No, this present has an impeccable pedigree. It's His Highness, Wilhelm von der Moritzburg—a Glarian wolfhound from the royal kennels, known to his intimates as Willy. I already met him in London, a noble beast. Lucas and Sophia thought Quest might like puppies."

"Puppies! Oh, Nicholas, she'll be the best mother. So the whole world is to have babies!"

Molly Hardacre knocked softly at the open door. "My lord? My lady?"

"Viscount Saxlingham has just finished breakfast, Nurse,"

Nicholas said. "Little Sophie still sleeps. We leave our two angels in your capable hands."

Molly gave a deep curtsey. "Yes, my lord. And they are angels, too!"

She bustled over to check on her charges.

Nicholas led Penny back to their room, closed the door and locked it. She slipped her arm about his waist and laid her head on his shoulder.

He turned her in his arms and kissed her, before taking her hand and leading her to the little door in the corner. Her blood began to pound in her veins.

She followed him up the stair to her old room in the tower. Sunbeams streamed across the desk and danced on the door that led to the roof, no longer guarded by soldiers.

Nicholas lay down on the narrow bed and smiled. "About that business with the cream—?"

Penny went to him and laid a hand on each muscled shoulder. She opened his dressing gown to press a kiss to his throat. The pounding in her veins became a rhythmic melody, singing of enchantment, of a fairy prince who had once stolen her away on his great black horse. Songs of love and passion, untainted by doubt.

"I'm so very glad your person is no longer sacred," she said as she lifted her head to kiss his willing mouth. "I do so like to touch you without asking permission. Now, my very dear Lord Evenlode, what was that you promised about tongues?"

Author's Note

There's something rather appealing about the lowly hedgehog.
These spiny little creatures were indeed sold at Covent Garden
in London in the eighteenth and early nineteenth centuries.
Since hedgehogs like to hunt in nooks and crannies for their in-
sect food, the ruins of old Rascall Manor would have been the
perfect habitat for them. They are also quite easy to tame. The
London hedgehogs had to come from somewhere, so why not
have Penny gather them in Norfolk?

This love story doesn't dwell on war or politics, but I did my
best to make Nicholas's predicament credible given the situation in Europe in 1814. Glarien and Alvia never existed, of
course, but they fit quite plausibly into the history and map of
the Alps. Though it doesn't appear in these pages, I invented a
history to explain why Alvia would be reabsorbed by France, if
there was no male heir. It then became obvious that in 1814—
with Napoleon exiled to Elba, just south of Alvia—the victori-
ous Allies would have been very concerned about the fate of
these little dukedoms. To put them both safely in the hands of
Grand Duke Nicholas, with his British heritage, must have
seemed a perfect solution.

What's far more important to my story, however, is
Nicholas's understanding of horsemanship. More horsemen

and women than I can name helped teach me what Nicholas knows: The outside of a horse is good for the inside of a man. But my real gratitude is to the horses who taught me to love and respect them. As Nicholas taught Penny, it's never the horse that must be mastered, it's the rider's own emotions.

Incidentally, Nicholas's description of the planets that includes the interestingly-named *Georgium Sidus* was taken word-for-word from a Regency text.

I love to hear from readers and may be reached at P.O. Box 197, Ridgway, CO 81432-0197. A stamped, self-addressed long envelope is much appreciated if you'd like a reply. I can also be E-mailed through my Web site: http://www.juliaross.net.